# Forty Years of
# Coronation
# Street

# Forty Years of
# Coronation
# Street

## A Collection of Memories

### Stephen F. Kelly & Judith Jones

B⬛XTREE

For

Nicholas
(who once appeared in
*Coronation Street* in his pram)

and

Emma

**Stephen F. Kelly** was born on Merseyside and worked at the Cammell Laird shipyard for more than six years before embarking on a university career that took him to Oxford and the London School of Economics. He subsequently became a political journalist with the left-wing weekly *Tribune*. In 1978, he joined Granada Television, where he remained for ten years, contributing to Granada's political and current affairs output. In 1988, he left Granada to pursue a career as a full-time writer. He has now published more than a dozen books, including biographies of Bill Shankly and Alex Ferguson, and has written a number of oral histories. He is also Fellow in Media at the University of Huddersfield.


**Judith Jones** was born in Liverpool and is a former television production assistant who worked for Granada Television for ten years, at its Liverpool and Manchester studios. During that time, she spent a year working on *Coronation Street*. She left Granada in 1988, but has continued to work in a freelance capacity. She is also Lecturer in Media Professional Studies at John Moores University, Liverpool, and has an MA from Manchester Metropolitan University. She has recently completed a study of cinema-going in Manchester during World War II.

First published in 2000 by Boxtree, an imprint of Macmillan Publishers Ltd,
25 Eccleston Place, London, SW1W 9NF and Basingstoke

www. macmillan.co.uk

Associated companies throughout the world

ISBN 0 7522 2311 9

9 8 7 6 5 4 3 2 1

A CIP catalogue record for this book is available from the British Library

Typeset by Blackjacks

Printed by Mackays of Chatham plc, Kent

# Acknowledgements

During the course of writing this book, we have interviewed at length more than 70 people. Names and details are given elsewhere. They were mostly interviewed face to face in a variety of locations – homes, pubs, offices, television editing rooms, restaurants – as well as on the telephone and even the Internet. We would like to thank all of these people for their time, their thoughts and their memories. Without them, of course, this book would never have been possible.

Our thanks also go to many others who offered assistance in the form of ideas, names, telephone numbers, addresses, hospitality and so forth. Among those are Thames Television, Katie Jones, Yorkshire Television, Irene McGlashen, Barbara MacDonald, Jim Walker, Claire Lewis, John Farnsworth, Clare Jenkins, Andrew Serraillier, Iris Frisby, Martin Wainwright, the staff of the Amblehurst Hotel in Sale, Graham Hobbs, Richard Hadley, Ann McAdam, Ian Barr, Melanie Barr, Ged Lalor, Jackie Lalor, Mark Leadbitter, Berni Leadbitter, Louise Sethi, Trina Williams, Jack Rosenthal, Malcolm Foster, Ken Wong and Cynthia Finch.

There are other people who gave assistance, but who wished to remain anonymous. Special thanks to them, and our appreciation for talking off the record.

We are also grateful to Emma Marriott, our editor at Boxtree, whose enthusiasm for this project and critical advice, as well as encouragement, have made this book a pleasure, rather than a burden.

As ever, we are deeply indebted to our agent, John Pawsey, whose support and help have proved invaluable, not only with this book, but with so many others over the years.

Our most grateful thanks, however, must go to our families – to our parents, Anthony and Marjorie Rowe Jones and Mary Kelly, and to our children, Nicholas and Emma, who have had to suffer a small amount of neglect during the lengthy process of writing this book.

Finally, it should be mentioned that any mistakes within the text remain the responsibility of the authors.

Stephen F. Kelly    Judith Jones

MANCHESTER, MARCH 2000

# A note on the research and editing of interviews

The vast majority of interviews contained within this book were recorded on a minidisc player. Each interview was then transcribed and broken into sections to be included in the relevant chapters. As little editing as possible has taken place. Where editing has taken place, it has been carried out in order to make the interview as coherent and readable as possible. Slang and dialect words have been kept in so that the character of the interviewee is retained. The interviews, however, have not been included in full. Some repetitions and irrelevancies have been deleted. The occasional correction has also been made (to dates, names and so on) in order to save the interviewee any embarrassment and avoid any confusion for the reader. People's memories are not always as accurate as they imagine!

Some interviews were also recorded over the telephone. Clearly this is not an ideal way to record an interview as face-to-face contact is much more natural for good conversation. It was only in instances where it was logistically impossible to arrange this that telephone interviews were conducted.

A number of interviews have also been included after a request was posted on the Internet, mainly via the New Zealand *Coronation Street* web page. Interviews were submitted in the form of a written statement based on a number of areas we suggested. It turned out that not only people in New Zealand read and submitted to their own chat pages, but also fans in North America and Australia. As a result, we have included interviews from these and other countries as well.

# Contents

# CHAPTER ONE

# The Pickwick Papers

That very English and much-loved poet Sir John Betjeman once described *Coronation Street* as 'The Pickwick Papers'. It was, he claimed, 'the best writing and acting I could wish to see. Thank God, half past seven tonight and I shall be in paradise.' Betjeman was as big a fan of The Street as anyone.

That The Street should attract the critical appraisal of none other than Betjeman speaks volumes for its popularity. He wasn't the only famous person to love the programme. Harold Wilson and, particularly, his wife, Mary, were huge fans, inviting some of the cast to Number 10 on more than one occasion. It was even claimed that he once conspired to close a crisis Cabinet meeting minutes before 7.30pm so that he could nip upstairs to watch a crucial episode.

Jim Callaghan was another prime minister who loved the programme. *Coronation Street* is not totally Labour territory, though, as Mrs Thatcher sent a message of congratulations when The Street celebrated its two thousandth edition. 'There must be few people in Britain who have not heard of the Rovers Return or become involved in the lives of Ena Sharples, Albert Tatlock, Annie Walker, Elsie Tanner and Ken Barlow,' she wrote. Later in the book, the former Labour Chancellor of the Exchequer Denis Healey heaps lavish praise and affection on The Street, emphasizing its important role in popular culture.

Cilla Black, Dustin Hoffman, Joanna Lumley, Cliff Richard, Lily Savage, Ringo Starr, Victoria Wood, Michael Parkinson, Billy Connolly, have all at some time publicly expressed their affection for The Street. Over the years, *Coronation Street* has attracted the plaudits of critics, poets, politicians, academics, writers, actors and, of course, the British public at large. In 1982, Her Majesty the Queen, rumoured to be a fan herself, came, wandering down a bunting festooned Street, to meet the cast and production staff.

The Street definitely has a special something. Ken and Deirdre's wedding in 1981 attracted more viewers than did Prince Charles and Lady Diana's, while a phenomenal 29 million watched to see if Deirdre was going to stay with her husband Ken or move out with Mike Baldwin. They even flashed the result of that little dilemma on the scoreboard at Old Trafford in the middle of a game.

It was not the first soap opera on British television. There had been others. Arguably, *Appleyards*, which began in 1952, was television's first soap, although it was actually aimed at a younger market and transmitted in Children's Hour. *The Grove Family*, which began in 1954 and continued until 1957, is the BBC soap most remembered from the 1950s. ITV's first soap, *Sixpenny Corner*, which began in 1956, was shown 15 minutes each day, but was dropped after 10 months. A year later came the highly popular *Emergency Ward Ten*, made by ATV, with a viewing audience of around 6 million. It continued until 1967, but by then it had long been surpassed by *Coronation Street*.

What made *Coronation Street* special was that it was different. For a start, it was Northern, unlike all the other soaps, which had been thoroughly Southern. It was also cast in the mould of kitchen-sink drama and caught the mood of the times. It was John Osborne, Harold Pinter and Arnold Wesker all rolled into one, with even the occasional touches of a Samuel Beckett. It was revolutionary. Although there had been soaps before it, there had been none like this. One director describes it as 'pure drama documentary'. *Coronation Street* was working class and proud of it, not like the lower middle-class soaps that had preceded it, which focused on squeaky clean nurses in squeaky clean hospitals and 'nice' middle-class families from 'darn South'. Northern, working class, kitchen sink – there had been nothing like this before on British television, which is odd because it was simply about real life.

The arrival of The Street in December 1960 coincided with a social and economic revolution. Television sets galore were being purchased by a new consumer generation. It was the 'never had it so good' era of Harold Macmillan. Television was about to become the new popular culture, and millions of new viewers, mostly working class, could relate to The Street. Once they were hooked, that was it.

For 39 years The Street has been one of the top ten favourite programmes, and for most of those years it has stayed at number one, which says more than any words. Why is The Street so popular? What is it about the programme that makes it the most loved of all soap operas? Why is it so endearing and so enduring? If only the phenomenon could be explained simply. Alas it can't, but at least we can try to offer some suggestions, and the contributors in this chapter clearly have their own answers to these questions.

Perhaps, as one former Granada Producer Jim Walker suggests, the magic is really in the fact that The Street still exists when so many of those familiar terraced Victorian streets that were common to most Northern industrial towns and cities have been bulldozed. In the process, those close-knit communities, where everyone knew each other's business and where there was curtain twitching and nosiness, have mostly disappeared. Maybe it is pure nostalgia, that The Street is about a lost world we still prize. The houses themselves and the grimness may not have always been so respectable, but there were values that were held in high esteem. Perhaps, also, that is why so many have taken against new storylines of recent years that destroy an otherwise idyllic picture we have in our minds of working-class life.

Nostalgia might be one ingredient, but The Street is many other things as well. It's had humour, by the bucketload on occasion, and, of course, it's had drama. There have been deaths – some downright tragic, many just sad. There have been marriages, some for the better, some for the worse. It's not always been pleasant. There have been violence, murder, cruelty, wife-beatings. There have been lies, adultery, money problems, fires and even a train crash. Heady stuff – and all before *EastEnders* and *Brookside* had even been thought of.

It may be dramatic, but it can also be therapeutic. Canadian Angela Larson testifies to how watching The Street helped her over the tragic death of her husband. For just half an hour, twice a week, she could escape her nightmare:

'When I was engrossed in the affairs of the Weatherfield contingent, I wasn't moping or worrying about my own tawdry life. Without trying to make light of it or expand on the horrendous circumstances associated with his death, it was only through the repetition of ordinary daily activities that I was able to function at all in those dark days. *Coronation Street* was a life-line for me then. I knew there would be at least 30 minutes when I could suspend the pain that was my life and focus instead on the activity of The Street.'

For another fan, Christabelle Embleton, living in Ramsgate, The Street provided a quick antidote to another kind of pain! 'My son was born about three or four o'clock in the afternoon and I was up watching it that night at half past seven! This was in the hospital. I didn't even have him in my arms, I left him in one of those cot things!' she says.

It's impossible to know precisely what the magic of *Coronation Street* is, but, undoubtedly, comedy plays a major part. Who can forget those memorable scenes with Hilda and Stan or their binman lodger, Eddie Yeats, as well as those with Derek and Mavis, Alec Gilroy or supermarket boss Reg Holdsworth. None was a deliberately comic figure – each had moments of drama as well as giving you a good belly laugh. They were simply well-rounded, superbly crafted characters, given lines that could tear at the emotions.

Then there has been the true grit of The Street. Ena and Elsie at it hammer and tongs – Ena with that jabbing, accusatory finger – Bet Lynch giving someone a piece of her mind; even Betty Turpin can turn nasty. Deaths, love, marriage, drama – we have seen them all on The Street.

Who could forget Martha dying in the pub, slumped over her milk stout, the trauma of it still etched in the mind of more than one person in this book. Also, that moment – perhaps the most poignant ever in The Street – when Hilda picked up the glasses case of Stan, realizing that he was gone forever, and slowly wept. Millions wept with her.

There has been love as well and plenty of it. Ken and Valerie, Ken and Deirdre, Ken and whoever was next, to say nothing of that convoluted love triangle with Mike Baldwin. Someone calculated that there had been more than 20 women in Ken's love life. Of course, there was Elsie with Len Fairclough, Steve Tanner, Alan Howard and, finally, Bill Gregory. In between, a host of odds and ends. Bet Lynch had her fair share of men as well.

Whether or not The Street is true to life doesn't matter. It's a community and we believe in it. After 40 years, we know the characters. There is a safety factor and maybe The Street itself is a safety zone. In an ever-changing world where technology leaps forward confusingly by the day, The Street offers stability and continuity, although, in more recent years, cast and storyline changes have shattered that stability. That, perhaps, explains why so many have taken against the new brasher storylines and characters. We like to feel that The Street is there and always will be. We don't mind the occasional upheaval – that, after all, is life – but not too many, thank you. Communities are important and all too rare these days. Maybe there is a little hankering for the past, for a time when neighbours took an interest, for a time when you could wander by yourself to the pub, knowing that you would meet someone you knew there.

Of course, there is the gossip, too. Where would The Street be without its gossip? As one fan, Graham Twyman, puts it: 'If you like Coronation Street you've got to like a bit of gossip, you've got to want to know what's going on, what people are talking about; you've got to like to know what's going on with other people. If there's anything going on that shouldn't be, you want to know. I think that's what grips the people, being in on all the gossip.'

Yet, if it is about communities – and very Northern ones at that – how come they watch it so avidly in Canada, Australia, America and New Zealand, let alone Kent. Sandy Charbonneau – once of Britain but living in Nova Scotia, Canada, for more than 30 years – claims that 'Coronation Street does not seem a million miles away. In fact, it's been on TV so long here that it is a natural part of life. The most important thing about the show is that it keeps home close and that is important when you are so far away.'

The show's long-time Executive Producer, Harry Kershaw, used to say that, for him, the real enchantment of The Street was jumping off the bus on his way home in the evening and wandering past the lighted windows of houses and seeing Coronation Street flickering on black-and-white television sets with families watching, spellbound.

The secret of The Street for Sir John Betjeman was that it 'never plays a false note'. The sets, he noted, were perfect, 'the interiors both as to colour and furniture are true to life.' It was the little things, though, that really captured his poetic imagination: 'the awful browns and oranges and greens' and the 'things displayed for sale in the corner shop'. And he was right.

It has been that concern and respect for detail that has placed The Street above all other programmes. It has always had all the expensive production values of a major drama. It has never been a make-a-quick-buck show. Even though producers have always complained at the inadequacies of their budgets, they will take time and care in getting the simple things right. The directors – many of them young, making their first attempts at drama – have gone on to make names for themselves in Hollywood and elsewhere. Directors such as Michael Apted, Mike Newell, Julian Farino, Charles Sturridge all cut their teeth on The Street.

Oddly enough, it's the simple things that are best remembered by viewers: Hilda's mispronunciations, especially the word 'murial', or Ena's emphasis on the 'e'. You can hear her now, telling Florrie Lindley, 'I'm not having any of them eee-clairs!' It has been about writing, about an ear for the dialogue of the streets. It's no coincidence that many of The Street's writers have since created some of the finest television drama over the years. Writers such as Jack Rosenthal, Paul Abbott, Jimmy McGovern and, of course, The Street's creator, Tony Warren.

It has also been about spot-on casting and exceptional acting, actors who can make us believe in them. Don't ever tell anyone that Ena or Elsie weren't real. Just to complete the picture, everything has always been backed up by a production staff dedicated to the highest standards. Former Granada presenter Bob Greaves maintains, 'it has always had quality – quality producers and most certainly quality writers; it's had a lot of quality directors, but, more importantly, it's had a lot of quality actors and actresses, many of whom had huge personalities.'

Yes, *Coronation Street is The Pickwick Papers*, with its litany of fantastical characters, large and small, its tales of grief and humour. It is, as one fan suggests, 'bedtime reading', a half hour of pure escapism when we can all forget our problems and indulge ourselves in sheer fantasy. Long may it continue.

## Norman Frisby
*Granada Press Officer*                         **THE COMMON TOUCH**

The actors, when they started, were unknown – they may have done small bits, but they were not famous. It used to infuriate them that they were always known by their *Coronation Street* names. I had to stop myself sometimes calling them by their cast name rather than their real name. I think they grew into the parts. Sometimes newcomers would come in and you'd watch them the first few times and you'd think, 'I'm not sure they are right' and then they would slowly but surely become right. *Coronation Street* has some magic ingredient.

I used to think it has survived because it is so true to life, but then I know that it isn't. My mother used to live in a tiny village in the Sherwood Forest and she was a great *Coronation Street* fan and I used to ask her what she saw in *Coronation Street* and she would say it was so lifelike and real. 'But,' I said, 'it bears no resemblance to the kind of life you live here' and she would say, 'But they talk about the things we talk about' and I think that is it – the common touch, it has a kind of real life, real things about it. It is real *even though* it is not true to life. I think that is its secret.

## Ken Farrington
*Actor, played Billy Walker*                    **A DOCUMENTARY DRAMA**

I never knew it was going to be such a success, but it was breaking completely new ground. They did 16 episodes at the beginning and I was written into the end of them. Originally, it wasn't what soaps are today – it was more of a documentary-drama, which was quite exciting. I don't watch *Coronation Street* today – it's changed too much, it's no longer the same sort of show – but I wouldn't mind going back, if they were to ask me nicely. If they want you, they can make a storyline, even if you're dead. If they want you badly enough, they'll bring you back, but I think it's probably too long now – it's 16 years.

## John Finch
*Scriptwriter, Script Editor and Producer*      **BEHIND THE**
                                                **LIGHTED WINDOWS**

Harry Kershaw used to say that, for him, one of the most exciting things was getting off the bus, going home in the evening and going past the lighted windows of the houses and seeing *Coronation Street* on inside. Suddenly you were plunged from living a fairly ordinary sort of life into something else; it changed everybody's lives. From being broke we suddenly had money. With the first script fee – which was £100 – we bought a washing machine for £99 and blew the £1 on a bottle of wine. To be able to look at something and think 'I won't be ashamed to write that.' The Street was a big step forward in television.

## Anne Reid
*Actor, played Valerie Barlow*                    **A BRAND NEW VOICE**

I think Tony Warren came in with a brand new fresh voice and a way of writing Northern comedy. The Street was a comedy show – it had moments of drama, but basically people watched it then because it had wonderful salty old characters in it and it was very funny. Now it's absolutely unrecognizable to me, nothing's the same thing at all, but then I suppose it wouldn't be. But when you think how brilliant Jack and Annie Walker were, what a wonderful duo they were and those old biddies in the pub, they were just wonderful characters. His dialogue and his way of talking, I do think that the others picked it up. I'm not saying they copied it, but he set the flavour of the thing. It might have been done before, I couldn't tell you because I didn't have a television set, but it always seemed to me that he'd started something off that was absolutely wonderful. Just the way they chatted to each other and then somebody would reply to something half a page later, a question that had been asked six lines earlier that everybody had ignored and then somebody else would come in and answer it. He was a wonderful writer, he was a really good writer, Tony.

## Bob Greaves
*Television Presenter*                                  **QUALITY**

I have a lot of affection for The Street as a series and a lot of affection for many of the people – some of whom are still there, but especially for many of the originals. It was obviously, and still is, an ongoing drama series – they hate the word 'soap' – it has always had quality. Quality producers and most certainly quality writers; it's had a lot of quality directors, but, more importantly, it's had a lot of quality actors and actresses, many of whom had huge personalities, most of whom were very likeable people.

## Alistair Houston
*Sound Engineer*                                **LIFE IN SALFORD**

Why do I think it's been so popular? In the early days, it was almost a replica of how people in Salford lived their lives and so people could relate to it. I always thought the programme would be good. I said to my mother-in-law that this is a programme that you'll really like and it didn't surprise me in the least when they extended it. It was different and Tony Warren just knew how people in the local pubs around Salford would react, how families in these streets reacted.

## John Temple
*Former Storyline Editor and Producer*               **COMFORT TELEVISION**

Granada Chairman David Plowright used another phrase to me, 'It's comfort television.' People love it because it makes them feel good. At the end of the episode, they'd end up feeling a damn sight better than they did when they started to watch it. I think there's a sad lack of that in television today. There's nothing better than making people feel good, making them feel warm and feeling they've been thoroughly entertained, had a good laugh, not made to feel uncomfortable. I know there has to be challenging stuff as well, but that's for some other area. The Street has survived, in my view, because of its warmth and its wit and its charm.

## Julie Jones
*Fan*                                               **CASTING CORRIE**

I think the success of *Coronation Street* depends on both the writing and the acting. They are renowned for bringing on writers. A lot of excellent writers have started there and I think the quality of the writing is more consistent than any other soap that I can think of, but I think the casting is brilliant as well. Obviously they're going to get it wrong from time to time, but I think mostly it's been spot on. They've got an eye for male and female crumpet and the young people they're casting, I think, are really good. From what I can gather, they are quite good at bringing new characters in that they will observe on screen for a while. They'll try not to give them too much to begin with so that they can pick up what they're like.

## Jim Quick
*Graphic Artist*                                    **THE IMMORTAL HILDA**

I would fight for the fact that if you put Hilda Ogden up against whoever they've got in The Street these days, she'd wipe the floor with them. The cutting might not be the same, the lighting might not be the same, there'd be no wobbly camera angles, you probably wouldn't have as much flexibility in terms of your outside broadcast shooting and your turnaround wouldn't be as quick, but you'd probably notice that the lines were delivered better, that you were believing in the character more, that each scene lasted more than 30 seconds, that the camera movements were developed, that the direction was better in the true sense of the word.

## Lynn de Santis
*Fan*                                                    **THE SIMPLE THINGS**

An episode that I remember is the one where Jack Duckworth was talking to his grandson. He had the babe on his knee and it was just him and this baby and he was talking to it and almost half the episode was taken up with Jack chatting and it was just fabulous, it was really so wonderful. It's things like that that really touch you because you get this bumbling character, poor old Jack, and you get this lovely touching moment where he is talking to this little baby about how wonderful the world is and how you're never going to make my mistakes.

It's lovely, things like that, and Hilda's mispronunciations – 'a murial' – and the way she used to sing when she was doing her cleaning – she had this awful high-pitched voice! They are very fond memories. The tragedy is far more effective because it is linked to the comedy – there's so much more poignancy and it's carried on with that. The scriptwriters have always been able to carry that on, as with the death of Jude. You've got the wedding with Ashley making jokes and then someone's dying, and it's that juxtaposition that's always kept it at the top. It's always been at the top of the ratings whereas the others, it's really hard stuff, it always so depressing, whereas in Corrie you've always got that lightness. It's a very rare episode that hasn't got some lightness in it and when there isn't, it's for a reason – it's to hammer home something that is particularly nasty.

## Robert Khodadad
*Director*                                                **SHOOTING STYLES**

There is a certain style for shooting *Coronation Street* and if you try to impose too much of your own style on it, it jars with the public. With any other drama, one of the major factors is the style in which you are going to shoot it and the feel that you are going to give it on screen and there is more individualism for you as a director, whereas on The Street there isn't. The Street is far bigger than you or I will ever be. There are different *ways* of achieving the same on-screen look, but, ostensibly, you will still achieve the same on-screen look.

## Ric Mellis
*Assistant Stage Manager, Floor Manager and Director*    **A WAY OF LIFE**

There are so many things that go into the making of the programme, it's such a massive team thing. It's about people and real life, in the way it's done. In the movies, people turn up, do their job and move on. In The Street, it's a way of life that you become a part of and it's a way of life for the people who watch it. That's why I don't want to do anything else in television. What I want to do is be involved in soaps because you can show people things, alternatives, how silly it is to behave in a way that you disapprove of, the results of careless behaviour – from a misplaced insult to killing somebody – and it can do all of that. It relates absolutely to real life.

## Robert Khodadad
*Director*    **NEVER IN MY WILDEST DREAMS**

When I started on *Coronation Street*, it was quite a strange sensation walking in through the doors of Stage One.

I was born and grew up in south Manchester, just six miles down the road from Granada, and I remember as a five-year-old watching television with the family. We used to watch *Coronation Street* and I never in my wildest dreams thought that maybe 30 years later I would be walking in through the doors to direct it. It is one of those programmes that is greater than any one individual who might be working on it. So many programmes are born and produced by one or two key individuals who then stay with it through the life of the programme. The thing about *Coronation Street* is it's perpetual, it keeps going by its own success and popularity. It is a part of British culture and that's why I think it's far greater than any one individual.

The other thing about walking into *Coronation Street* for the first time – and it can be quite daunting, even as a director where you've worked with a lot of well-known people in the past – when you walk into the Green Room of *Coronation Street* for the first time, you see the 30 or so actors who you've seen on the screen for years, all sat there together, and it can be unnerving. They're just ordinary human beings like the rest of us, but, even as a director, although you get desensitized to stars, to walk into the room for the first time and see 30 of the most famous people in British culture and a big percentage of them who were very prominent even in my own childhood, it's quite an interesting experience.

## José Scott
*Casting Director*                                    **SNOBBISHNESS**

The Delfonts and the Grades were all friends of the Bernsteins and I remember Cecil coming in one day and saying, 'I've had a funny call, an interesting call' from either Bernard Delfont or one of their wives, saying, 'Come on Cecil, what does happen?', because they were all addicts. 'Come on, please tell us, because we're going away and we won't be able to see it', and he said, 'I'm sorry, I can't tell you.'

There was a certain amount of snobbishness at the beginning, when people would say, 'Oh, *Coronation Street*, yes. Well, I don't watch it, of course, but I know quite a number of people, my cleaner watches it and she tells me.' And you'd think, 'Lying bugger, you've been watching every moment of it'!

But then, eventually, of course, people started to say, 'Mmm, yes', because there was nothing offensive about it. I mean it's just working class. You talk to people now who were very young when *Coronation Street* started and they loved it, but they don't like it because they don't want to hear this awful, coarse, rough language.

## Harry Whewell
*Northern Editor of the* Guardian          **MEAN STREETS AND
                                          A BIT OF THE WHIPPET**

There used to be a feeling that *Coronation Street* stereotyped Manchester and that Manchester is not really all like *Coronation Street*. That is perhaps a bit of a middle-class view, but it is also true that somewhere like Manchester is not really that much different from Leeds. I do think it is true that *Coronation Street* stereotypes the North – mean streets and a bit of the whippet. That's what people think of the North. Maybe *Coronation Street* occasionally plays up to that image, but, if I was a young person who had grown up in the *Coronation Street* era and I went abroad, I would walk tall. *Coronation Street* has given much to the area.

Many of the characters in *Coronation Street* had the right values, and there was a lot of subtlety in those characters. They weren't pantomime characters. They would slip something in that gave them an extra dimension. I think the writers must have been proud of themselves because what they were doing was something that no other writers were doing at the time.

I often wonder what Manchester has done for *Coronation Street*, but certainly *Coronation Street* has done much for Manchester. It gives a focus on Manchester in a way that Leeds, for instance, does not have. Go anywhere and ask people about Manchester and, after 'United', they will think *'Coronation Street'*.

What has always interested me is whether it has made Mancunians see themselves differently. I'm sure it must have. When you think of Manchester, you think of *Coronation Street* and Manchester United. I'm not sure which of them has the stronger draw, they both attract a huge amount of space in the newspapers, particularly the tabloids.

## Lord Doug Hoyle
*Former Labour MP*        **THE WRONG IMAGE?**

I think it's a tribute to the North West. When it started, there was an outcry in the North West that it was portraying the wrong image. The backstreets of Salford and Manchester were not what the North West wanted when they were trying to attract new people and new industry into the area, but I don't think that criticism was true. I think it *did* depict people accurately at the back end of that era, but it has changed over the years and is still as popular as ever.

I think it is far more of a reflection on life in the North West nowadays than it was some years ago. They have introduced more middle-class characters into a working-class soap. In the past it was all apple pie and laughs all around. But now they do try to look at real situations, people getting divorced, having affairs and so on. It is far more up to date although they have retained a sense of humour which other soaps do not have.

I do think it is important to our region and I think it has been helpful. Go anywhere in this country, as well as many other countries, and they know about the North West, about Manchester, and I think as a politician that that is important. I tell you what is interesting is that if someone has appeared in *Coronation Street* but goes on to appear successfully in other programmes or films, they are still remembered for appearing in *Coronation Street.*

I think in terms of popular culture it has been very important. It has been important to people as they relate to the characters and can see themselves in the characters. The characters have not been too remote from the average viewer and they have been able to identify with them. With 14 million viewers over a period of 40 years it has to be one of the most important areas of popular culture in this nation.

## Ian White
*Director*                                              **'SHE'S STAYING!'**

I think the Ken and Deirdre and Mike Baldwin three-way affair was during [Producer] Bill Podmore's time. I remember being at Old Trafford, watching a football match, when that came up, and I wasn't a Street director then. I was watching Man. United v Wolves and it was nil–nil at half time and then they put the thing on the scoreboard, saying, 'She's staying!' That's how important The Street is.

## Ian White
*Director*                                      **ENTERTAINING GRANNIES**

There have been times when I've worked on *Coronation Street* and it's almost brought me to tears because you feel quite close to the soul of the programme. You have a responsibility to a large number of viewers, and also to your granny. Both my grannies were watching it throughout my time on the programme and I would get rung up about it afterwards. You were trying to do your bit as part of your generation to entertain the largest number of people with the highest quality.

## Lord Denis Healey
*Former Chancellor of the Exchequer & Labour MP*    **REFLECTING SOCIAL CHANGES**

I think its role has been very important as a strand of popular culture. What was really very good about it was the way they adapted both the plot and the scenery and everything to the social changes that were going on at the time. You know when people started having fitted carpets, for example – only Tories had fitted carpets when I started! It reflected all those social changes and did change as the society it was reflecting changed. It was the petit bourgeoisification of the working classes! We're all middle class now, you know! Granada was a very good company and Sidney Bernstein, who I knew a little, was a very impressive man. He took risks to do what he thought was sensible and right; he worked by instinct.

## Gary Parkinson
*Fan*                                          **REVOLUTIONARY DRAMA**

I think you can watch *Coronation Street* on two levels. You can watch it purely as a soap and enjoy it, but I also think you need a healthy sense of irony to appreciate it properly whereas I don't think the other soaps have that sense of irony about them. It's almost like a post-modern thing with *Coronation Street* in that, if you take it at face value, it can look incredibly naff and the characters can look like pantomime characters, but if you look at it from a bit of distance, it can be fantastically outrageous and it's got a real sense of bizarre, which something like *EastEnders* doesn't have.

It would be great to see a move back to social realism, because that's where it came from – it came from all of the kitchen sink Northern drama. When you look at those old episodes, a lot of it really is quite gritty and bleak. That was Tony Warren's original vision of it. Those episodes where David and Irma Barlow have been involved in a car crash and everyone's waiting to see if they've survived. They're so weighty those episodes and they are the solid foundation that The Street is built on, so a move back towards that I'd love to see.

In terms of popular culture, I think it is less important these days than it has been. I think in 1960 it was an incredibly important programme and throughout the Sixties it was revolutionary, just in terms of television drama – no one had seen the like. People's experiences of television soaps were *Peyton Place* and American imports and things like that, it must have looked quite shocking at the time. With films like *A Taste of Honey*, it was right at the forefront of that movement, of that British social realism, so I think it was fantastically important then. These days, it's become an institution and I don't know whether it's important at all. It still gets the highest ratings – 16, 18 million – so a hell of a lot of people still watch it on a regular basis, but I don't think you could say it was important really.

## Dionne Spence
*Fan*                                              **THE REAL STREET**

My friend lives in Droylesden, in Manchester, and it reminds me of *Coronation Street*. They're all terraced houses and the neighbours know each other's business and they all go to the local pub. When I think of where I live now, it doesn't remind me of *Coronation Street*, I can't relate to it at all, but when I go to my friend's house, yes, it is very much like real life down there. The pub is the local meeting-place and people are just generally friendly.

# Julie Jones
*Fan* **LIKE REAL PEOPLE**

*Coronation Street* is the one programme that I actually bother to watch. Anything else I'm not really concerned about. Part of it with Corrie is that I've got some hardcore mates who are very into it as well, so the first conversation when you meet up is, 'Did you see Corrie?' I know it's really sad, but you've got to do it. You speculate on who's done what and why, do we believe it, if not, what should have happened? If we do believe it, what might happen next and then we've got that done and we can get on.

It's the lack of sense of community now and the lack of people taking responsibility for each other – it's almost like you need some common ground, and I think, unfortunately, we're getting it through telly and things like Corrie. I know we've actually discussed these people as if they're real and that's pitiful because we're supposed to be quite intelligent, but it becomes part of your life. And if you happen to see an actor while you're out, there is that kind of thing that you think you know them. You're about to go, 'Oh, Hi' and then you think, 'This person's on television, they don't know me and I don't know them', and it's totally mortifying. You can see how some people really do believe in them and mob them in the supermarket.

It's not acceptable to a lot of people to admit you watch it. It's still, like, 'Oh, the soaps', but they secretly must watch it themselves because where are those 18 million coming from, somebody's got to be watching it. I would admit openly that I watch it and I think it's great, but I think people are quite snotty about it or say, 'I'm watching it in a post-modernist, ironic sort of way and that's OK.'

I'll put it on and Richard will watch it if it's on and Oscar's just making as much noise as he can so I'll probably catch about half of it in any episode. But I used to love watching it quietly, uninterrupted – and if somebody rings at half seven it's, 'How well do you know me? Is it half seven and is it Wednesday? Well, sod off then!' Five nights a week would be too much of a commitment. I wouldn't like it if it was five nights a week. I know it's four now and you'd think it wouldn't make a lot of difference. Mind you, before that seemed like too much, but we've got used to that. My mum still watches it, but I don't think she's *got* to watch it like I have. If I go away, I'd make sure I'd get it taped. It would be an absolute feast, watching all those episodes, it would be fab.

Me and my pal Gary, we've been to the World of *Coronation Street* in Blackpool twice, that's how sad we are. If I went to Blackpool again, I'd probably go again. He once bought me a spoon with Brian Tilsley's head on it, which is a fabulous thing to have, but I've not gone to tea towels yet. He's made me T-shirts with various characters on saying things and he makes me cards with characters. We like it because it's camp.

## Christabelle Embleton
*Fan*                                                   **I *NEVER* MISS IT!**

I love it, I never miss it. One of my sons was born on the Wednesday and I got up a few hours later to watch it. He was born about three or four o'clock in the afternoon and I was up watching it that night at half past seven! This was in the hospital. I didn't even have him in my arms, I left him in one of those cot things! Even when I'm on holiday and I'm in a hotel, I rush back to watch it at half past seven. I then get told off! I never go abroad – I'd miss it! I prefer The Street to all the other soaps. My mum, who's 20-odd years older than me, has never watched an episode. We started off watching it together and I said, 'Oh, this is good' and she said, 'It's a load of rubbish' and she's still not watched it, she still doesn't like it. Strange.

## Nance Green
*Fan*                                                          **A PART OF ME**

I feel a mixture of embarrassment and pride to confess that I watch it to people who don't – it feels like a weakness that I have to admit to, but, actually, it's because it's different here. I come from up North, you lot don't understand it's something we do and it's an important part of me. I would be quite happy if someone decided to axe the show, then I wouldn't have to watch it any more and I could do other things in that time. For as long as they carry on producing it, I'm going to have to watch it!

One of the reasons why I stick with it, why I'm faithful to it, is because I live in Manchester. There have been times when I've thought, 'Why on earth do I carry on watching this programme?' and I think I'd feel disloyal if I stopped watching it and just watched *EastEnders*.

If *Coronation Street* went to every night of the week, I'd carry on watching it, I'd find the time. If I go away I'll set the video and record, that would be a priority. And I take videos with me if I'm going to stay with family, for example James' parents, and they say, 'Nance has got to have her soap' and people end up saying, 'Your programme's on.'

## Lynn de Santis
*Fan*                                        **IT'S GONE FOREVER**

I kept watching it through my teens – probably in my twenties may have drifted off, simply because, late teens and twenties, I was going out and maybe not around quite as much – but, really, I've always followed the plots. You always know what's going on, even though you may not watch it for a while. You pick it up again when you start watching; it's part of your life really.

I think the rest of the family watch it tolerating it really – they enjoy it, but they wouldn't go, 'Oh, it's half past seven, it's Corrie', it's me who does that. My husband would never dream of putting it on, but, if it's on, he'll watch it and he'll enjoy it and he'll laugh at the right characters and go ooh and ah at the right scandal bits, but, really, I'm the one who's addicted. I don't watch, I dabble in, *Brookside* occasionally. Slightly more than *Brookside* I watch *EastEnders*, but, Corrie, I've got to be there, I've got to watch it and if I do miss an episode, I have to watch the omnibus. If I miss the omnibus, I'm a bit put out by it. If I miss a Friday night *and* the omnibus, then it's gone forever. You don't get repeats of *Coronation Street*, whereas, if you miss an episode of *Casualty*, you know in three months' time its going to be back, so I do get quite upset, but it's a soap and it's easy to pick up the story.

## Gordon Burns
*Television Presenter and fan*                **VISITING THE STREET**

I didn't watch the show when I was living in Northern Ireland. I was aware that it was on, but I was young and out and about doing other things. I was a slight latecomer to *Coronation Street*, I suppose. It was really only when I joined Granada Television in 1973 that I started watching – partly because I was in the building where it was being made – and I bumped into the stars in the lift every day and got to know them. I got into it and got hooked.

The street which is there now isn't the original. They knocked the original down and sold off the bricks. In fact I tried to buy a brick but failed! But it was always something you went to see. If a friend or relation or my Mum or Dad came over from Northern Ireland to visit I always took them to see the Street. This of course was before the Granada Studio Tours. So it was always a great treat if you could go and stand on Coronation Street and have your photograph taken. Because there weren't the tours in those days; it was unique and there was some kudos in being able to do that.

## Dionne Spence
*Fan*                                    **BEING PART OF *CORONATION STREET***

Wherever we are, Gerald and I, we both get back for *Coronation Street* or we don't go anywhere until *Coronation Street* has been on. If we do happen to miss an episode, we catch up on the Sunday. We all sit round and watch it and then afterwards we will talk about things that have happened in the show and look forward to the next episode. If we go on holiday, we have to get somebody to tape the Sunday episodes for us. I know it sounds really sad, but its true, we are avid. I think it will pass on to our children.

Going down the Street was fantastic, it was brilliant actually seeing where these people supposedly lived and going in the pub. It was just great being in there. It was eerie in a way being in that pub. I know it's a new set but all those memories that are there of all those previous characters. I felt that I could be a part of it myself.

## Steve Embleton
*Fan*                                              **A BIRTHDAY TREAT**

I am an obsessive viewer. If I go out, I tape it. If I miss *EastEnders* or *Brookside*, then I miss them, but I do tape The Street – I won't miss that. I watch all four episodes every week. The shift to four episodes has been good as far as I'm concerned. I don't think the programme has lost anything – the storylines are still there, the characters are still there and it moves along just as well as when it was twice a week.

We went to see The Street on 2 July 1993 – I remember it because it was my birthday. We went on a three-day break and spent a day in Granada studios. When I got on The Street, I just couldn't believe I was really there. It was such a big impact. You just walked around a corner and you are there, actually on the set. Then we went to my friend Graham's a few days later, who had come with us, to see the photographs, and he had the whole house decked out like The Street. He had the theme music playing as we walked through the door – it was like reliving it again. I had taken well over a hundred pictures and they had taken just as many.

I've also got a load of pictures of the cast. I've got a whole album and letters that they have written to me. Sometimes when you write in and ask for a photograph, they put a little note in as well, saying thanks and so on. There's not many I have not received anything from.

## Gordon Burns
*Television Presenter and fan*                    **THE KRYPTON FACTOR**

I am proud to say that I have appeared on *Coronation Street*. It was a bit sneaky, though. When I was presenting *The Krypton Factor*, we had a producer who was very sharp on how to sell programmes. He persuaded *Coronation Street*, in one scene with the family sitting in the house, that there would be a television on in the corner and he persuaded them to have *The Krypton Factor* showing. It was just in the background, but you can recognize my face and my voice while Hilda or Stan, or whoever it was, are having a discussion. So that was the great thrill of my life – to have appeared on *Coronation Street*, albeit in the corner of the room on a television set. My greatest moment!

## Graham Twyman
*Fan*                                  **MAKING 'CORRIE' AT HOME**

My trip to The Street was a miracle. To be quite honest with you, as a child, having grown up with it, it was something we thought would never come true. It really was a miracle. We went with three or four friends of ours on a coach trip to *Emmerdale,* which my wife watches but not me really, and then *Coronation Street*. When you've watched it for 30-odd years, when I got off the coach, well, I still think about it now. We entered the studios and, all of a sudden – we went round the corner, round this brick wall – and you saw the fascia of the Rovers Return. It was unbelievable. You can't believe, after watching it for so long, that you are there. I can't explain it. It was a miracle come true.

We went down the Street, we went in Derek and Mavis' and Des Barnes' houses. We weren't supposed to go in there, but someone had knocked the wall down, so we sneaked in the back. Then security came along and made us come out. Nobody has probably ever been in there, but we did. We got a photo of myself looking through the front window – I should never have been in there. You walked down the Street and you go in the pub – you've seen it on the telly for 30 years and then suddenly it comes real.

I'd been with my wife and three friends and we decided we shouldn't show each other our photographs until we'd all got them developed, so we arranged for a special night. We didn't tell any of our friends, but we put green and yellow paper chains on the ceiling, then did the house out with things from The Street, such as beer bottles done up as milk stout, *Coronation Street* mirrors and pictures – we did the house out like the snug. When our friends arrived, we'd made a tape of the signature tune and played it as they came in. Then we showed each other the photographs, then we watched a video of *Coronation Street*. If anyone was to hear this, they would think we were mad! We are obsessed by it.

I have never missed an episode. We go on holiday and we get my friend's mother to tape it and when we come home we have to have time off work and stay up all night catching up with it. We can't miss an episode, we daren't. You might find this hard to believe, but it's absolutely true. I'm a funeral director, but if there is a funeral or a wedding in The Street, I go out at eight o'clock for an hour to have a glass of wine or something at my local club, and Lynn and I always have cheese and biscuits or a glass of wine. Now we start the tape. If we're going to eat, we don't eat until we get back to the buffet at the funeral or the wedding because we think we're there. We can't eat our food until they all get back. We grieve with them, because we've seen those people for years, especially me being in the funeral business. When we get back, I say to Lynn, don't you eat your food until I get back. We'll eat it together cos we're there with them.

You miss the ones that are gone. It's nice to see new people come in, but it would be nice to see some of the older ones come back. I don't want it to get too much like *Home and Away*. The Street's still good, but I'm worried that it might lose it a little bit. We want some pensioners – Percy Sugden, Phyllis with the blue rinse, we want some of them in it. I wanted to frost my front window over like the Rovers Return, but my wife wouldn't let me. I wanted to paint the house green as well but she said 'no'.

# Gary Parkinson
*Fan*                                            **THE STREET IN THE STARS**

I've got a collection of videos. There was a series and they did one every couple of months and it was based around one character, so you'd get a whole tape of Bet clips and then a whole tape of Stan and Hilda clips. I've got about 12 of those. I've got a couple of videos that were made around its twenty-fifth anniversary, which involved some character, who supposedly lived in The Street in the Fifties and had since then emigrated to Australia, who came back to visit and she goes into the pub and meets Hilda and Betty and they reminisce and it goes into clips from the past. I've got pretty much every book that was ever published on *Coronation Street* – the twenty-fifth anniversary celebration book, the excellent *Weatherfield Life*, which charts the history of The Street from when it was built in 1902 up to the present day. I am a bit obsessed with it. I've not actually been to the real set. I've been to the World of *Coronation Street* in Blackpool three times, which has got a full-size replica of the set, but I've not been to the Granada Studios Tours.

I've been an astrologer for 15 years and I thought I'd combine my obsession with astrology with my obsession with *Coronation Street*, so I did a chart for the first episode and looked at that and then I realized that most of the long-term characters, they give their birth dates, so you can theoretically draw up a chart for the character rather than the actor. So, I started doing that and they work. Three years ago, I made predictions for about ten of the major characters and we were trying to get it in a newspaper and no newspaper would take it, but just about every single character prediction that I made has come true. It's really quite alarming. I predicted Martin Platt, his career would be in trouble, which it was with Les Battersby who took an overdose when Martin Platt was supposed to be looking after him so he lost his job and has since got it back. Mike and Alma Baldwin would be divorced by the end of last year. I predicted that Bet would come back, which she did only for a week-long episode, but she did come back. Loads of things, it's quite odd. I know for a fact that they don't have an astrologer working on The Street, so presumably the birth dates are picked at random, but the character traits fit them as well.

## Nance Green
*Fan*                                                    **MY BEDTIME STORY**
..................................................................................................................
Watching it, I think, is a time to stop and do nothing. I've always looked at it as being my bedtime story. It's like, if you haven't got time to sit and read a novel for half an hour a day, at least you can have that input

where you don't have to make an effort and you can even do other things while you're watching it and you can still keep up with the storyline, which is the important thing, and make sure you know what the characters are up to.

When I first had children, ten years ago, I always recorded it and, at the end of the day, when everything was done, I would sit down and watch it at my leisure and it was my bedtime story. When you asked me about this, I worked out I have spent three months of my life watching *Coronation Street* and just think what I could have done in those three months!!

## Norman Frisby
*Granada Press Officer* **THE QUEEN'S VISIT**

The most enormous highlight was in 1992, the day the Queen came. We had moved into the set near the Granada Tours. I thought that was it. I could not believe my eyes that here was the Queen and the Duke of Edinburgh walking down Coronation Street. Obviously she knew who the characters were because she was well briefed, but I shouldn't think she's time to watch *Coronation Street*. No doubt the *Sun* and the *Mirror* would think that she would watch *Coronation Street*.

## Jim Walker
*Granada Television Producer* **STILL THERE**

My most enjoyable brush with The Street came on a summer's afternoon when Roland Joffe – who later won an Oscar for *The Killing Fields* – came to see me in something of a panic because he'd been asked to direct a few episodes of The Street and confessed, in his cut-glass accent, that he had no acquaintance whatsoever with working-class life. Would I give him an insight?

I took him to Gledhill Street in Ordsall, Salford, which was identical to Cresswell Street where I had lived. We sat on the kerbstone while I showed him the joys of dropping pebbles down the grid and of excavating tar from the melting street. I talked to him about the last 'knocker-up' who had only just retired. I asked him to imagine all the thousands of people who had lived and died here and had never seen London, let alone a desert or an ocean. We talked to the housewives whose community was about to be demolished against their will. I think Roland found the tiny rooms and narrow ginnels quite a shock, but he didn't show it.

As we left, we promised to campaign to save Gledhill Street, but, needless to say, it's gone now. And so, for that matter, has Cresswell Street. And that's the crucial point – Coronation Street hasn't. That's why we like to know that *Coronation Street*, at least, still survives.

## Jim Quick
*Graphic Artist* **THE STREET OF THE FUTURE**

*Coronation Street* in the year 2050 – will it have any actors in it or will they all be virtual or will it be done on the Web? The future, I think, is more important than the past when you talk about how soaps are going to be delivered. When they offer us the choice with true interactive digital, the choice of six cameras to cut from, are they going to do the same with soap operas? Is the next stage to say, Do you want a happy ending and will you just concentrate on the characters you're interested in? Do all the characters need to go into studio any more or could they just sit in front of their webcam and deliver their lines and put their face on to a robot model? Will people care, because are they real characters now? Part of the fun of watching *Coronation Street* was they were partly cartoon, there was that spin put on it. With Bet Gilroy, the brooches were just slightly too big and the necklines just slightly too plunging – they were caricatures – but in virtual reality, do you want to be part of it as a new character?

So, where to next for *Coronation Street*?

# CHAPTER TWO

# Florizel Street

It all began, as everyone surely knows, as a 16-part series, created by Tony Warren, and initially called *Florizel Street*. Warren was a young writer in the Promotions Department at Granada Television, working alongside Jack Rosenthal and Geoff Lancashire – two other young men who in later years would also write for The Street.

Warren had joined Granada in 1958 at the age of 21. He had originally been interviewed by Casting with a view to offering him a role, but his baby face and beanpole figure hardly suggested much in the way of parts. Casting Director Margaret Morris then surprised him by not only being aware that he was writing, but asking if he might be interested in talking to Harry Elton, a producer who was trying to build up a team of writers at Granada. It wasn't long before Warren had been taken on by the new Manchester-based television company and was writing for a series called *Shadow Squad*.

Sir Denis Forman, then Programme Controller of the company, later Chairman, remembers Tony Warren at the time as 'a willowy figure with a long cigarette holder and a cane, who affected the style and manner of speech of Noel Coward'. He was 'unmistakably a grown-up child actor', he adds.

Warren had indeed been a child actor, though maybe more acurately described as a bit actor, who had also turned his hand to writing. Back in 1956, he had written a script called *Where No Birds Sing*, a yarn about life in a Northern backstreet. It was the seed from which *Coronation Street* would later grow. The following year, he developed that same script, giving it more humour and called it *Our Street*. To cut a long story short, the script was sent to the BBC, but, typically, Warren is still awaiting a response!

Elton, however, thought that Warren might benefit from a stint in the Promotions Department – a unique training ground in the mysterious ways of television. Warren was still only 21. Over the next year or so, he wrote scripts for the local news magazine programme *People and Places* and was also given an exclusive contract to write episodes for *Biggles*. It was good money – £30 a week – but Warren was not altogether happy. Perched on top of Elton's filing cabinet one day, he demanded to be allowed to write 'what I know about'. Elton ordered him down and recklessly gave him 24 hours to come up with an idea that would take 'Britain by storm'.

Warren returned to his old script and the idea that had continued to burn in his mind. Here were the characters of The Street – the lady who ran the corner shop, old women like his own granny, the street floozie, ordinary families with their problems, young lads struggling to escape the parochialism and suffocation of working-class Salford. It was almost a Manchester version of Damon Runyan's New York. These were the real people who existed in the Victorian, back-to-back terraced houses, that could be spotted in any large industrial city or even town. It wasn't just Salford, it was Birkenhead, Wigan, Middlesbrough, anywhere in the North. The place didn't matter; it was the characters that mattered – their problems, their struggles to make ends meet, the monotony of work, their relationships, their leisure time.

Warren began with one household, one family, then added a second, a third, a fourth, then a corner shop, a pub and so on. Very soon he had a whole street, a whole community. *Coronation Street* had been born – or, rather, *Florizel Street* as he called it.

When Warren walked in and presented Episode 1 of the script, Elton immediately fell in love with it and promptly showed it to Stuart Latham, one of their more experienced drama producers, who was equally ecstatic. An idea had been born and, thankfully for future generations of television viewers, had been recognized by someone. Now, though, they had to convince the powers that be at Granada to give them the go-ahead to make the series.

Both Elton and Latham went to see Forman. 'Read this,' they told him. 'Give me 20 minutes then,' he replied. They returned 30 minutes later. 'Good characters, good dialogue,' he told them in a strangely non-committal way. Elton and Latham were not too taken by his lack of enthusiasm. Faces were pulled. 'Is that all you've got to say?' they asked. Forman continued to hedge his bets, but at least agreed to take the script to the Programme Committee, which decided future projects, but added that they should certainly find a better title than *Florizel Street*.

True to his word, when the next Programme Committee met at Granada's office at Golden Square, in London, *Florizel Street* was on the agenda, but, again, there was a lukewarm response. Forman, who was now sold on the idea, remembers Alex Bernstein being dismissive: 'Dreary, trivial, downbeat.' Victor Peers was also not impressed, concerned that people down South would not be able to understand the accents and idioms of Salford. Sidney Bernstein was vague – it wasn't his cup of tea, he said, others should decide. Company Secretary Ken Brierley didn't sound enthusiastic either. However, Cecil Bernstein was impressed and gradually Forman and his one ally began to work on the rest of them, finally persuading the others to at least give it a try. Reluctantly, the Programme Committee agreed that it could go ahead, though only as a seven-part series and only if they changed the title.

The news hardly generated much confidence back in Manchester. There was a feeling that the company was only half committed to an idea that they reckoned 'a miracle'. At least they had not given it the thumbs down, though, as they would later to another proposal – *Z-Cars*. (Writer Elwyn Jones finished up taking that to the BBC.)

To get production under way, a team was quickly assembled. Harry Latham was to be Producer, while a young scriptwriter called Harry Kershaw (later better known as H. V. Kershaw) was appointed Script Editor. Tony Warren would, of course, write the scripts. Denis Parkin was to design the sets. This was a crucial a job, as time would prove – Parkin had to get it right.

Today, Parkin remembers how he and Tony Warren 'used to wander round Salford'. They homed in on a row of terraced houses in a street called Archie Street. It met precisely their notion of what Coronation Street should look like. The local MP, Frank Allaun, was, with some justification, to proudly call himself the MP for Coronation Street for many years, until Archie Street was demolished in the late 1970s.

They even 'found a pub that would be the Rovers Return, and then we found a street to film the opening titles, which didn't have a pub at the other end, but film was in such a state then that you couldn't see that far.' Having established the exterior character of The Street, they then set about designing the interiors, looking at each of the characters and deciding the kind of furniture and decoration that would be most suitable. Albert Tatlock, for instance, would have heavy Edwardian furniture, but Elsie Tanner would be a little more modern, but not too house-proud. 'The Barlows,' remembers Parkin, 'were the opposite ... the Hardmans' was a bit gloomy because the mother was slightly odd. Esther Hayes was The Street's agony aunt, a bit nondescript. Harry Hewitt didn't have a wife, so he was a bit untidy' and so it went on. Characters and their homes, built brick by brick. What about the names of the characters? 'Well, they came from Pendlebury Church in Salford, from the gravestones,' he told Geoff Lancashire.

Casting was assigned to José Scott, who had been at Granada since 1959, working as Booking Assistant to the Casting Director, Margaret Morris. It was a big break for José who was really only given the task because she was a Northerner and Margaret Morris, who came from the South, thought José might have a better idea. She was enthusiastic from the start: 'As soon as you read the script, you knew. It was like being in a weekly rep – "Ooh, I'd love to play that part!" '

She decided that the accents had to be genuinely Northern and started scouring the repertory theatres of Lancashire and Yorkshire for actors with genuine ability and accents. She also decided that the street itself was to be the star of the show and, consequently, did not want any well-known actors. One by one, the characters were filled. Bill Roache was spotted in rep at Oldham, Doris Speed was an old friend, and José also knew Pat Phoenix.

When José suggested Pat Phoenix for the part of Elsie, she met with some resistance. Margaret Morris was 'absolutely adamant that she didn't want Pat in the thing. She said, "Oh, she'll go miles too far, she'll go right over the top ... we don't want anyone going too far" and Tony and I fought like mad. I had been in rep with her and I said, "I'm sure she won't", because Pat had got a tremendous sense of the theatre.'

Casting Ena Sharples was also difficult, until Tony Warren had a brainwave, remembering her from his days as a child actor at the BBC. Violet Carson had also played piano for Wilfred Pickles in *Have A Go*. With Ena, Elsie and Annie cast, they were well on their way.

Granada's music man Eric Spear was asked to write the music for the opening and closing titles and Tony Warren continued with the daunting task of writing the scripts. Dry runs were organized to audition and test actors and two pilot episodes were to be made. However, when they were completed, they were not well received by Granada's executives. The whole project stood on the brink of collapse.

As the Sixth Floor still had its doubts, Harry Elton came up with a novel idea: he would show the programme on television sets throughout the building and canvas opinion. Pompous Sixth-Floor executives might not appreciate it, but he was convinced that ordinary Northern folk would love it. Questionnaires were organized and the showing of the programme advertised around the building. Elton wanted everyone to see the show, from cleaners to visitors. When the results came back, opinion was overwhelmingly favourable, even though it clearly showed a distinct split between those who loved it and those who hated it. There seemed to be no in-between.

Sound engineer Alistair Houston vividly remembers his reaction: 'We did two dry runs as *Florizel Street* and the thing that I remember about it is that, after we'd done the first dry run, I came home and told my mother-in-law, who came from Salford, that we were about to do a six-part series called *Florizel Street* and that she would love it because it was just the sort of thing that people of her age would get involved in, never dreaming that it was going to be what it ended up.'

When Elton took the results of his straw poll upstairs, the executives climbed down. On 25 August 1960, it was formally agreed that *Florizel Street* – as it was still known – could go ahead and be extended to 16 episodes. By mid October, Tony Warren had finalized the first six scripts. Everything needed to be completed by the end of November so that rehearsals for the first show could begin on the morning of Monday 5 December.

By November 1960, a title had still not been chosen. In truth, they hadn't really put their minds to it, but time was now pressing and a suitable title was needed. Harry Kershaw in his autobiography remembered that the three Harrys – himself, Harry Latham and Harry Elton – locked themselves in a room, with a bottle of Irish whiskey, determined not to emerge until they had decided on a new title. All three agreed that it should follow the initial suggestion and be the name of a street. Various names were thrown into the ring, but two emerged as clear favourites – Jubilee Street and Coronation Street. A vote was taken and all three retired for the evening. Next morning, when they came into their office, there was a memo confirming the name of the programme. It was to be called *Coronation Street*. Kershaw spotted Harry Elton, already at his desk: 'So it's to be called *Coronation Street*, then,' he said. 'Personally, I voted for *Jubilee Street*.'

'That's funny,' replied Kershaw, 'I'm damn sure I voted for *Jubilee Street* as well.' Given that there were only three of them, it was clear that the show's Producer, Harry Latham, had pulled a fast one. Of course, it didn't matter in the end. *Coronation Street, Jubilee Street*, whatever it was called, the programme would have been a success, although maybe *Florizel Street was* a bit of a mouthful! That's the official story. Denis Parkin, who was designing the sets, has another version, not much different and again involving alcohol!

It was now full steam ahead. All 22 characters were cast, the set was constructed and the directors appointed. On the morning of 5 December 1960, they all gathered in the studio to be begin rehearsals. The show was to go out twice a week, on a Friday and Monday evening at 7pm. Both episodes were to be done on the Friday evening, with the first show going out live, while the second would be recorded, 15 minutes later, as for live, but transmitted on the Monday.

Although recording facilities were available, editing was not. It put tremendous pressure on the actors, though, thankfully, their backgrounds in the theatre at least meant they had plenty of experience of live performances. None the less, there seems to have been some surprise when Stuart Latham informed them that the first show would be going out live. Philip Lowrie, who was to play Dennis Tanner, was later to describe it as 'the most frightening moment of my life, ever'. Another actor described it as 'being thrown in at the deep end'. There was no room for mistakes. If the scenery fell down, so be it; if lines were fluffed, they had to make do as best they could; if a camera went down, they would have to switch cameras. It was an adventure, living on your wits.

Bill Roache remembers the cast squeezed into the wings of the sets: 'You had to freeze, you couldn't cough or anything. Once your scene was finished, you froze. It was the most terrifying ordeal.' By the second episode, recorded a little later, everyone was beginning to feel a touch more confident, a shade more relaxed. Within a few weeks, most of the nerves had disappeared.

So the show went out, beginning on Friday 9 December at 7pm. Although it had been offered to the ITV network, not everyone wanted it. Some thought it too parochial to Manchester. Both Tyne-Tees Television and ATV in the Midlands opted out. Tyne-Tees joined three months after the start, while ATV came in a further three months down the line. At that point, the programme switched to 7.30pm on Mondays and Wednesdays.

Former Granada Press Officer Norman Frisby remembers that Cecil Bernstein 'decreed that we were not to publicize it very heavily because we were a bit nervous and we didn't want to make a big song and dance about the programme if it was not going to succeed. So, we didn't have any billings in the *TV Times* for the first few weeks and we certainly didn't have any press releases or a press launch. We didn't push the boat out with the publicity – far from it, we kept it under wraps and, of course, the newspapers themselves in those days were not all that interested in television, so they didn't pursue us in the way that they did subsequently.'

With so little pre-publicity, the result was that the show went out almost unnoticed, except in the *Daily Mirror* where Ken Irwin, the following morning, gave it that now famous scathing review: 'The programme is doomed from the outset,' he predicted, 'with its dreary signature tune and grim scene of terraced houses and smoking chimneys.'

Irwin has come in for much ridicule, but, in all honesty, he wasn't alone. Clearly Granada itself was nervous, especially on the Sixth Floor, while others, such as one of its later writers Tom Elliott, were also not too taken: 'My very first impression when I saw it was "It's not about Manchester", because of the accents. There was a lot of dialect, too, and Mancunians don't have dialect to a great extent. I was not impressed by this depiction, or this distortion, of my home city. I was born in Gorton in Manchester, so it was bogus as far as I was concerned.'

Warren's friend and work colleague Geoff Lancashire was another who didn't take immediately to the show: 'Like everybody else, I didn't think it would last,' he says. 'I remember talking to Tony Warren and he was thinking what I thought and I said, "I don't think so Tony, no one south of Stockport will understand you. But I like the characters, I like the names."'

Whatever the reaction, *Coronation Street* was under way. The memory of that first night was to live on in the minds of all those who witnessed it, whether production staff, actors or even viewers. It was recalled by Tony Warren some years later: 'the sort of night legends are made of. The show went out live, and there was an excitement around the building that I have never known before or since.'

## Bob Greaves
*Television Presenter*                                    **A CHARMING MAN**

Harry Kershaw – H. V. Kershaw – the original Script Editor and later a Producer for many years, I think he wrote it as well. He was just a funny, amiable, guy who was lovely to be with. It was always a pleasure to be in his company. He had wit, he had charm, he had urbanity. He was simply very funny. He did a good job. He probably took it seriously, but he never, ever gave the impression that he took it *too* seriously. He never gave me the impression that the job ever created problems with the personnel, the management; he just sailed through it quite serenely, a charming, charming man and I miss him dearly.

## John Finch
*Scriptwriter, Script Editor & Producer*   **THE DOUBLE-HEADED PENNY**

I sent a play in to Granada and Derek Granger [*Coronation Street* Producer] wrote and said he wanted to see me, so I went and had a chat. He offered me all these different series they were doing at that time, but I didn't like any of them, so I said 'No'. Then he said, 'We're doing this thing *Coronation Street*.' It hadn't gone out then – Tony was still writing the script – and he gave me a copy of Tony's first script. Straight away after I'd read it, I said, 'This is it, I'll do this.' The characters were fantastic. So I saw Harry Kershaw, who was Script Editor, and he commissioned me to do Episode 24.

The characterization in that first script was terrific. Up to that time, I'd always had great difficulty in constructing a play, I had loads of half-finished plays that had no endings and the BBC tried to encourage me. They said, 'You're like an exciting boxer – you come out from the corner, with your fists going, and then nothing happens.' *Coronation Street* taught me construction, Harry Kershaw in particular. Harry was very good at construction. Jack Rosenthal says the same. Apart from being able to earn a living, I owe *Coronation Street* that debt.

There must have been a dozen or 18 writers on *Coronation Street* at that point, coming in and out, but I was the only one who survived that first stint. They were trying people out. You did a trial script.

I always remember, it was Christmas Eve when the phone rang at home. My wife and I were absolutely stony broke and Harry Kershaw was on the phone and he said, 'We like your script, we'd like you to do another.' A couple of weeks later, they offered me a year's contract, so I said 'OK'. I went back to the engineering firm where I was working in Rochdale and said, 'I'm sorry, but I'll have to resign because I've had this marvellous opportunity', and they said, 'Would you come for a half a day a week and we'll pay you the same as a consultant?' So, I carried on for a year, running the two things side by side.

In the very beginning, it was just a dozen people crammed into this tiny office, with Harry Kershaw sat behind a desk and everybody tossing ideas around and he was writing it down and sorting it out into episodes and scenes. Then he shoved it into the Typing Pool and then he gave trial scripts to all the people who were there. When I saw him, it was a one-to-one thing, so I was lucky. Out of that first dozen or so, everybody fell by the wayside except me.

Harry and I then used to meet and work out a storyline for two episodes between us and then we'd toss a coin to see who did which, because the second episode is always the best episode to write. The first episode was setting up and the second episode was really the guts of the thing. I always reckoned he had a double-headed penny because he always got the second episode.

## José Scott
*Casting Director* **FINDING THE CAST**

I started working at Granada in 1959 and I was the Booking Assistant to Margaret Morris, who was the Casting Director.

Tony had been talking to me about *Coronation Street* for a long time and I'd read almost all the episodes because I think he wrote the first 26, so we'd talked about it. In fact, we'd spent many hours discussing what it would be like if it ever got off the ground. When eventually they got the go-ahead to do it, Margaret Morris said, 'Well you're the expert on the North [she was a Southerner], so try your hand at this lot, but I'll be there to give you a hand', which, of course, she was. But she really gave me my head and, after a very short time, once it had all got going, I got made up to Assistant Casting Director and took over. Margaret was instrumental in being part of the beginning because she was a very good Casting Director and she eventually became a producer of The Street.

Tony had given me the scripts, of course, to read and the characters, which he'd talked about, and, of course, the characters he didn't need to talk about. As soon as you read the script, you knew. It was like being in a weekly rep – 'Ooh, I'd love to play that part!' There were quite a lot of plays then that were being done that were purporting to be from the North and you would hear this awful accent and it was nowhere nearer Yorkshire or Lancashire than the man in the moon. So, we both said, 'We're certainly not having anything that isn't the genuine article, they've got to come from the North. It doesn't matter whether they're Liverpool or Manchester or Yorkshire or wherever, but the proper North, and nobody particularly well known.' Of course, nobody particularly well known wanted to do it anyway – it was only this try-out thing. So that was how it all started and we held tremendous auditions for weeks and weeks.

Before a casting session, I would have been to the theatre or whatever – we went all over the place. It wasn't at all unusual to set off on a Friday and go to Liverpool and then go to York and, of course, we always kept notes and things of everybody, photographs. I would get a list of people who might be possible and then we'd ask them to come and see us and then they would make a short list and say, 'Well, right, we'll put you on camera, give you a camera test.' It's odd to think that Ken Farrington was very highly tipped as being Denis Tanner and then Philip Lowrie finished up as the perfect Denis Tanner and Ken Farrington became Annie's son. Casting is a gut feeling and the whole thing was something so new to all of us really.

Once it took off, there were actors who we would have liked to audition, but we made it quite clear that The Street was the star. I know there were quite a few stars who do come from the North and say, 'Well, I've never been asked to be in it', but that was the reason, they were already stars and we didn't want to make it unbalanced because, really, nobody did.

Strangely enough, I don't think it was difficult for theatre actors to trans-fer to television. Probably the ones who got in were the lucky ones who didn't give off a performance, they just got hold of the script and said, 'Oh, hello mother, how are you?' It was very fortunate for actors in those days, or would-be actors, because we were doing quite a lot of other programmes, like *The Verdict is Yours* and *Magistrates Court* and things like that, and there were always small parts that needed to be played and so I would put them in that little part and we would get a chance to look at them. Even if it was only a maid or a stewardess or something like that, maybe they'd only have two or three lines to say, so that was another showcase for them. Ones who did find it difficult didn't get in. I suppose it was like being in the theatre. You know you've got to go on, come what may.

In the very early days, it's interesting to think that people like Pat Routledge and Prunella Scales were on The Street, but a lot of them seemed to want to stay [on The Street]. There was something very cosy and comforting and, of course, there was the security.

It's amazing to think that, actually, Bill Roache was the most attractive young man. I remember going to see him at Oldham and thinking 'My God'. He would be about 26, 27, when he was there, because he had been in the Army, and Anne, his wife, was there. But he really was quite magical, actually. I'm always amazed that Bill has just stuck in The Street. When people say he's very dull, it amazes me to think how he wasn't dull in the early days, he really was quite sensational and a very good actor, but I think a lot of them, in a way, settled. They obviously enjoyed it very much being the characters that they were and settled for as long as they could stay there.

## Geoff Lancashire
*Scriptwriter* **EARLY DAYS**

The Street started in 1960 and, like everybody else, I didn't think it would last. I remember talking to Tony Warren and he was thinking what I thought. And I said, 'I don't think so, Tony, no one south of Stockport would under-stand you, but I like the characters, I like the names. Where did you get the names from?' He said, 'Well, they came from Pendlebury Church in Salford, from the gravestones.' I said, 'Really? Well they're good names.'

It was beautifully cast, José Scott was the Casting Director. They wanted everyone in the cast to be from south-east Lancashire and, by and large, they were. I think Bill Roache was at Oldham Rep – he came down for an audition. Pat Phoenix was touring in some show – she wasn't using that name, though. She came and auditioned and was perfect. Ena Sharples, I suppose, was difficult because the way Tony described her didn't fit, but Tony came up with the answer. He said, 'How about Violet Carsons?' I remember thinking at the time, 'She's the pianist in the Wilfred Pickles show.' Tony said, 'She's also Auntie Violet on BBC North and I remember her being in a quiz once.' She came for an audition and she put the hairnet on for the audition.

The show started and it was amazingly successful from the word go. It went out at seven o'clock on Monday and Wednesday. In those days, the transmitters would overlap. If you were in an ATV area, but quite north, you could get Granada, so people were picking it up [in the ATV area]. At the end of 13 weeks, ATV said, 'We'll take it' because, at the beginning, some of the companies weren't taking it. It was in the Top Ten and the press picked it up.

The term that no one used in those days was 'soap opera' – that was a very American idea, to do with radio in the 1930s. It was seen as drama. Granada's drama output at that time was amazingly good. The first play that Granada did was *Look Back in Anger* and that set the pattern for the next ten years.

Tony had written 26 episodes while he was in the Promotions Department and, at the end, he was just absolutely exhausted – 'I can't seem to go anywhere else, that's it' – but I think Granada already knew that he obviously needed help. That's where Jack Rosenthal came in and Harry Kershaw and then John Finch.

## Norman Frisby
*Granada Press Officer*                                    **PART OF A TEAM**

All the programmes that we did were new – *My Wife's Sister* and *Skyport* – lots of attempts at doing series, maybe 13-part series involving a close community. Then Tony Warren, who worked in the Promotions Department, apparently came up with this idea and went to see Harry Elton, the then Programme Controller. We didn't have titles in those days, so it was difficult to pin down who was who. Tony sold him the idea of this and we had rehearsals, dry runs, and it was thought that we perhaps ought to show this ambitious new idea, which I think was going to be 13 parts, we ought to show this to the staff and see what they made of it. I think there was a bit of nervousness upstairs with some of the metropolitan people who were then working on drama that it was too Northern, that people wouldn't understand the Lancashire dialect.

So, television sets were installed in the canteen and around the building and we all had to sit down and watch it and then write a piece on what we thought – whether the accents were too strong or whatever. I think probably as a result of that, it was a bit watered down, I think it was more Lancashire and some of the cast were changed as well. The woman who played Ena Sharples was changed after the pilot programme when Violet Carson was brought in.

We used to interview all the artistes, looking for stories for the newspapers, and we had never been confronted before with a cast of 15, 16 maybe 20, all working together on one thing and all of equal prominence. It was stressed to us that there wasn't going to be a star of this show, they were all a team.

We actually produced a form that was circulated to all these actors, asking for their names, addresses, phone numbers, previous jobs, likes and dislikes, hobbies and holidays, things that Press Officers are looking for. We used to jealously guard these things as the years went on because it was wonderful to have Violet Carson's biography written in her own hand and details like where it said 'Age' and she had written, 'What, really?' or something.

We also got together that wonderful photograph, which is still used in books, of the whole cast sitting together. We had to doctor it because two of the people in the photograph were actually dropped between the taking of the photograph and going into the studio, so we had to paint out two people. I think they were only extras, but they rather spoiled the photo.

Then this dry run was made and we all viewed it and I think Joyce Wooller [Granada Executive] said she thought it was an absolute disaster.

## Denis Parkin
*Set Designer*                                    **BUILDING THE STREET**

It was great for the actors because it was the first time they'd done television. Most of them came from Oldham Rep and José Scott cast the kinds of people that the characters were. I did think it was going to be a success because it was the kind of thing that Northern people liked to watch. This is the life I knew, so there must be thousands of other people that feel the same. Ken Irwin at the *Daily Mirror* didn't think so – he savaged it, but he was proved wrong.

It was a wonderful time because we always said we did it in spite of Granada rather than with their help. They just left us alone to do what we wanted, like our own television rep company. Everybody knew everybody. The cast and crew were as one. We used to go with Pat Phoenix on her PAs [personal appearances], go to her house, and people came to ours. It was lovely. We used to do things for them and buy presents for them at Christmas and birthdays.

What they used to do at the PAs, a few of them, they had raffles for the public to raise money for charities and the prize was usually a tray with a glass top and wickerwork around it. And what I used to do was have one of my sketches of The Street photographed and put it under the glass and they all autographed it and that was the prize for the raffle. We did dozens and dozens of those.

I started off by doing the ground plan of a house to fit it into the studio because mentally I knew what the rest of it was going to look like so it was just a matter of fitting it in. In those days, the sides of the set had to be splayed outwards because of the size of three cameras. Also, the layout had to be, as far as possible, so that one set wasn't next to the set that was going to be in the next scene because you had two booms each end of the studio and if that couldn't be done, the boom had to swing from one to the other, which is why, if you watch the old ones, there are so many scenes with people stirring cups of tea until the boom gets there. Sometimes you could hear it, too. And you needed space for three cameras and you couldn't have any ceilings because you had to have a lot of lighting. Most of the lighting directors, one in particular, used to light every square foot to the same intensity and if anybody was reading newspapers they had to be sprayed down until they were nearly black otherwise they flared all over the place.

The director had to work out time for lens changes. One cameraman, Phil Phillips, was wonderful because he could set his camera off like going on a scooter and ride on it from one end of the studio to the other, changing his lens at the same time, and it would stop in exactly the place he wanted it to be. He was brilliant. Everybody was.

In the beginning, the set used to be taken down after the programme on Monday and there were other programmes in the studio because that was the only studio there was. There was *Criss Cross Quiz* on Monday, *Spot the Tune* with Marion Ryan on the other, and then *Coronation Street* went back in.

Nobody ever thought about continuity – it was up to the prop men to remember where everything was. We hired the original props because we didn't know it was going to last that long. In fact, the workbench in Len Fairclough's yard, we were hiring that for about ten years. The same with Albert Tatlock's sideboard, that was hired.

I think most of the viewers thought it was real. It was Archie Street in Salford, the first street. A couple of blocks away from that was either the Kellogg's or the Palmolive factory and there they used to think that we took our cameras into the houses and filmed whatever happened to be going on at the time. I don't know whether the sets were better or people's knowledge was a lot less, but I never got any letters about the set or what was wrong with it, so it must have been right.

After about a month, I thought it was going to go on a bit longer because Tony started to panic about being able to write that many. We had Vince Powell and Harry Driver [writers who went on to work for Thames TV]. The script conferences used to be hilarious because there were all sorts of suggestions that were impossible that people came up with. Harry Driver was a great comic. I had to go to those, tell them what they could have. I don't think I started doing the studio layouts until the script arrived, which was about three weeks before. As far as I can remember, the budget was £175 a week, but that was just materials, we didn't pay for labour, but, still, it wasn't a lot.

I needed to know about cameras and lenses, where booms could reach, where people could be. For the funeral of Ida Barlow, we had to build from one end of The Street to the other. We had about a fortnight to do that. We were always working on three episodes at the same time, or maybe four. One was in the studio, one was in ground-plan stage for the directors, another was in construction and the fourth one was still on the drawing board. That was non-stop – not as much as it is now, it's seven days a week now – but it was great fun and knowing about construction was a great help – you knew about short cuts that nobody else might know about.

By the time of the train crash, we were out where Granada Tours is. Another designer put my set out there – that was in the days when the cobbles were triangles. I can't imagine why he ever did that because there was room to put it the right way round. And then, to try to weatherproof it, he put vacuum foam plastic bricks all over the front and it stayed like that until we went into colour in 1969 and we did tests on it and all the bricks looked bright red. I think mostly it was because the engineers didn't know about turning the colour down, so we had a hell of a time working with that.

I went back to The Street when they changed to colour because they said how awful it looked. Harry Kershaw was producing it. I said, 'Why don't we build it in real brick out there?', so I found a couple of bricklayers. I think we put a new Mission Hall [where Ena Sharples was the caretaker and lived] on at the time and the block of flats stayed as they were and it stayed like that until they wanted to pull it down and put it where it is now.

I used to enjoy doing exteriors in Studio Two. Underneath canal bridges, for when Lucille Hewitt got lost and when Peter Adamson wanted to commit suicide. Exteriors in the studio I did enjoy doing because they were a challenge. The outside of Leonard Swindley's shop I remember we did once, and I also did a perspective street, which ramped underneath that low part of the studio, with a model bus that I borrowed from Manchester Corporation – I think that was for when Lucille got lost, too, so the bus trundled along with its lights on. It worked in those days in black and white; it wouldn't work now. You could get away with more in black and white – at times we even used to extend the set with cardboard. It was too late if anybody noticed.

## Denis Parkin
*Set Designer*                                          **CHANGING ROOMS**

I'd read an article about television design and, a few weeks after that, Roy Stonehouse found an advert in the *Guardian* for a draughtsman at Granada. He showed it to me, I wrote off and got the job. There were two other designers there then from the theatre who used to do all the drawings. I found out very soon that I knew as much as they did, probably more about construction. We had a Head of Design who was a Canadian. He took me out to Kendals to tea one afternoon and said, 'We've got a new programme' – they'd bought it from Associated Rediffusion – and he said, 'If you can find another draughtsman, you can design that.' That was February 1957 and Granada had started in May 1956.

Then, jumping forward to 1960, we did this series about Biggles. Tony Warren wrote those, but, at the time, he was a continuity writer, but he always had this thing about what he called *Florizel Street* then and his office was about half the size of this room with only one chair and a desk, so, when I went in there, I used to sit on the floor and he'd read all this dialogue out to me. We were doing *Biggles*, but it was a series about flying and we never had any film, so it was all in studio and then, in the end, the network refused to take it any more because the viewing figures were so awful. And that was the reason *Coronation Street* started because they had to have something to fill in for this.

Harry Elton gave Tony the chance of doing *Coronation Street* and, at the farewell party for *Biggles*, which was in a pub up Bootle Street, that's when we decided on the name of it. We were probably all half pissed at the time. We decided on Coronation Street because we were talking about when the houses would have been built, so various things came up. Mafeking Street, but they thought it might be open to misinterpretation, Jubilee Street and all around that period, but we ended up with Coronation Street, with that being the coronation of Edward VII, when the houses were built.

We did two dry runs. We had about six weeks to do it and we were still doing *Biggles* at the time, so we worked hard in those days. Tony and I talked about the kinds of houses they were [in Coronation Street] and he knew what kinds they were and I knew what kinds they were so we used to wander round Salford. He found a pub that would be the Rovers Return and then we found a street to film the opening titles, which didn't have a pub at the other end, but film was in such a state then that you couldn't see that far.

I went through the scripts that were there, finding out what the people were like and from what Tony told me and then designing the kinds of houses that they would live in, the kinds of things that they would have and, from the scripts at the time, working out which way round the house would be, whether the fireplace was on the back wall or opposite was the back wall. It had to be one or the other because there was no room to put entrances on the back wall, they had to be each side. And we could only get six sets in the studio at the time, in Studio Two. Because of that, I had to go to script conferences, because it depended on the studio space, what sets they could get in and what they could write about. It worked quite well. It was a lot more work than it is now because now they just design a set and shoot everything in one set and then move on to the next.

Albert Tatlock's house was easy because he was old-fashioned – he must have been there for umpteen years. Elsie Tanner was a bit flash and not very house-proud. The Barlows were the opposite, even though, in the first episode, David was mending his bike in front of the fire, so that gave us which way round that one was. The Hardmans' was a bit gloomy because the mother was slightly odd. Esther Hayes was The Street's agony aunt, a bit nondescript. Harry Hewitt didn't have a wife, so he was a bit untidy. The Mission Hall goes back to when I was very small and my father had an aunt who lived the other side of Leeds, which was where I came from, in a little back-to-back house and, opposite it, was what they called a tin tabernacle, it was a Mission made of corrugated iron. And I remembered that, and I also remembered this aunt had a horse-hair sofa and, when you were a little lad, with short trousers on, all those bits used to stick in your legs, so that was the basis of the Mission. The railway arch at the back was always in Tony's scripts.

## Alistair Houston
*Sound Engineer*                                          **THE SOUND MAN**

I was part of the Sound crew in Studio 2, which was where the programme first started. We did two dry runs as *Florizel Street* and the thing that I remember about it is that, after we'd done the first dry run, I came home and told my mother-in-law, who came from Salford, that we were about to do a six-part series called *Florizel Street* and that she would love it because it was just the sort of thing that people of her age would get involved in, never dreaming that it was going to be what it ended up being. Then, when we came down to doing the actual programme, they decided to change the title to *Coronation Street*.

It was very cramped in the studio because it wasn't a very big studio and we had to have everything there – the street was built in there, the Mission Hall, all the other sets were there and, in commercial breaks, sets would be struck and another set put in.

From a sound point of view, the one thing that I always remember is that the theme music was a bone of contention right up until the dress rehearsal of the first transmission. The *Coronation Street* theme had been specially written, with the various links, ends of parts or between scenes indicators, closing music and the rest of it, but there was also an LP of the CWS brass band and one of the tracks on that, we got themes from it. I can't remember exactly the track, but there was an argument between all the production staff as to whether we were going to use the brass band or the specially written music and, right up to the dress rehearsal, a decision hadn't been made because, for all the rehearsals, we'd play one lot of music on one and another lot on the other, but before dress [rehearsal] Stuart Latham [Producer] and Harry Kershaw [Executive Producer] came in the sound control room and they listened to them all through and the decision that swayed it was the fact that we've paid for this specially recorded music, we'd better use it.

They then didn't have a suitable piece of music for the ends of parts and, in the sound control room, Mike Dunn was doing the sound mixing and I was doing all the tapes and sound effects. The opening of the programme, you never hear the end of the music because it always fades under the first scene, but the end of the opening music ended and there was nothing like that for an end of part because all of the ones that had been written were upbeat like openings, so I suggested that we cut the end off the opening music and play that in. Just by sheer fluke, it lasts five seconds and it worked and so that's my permanent contribution to *Coronation Street*. It was my idea to put that on the end so, from then on, the brass band was never thought about again.

## Norman Frisby
*Granada Press Officer*　　　　**CREEPING INTO THE SCHEDULES**

There were only three of us in the Press Office – a secretary who typed the press releases, me, who did virtually everything single-handed, and I had an assistant, Glyn Standford, a young lad who'd been a messenger boy, virtually a school-leaver, who was at the beginning of a great career for him, too.

Cecil Bernstein was the great power behind Light Entertainment in Granada and he took *Coronation Street* under his wing. He decreed that we were not to publicize it very heavily because we were a bit nervous about it and we didn't want to make a big song and dance about the programme if it was not going to succeed. So, we didn't have any billings in the *TV Times* for it for the first few weeks and we certainly didn't have any press releases or a press launch. We didn't push the boat out with the publicity – far from it, we kept it under wraps and, of course, the newspapers themselves in those days were not all that interested in television, so they didn't pursue us in the way that they did subsequently. So, it got off to a fairly quiet start.

It was reviewed, though, and there was this famous review in the *Daily Mirror* where they said that this thing is never going to take off, it's dreary and nasty and sordid and it's a great disaster and Granada doesn't know what it's doing. On the other hand, there were people like Mary Crozier of the *Guardian* who said, 'This sounds as though it could be good.' It crept on to the screen and, of course, it was only screened in the Granada area. It was virtually a local programme.

ATV didn't take it in the Midlands and I remember companies like Tyne-Tees coming in after a while when they were sure it was good and worth taking. It was quite a while before it was seen in London. It crept on to the network in that way and we had to make special episodes for people that joined after it had been established to fill in the background to it.

It started in December 1960, so it didn't get into the Top Ten until March 1961, by the time it got down to London. The first episode went out on a Friday and then they telerecorded the episode, which I think was for the following Wednesday and I know that we changed the schedule of it to fit in with other companies on the network to make it more acceptable to them.

## José Scott
*Casting Director*                    **ALL DONE FOR PEANUTS**

Everybody so loved the idea of it and they were all Northern people so they knew somebody who was like that.

To start on something totally new is very, very exciting, to be part of it. I think the most nerve-racking thing was that we weren't able to see – now, you see an episode and you have a preview; then there was no preview. Seven-thirty came and you were off, everybody was sitting in the viewing room.

I think it was seen as a success fairly overnight. Within a month, it really was – people started to show an interest and agents would ring up and say, 'You did know that so-and-so came from Preston didn't you?' and you'd think, 'Well I did, but you told me they didn't', because it was really not the thing to be a Northerner. It was so different really because it was sort of not quite of this world and yet it was so down-to-earth but it was fun to watch.

It didn't seem very long before we were all summoned to Denis

Forman's office and he said, 'Congratulations everybody, this has stunned us all.' I think Cecil always thought it would work and Denis thought it might, but nobody had ever done anything like that before, nobody had actually ventured into that kind of a thing, so it was all done for peanuts. We didn't pay anybody anything much – well, of course, nobody got paid much in those days. It was better paid than the theatre, but I think they got £20 an episode and you didn't have to be a member of Equity in the very early days.

I can remember the time when I used to think how lovely, I'll rush home, I'll have a drink, sit there and I'll watch The Street and now I couldn't care less.

We were lucky that we had that period because it will never come again.

## Tom Elliott
*Script Editor and Scriptwriter*  **A VIEW FROM THE BILLET**

I was in the Army when *Coronation Street* first began – that was in 1961. It was being networked then and we were stationed near Aldershot. I was on detachment at that time and I remember driving back in a three-ton truck and passing a few of the lads. One of them said, 'Where have you been, the Rovers Return? Have you been out with Elsie Tanner?' and I thought, 'What are they talking about?' and then I got into the billet. There was this programme – we had a little black-and-white telly stuck up on the wall – and it was all about Manchester. My very first impression when I saw it was, 'It's not about Manchester', because of the accents; there was a lot of dialect, too, and Mancunians don't have dialect to a great extent. And I could pinpoint, he's from Bury, he's from Oldham, she's from Rochdale, so my first impressions were I was not impressed by this depiction or this distortion of my home city. I was born in Gorton in Manchester so it was bogus as far as I was concerned.

## Les Chatfield
*Cameraman and Director*  ***FLORIZEL STREET***

*Coronation Street* was suddenly just there – it was called *Florizel Street* then. We were going to do six, I think, and we did the first one and nobody thought it was anything out of the ordinary – full of all these unknown actors and actresses from the North who José found – and, then, before you knew it, it took off.

The Street was more an experimental thing than the plays we'd been doing because they had all the new young directors on it and they used to try various things because they were new and wanted experience.

Suddenly, *Coronation Street* was there all the time. Then, I think, we only did two a week. As a cameraman, you went to a technical rehearsal and did it the next day. We used to start on a day at lunchtime, rehearse till about seven o'clock and then come in the next day and do it. The worst thing as a cameraman was that the studio was so tiny and you had the street down the middle and all the houses off the sides. It was very cramped and there was a lot of rushing about, so I think it was pretty noisy. I remember the Director, Peter Plummer, deciding one week he wanted to do everything on long lenses, so it would compress everything and make everything look smaller, which made it far worse for us. He thought it was a success, but I don't think anybody else took it up.

The actors and actresses were different because they weren't names. They were nice people. I remember Pat Phoenix was so different when she started. She was blowzy, but she was obviously good for the part, she was ideal for it. I think that's why it was so successful, because it was the women who were the big strong characters, which was unusual on television then. I think the three old ladies and Pat Phoenix were the stars then and all the rest were coming up – Bill Roache and Alan Rothwell.

I can't remember anything really of the early episodes, except for rows between Pat Phoenix and Violet Carson, Elsie Tanner and Ena Sharples within the story. I think it was quite a bit later that rows started coming within the cast.

I was a cameraman for about seven years on *Coronation Street*, I suppose. Over those seven years, videotape made an enormous difference allowing programmes to be recorded – I can't remember when that came in. It became more sophisticated because it had some pretty good writers in the early days – Jack Rosenthal and Geoff Lancashire, Jim Allen, Peter Eckersley, John Finch – they were a pretty strong team of writers.

## Sandra Gough
*Actress, played Irma Barlow*      **BELLY-DANCING INTO THE STREET**

It was fantastic going into *Coronation Street* – I was so excited, I was over the moon. It was really nice in those days, easier, calmer. The people weren't so frantic and everybody was friendly at Granada.

I did a belly-dancing thing and then I went for an audition with Dennis Tanner for this club he ran. I sang and it was dreadful. And then I started coming in as one of the girls from the factory. Then they wanted to keep someone, so they got myself, a dark-haired girl, and another blonde, gorgeous-looking girl. They were trying the three of us out at the time. We were trying to be nice to each other and thinking, 'I hope it's me!' And they chose me.

Then they put me in the pub behind the bar, serving, and said I had a secret and I was calling myself Freda then. They said it was because I was ashamed of my mum and dad who eventually would come into it. Then I auditioned with lots of people and eventually they put Bernard Youens and Jean Alexander with me and we went from there. Nobody knew where I lived, because of the shame, and then they came looking for me and saw me in the pub. Then they got a house in the street and I had to live with them. It was great then, I really was happy.

Monday we'd start blocking it, Tuesday rehearsals, Wednesday morning rehearsals, Wednesday afternoon was the technical run with the Producer, the cameras – they'd like to see how it was going. Then you'd have notes after that and if they wanted to change anything or if the Producer particularly wanted some more put in, cut out, timing and everything. Then we had Thursday morning off. Thursday afternoon was the run through in the studio, while the others were upstairs in the rehearsal rooms for cameras. It was a long day because, although we went in at lunchtime, we finished very late. Then Friday dress rehearsal, tape it, have lunch, then the same in the afternoon. I didn't get nervous, just excited. I realize now that I'm older, I've always been a talker. I thought that some people were being nasty and funny when they said, 'Oh go away', but I am the type of person who needs to charge my batteries up from people and talk. I realize the strain of it for someone older and for someone young to go on chattering like that, it can be annoying. They were preparing in their own way and I thought they were miserable buggers.

## Phil Redmond
Brookside *creator*                                   **LOOKING BACK**

I think *Coronation Street* started in 1960 and that was just when I was going to secondary school and TV was just starting to become ever present in everybody's homes, so, yes, we watched it.

I used to watch it quite regularly because it was a very hard social commentary at the time within the context – Ken's sauce bottle episode that everybody talks about. It was also part of that school of television that was coming out then in the early Sixties where people like Ken Loach and Jim Allen [writers] came through and *Z-Cars*, of course, which had Fancy Smith [character in *Z-Cars*] throwing his dinner against the wall and the nation up in arms that policemen should be portrayed in this way, shaking the *Dixon of Dock Green* view of life.

So, I used to watch *Coronation Street*. I don't remember it in that great detail because I was only 11 going up to 15, but I remember the big things, like the train coming over the viaduct, Harry Hewitt being crushed by his car. Of course, then, it was put down as a good story. Now, we'd be doing a social issue on it, there'd be a helpline for how to jack your wheels, if you know someone who's been crushed by a car, phone this number.

I think all that played a part in my formative thinking about television and, when I wanted to write and wanted to get into television, that's the kind of stuff I wanted to write. When I watched *Coronation Street* develop over the years, off and on, I always say it settled into its rut in about 1968. I don't mean 'rut' in a pejorative sense – its groove, I suppose, about 1968. All the first lot – the Jack Rosenthals and all them – had obviously moved on and it sort of stayed there. There's nothing wrong in that and it sort of stayed and just moved along from there. It's kind of, 'Co-ee, chuck' and popping in and out to borrow sugar – it stayed still in 1968.

Of course, it's never had that kind of drive for reality that I wanted in Brookie. The one thing that I remember in *Coronation Street* that was quite funny was that fact of the 'Co-ee, chuck' borrowing the sugar thing, because, if anybody in our area had walked into somebody's house like that, they'd either be dead or arrested – one of the two. So, already, even in the Sixties, it was slightly looking backwards, but, for what else was around, it was quite powerful.

# CHAPTER THREE

# The 1960s

## *The gritty Northern drama*

'It didn't seem very long before we were all summoned to Denis Forman's office,' remembers Casting Director José Scott, 'and he said "Congratulations everybody, this has stunned us all." I think Cecil [Bernstein] always thought it would work and Denis thought it might, but nobody had ever done anything like that before, nobody had actually ventured into that kind of a thing.'

The show had become a huge success. In March 1961, just four months after it had first appeared, it was in the charts and, by October, it was at number one, the top-rated TV show in the country. By then it was being shown throughout the ITV network and had shifted to Mondays and Fridays. It was clocking up an audience of almost 7.5 million. By 1962, it was up a further million. Since then, it has rarely been out of the Top Ten.

What caught the public's imagination was that the show was so dramatically different to anything else that had appeared on television before. Harry Whewell, who later became Northern Editor of the *Guardian*, remembers it being so like his own street in Salford: 'It was the feeling that here was something which was quite different and which we had not seen on the telly before. The characters were different, but they were 99 per cent like the woman who lived down the road – in our street anyway. Here was this kind of slight tension between the respectable ones and the unrespectable. In our street we had the Dowds, who were the unrespectable ones who were three doors away, and the Foggertys, who were so respectable that, when my mother called – and this was a council house – he would put his jacket on. That's how respectable they were! People were like that, but I recognize the characters in *Coronation Street* as people who lived on our council estate in Stretford, near Trafford Park, just a stone's throw from what would have been the real Coronation Street in Salford. The feel of *Coronation Street* was like the feel of my estate.'

Even someone who did not live near Salford could feel the same affinity. Fan Graham Twyman claims, 'You could relate to the characters like people you knew living down the road. Albert Tatlock was like some elderly chap down our street, Ena Sharples, well, there's an Ena in every street. That was the beauty of The Street in the early days – you could look at any of the characters and relate them to people who lived in your street, specially someone like myself who was brought up on a council estate.'

For those who lived down South, the show was a real eye-opener. Life-long devotee Christabelle Embleton, who lived in Ramsgate, remembers the shock on seeing this alien way of life: 'We were down the South where it is a totally different way of life. Down here we were always very reserved, but they were not up there. It was as it is, it was friendlier; they would fall out with someone one day and the next day they would be buying them a drink. The houses were exactly as they were like where my husband comes from. The coal would be delivered in the streets and you hang your washing out. I think that's why it caught on because we down in the South didn't know anything about that way of life. We didn't have streets like that down in the South. Accents were also totally different. We thought everybody spoke like us down South or the way they did on the BBC, you didn't think people had accents.'

Joan Le Mesurier, who also lived down South, had been evacuated to Lancashire during the war and *Coronation Street* suddenly brought back memories of Oldham: 'When I first saw *Coronation Street* it rang a bell. For starters, there were the cobbled streets, the corner shop, all those things were there in *our* street. We didn't have a pub in our street, but we had a social club. So, I loved it immediately. I thought it was evocative of that way of life.'

For so many people, particularly in the North, *Coronation Street* was a counterpart to their own communities. Every street had an Elsie Tanner, an Ena Sharples, a corner shop and a pub. Old men and widowed women would wander down to the pub of a night for a gossip, a drink and companionship. For *Coronation Street* read any street, anywhere in the North. For a time, people would argue as to where the real Coronation Street was. Some said Liverpool, others Oldham, even Leeds was suggested.

The other thing that people found novel was the continuity. Christabelle Embleton again: 'It was a new thing, it was something which didn't finish. Before that, programmes finished that night, whereas this came at us and carried on. It was a different concept of television, it was the first soap really. You had all those detective programmes on, but they finished and it was the end of the story. With this you had something to look forward to later on in the week.'

For Mike Newell – who directed The Street in the 1960s and later went on to direct the Oscar-nominated *Four Weddings and a Funeral* – it was the rawness that was most appealing: 'The first six episodes did have the force of a great truth and it was looking at a kind of life that hadn't been looked at before. It was like watching *Saturday Night and Sunday Morning* or any of those marvellous films from the early Sixties. It was much grittier than it very quickly subsequently became. It drifted, I think, into something which was "comedy drama" and, indeed, that was, for the most part, due to the talent of the writers.'

In its first year, Ken Barlow had an affair with a librarian and his mother was crushed to death under a bus, Elsie Tanner became a grandmother and the entire street had to be evacuated to the Mission Hall following the discovery of a fractured gas main in Mawdsley Street. By the end of that first year, Ena, Elsie and Annie Walker had become household names. It wouldn't be much longer before they were icons. They began to make personal appearances – around Salford to begin with, but then further afield as their fame spread. Violet Carson even switched on the lights in her own beloved Blackpool, and was mobbed. Coronation Street was as famous as Downing Street.

The programme was still being made live to begin with, but, as the 1960s unfolded, new technology was introduced, making life slightly easier for everyone. 'When I joined, it was live,' remembers long-time Director Wally Butler. 'Then we went very quickly to pre-recording. On the Friday we'd do two episodes. It was tele-recording at that time, but the thing was you weren't allowed to stop the tape when you felt like it or for an actor's mistake – only for a technical error – so you very rarely stopped. You went in and did a quick run through for positions and it was my decision then to say, "Right, we're going for a take" and we went right through the take. Because of the fact that we couldn't stop, everybody did it rather well and we got through in just over the half hour and they were off. It was marvellous and they were pretty faultless – they knew their lines, they knew their moves.'

At least if there was a technical problem you could start again, not like the old days when you simply had to plough on: 'They'd only let you edit if something went wrong,' says Director Les Chatfield, 'and the cast soon cottoned on to that and swore and then you had to edit. They were only "knife and fork" edits. It was reckoned to be a calamity if you had to edit because you couldn't use the tape again.'

There were others complications as well. Studio cameras had fixed lenses and there was little movement. You couldn't zoom in as you can nowadays by pressing a button on the camera. Instead you physically had to move the camera. Inevitably it would shake or never run at an even pace.

Everything was also shot in the studio and it was not until the 1970s that directors contemplated moving outside to give an added dimension to The Street. Even the sets occasionally wobbled.

Sound also caused a few problems, as Alistair Houston recalls: 'In those days, you didn't go into dubbing and put sound effects on, everything had to be done live, so you would have quite a number of tape machines and discs during the programme and it was sound effects of the exterior if you were out in the street – traffic noise, people boiling kettles, all these things had to be on, so it was quite a busy job.' It was very much primitive television, hampered by technical restrictions, as well as the odd union demarcation.

As for the viewer, there was also more of a ritual to watching programmes in those days. Entire families, from grandmas down to the youngest grandchildren, would huddle around a flickering black-and-white set in the corner of the room. Watching TV was a family event, especially in many working-class families where the extended family still flourished. Television was novel and sets still an expensive luxury, with the top-rated programme only attracting seven million viewers, well under half of what such a show attracts today.

For Hollywood director Michael Apted, being given the opportunity to work on The Street then was his first break into the world of drama. It was something that he never forgot and, in particular, he remembers the writers: 'It was a wonderful period for writers when I was on it, like Peter Eckersley and Jack Rosenthal and John Finch, and Harry Kershaw was around as the

Executive Producer, Geoff Lancashire, John Stevenson. I think it was a vintage time for writing. I don't think the writing on The Street had ever been in better shape than the time that I was on it, so I was lucky there. That was a valuable lesson to learn, how to make material your own even when it is something that's done twice a week on fairly minimal preparation and rehearsal and shooting, but, none the less, you still had to learn to work with writers to get the sort of material you wanted.'

In the early 1960s, the writing had a rawness about it; it was moody, kitchen sink, even slightly political. There was less of the comedy that was to filter through in later years. Although social realism was to become the style of The Street of the 1990s, it was present in bucketloads in the 1960s. One writer, John Finch, recalls Jim Allen, then working for The Street, who would later become one of the most polemical writers in TV and film drama: 'Jim Allen and I were political opposites, but we got on very well. Jim was very hard-line, but we used to debate things in scripts. I'd see a script of Jim's where he was pushing this point of view and then I'd use my next script to counter his arguments. Then he'd come back. Nowadays they're talking about using The Street for social issues – we were doing this very early on. I remember we did a whole episode on the population theory, Malthus – they wouldn't do that now. The Street wasn't as much pure entertainment as people think.'

By the close of the 1960s, *Coronation Street* was a fixed item on most people's viewing agenda. Its stars had toured Australia, mobbed by banner-waving crowds wherever they went, and had tripped, starstruck, down Downing Street. Ratings had risen steadily, thanks to Ken spending seven days in prison following his participation in a banned student demonstration, Elsie marrying her Yank, Steve Tanner, and Emily Nugent jilting Leonard Swindley at the altar.

Arresting writing, quality acting, but if any one individual is to be associated with the success of The Street, particularly during the 1960s, it was to be Harry Kershaw. H. V. Kershaw, as he was known, was the man who took Tony Warren's basic idea, shaped it and made it happen, week in, week out. 'If Tony was the father of The Street, then Harry was the midwife. He set the standards,' says Scriptwriter Geoff Lancashire, who knew both men well. Writer Jack Rosenthal claims that 'for unflappability, he made Harold Macmillan look like a panic-stricken Woody Allen. He was our man from the Pru; a gentle man and a gentleman. His unselfish generosity of ideas to all of us should have got him drummed out of the Writers' Guild.'

One *Sunday Times* critic summed the programme up perfectly: 'She may live in a world of her own, but she knows what matters: family, frugality, neighbourliness, values that posit a communality of interest between anyone born into a time and place and an income bracket.'

# John Finch
*Scriptwriter, Script Editor and Producer*     **SHAPING A SCRIPT**

Constructing a script was a bit like learning computing for the first time. You go through a process where you don't understand the thing at all and then, suddenly, the light dawns and the whole thing clicks into place. I found that very quickly I absorbed this business of shaping a script. When I first saw the cast actually playing the parts, that's really when it became almost a doddle because they were so good that you just wrote them. They were so real, so recognizable. I used to love writing for Violet Carson. I once wrote half an episode with one speech from Vi where she talked about being a half-timer in the mill. That was the sort of thing you could do on The Street.

Jim Allen and I were political opposites, but we got on very well. Jim was very hard-line, but we used to debate things in scripts. I'd see a script of Jim's where he was pushing this point of view and then I'd use my next script to counter his arguments. Then he'd come back. Nowadays, they're talking about using The Street for social issues; we were doing this very early on. I remember we did a whole episode on the population theory, Malthus – they wouldn't do that now.

The Street wasn't as pure entertainment as people think. Derek Granger was tremendously interested in the comedy aspect of it. Derek was the Producer when there was the episode where Elsie Tanner comes in from the kitchen and says to Dennis, 'Why's there a gorilla sitting in my sink?' Derek was very strong on the comedy. I was his Script Editor at the time. It was an absolute nightmare to work for him because he was a bachelor and he used to work until three o'clock in the morning and he expected everybody else to do the same. Derek's stint on The Street was very good – he had enormous prestige amongst journalists.

Usually you were given a couple of weeks to write an episode, although, in dire circumstances, you'd write one in a few days. When I first started, the first scripts I did, I hadn't seen the actors and, what I did, I couldn't visualize them – they were there on the page, but I couldn't give them this extra dimension that made them alive. So, I got this picture of Peter Adamson [who played Len Fairclough] and stuck it in front of my typewriter and glared at it until it started to move and then I was away and I began to visualize the characters, but, initially, I had to visualize them from the page. Strangely, there was a kind of internal clock, which seems to work, and I was always within half a page. Also, I was pleasantly surprised that there was very little rewriting in the early days, whether that was pressure of time or not … It was just very exciting to then watch it so close. I was talking to Jack Rosenthal on the phone not very long ago and he was saying that, nowadays, you know that if you go in with an idea, you're not going to see it for 18 months and you can't get excited about it.

Harry used to bridge the differences in people's styles, but, in the early days, I don't know to what extent it's true now, but even the audience used to say, 'We know who's written that before we've seen the name.' Harry's style was distinctive, so was Adele's. Harry's was always beautifully constructed, Adele's always had a lot of women's stuff in that men wouldn't know about, so she had one up on us when it came to the women. That was the striking thing about her, suddenly you'd see a line and think, 'Well, either he's been talking to his wife or Adele's written it.' Jack's was always funny. People used to say that they could tell mine, but I could never say why.

I remember my first episode there was a part in the storyline where Pat didn't understand how to do the football pools and Denis was trying to explain it to her. I didn't understand how to do the football pools and I thought I ought to see somebody about this and then I thought, 'I'll try and write it because *I* don't understand' and it worked like magic. I remember how desperate I was to get that first one right and I only had two weeks to do it. I'll never forget Harry ringing up and saying, 'We want to commission another.'

# Mike Newell
*Director*                                       **WORKING WITH WRITERS**

I started working for Granada in 1963, when I was 21, as a production trainee, which was a sort of scholarship. *Coronation Street*, at that time, was very new still – no more than three years old. All the original people were in it. It was one of the two or three shows around that was enormously generally popular throughout the nation – particularly in the North, but it had already broken out of that. Anyway, the North was cool then because there was also *Z-Cars*, which had, I think, pre-dated it slightly, and *Z-Cars* was being written by a lot of good people who then turned into real serious dramatists. It was a cradle of writing, and *Coronation Street* was the same.

It was a different kind of programme. It was a soap opera, not a weekly drama series, it ran 52 weeks of the year and it didn't have the social content that *Z-Cars* had, nor the excitement, and I suppose, what it was, *Z-Cars* felt like it was the solid drama and *Coronation Street* felt like it was the comedy drama. I think it always had that 'there's nowt so queer as folk' attitude to it. It was quirky and there was a joke behind it.

The interesting thing was to watch, as we did, some while after we got into the company, we watched the first six episodes of it, which were made in black and white, and you could still see the hunger marks in the actors' faces. They hadn't grown into the fur coats, the way they had by the time I had arrived. By the time I arrived, they were paid, by those times, a lot of money. They were big stars, they were the show that kept the company perky. But the first six episodes did have the force of a great truth and it was looking at a kind of life that hadn't been looked at before. It was like watching *Saturday Night and Sunday Morning* or any of those marvellous films from the early Sixties. It was much grittier than it very quickly subsequently became. It drifted, I think, into something which was 'comedy drama' and, indeed, that was, for the most part, due to the talent of the writers who were working then.

I started working on *Coronation Street* in 1965 and I did it over about 14 to15 months; I did 22/23 episodes. I had been directing for a couple of years by that time and so, technically speaking, I wasn't as green as I had been. I was very green in all sorts of other ways. What I didn't know my way around with was the actors or the writers. The actors were very sweet. Jean Alexander was just beginning, those two, Stan and Hilda, were just beginning while I was on the show and she was always really sweet – she was an adorable woman – and I remember thinking that some of the actors were very good. I remember there was a very strong sense of superiority over the other big soap operas of the time, especially that thing about a motel, *Crossroads*. I think we all felt mightily superior to that.

The actors were very kind. I suspect they took notice when they thought we had something to offer and they simply blanked it when they thought that we were crazy. There was a pretty solid strait-jacket of character and weekly story development that we had to get through anyway, so we couldn't screw around and it wasn't possible to make an art movie of the thing. It was only possible to show individuality in little flashes. They were box sets. Towards the end of my time there, we were much more ambitious with film.

We had a lot of dealings with the writers. From where I stood, the big profit for me was dealing with the writers. The first week was script and you weren't allowed a tremendous amount of leeway in any of this because they were working to storylines that had to unroll in a comprehensible way or the following weeks would be prejudiced, but there was little bit of stuff that you could do. Also, everybody was very game. There was a writers' floor and these guys, Peter Eckersley and Jack [Rosenthal] and John Finch and John Stevenson and Adele Rose, and so the big bang that I got out of it was actually working with the writers – that's the thing that I've taken away from it most.

## Sandra Gough
*Actress, played Irma Barlow* **A LOAF AND A TIN OF PEAS**

The writers would copy what you said a lot. They wouldn't ask you what you thought your character should do, they'd listen to you and get in conversation. I certainly never suggested something I could do because that's not my job – the writers are the writers, the directors are the directors, I'm there to do as I'm told to the best of my ability, it's a different job. A writer's not going to tell me how to act, but if it was something really ridiculous, you'd say, 'I genuinely feel this is ridiculous.' They might still make you do it or they might say, 'Why?' and if you gave a good enough reason, they'd work around it. It would get passed on to the writer by the director, but a lot of actors, just through nerves, would say, 'This speech is ridiculous' when it was just a lot to say. Some would have the cheek – it was Pat mainly. I used to stay in to learn my lines. A lot of actors like to have their moves before they learned the lines, but I've got to learn my lines and have a good idea of how I'm going to do it and then I can listen properly about movement. You'd learn it and you'd come in and she'd say, 'I've changed all this and I've changed this scene' and you'd be gutted.

You'd be so angry, but everybody was scared of her because she'd throw tantrums and be funny.

I think I'm the most proud of when it was boring, when it was the same each week but you could still make something of it. Ken Farrington, who played Bill Walker, was lovely, Annie Walker's son, and I'd like what we'd do because he'd have to come into the shop and say, 'A loaf and a tin of peas, and will you put it on the slate for me mam?', and you'd say, 'Yeah, OK, how are you Billy?' and that was the end of it. And you'd done that last week and the week before, so we decided between us he'd be Humphrey Bogart and I'd be Jimmy Cagney and, as he came in, I'd just add, 'OK, you dirty rat, what do you want?' and he'd say [as Bogart], 'Have you got a loaf, a tin of peas and put it on the slate for my mum', and then we'd laugh and talk in the character, which you can do in life anyway. It just spiced it up. I liked to do things like that. I liked a lot of the comedy.

I think all the writers were good and the directors were great then. There were a lot who'd just come from university and are doing films now. Mike Apted and Mike Newell, we used to go out with a few friends and have a laugh and a joke, they were nice.

## José Scott
*Casting Director*                                    **BOOK HIM!**

Graham Habberfield, who played Jerry Booth – scenes that he was in were lovely – and Ken Coates 'Sunny Jim' – that was always a lovely relationship with Martha. And Gordon Rollings, too, he was. Trevor Bannister – I think he was a decorator – he was incredibly funny. The relationship between Jack and Annie Walker, when they'd had a bit of a row and she'd say, 'You can take your bowling bag with you', and then there was a wonderful episode when they did a cod *This Is Your Life*. Michael Barrington from *Porridge* appeared and they sang 'Only a Rose' or something daft like that. It was not real life, yet it was in a way.

I suppose one of my favourite characters was Arthur Lowe because he was so funny. He was such a love, too. He was quite well known, he probably was the most well known of any of them. Jack Howarth had been around a long, long time. People would be dilly-dallying and messing about, 'What about so and so?', and Margaret said, 'Arthur Lowe, get in touch, see if he's available' and you'd say, 'Yes, he's available.' 'Book him', that was it, she was absolutely right. Only every now and then she would do it and, of course, he was absolutely wonderful, Swindley working for that Mr Papagopolous.

The important thing in casting is being able to weigh up people. I used to think some of those times when those girls were working in the factory making the frou frou skirts were very funny because those girls were funny – Angela Crow and Eileen Mayers and, of course, Christine Hargreaves. That was a terrible tragedy, when she was taken so ill, because she was very funny.

The writers would come in and talk about casting. Tony you knew automatically, but sometimes the writers could be very difficult. I used to think sometimes they got rid of people who were very good because they couldn't think of anything more for them to do. They could be quite tough, the writers, and say, 'No we don't like her, we don't like him.' Everybody had a say in it, it wasn't just you, it was the director and the producer and everybody else making up their mind who they were going to have.

## Wally Butler
*Director*                                    **DIRECTING THE STREET**

I went to Granada in the Sixties. *Coronation Street* was already up and running, but it was still the original cast. I did some programmes for them before I went on to The Street, but it was still quite early in the development, they were just settling down.

It was perceived as the staple diet for directors – it wasn't high-flying, it was a good, solid, staple diet for the company. They started off by using myself and one or two others who were theatre types, then they got more adventurous. They got a bee in their bonnet about graduates and started bringing in graduates and there was a bit of a revolt by the cast. There was a fellow who wanted to give them half an hour of warming up – 'I am a snake and you're a boulder.' The cast went up to the office and said, 'We're not having this.' Then there was another fellow who, for some strange reason, brought into the rehearsal room a series of rostrums and he used to make the cast work on the rostrums. I don't know whether he was looking for lower angles or what. They got fed up with this so he went. And there was another fellow who had a bee in his bonnet about being factual and he wanted to bring in things like real hotpots and real beer and he wanted the real thing.

The reason I got a reputation for finishing early was, quite simply, that these people knew what they were doing and you said, 'Right, we're going into the Rovers now' and immediately they took up their positions. All I had to do was let them go, to a degree, pick up the angles I wanted, make a few suggestions about business which they were quite happy to do, which didn't alter the positioning, then we'd move to the Corner Shop and we'd take up the standard positions which they used. So, it was an easy rehearsal and I just picked up the shots, marked them down, gave them to the PA, made up the shot list and on we went. Down on to the floor we went, they moved immaculately into position. They knew about eyelines and things like that because they'd got used to it and, in those days, we were working with sets which had a background and only about two and a half feet reveal on either side, so there was a degree of standardization about the shots because there were only certain shots you could take because otherwise you shot off the set. The actors knew this and they worked accordingly, they worked around it, so my job was made easier. It was also made easier by the rapport I had with the actors. Most of them I had no problem with because they knew that I knew what I was doing and I gave them the courtesy of knowing that I wasn't going to whip them into submission. They just moved beautifully into the positions.

When I joined, it was live, then we went very quickly to pre-recording. On the Friday, we'd do two episodes. It was tele-recording at that time, but the thing was, you weren't allowed to stop the tape when you felt like it or for an actor's mistake, only for a technical error, so you very rarely stopped. You went in and did a quick run-through for positions and it was my decision then to say, 'Right, we're going for a take' and we went right through the take. Because of the fact that we couldn't stop, everybody did it rather well and we got through in just over the half hour and they were off. It was marvellous and they were pretty faultless – they knew their lines, they knew their moves and if they moved slightly out of position, I could always compensate for it, knowing what the parameters where, so there were never any hold-ups or stopping for discussions. I always made sure that, between the run-through and the dress, I used to go round all the dressing rooms and make quick notes. These people were used to notes and you could go into someone's dressing room and say, 'Now, you know when you come in that door there, remember, go to your left as far as you can. When you pick up that cup, put it down straight away because you're masking your face' and they'd clock it and everything would be fine. So, I didn't have to stop rehearsals and go down on the floor. I used to wait and take notes copiously and then go round all the dressing rooms in the break before the dress or the take and they took it on board and away we went.

## Bob Greaves
*Television Presenter*                                    **THE CANTEEN CULTURE**

I joined Granada Television in 1963 as News Editor and my connections with television before that had been nil. I had worked in newspapers all my life, so it was a culture shock. I didn't know what I was entering into, but, from day one, I was privy to the canteen culture at Granada and there I used to meet, and eventually join at their tables, the *Coronation Street* cast of those far back days.

My impressions were that the cast in the Sixties were themselves a community. They got on well, though, yes, you used to hear about the odd argument and dislike between one person and another, although that's natural in any group of people who are working together, whether on a building site or whatever, but most of them were a real-life community – they socialized together, they worked together, they had their lunches together in the canney.

Most of them had no side on them. You'd go and sit with Arthur Leslie, who played Jack Walker, who simply was a very, very nice, interesting man. He hardly knew me, but he would welcome you to his table and regale you with stories.

Some of the people haven't always been very nice. Arthur Lowe, who played Leonard Swindley, always seemed to lord it to me. Brilliant actor, but a difficult man. Knew what he was, what he wanted, not the most charming of people.

Pat Phoenix was one of the queens and, of course, both she and Ena were big women. Violet was not as tall as Pat, but they both had that 'I'm someone special' air about them. You had to open doors for Pat Phoenix and she would give you that smile and say, 'Thanks chuck' or 'Thanks pet.' Doris Speed, who played Annie Walker for longer than I care to think, was another one in the queenly mode. They had a whole series of these big, strong female characters.

# José Scott
*Casting Director*                    **A NICE COLD COLLATION**

I think, like any little community, it was like a weekly rep – everybody gangs together. Obviously, over the years, people would have their little differences and people would do silly things, get drunk or whatever. Wherever you are, there's always somebody, but they seemed to have a wonderful community spirit and it was terribly unsophisticated really. On a dry run, they would go and have afternoon tea in the Green Room and then, on a Friday, they would do the first episode and they would have lunch and I would go down and we'd all play bridge in one of the conference rooms. It was all very chummy, but then the whole company was all very chummy. When you went into the canteen, it was just a different place – there were these tables and you put another table together and another table and perhaps even Sidney Bernstein or Denis Forman [Company Directors, Granada Television] would join us. It was quite a different atmosphere. It was wonderful working on any programme, but that was particularly wonderful.

Every month we used to have a story conference and everybody would turn up, even Cecil [Bernstein, Company Director, Granada Television] – it was his baby. So Cecil would be there and Peter Eckersley and Jack Rosenthal, all the writers and all the directors. At the time, we didn't realize how exciting it was. It was like any story conference. We'd say so and so is going to do this and we had an idea, what do you think about this? Everybody chipped in, everybody had a chance to chip in. We'd have a very nice cold collation and a drink.

Those were lovely days because it was so relaxed in a way that, however lowly anybody was, if they were part of the production team, they were there, the designers, everybody who was concerned was there and they all could say what they wanted to say.

The first character who was killed off was Joan Heath, May Hardman. I'd been in rep with her; she was a very nice actress, too. I forget the sequence of it now. It came as a surprise. It was very rare that the news was leaked. The loyalty element was there. You didn't want people to know that somebody was going to have some fatality because that added to the spice of it all. Of course, it had not been going all that long. The next one was Noel Dyson, when she was run over. I believe the bloke – Bernard Kay, who was the bus driver – had a terrible time. People were stopping him in the street and saying, 'You killed Ida Barlow, didn't you?' and it was a long time before he worked. Noel was a charming woman. That was very sad.

## Anne Reid
*Actress, played Valerie Barlow* **GIDDY GIRLS**

I had a friend called Angela Crow who was playing Doreen Lostock in something called *Coronation Street* and she and I were friends. We actually shared a flat and she went off to be in this thing that I'd never heard of. I really had no idea what it was. I just heard that they were looking for somebody and I went up for an interview and went into it.

When I arrived on the first day, I really didn't have a clue and I didn't have a clue how popular it was until, I don't remember how long I'd been there – about three or four weeks – and Frank Pemberton, who played Frank Barlow, said, 'Would you like to come on a PA?' and I didn't know what he was talking about. We went to Blackpool and, on the train, he said to me, 'Have you got your speech ready?' and I just laughed. I didn't know what he was talking about. When we got there, it was actually a personal appearance and I was absolutely stunned, I'd never been to anything like that. I think it was the same year that they turned the lights on and I realized how popular it was. I'd never seen it because I didn't have a television set. In a while, I was recognized all the time. To begin with I thought it was great fun, but I got a bit fed up with it in the end, as you do.

They tried me out for three weeks to start with. Dick Everitt directed the first one I did and Howard Baker the second. I think it was at the end of the second week that they said they were going to keep me on, but they said it was a try out and was just brought in as Albert Tatlock's niece, who was visiting from Glasgow. I think they'd brought this character in with the intention of being destined for Ken, but it wasn't until they could see Bill and I together and, in actual fact, we'd been to brother and sister schools in Colwyn Bay, North Wales, which was a strange coincidence and Jack Howarth's son had been to the same school, so we had a common bond.

We came in and there was the Equity strike and I had to leave, so I went back to London and I didn't know whether they would ever bring the character back again. I think it was the following July when they asked if I would come back. They had a nucleus of people who'd signed the contract before they were notified by Equity that they wanted more money. Anybody who came in after that date had a clause in their contract saying, 'If there is no more money, then we are going on strike', but the people who'd signed before that, like Bill and Philip Lowrie and Pat Phoenix and Doreen and Ivan and the three old ladies and Jack and Annie Walker, maybe all the Tanner family, I think that was more or less it, could stay. Of course, they went through a very difficult time because I think it went on for three months and they couldn't bring any new actors in, so they used things like chimpanzees. I was fed up because it was such a good job and suddenly I was having to leave it. So, I was very, very glad when they asked me back the following July, and Bill and I got married, I think, August 1$^{st}$. I think the wedding has been shown on television a few times. It's very popular. All I see now when I see it, I can't believe my waist was ever as small as that.

We had both programmes done by Friday night because then we used to go out and have a meal and go to the Everest restaurant – John Finch and Jim Allen and a lot of us. Then start again on Monday morning. It used to go out, to begin with, on Monday and Wednesday of the following week, but then, as time went on, they did four in one week and got ahead of themselves so they had a gap then. Well, I liked it better then because there was more rehearsal.

It was OK then, but of course, nowadays, I don't think they get any rehearsal at all. It was all right to start with, but when you go on year after year, playing the same character, I just got bored quite honestly. I didn't care what happened to her. I never got a laugh, that was the thing, and comedy is the thing that I've always liked to do, but it was fun and Bill and I got on very, very well together. I hope he will say the same thing because we had a very, very happy eight and a half, nine years together. I don't think we ever had an argument about anything. It sounds boring, but I think we were very similar in many ways, fairly laid back about it. I used to get much more nervous than he did, because I'm like that, and he used to pat me on the head and say, 'Calm down.' There was once I dried and we had to go again. At that stage, I think we did a quarter of an episode and, if you dried, you had to go back to the beginning of the episode, but I didn't usually dry, because you're young and you remember it. As the machinery and the cameras and the editing equipment became more sophisticated, it could be done in shorter and shorter bits and it was much easier on the actors when you could do retakes. I just remember 1968 we went into colour and that was fun because suddenly some of us don't look so hot in black and white. Some of the girls with the beautiful bone structures and the black hair look wonderful in black and white, but the blondes look better in colour.

I got to know the writers very, very well because there was pub called the New Theatre Inn, which was a famous theatre pub and just round the corner from Granada. There were a couple of people from The Street who used to go and drink there, but, mostly, they weren't pub people. I come from a family of journalists and Christine Hargreaves, who played Christine Hardman, and I were sharing a flat by this time and we were giddy girls having a good time. We used to go over to the pub and all the people would come over, like Mike Parkinson and Bill Grundy. So, I got to know the people from Current Affairs and the writers like John Finch and Jim Allen and Harry Kershaw, and it was simply the way we spent our leisure time. So, I got to know them very, very well and that's how I met my husband. I don't recall us talking shop, I don't ever remember us talking like that.

## John Finch
*Scriptwriter, Script Editor and Producer*     **ISSUES AND DEBATES**

I've always thought it's quite possible to be good *and* popular. What held us back in the early days was management's attitude. They had this business of looking down on the audience. I know a couple of times I got mentioned in the House of Commons – once in a negative sense when they said somebody ought to shut this bloke up and the other one was complimentary when they said, 'If you want to know what the Poor Law's all about, watch so and so.' I think there were a few mentions over the years.

Harry Driver was never interested in doing social issues and he used to say, 'Shut up, John, and take the money.' I was always very strong on doing things like that. Harry Kershaw was in the middle, weighing up the balance, listening to the arguments, very good like that. Jim Allen and I were on the Left in politics. Jim was much more Left than I was, but Harry Driver was a true blue Conservative. Now you wouldn't have thought that somebody like Jim and Harry would get on, but Jim had enormous respect for Harry and Harry for Jim and it would be most unusual for Harry to change anything of Jim's. He might say to him, 'This is a bit strong', then Jim would find another way of saying the same thing. That was a debate that went on within the team. Peter Eckersley joined when I was Script Editor, because he wrote to me and said, 'I'd like to do a trial script' and it went from there and he was always more interested in the comedy, as was Jack.

I was really the one who was interested in social issues. I often lost out and they used to argue me into the ground. I think the success of *Cathy Come Home* probably influenced The Street to some extent. We did homelessness. There were certain actors in The Street who you could do social issues with more than with others. You could do quite a lot with Violet Carson because she had this memory that went back beyond The Street, so I could write half an episode as one speech from Vi. You just knew how she was going to do it and the great thing with Vi was that you used to be able to write silences because the camera would always find her face at the right time and this face said it without a line. In fact, it was much stronger without a line and I used to work to that deliberately. I used to know that, in the end, there was a line that was silence and Vi's face would say it. That really is a good example of one of the pluses of working in a long-term thing with actors because you know what's going to happen and the actor knows when they see it on the page. They know that you've recognized this and they know what they're going to give.

You can't get that now. I should imagine you have a big flashy story conference with about 20 people sat around the table and you're supposed to be talking about big human issues and how do you concentrate it from this diversity? I suspect that things either get bland or they get trivialized. It's all got very frenetic.

I always remember speaking at Harrogate Arts Festival and on the platform were me and David Rudkin, who was a very up-market dramatist. We were answering questions from the audience and I was very much aware that Rudkin, because I was in television and an ex-*Coronation Street* writer, was looking down his nose at me, until I said why television was getting more and more frenetic and why this was a bad thing and, suddenly, I realized he was looking at me with some respect. That really is what's happened – there's no quiet reflection or very rarely.

## Les Chatfield
*Cameraman and Director*     **THE *CORONATION STREET* SCHEDULE**

After a year as a director, I worked on *Coronation Street*. I did a year on things like *All Our Yesterdays*, the local programme – I can't remember whether it was *Scene at Six Thirty* or what it was then – with Bill Grundy, Michael Parkinson. *Coronation Street* was looked on then as a training ground for people who wanted to do drama and it was not like now, it was something you didn't actually talk about. If someone asked you what you were directing, you'd whisper *Coronation Street*. It was looked down on, soap operas in those days. They were still pulling the ratings, but they weren't regarded as great art as they are nowadays.

I did two years on The Street before I directed any plays and then it was really drama series – I started on *Family at War*, things like that – but I was very lucky working with Jack Rosenthal, John Finch, Jim Allen, people like that. It was fairly easy and also the cast were well bedded-in by then and they were pretty good in those days.

We had a three-week turnaround. First of all we used to attend storyline meetings and you were allowed to chip in – I don't know if that still happens – you were allowed to put forward ideas. All the writers were there and I remember Adele Rose used to bake cakes and bring them into the meetings. That would be the first thing. On the Monday you'd get two scripts and the second day you'd go and see Harry Kershaw, the Producer, and talk about the scripts and he'd have ideas of rewrites and listen to any you had. Then they'd go back to the writer. And you used to have your own production assistant from the first of the three weeks – everyone was on a three-week turnaround then – and then the second week would be spent doing your blocking, working things out because the first week the designer would have got a floor plan out and everything. Any casting that had to be done, would be done. Then the third week you started rehearsal. Read-through was done at lunchtime on a Monday, then blocking to a producer's run on a Wednesday afternoon (blocking is the process of working before-hand all the logistics of actor, camera and scene movement), tech-run on a Thursday morning, in the studio Thursday afternoon and, hopefully, block the two episodes Thursday afternoon and early evening, seven o'clock finish, I think, and, then, the next day, come in about 12 o'clock, rehearse them again, do a dress rehearsal and then do one live and one as for live. I'm sure there was a time when we used to do both live.

It was a long time before they let you edit them, even when editing came in. They'd only let you edit them if something went wrong, and the cast soon cottoned on to that and swore and then you had to edit. They were only 'knife and fork' edits. It was reckoned to be a calamity if you had to edit because you couldn't use the tape again. When we used to get to a commercial break, the running time would be given to the cast and they would have to gallop through or slow up. One famous one that I did in a live show with a floor manager called John Oakins, we got to the commercial break and we were something like nearly 2 minutes over and I told him that we'd got to get a move on. I heard him say to the cast, 'Right, we're 2 minutes over, that's 120 seconds, there's 18 of you in the cast, so, if you all save so many seconds, we'll be on time', and I remember saying to him, 'But what happens, John, if 2 of them save 10 seconds at the same time?' But that's what you used to do and, if you were under, I remember Harry Kershaw always used to say, if you were under, put a pan in, so, if you look at any of the old episodes and you see a scene start with a slow pan shot [a horizontal moving shot] round … There was the odd occasion when someone would come out with a line you didn't recognize or you thought, 'That's the wrong episode or something', or they'd gone back to last week's lines. That didn't happen a lot, but it was known to happen.

## Alistair Houston
*Sound Engineer, retired*                                    **FISH AND CHIPS**

In those days, you didn't go into dubbing and put sound effects on – everything had to be done live. So, you would have quite a number of tape machines and discs during the programme and it was sound effects of the exterior if you were out in the street, traffic noise, people boiling kettles, all these things had to be on, so it was quite a busy job. At one stage, there was a fish and chip shop featured in it and they used to be battering fish and dropping them in, so, every time they dropped them in, you had to have the splash of the fat. We'd been to a chip shop to record the sound effects and I remember the technical supervisor then was Jack Whitworth. He came in one day and said, 'These effects are very realistic, I had a terrible argument with my mother-in-law last night that they really cook these fish because, every time they dropped the fish into the pan, they heard the fizz and the splash of the fat.'

## Michael Apted
*Director*                                          **WORKING WITH ACTORS**

I started working at Granada at the end of '63 on the production training course. I didn't go on to *Coronation Street* until 1966, but my impression then was that it was already part of the foundations of the company. It seemed to be a very important part of the company's agenda and highly thought of, incredibly popular. The stars of it were some of the biggest stars on television. It already had a central part in the franchise and an important place in British television.

*Coronation Street* was the first drama I did as a director. They were using it as a first step for potential drama directors. It was fantastic because everybody was very helpful. It must have been hard for them having trainee after trainee coming in, but it was great experience because, in many ways, it ran itself. Technically it was incredibly difficult because, when I was on, you weren't allowed to edit. At least it wasn't live, but you had to get through half the programme in one take, so, technically, it was very demanding.

I remember we were in a very small studio, Studio 2 as it then was, but it was great training because they knew what they were doing. They would respond to what you said and if they didn't like what you said they'd just get on and do their own thing because they knew what to do. The crew was very expert at it by this time – they'd been going for six years when I went on it. You could offer such stuff up and if you didn't know what you were doing it ran itself.

You had such a huge variety of actors. You had big stars like Violet and Pat Phoenix and Peter Adamson and you had some terrific young actors, Graham Haberfield, Annie Reid and Bill Roache, and Philip Lowrie. You had those who loved being directed. It was fantastic training because you simply dealt with different sorts of actors and it would prepare you for everything that would lie ahead. Difficult actors, starry actors, responsive actors, unresponsive actors, the whole thing, and yet it was a well-oiled machine, so, at the back of your mind, you thought that there was so much support for it. If you were messing up, then still the stuff would get out.

For the train crash, we moved into a bigger studio because it was a big event. It was a big deal for me and it came towards the end, so I had been there for some time. I was on it for nine months. What happened was I'd always wanted to have a go at drama and Mike Newell went on holiday, so I went and asked Julian Amyes [Director of Programmes] if I could do holiday relief. I think he thought it was funny and said, 'Why not?', which was one of the joys of working at Granada – a small company and very flexible, it wasn't like if you trained at the BBC where you'd become compartmentalized in something. So, I did his holiday relief and it went well. I said I'd like to do it on a regular basis and they thought that would be a good idea, so I had to go back to *World in Action* and, a few months later, a place became free and I went on.

I loved directing in the pub, I loved Doris Speed – she was always very sweet to me. It was a wonderful period for writers when I was on it, like Peter Eckersley and Jack Rosenthal and John Finch, and Harry Kershaw was around as the Executive Producer, Geoff Lancashire, John Stevenson. I think it was a vintage time for writing. I don't think the writing on The Street had ever been in better shape than the time that I was on it, so I was lucky there. That was a valuable lesson to learn, how to make material your own, even if it is something that's done twice a week on fairly minimal preparation and rehearsal and shooting, but, none the less, you still had to learn to work with writers to get the sort of material you wanted. So, that was a big lesson, and I was lucky that I had people who I then got to go on and work with in other ways. For me, it was the beginning of a very long relationship with Jack Rosenthal and also with John Finch – I did a lot of his stuff later on. Also with Peter [Eckersley], who became Head of Drama, so, for me, important personal relationships were cemented there which kept me going for the next five or six years or even longer.

I think now soap operas tend to be factory-driven, but then there was enough time to give it care and attention. It didn't have that kind of brilliant rough edge that those early ones had, but it was still in pretty good shape. It was still good, funny, potent stuff.

## Alistair Houston
*Sound Engineer*                                         **A GREAT DIRECTOR**

One of the best scenes I think is the one Michael Apted did with the rail crash and the train came off the line and Ena Sharples was trapped. That was a great episode to work on, with all the effects, and it was one which really established Mike as a top director.

## Jim Quick
*Graphic Artist*                                   **STAYING TRUE TO CHARACTER**

I do feel that the Geoff Hughes group was my favourite group of people on The Street and, going back to the early days, the triumvirate of Ena, Minnie and Martha. I recall them as very good actresses, people who could deliver a line and work off each other. Those early days were a bit more depressing as well. It was the bit-part players as well, the people who came in, stayed five minutes and went. They're all famous and they've done their bit. Joanna Lumley's performance, I thought, was lovely, when she became Ken's paramour for a while. I thought that was a lovely little cameo. I don't honestly think you can say you had a favourite character because it would depend on what they were doing, how they were behaving and whether or not you thought they were behaving in the way the character should behave. Because there was a lot of ownership, you don't like to think that your hero is behaving out of character.

## Lord Denis Healey
*Former Chancellor of the Exchequer and Labour MP*      **AN MP'S VIEW**

I started watching *Coronation Street* almost as soon as it began, back in the early Sixties. Edna and I watched it together, the children less so, as I think they were away from home at that time. *Coronation Street* was exactly like the streets in Harehills in my constituency in Leeds. Liz Dawn, who played Vera Duckworth, actually came from Harehills in Leeds and I actually knew her as she was a constituent of mine. So, I enjoyed it very much, although I don't watch it much now. But, in those early days, I found it very interesting and, as I say, so much like my own area, even though it was made by Granada in Manchester, over the Pennines from Leeds. I once met some of the actors when I was doing something at Granada. It was wonderful.

The character I remember best was the barmaid, Bet Lynch. She was so typical of the girls who were in the pubs in Leeds. I was also very struck by the girl who played the sexy lady, Elsie Tanner. She was terrific. They were all good, and Mike Baldwin was also very good. Then I also liked Ena Sharples and her pals Martha and Minnie – they were part of the old world. But it was very well done, particularly the street scenes and the pub scenes. They were like any pub in Leeds or the whole of the North of England really; there's not much difference between Yorkshire and Lancashire, you know, except in speech.

Nothing reflects everything, but I think it was perfectly realistic, remembering that it did not cover the whole of life. Comedy was, of course, very important, especially the barmaid, Bet Lynch. It was comic realism. The industrial North of that time was just like that – terraced houses and row after row of streets with all those similar characters. But The Street has accurately adapted to changes.

## Jim Allen
*Scriptwriter*                                   **'STILL HAVEN'T BEEN PAID'**

For me, writing became a political necessity. When I worked down the pit, a bunch of us started a rank-and-file paper called *The Miner* and, after we bought a typewriter on the hire purchase, big Joe Ryan, who I'd worked with on the docks, shoved it into my hands and said, 'You got us into this, you edit.' So, I was thrown in at the deep end. I'd learned to type with two fingers and was compelled to find the words to express the politics. For four years, we published our paper and were a bit spellbound when we saw our names in print. Kicked from pillar to post by management, chased by police at different pits and attacked by union leaders, we enjoyed every minute of it. Then, in 1960, I was blacklisted and this led me into television.

I was working in the building trade as a scaffolder's labourer when my name came to the attention of Granada and I was invited to write a trial script for *Coronation Street*. In January 1965, it was transmitted and I still haven't been paid for it – although I did get a contract.

I forget how many scripts I wrote, but I stayed there for about 18 months before I 'broke out'. I had seen and lived through much and was eager to give expression to something more substantial than cardboard characters filled with self-admiration. With one or two exceptions, the actors were all working-class Tories, acting like thirty-bob millionaires. When a new face joined the writers' team, he was looked upon as a threat, but, in my case, they needn't have worried because I had no intention of staying long.

The one writer who didn't give me the hard stare was John Finch, a bald-headed Yorkshire man with real talent and a great sense of humour. We became boozing buddies and it was John who introduced me to BBC Producer Tony Garnett. For a year, I'd been trying to persuade Granada to commission me to write a script about the Lump – a brutal anti-union labour-only system of work in the building industry. My pleas fell on deaf ears and I was desperate when John suggested Garnett. In 1967, the BBC showed *The Lump* on the Wednesday play slot and it was a huge success. It was through Tony that I met Ken Loach and, together, we made *The Big*

*Flame*, a film about Liverpool dockers taking over the port. It was after that that I made my break from The Street and went freelance.

Writing for *Coronation Street* was a great learning experience. It taught me the grammar of television and the economy of language. It also paid the bills. Nowadays, I never watch it. When I do, I find the characters lifeless and predictable and the stories dull. Perhaps, to spice it up, they should reconsider a suggestion I made when I was serving my time there: pack all the characters on to a bus and send them on a 'mystery tour' to the Lake District, then drive the bus over a cliff and kill them all off. In today's battle of the ratings, that would be a winner.

## Barrie Holmes
*Fan*                                                    CHANGING TIMES

I can certainly see that 1950s kitchen sink drama in The Street, concentrating on the Northern working-class environment. I think at first it was straightforward Northern characters. I don't remember a great deal of humour when it started – that came later. It was almost like a mini play each time, and it gradually pulled together and the characters came to life. It's amazing when you think back that it was done live.

I remember in the early days when Ken Barlow had just come back from university and announced that he was going to be a schoolteacher and his father, far from being proud, thought he was getting above himself, it wasn't his station in life. He was the only one of the cast who attempted to be socially mobile, whereas now it is very different. I think that reflects the way society has gone. I imagine in 1960 when it started that you could have gone down to Salford and seen the characters that are portrayed. I think if you went down a Salford street now, I don't think you would find an Emily Nugent dropping in for a glass of sweet sherry or whatever! So, it has changed. It was probably truer to life then than it probably is now. I think it was a fair reflection of life in the Sixties.

I think the other thing when it started was that it was all done in the houses in that street, the pub and the corner shop and that was it. If anyone wanted food, they went down to Jackson's chippy, but you never *saw* Jackson's chippy. There was a lot more left to the imagination, whereas, now, they have developed more scenes and sets – they've built up the other side of the road and so on. It's been an evolutionary development. All the characters gradually developed as well, each with their own characteristics.

## Les Chatfield
*Camerman and Director*                    **A GOOD BONFIRE**

I can't remember when they actually built The Street. The first time I can remember working on the lot, I knocked down the Mission Hall. I remember we hired a firm called McGuinness, who were the big demolition experts in Manchester at the time, and we had this blooming great bulldozer-type of thing and the idea was we were going to film him knocking it down and then we were going to burn it all because it was all wood and I remember saying to this Irishman who was driving it, 'Now, we're just going to rehearse, when I say "Action", don't do anything', and he said, 'Right' and I said, 'Action' and he went straight into the Mission Hall, so we had to start the scene with the bulldozer embedded in the Mission Hall because, if he had pulled out, the whole thing was only a shell, it would have all fallen down, but it was a good bonfire.

## Ken Farrington
*Actor, played Billy Walker*          **CASTING FOR DENNIS TANNER**

About a year into my career, I was due to go to the Library Theatre, Manchester, and José Scott asked me to come in for a reading. I am a Londoner by birth and I'd never been up North except for two weeks with the National Youth Theatre, but I had been at drama school with Albert Finney. We were quite pally and I went to this reading and José read the other character. She said to me, 'Can you do a North country?' and I said, 'Sort of' and so I did my Albert Finney voice. The Street was originally set in Salford, not Manchester, and Albert Finney was Salford so that fitted rather well. Then she said to me, 'Listen, I'm going to put you up for a test, but they're very keen on getting local people, so don't tell anybody that you're not from up there', so I didn't.

So, I went up and I didn't get Dennis Tanner, but they wrote a part in for me. Harry Kershaw wrote it because he'd seen the way I did my test and said, 'Right, we want him and we'll write him in', and they wrote me in another character. It wasn't until about three months after I'd been in it that I told anybody that I wasn't from up North.

# Alistair Houston
*Sound Engineer*                              **A ROW WITH PAT**

I had a bit of a row with Pat Phoenix once. In those days, the unions in television were quite strong and Studio 2, being so small, had got extremely hot in the summer. The only ventilation were two huge fans, which you couldn't have on because of the noise they made, and there had been a very long Equity strike, in which the permanent cast weren't involved because they were on permanent contracts. They continued working, but there were a lot of actors who were out of work for a long time. One particular day, the studio got so hot, the union called a halt and said, 'There's no way we can work in this' and they abandoned the recording. We started to de-rig and Pat had a go and I had a go back about not being on strike with Equity, but taking all the benefits that the strikers had got. I broke it off and turned around and Julian Amyes, who was both a programme director and a company director, was standing at the edge of the set with a smirk on his face. But she was a real character.

# Gillian Jones
*Fan*                                      **ANNIE AND MY MUM**

For as long I can remember, I've watched *Coronation Street*. We all used to watch it. The one that stands out was Ena Sharples. I don't know whether I liked her, but she was one of those characters that, although she was quite nasty, there was a soft side to her. Although she used to argue with Elsie and be quite nasty to her, she was always trying to look after her. Annie Walker, of course, because she reminded me of my mum, although my mum didn't think so. In the old ones, she's got a much more Northern accent. She changed gradually, but I never noticed it happening. And, of course, Jack who was always sensible. I quite liked Len – he was a bit of a rogue; his relationship with Elsie was always bubbling under. I remember Elsie getting married and how smart she looked. I remember Mr Swindley in the shop and Emily had a thing for him – he was quite good. Hilda's son, David, and Lucille Hewitt – she went very abruptly. Irma reminded me of my sister, Pauline, at the time, with the big, bouffant hair. David was the studious one ... and Valerie Barlow, she died in something to do with a hairdrier.

# Lord Doug Hoyle
*Former Labour MP*                                    **FAMILY VIEWING**

I probably started watching The Street at the very beginning, in 1960, but I must tell you right away that I'm not a regular weekly watcher these days, but I've always watched it off and on because I've always felt it was the soap to watch.

We would have watched it as a family in the Sixties – it was family viewing. Families did watch television together, even though I would be in and out as a young person. I still think older people watch it, but I have no idea about whether young people watch it.

The character I remember most was Elsie Tanner – she has to stick in everybody's mind – and, of course, the Rovers and all the characters there, in particular the Walkers, who ran the pub. I always related to the Rovers because it was like the pub down the road.

# Joan Le Mesurier
*Former wife of actor Mark Eden, who played Alan Bradley*     **OUR STREET**

I used to live in Chadderton, in Oldham. It was *Coronation Street* country. I was born there, but, when I was one year old, I came down South, so I didn't know anything really about Oldham until the war came. I was eight then and we were sent back up there with my mother to live for about four years. The contrast between living in Folkestone and seeing all those 'dark satanic mills' was a real culture shock. I used to think it was so depressing, but the people up there were lovely, they wished you well. There was more of a community spirit. If somebody died in the street, everyone would go to see the body, because it was laid out in the home.

When I first saw *Coronation Street*, it rang a bell. For starters, there were the cobbled streets, the corner shop – all those things were there in *our* street. We didn't have a pub in our street, but we had a social club. So, I loved it immediately. I thought it was evocative of that way of life. Looking back, maybe it was a little far-fetched really. It was rather depressing. I think it still is in a way because you think, 'What awful, sad little lives we all lead?', but maybe it makes you think a little better about your own lot.

There was definitely an Elsie Tanner in our street, there's always the tarty one that's no better than she ought to be with a bit of scandal. I had an Auntie Jean who was no better than she ought to be! There was the old do-gooder and the one with a sharp tongue like Ena. I had an Uncle Billy and a boring old Uncle Hector.

I can still remember the early black-and-white *Coronation Street*. We must have seen it from the very, very beginning. It was definitely my mother's favourite, so we must have seen it from the off. Martha Longhurst, the three old ladies sitting in the pub with their pints and hairnets. I would be in Ramsgate by then. We lived here all the time after that, apart from those war years. *Coronation Street* was my mother's little lifeline to reality, nostalgia.

## Alistair Houston
*Sound Engineer*                                    **HAPPY MEMORIES**

I'm sure it was an instant hit with the public, which is why they decided six episodes weren't going to be enough. Tony just continued to write it and it pulled in the viewers. I think the production schedule stayed pretty much the same over those three years. It was always two episodes and I'm sure we just had the two days to do it in because, in those days, you spent the first day rehearsing the two episodes right through in studio with cameras. There was a technical rehearsal on the day before you were in studio.

People liked working on it, they were all quite keen to do it. It was so busy in the studio because it was continuous. Say we had three cameras and two booms in the studio, which was a much tighter area with the sets to work in, about 30 seconds before the end of one scene, one of the cameras was released to get ready for the next scene and then there would either be a boom waiting to start that next scene or it would be a case of holding the shot while the boom swung across to the next set, so it was quite fast moving. I think people had to be much more professional. If you take the stagehands, they've never been used to moving sets and props quietly while you're recording in another part of the studio and that had to happen. They were resetting things while you were actually taping at the other end of the studio. People just wouldn't know how to do it today. You had to be much more alert, both in the sound and vision control rooms, because it had to be right. If it wasn't right, it went out as a big mistake. A lot of the actors and actresses had done a lot of stage work, so they were professional enough to fumble through it if they forgot their lines.

In those days, my favourite characters were the three old ladies in the Snug and Doris Speed and Arthur Leslie. Some were quiet and, if you passed them in the corridor, a bit withdrawn, but others were so friendly. In the early ones, Philip Lowrie, who was Dennis Tanner, was a great guy. I always got on very well with Thelma Barlow and with Bill Tarmey. In later years, I moved into the music studio and Bill, having been in music, was always coming in.

There used to be a lot of scenes in the Mission Hall, which was converted into the factory. The screaming in the street between Pat Phoenix and Ena Sharples, they were really good, and all the traumas that Pat Phoenix went through with her men. I've got no bad memories of working on *Coronation Street*.

## John Finch
*Scriptwriter, Script Editor and Producer*

### THE DARK SIDE OF THE STREET

I think I wrote the episode after the funeral of Martha Longhurst. I didn't agree with her death, but we had to go along with it. Vi Carson didn't speak to me for two years. I thought it was a mistake. I did the funeral of Ida Barlow – The Street peaked at that point, we got an enormous audience. She went under a bus. Harry Kershaw and I sometimes used to disagree on things like that – like, when the Hewitts' baby disappeared, I wanted it to be found dead because I thought that would make people more aware of their responsibilities. Harry thought it would be too upsetting for the audience.

## Christabelle Embleton
*Fan*

### DEATH IN THE SNUG

Martha Longhurst dying in the Snug was ever so sad and moving. I think that was one of the first deaths in The Street. We all felt we knew her. We didn't have video recorders in those days either and it was a total shock – goodness gracious, what's happening? It hadn't been in the newspaper like it is these days.

## Lynn de Santis
*Fan*

### COBBLED STREETS AND BACK-TO-BACKS

We always had a television, so, although I don't remember the first episode, it would be from then that we would have watched it as a family. I can remember my mum talking about *Florizel Street*. I think she did identify with it because it was Salford, but, also, because they had moved out from the cobbled streets and the back-to-backs. They'd got this semi, so it was seen as a reminder of what they had left behind. They had taken a step out of that so they were looking down on it – not in any superior way, but they were a bit removed from it, which I think was nice for them because it was very much how they had lived in the two up, two downs and what the communities were like. She still says about people, 'I know somebody like that.' I remember the Ena Sharples character was actually my auntie, we had an aunt who was Ena Sharples – she didn't wear the hairnet, but she always wore the coat and drank stout.

I remember Elsie Tanner and Ena having rows, Elsie and her children, I remember Dennis Tanner being a sort of rogue. I can remember the rows within the Barlows – Ken Barlow going to college and getting a bit above himself. All that sort of stuff about the sauce bottle and bringing a girlfriend round – she was obviously a bit upper crust, middle class, and he was obviously embarrassed.

The big one I always remember was Martha Longhurst popping off in the Rovers. I don't know what year that happened, but I can distinctly remember it. It was the first programme where characters became a member of your family because they were appearing once or twice a week, so they were in your living room very regularly and they became part of your family more than things like Dick Van Dyke and the other American sitcoms because they were so removed. I can remember when Martha Longhurst died, everybody took it really personally and I can remember kids at school being quite upset – not crying or anything, but just, 'Oh wasn't it sad?' I suppose to some kids it was the first bereavement they had ever had, Martha Longhurst popping off in the Rovers.

## Graham Twyman
*Fan*                                        **THE NORTH–SOUTH DIVIDE?**

I started watching *Coronation Street* when it first started. My early memories are quite traumatic really. I know this is a stupid thing to say, but it is quite true – my first memory was when Martha Longhurst died in the Snug. I was nine. It was one of the first deaths I had ever experienced and it was quite traumatic. At that age you believe it.

We watched it as a family, living on a council estate in Ramsgate. They were like your neighbours, it was like something happening around the corner. It was the only thing that was real on the telly in those days. As young as I was, it was real. The North–South divide didn't matter, that family came into your home. We had the same houses in Ramsgate. You could relate to the characters like people you knew living down the road. Albert Tatlock was like some elderly chap down our street, Ena Sharples, well, there's an Ena in every street. That was the beauty of The Street in the early days – you could look at any of the characters and relate them to people who lived in your street, specially someone like myself who was brought up on a council estate. You could also relate to your local pub. If you were to come down and walk in my office now, you'd see a photograph on my desk and it's the first thing you see – it's Ena Sharples, Minnie Caldwell and Martha Longhurst in the Snug. It's there in my office. It takes me back to the beginning when it started, my favourites.

## Mike Newell
*Director*                                           **ALL FOR A BET!**

My time on it was when it just happened to be ticking over. What I do remember is that there were big conferences about storylines while I was there. I remember them losing one of the three fates – she had a heart attack in the Snug; Martha. I also remember the Producer, who was a pal of mine. We were all very young – there probably wasn't anybody who was more than 34, 35 who was on it. I remember this guy being pissed in one of the pubs that we used and saying, 'I bet you don't think that I can kill Martha Longhurst in the pub on Christmas Eve, but I'll show you' and he did! It was all down to a bet!

## Bob Greaves
*Television Presenter*                 **UNCLE ALBERT CATCHES THE BUS**

There was Albert Tatlock, played by Jack Howarth. He was always a bit of a crusty man – not the character, the real man. Not an easy man to get on with, but I'm maybe maligning him. He played a grumpy character and he could be a bit grumpy in real life as well. Legend has it he and his wife used to stay at the Midland Hotel – because he and his wife lived in Wales, so they stayed in the posh Midland hotel, just up the road from Granada, 800 yards or so away. He used to take the bus from the Midland to a bus stop outside the side of Granada's building. Why he didn't take a taxi on wet days, which in those days would have cost him a quid or so … What I do know is that he used to get on the bus and apparently argue with the bus conductor at having to pay a fare. He would say, 'I'm a pensioner, you're charging pensioners!' This was in the days when there were no concessionary fares for 65-year-olds. He used to resent paying his bus fare, which was probably two pence.

## Prunella Scales
*Actress, played Eileen Hughes,*
*girlfriend of Harry Hewitt*

**HARRY HEWITT AND**
**THE BUS CONDUCTRESS**

I was in, I think, Episodes 13 and 14; it was 1961. I played Eileen Hughes who had a crush on Harry Hewitt. I thought I was going to get him and become a national figure! I was a bus conductress. I had done a film by then – *Hobson's Choice*. I spent a lot of my childhood in Yorkshire, so I could do a Yorkshire accent, but I had to learn a Lancashire accent for the show – in fact, both for *Hobson's Choice* and *Coronation Street*. I'd obviously been to Lancashire, so it wasn't too much of a problem.

It was a happy time. I was in two episodes and it was fun. I remember the canteen and Violet Carsons. I remembered her because she played the piano for Wilfred Pickles.

Derek Bennett directed – he was quite young. Before we did the reading, we had a little chat and he said it's doing very well and getting good ratings. He was very positive. He introduced me to the whole cast, but it was very early on and, of course, in black and white. I wanted to be in longer, but I didn't break my heart when it didn't go on – I was quite busy anyway – but it was fun. At the time, I would have enjoyed being one of the regulars, but now, as I look back, I'm quite grateful that I wasn't. I think I've had a more valued working life. It was a lovely show to have been in and I do enjoy it. Granada was such a wonderful television station in those days and I did some wonderful things with them. It was always fun going up there and meeting Violet again in the canteen and chatting about old times.

I remember waiting at the bus stop, going back to my digs after rehearsals one day, and a whole flock of starlings came out as the sun went down. The woman in the bus stop standing next to me said, 'I always think they look like kisses.' I said, 'What?' and she said, 'They look like kisses.' I thought that was such a lovely thing to say about these birds in the sky and

I told the writers, hoping they might be able to use it, but I don't think they ever did.

In those days, in films such as *Hobson's Choice*, you didn't see yourself on screen until the première. I wasn't grand enough to be invited to look at the rushes, whereas, nowadays, they'll video you as you shoot and you can look at it and correct yourself as you go along. That's very useful. I enjoyed it and I'd like to think that I was good enough, but I'd have to look at it again to really know – if, indeed, it still exists.

I don't remember it being rushed. It was pressurized, of course, but all television is, and, of course, we had to get it right because there was no editing. I liked the cast, I liked the part and I slightly hoped it would go on. Ivan Beavis was lovely and it was a happy experience, but it was quite healthy, probably, not to have become involved. The work I did subsequently was more varied and there was stage work with the theatre as well, but I was very proud to have been in it.

## John Temple
*Storyline Editor and Producer*               **COMEDY AND DRAMA**

At this time, *Coronation Street* took on more of a comedy vein, but in the Sixties it always had a blend of comedy in there. It has always boasted that it was this strong mix of comedy and drama – that was its major strength. I think in the Sixties that comedy was much more rooted in the realities of life and *Coronation Street* was in a little world all of its own. It didn't often touch on the outside world, simply because of the limitations of shooting. It was limited to the amount of exteriors and mainly they were on The Street itself. This was fine. You very rarely got outside in The Street and, really, up to 25 years on – I was there when we changed from film to video. Even in the Seventies, when it was all done on film, the exteriors, you could see the difference in the picture quality and it didn't sit comfortably with the studio stuff.

I think in the Sixties it was more rooted in reality and the writing was, if anything, the best it ever was. We had people like Jack Rosenthal, Geoff Lancashire, John Finch, Peter Eckersley, Adele Rose and these people all had a real feel for the North, for the programme. There was a truth in it. It was an unreal world really. The Street has always been regarded as heightened reality, but, in truth, it was a fairly unreal world but wholly believable within itself, within the confines of The Street.

# Christabelle Embleton
*Fan* **REAL CHARACTERS UP NORTH**

I started watching The Street when it first began. I watched the very first episode and straight away I loved it. The characters were characters then, not as they are now. I think Ena Sharples was a real character and the Rovers with the Walkers and the Barlows – they were all real characters. They were also families – you saw the whole family, you didn't get just one character.

It was different to what we knew. The North was very much up North and the South was down here. I didn't have any associations with the North then, although I did later marry a Northern man and used to go up there with him – he comes from Newcastle – and it was just like it was.

It was a new thing, it was something which didn't finish. Before that, programmes finished that night, whereas this came at us and carried on. It was a different concept of television, it was the first soap really. You had all those detective programmes on, but they finished and it was the end of the story, but with this, you had something to look forward to later on in the week.

Everybody spoke about it. We didn't have the *TV Times* and a lot of people couldn't afford newspapers and, anyhow, they didn't tell you what was going to happen, so it was total surprise when it actually happened.

We were down South where it is a totally different way of life. I know from experience, having later gone up there, that you were taken into these people's homes and you were just one of them. Down here, we were always very reserved, but they were not up there. It was as it is, it was friendlier; they would fall out with someone one day and the next day they would be buying them a drink.

The houses were exactly as they were like where my husband comes from. The coal would be delivered in the streets and you hang your washing out and all the kids would drive along on their bikes and bang into it because it was hung from one back alley to the other. I think that's why it caught on, because we down in the South didn't know anything about that way of life. We didn't have streets like that down in the South. The houses were the same inside and I lived in a similar house to those in *Coronation Street*, but the streets themselves were different. Accents were also totally different. We thought everybody spoke like us down South or the way they did on the BBC, you didn't think people had accents. I've got three boys and the middle boy was absolutely spellbound by the accents.

We watched it as a family and they still all watch it and my grand-daughter now watches it, so that's three generations. She'll say to me things about the different characters – she knows all the characters now. That's the beauty of The Street, it just goes on.

## Harry Whewell
*Northern Editor of the* Guardian                      **ROGUES AND MORALS**

No one can forget the Snug and the Rovers Return and the old women with hairnets. That just sticks in my mind. It was the feeling that here was some-thing which was quite different and which we had not seen on the telly before. The characters were different, but they were 99 per cent like the women who lived down the road – in our street, anyway.

There was this kind of slight tension between the respectable ones and the unrespectable. In our street, we had the Dowds, who were the unre-spectable ones who were three doors away, and the Foggertys, who were so respectable that, when my mother called – and this was a council house – he would put his jacket on. That's how respectable they were! People were like that, but I recognize the characters in *Coronation Street* as people who lived on our council estate in Stretford, near Trafford Park, just a stone's throw from what would have been the real Coronation Street in Salford. We had rogues as well, Mr Cowden, who was a painter and decorator, and he would come home with large cans of paint that he would distribute to every-one. The feel of *Coronation Street* was like the feel of my estate.

There was also a morality to the programme. It was a working-class code of morals – many people who have written about the working class have never fully understood. For instance, people are not 'used' in the programme. One of the things that amazed me when I strayed into the middle-class world was the way people *used* their friends shamelessly and expected themselves to be used. This didn't happen in my background.

Language as well – there is little bad language in The Street and, when I think back, I never heard anyone swear in my street, unless they were drunk, and certainly my father never did. People didn't. It was very respectable and The Street mirrors that kind of respectability.

# Linda McAleny
*Fan*                                    **THE CONTINUITY OF CHARACTERS**

We were BBC only, so we were one of the last to get ITV. We used to dash to my grandma's, who was renting one from DER, so that we could watch *Coronation Street* and adverts. It was round about your Ena Sharples time and Minnie Caldwell in the Snug. When we had ITV ourselves, we would all watch television together.

The three characters in the Snug stand out mostly and, then, as time goes on, I remember Elsie Tanner and the Ogdens, but I think it's the humorous characters particularly that would stand out. I think Emily Nugent was one of the early ones, and Ken Barlow, obviously.

I remember when the Ogdens had the lodger, Eddie Yates, and the comedy in that was particularly interesting – maybe because those sorts of characters everybody knows. There are those sorts of people in your street like them and now you've got Jack and Vera and the Battersbys that have taken over on the humour side. I think that's what keeps *Coronation Street* going, because it's more true to life than a lot of the other soaps. Not so many dramas, but more things that you can identify with. You can look at your street and you can see all these different characters in your own street. Maybe that's what makes it popular as well, because a lot of these characters have been there for 30 years and there's a continuity and you can follow it right through.

# Gary Parkinson
*Fan*                                    **THE SILENCE AND THE TENSION**

I would have been quite a young child when I started watching *Coronation Street*. It was one of those things that, as a kid, was a regular thing. It used to be like the Royle family in our house – we'd all cram on to the sofa to watch *Coronation Street*. It was on two nights a week then – Mondays and Wednesdays. We'd all cram on to the sofa – Mum and Dad and me and my brother – it was like a ritual. We all enjoyed it. It would be a talking point at school as well the day after, which I can't imagine people doing these days. I can imagine kids talking about *EastEnders*, but not *Coronation Street*.

I do remember quite dark episodes, like there was a fantastic episode, which must have been in the Sixties, which I've probably seen since then because I won't have remembered it at the time, of David Barlow's death,

Ken Barlow's brother. He and Irma had emigrated to Australia and Ken Barlow gets a phone call to say they'd been involved in a car crash and they're waiting to hear whether they've survived or not and, in the end, David Barlow and their son are killed and Irma survives and it's just like a Harold Pinter play. It was still in black and white in those days and it's just filled with these fantastic protracted silences, people just standing around in corners waiting for the phone to ring, and it's the Barlow family and the Ogden family because Irma Barlow was Stan and Hilda's daughter. It was unbearable, those silences. The tension was fantastic.

## Lynn de Santis
*Fan*                                  **THE REAL CORONATION STREET**

My sister got married very young, so all that they could afford – much to the dismay of my mum – because, obviously, they'd come out of that and my sister was going back – was a two up, two down in Archie Street, which was the original street that they used [for the opening titles]. There is actually a Coronation Street in Salford, but that wasn't what they used, they used Archie Street, and there was the shop on the corner. They used to get people knocking on the doors, asking them how long they'd lived here and what was it like living in *Coronation Street*. The shop on the corner did brilliant business because people would be going in just to say they'd bought things from the shop on the corner of *Coronation Street*. Next door to them were Mr and Mrs Colman, who were Eddie Colman's parents – he was one of the United players who had been killed at Munich – and they had been there all their lives and they used to tell Brenda that, right from the start, they had this small tourist industry.

There was a time in the late Sixties and the Seventies where I think there was also a little bit of resentment in Manchester that this was the way that people would see them – they wore cloth caps and talked over the yard wall sort of thing. I think there was a lot of that about at that time, but they have changed over the years. I think the characters are very true to life for Northerners and I like the way they haven't really changed their accents. I believe at one time, when it first started, they almost had to have subtitles. I can remember them saying things like 'Stop mithering', which I knew what they meant, but had to be translated almost.

They didn't used to have many children in the early days, but you've got the young storylines in there now, which you never used to have. Ken Barlow was a bit of the rebellious teenager, but there weren't any kids. I think the fact that there are so many characters that have kept all the way through, like Ken Barlow and Deirdre, so many of them have been around for so long, so it's always the new ones who tend to get bumped off.

# Phil Redmond
Brookside *creator*                                              **THE GOLDEN AGE**

I suppose in terms of characters, I have to go right back to those early days. The Tanners, I thought, were a great clan. Ena obviously was a great icon character. The three witches – Ena, Minnie and Martha – Stan and Hilda. I think Stan and Hilda were great when they first started, but, again, the caricature came in towards the end. I think Mr Street himself, Ken. I remember being at that Lifetime Achievement Award thing and finding out he'd had affairs with 26 women and you go, 'What? Whoa.' They all have these iconic characters. The favourites just go back. It's the rule about the golden age of television – there's only one golden age and that's the one that you grew up with.

# CHAPTER FOUR

# The 1970s and 1980s

## *The comedy years*

In June 1970, *Coronation Street* celebrated its thousandth episode. It had firmly consolidated its position as the nation's top-rated television show with roughly eight million viewers. It was also being sold to ten countries across the world, from Sierra Leone to New Zealand.

During the 1970s, the strong storylines continued. Elsie, Ena and Annie continued at the helm, although actor Arthur Leslie, who played Jack Walker, died very suddenly. Elsie married, Len and Rita also tied the knot, and Ernest Bishop was brutally murdered. A young Bet Lynch – slim, fresh-faced and oozing sex appeal – had been introduced to viewers and a lorry had crashed into the Rovers, causing mayhem. Despite all the drama, there was still much to amuse.

Comedy was always an essential element of The Street. Even in those angst years as a gritty Northern drama, there was usually something to laugh about. There may not have been so many deliberate comic characters, but there were plenty of incidents and enough light-hearted characters to carry the comedy along. Even Ena Sharples had her moments. She may have been earnest, but, beneath the solemnizing, you couldn't help but laugh. That was her beauty. In a way, she was a figure of fun; the old world of conformity confronting the new world of informality, adventure and the breaking down of the old barriers whether social, gender or class. You had to smile as she confronted Elsie with her looser morals, neither of them afraid to speak their own minds or stick up for their beliefs. They just happened to be irreconcilable, worlds apart.

Comedy was a vital ingredient. 'I think that is what sets *Coronation Street* apart from the other soaps,' argues fan Barrie Holmes. 'Firstly, there is excellent acting and good scripts, but they have this weave of comedy in the scripts and the characters. In the Seventies, that was particularly strong. They did it in a very clever way. They would have a character who had the main comedy role. Geoff Hughes as Eddie Yeats was particularly good at that. He took over from Ken Cope, who had played Sunny Jim. Since then, we've had people like Reg and Alec Gilroy.'

The humour had been there from the start. Harry Driver and Vince Powell, who had written regularly for The Street in its first four years, eventually left to become comedy advisers to Thames Television. It was no coincidence that, during the Seventies, one of The Street's chief writers – Geoff Lancashire – also happened to be a fine comedy writer. Geoff, who had worked in the Promotions Department at Granada alongside Tony Warren and John Temple (later to be a producer and script editor of The Street), also wrote the much acclaimed Granada comedy *The Cuckoo Waltz*, as well as *Foxy Lady*. Lancashire had as fine an ear for dialogue as any writer in The Street's long history, apart from the incomparable Tony Warren.

Born in Oldham, he understood, like Warren, the natural humour of the street corner, the pubs and the workplace. Lancashire simply loved to let The Street amble along at a gentle pace, carried forward by moments of humour. The Street was not in those days so plot-driven – so many scenes were simply colour; they didn't take you anywhere in particular, they didn't carry the story or any of its plots any further. What they did do was to give you an insight into character, they were scenes that developed characterization – a necessity acknowledged by every playwright and scriptwriter from Wilde to Beckett. Beckett had also recognized that there is humour in everything. Humour is an essential tool in the writer's portfolio. Another Street writer, Jack Rosenthal, was widely regarded as a writer with biting wit, rather than whimsical humour.

Under Lancashire and John Temple, The Street devoted more time and more scenes to humour. Comedy characters also emerged. Eddie Yeats – the Scouse binman, played by Geoff Hughes – was introduced to viewers in 1974 as Minnie Caldwell's lodger. He would remain for the next 13 years, helping Stan Ogden with his window round, and initiating many a get-rich-quick scheme with Stan while charming the often gullible Hilda and Minnie.

Stan himself, played by Bernard Youens, was as rich a comedy character as any, with his varied repertoire of careers, from milkman, to coalman, ice-cream man, Father Christmas and all-in wrestler. Hapless, irascible, but loveable. Then there was Hilda Ogden, The Street's veritable gossip. There wasn't much that Hilda didn't know and, when she found out, it spread like wildfire. Gossip, and the telling of it – always a good tool for comedy.

Throughout the Seventies and Eighties, The Street became recognized as much for its humour as for anything else. It was critically dubbed a 'folk opera' and The Street somehow seemed cocooned from the real world. The problems that afflicted the rest of British life rarely touched those in The Street. Burglaries, car thefts, these were rare rather than everyday occurrences. Of course, there were incidents – a lorry crashed into the Rovers and Betty Turpin was mugged – but, generally, The Street was a peaceful place to live. It was certainly a safe zone. On reflection, maybe that was a more accurate picture of life in the North than the one of endless grime and crime we saw elsewhere. Nevertheless, The Street's portrayal of life was to bring its critics. There were no black families, for instance, and it was rare to see a black face in the programme – hardly an accurate reflection of life in Manchester, though, some might say, it was a fairly accurate reflection of some parts of Salford.

*Coronation Street* was a family show, suitable for every family. Even swearing was banned, although Geoff Lancashire recalls a battle to get the first 'language' into the programme when Valerie Barlow was electrocuted. It was, he says, 'one of Harry Kershaw's foibles that there was no swearing in The Street'. Geoff wanted a distraught Ken to stand over Valerie saying, 'Oh God.' Harry Kershaw wasn't happy, but, after a long discussion, finally relented: 'I think it must have been the first time a swear word of any kind had been used in The Street,' says Geoff Lancashire.

Sex never happened either or, if it did, it was off screen. The Street always had a moral streak running through it and, although there were affairs and relationships, there was never anything remotely *risqué*. The baddies always lost.

The Street took pride in its regional identity, although some criticized it for stereotyping the region, as if the North was all whippets, Hilda Ogden and too many nosy people. Harry Whewell, former Northern Editor of the *Guardian* newspaper came across this view on more than one occasion:

'There used to be a feeling that *Coronation Street* stereotyped Manchester and that Manchester is not really all *Coronation Street*. That is perhaps a bit of a middle-class view, but it is also true that somewhere like Manchester is not really that much different from Leeds. I do think it is true that *Coronation Street* stereotypes the North – mean streets, and a bit of the whippet, that's what people think of the North. Maybe *Coronation Street* does occasionally play up to that image.'

In the Eighties, the storylines were as strong as ever. There were wedding bells for Ken and Deirdre and then there was the infamous love triangle when Mike Baldwin became embroiled. At an Edinburgh Television Festival, TV bosses were asked to nominate their all-time top ten television drama moments. Top of the list was Ken discovering Deirdre's affair with Mike. The viewers agreed, with the show hitting an all-time high of an audience of 29 million. The storyline caught the public's imagination. Street Director Ian White remembers going to see Manchester United that Wednesday and the result of Deirdre's dilemma was flashed up on the scoreboard at Old Trafford. A roar of approval went up from the Stretford End. Another fan, Salford-born Lynn de Santis, remembers it vividly as well: 'I don't think there was a dry eye in Manchester on that night when he's throwing her out and she says, "I don't want to go", and Uncle Albert's there as well and he's crying. That was fantastic, that was really good stuff.'

There were other memorable moments. Elsie left, the Rovers went up in flames, Mavis and Derek married, Gail had her marital problems and Bet Lynch became Queen of the Street, taking charge of the Rovers. Julie Goodyear had perfected the character of Bet – likeable, vulnerable, unique, even though there was a Bet in every Salford pub. The Eighties, as fan Gary Parkinson recalls, was 'Bet Lynch's decade when she ruled the roost at the Rovers … she became this fantastic galleon. She got a new wig and she got all those posh new suits. She was like "cock of the walk", I always remember her using that phrase, "In my pub, Vera, I'm cock of the walk".'

Yet the period also brought some sad losses. Ena, Elsie and Annie all retired from active life in The Street (all three died some time later), Hilda also left and that great Street anti-hero, Len Fairclough, was sacked. Another great loss was Bill Podmore, who, in 1989, decided to retire. He had been Executive Producer of The Street since 1976. His old friend Bob Greaves remembers him fondly as a man of 'great mental agility, charm …

and an able soul'. All these changes would present problems that would have to be confronted in the Nineties.

The Seventies and Eighties also saw the introduction of new technology. For a start, there was colour. It had actually been introduced in November 1969, but only a handful of homes had colour sets then. It was not until the Seventies that it became the norm. So, the old black-and-white grittiness gave way to sunshine and flowers. The Street had always reflected the drabness and greyness of the North and there were plenty who feared that colour would bring a new light to The Street, exposing its darker side. Bill Roache for one remembers that 'everyone said it was a black-and-white show, that colour would not assist it. There was always a sort of reluctance to change.' But change they had to, even though one television critic in *The Stage and Television Today* reckoned that people had lost 'a touch of their authenticity' and that colour had not improved The Street. However, if viewing figures were anything to go by, it made little difference.

Wally Butler – who directed more than a thousand episodes of The Street during this period – remembers there were other innovations, such as the replacement of fixed camera lenses with zoom lenses. Editing techniques also improved, although the major leap forward would not really take place until the Nineties. As graphic designer Jim Quick explains, the beginnings of computerization were happening in the mid-Eighties, changing the workload of the Graphics Department and making life considerably easier.

Oddly enough, in this period The Street was not regarded by television staff as a show that you would aspire to work on. At least two employees testify in this chapter that it was sometimes regarded as the gulag of Granada – not very glitzy, hardly challenging and spelling the end of expenses! It was routine work, but all that was about to change. The new technology, which was improving almost by the day, offered new, exciting opportunities. Colour had ushered in the 1970s, but the change that was to usher in the 1990s was to be one of the most significant in the programme's history. In October 1989, a third episode – on a Friday night – was transmitted.

## Jim Quick
*Graphic Artist*                                    **READ ALL ABOUT IT**

In late 1972, I was given the great glory of working on The Street, which, it turns out, wasn't the great glory. The one thing every graphic designer hated about *Coronation Street*, the biggest bore in everything you did in those days, was the end roller caption, which was literally a long black toilet roll that you Lettrasetted on to and ran vertically through the field of view of the camera and punctuated between the end of the programme and the start of the commercials. The problem with doing the *Coronation Street* roller was that it was centred. That literally means that one line of type was centred under another line of type, so 'Graphic Designer Jim Quick' was in the centre of the roller. You had to work every single line of type out, you had to trace every name on. You wouldn't believe this – it took three days to do a *Coronation Street* roller. So they were employing so-called 'creatives' in mindless, repetitious activities, but it was the way the industry was.

*Coronation Street* wasn't a great show for a title sequence. They had their opening super-caption, which said 'Coronation Street' and then you were into the show. Our other contribution came at that time when they wanted what they called 'props', graphic props. So, if they wanted something which said, 'Steak and beans in the café – 1/6d', that's what you did and you used your skill in visual terms with a brush or a pen or a camera. Somebody might say in the script that there was a kid's drawing on the fridge, so you'd do that, or if it said there was a family photograph with so and so in, you'd con the photograph up. If it was Elsie in Blackpool and you didn't have a picture of Elsie in Blackpool, you'd make a photomontage, put it in a frame and stick it on the mantelpiece. Really, what you were doing at that point was acting as 'unpaid' assistants to the set designers, because the set designers would control the production requirements. The set designers would tell you or indicate a request for graphic props. We even did Weatherfield newspapers, '*The Weatherfield Gazette*' was produced entirely within Granada's Graphics Department. We used to use the body of copy from the *Manchester Evening News* and we'd make up front pages of newspapers which said, 'Ken dies under lorry' with pictures of the victim. We'd get these printed off and we'd get ten of them. One of them would be used on the show and the other nine would probably be taken home by people as souvenirs. For that one shot, that might have been a three-second shot halfway through the show, you'd have sent it out to print, you'd have done the photography, the headline, you'd have mocked it up – attention to detail, it mattered in those days.

# John Temple
*Storyline Editor and Producer*        **THE ART OF STORYLINING**

The three years I spent as a storyliner on The Street was the most beneficial period of my entire working life. I always said to writers, 'If you get the chance, the discipline of churning out storylines for something like *Coronation Street*, day in, day out, week after week, 52 weeks of the year, is an unbelievable learning curve.'

The Street has almost been unique in its creative system and its approach to things. None of the others has followed it so tightly and religiously and I think to their cost. I give all the credit for it to Harry Kershaw. If you look back, you will discover that, right from the beginning, he was pulled in as a Script Editor on The Street. They only had about 13 scripts to start with and Tony had written all of them. They brought in Harry, who was an insurance man, but had written quite a lot of one-off things for ABC and for Granada, and it was Harry who set up the system that works to this day. Granada always went for writer-producers to handle The Street.

All that has been weakened in recent years. What it needs is somebody who understands scripts. In my time – and I'm not alone in this and I know this is why I got the job as much as anything else – they knew I would continue to handle it that way.

You would have conferences and ideas were thrown up. We would look where we were in everybody's lives at that moment in time. We were only discussing six episodes, we'd only do three weeks' worth of episodes, what was going to happen to the lives of these characters over the next six weeks, picking up all the threads that were ongoing, who needed a story, who needed a break. There were logistical things entered into, so it was quite an exercise. Writers who had formed allegiances to particular characters would fight like cat and dog for these characters. Again, I think this has gone from the show now, but it was very rooted in characters in those days. There was no bending of characterization to make a plot work for some short-term gain and there's a lot of that goes on now. You knew where you stood with everybody in *Coronation Street* and they all had writers who fought tooth and nail to be true to them, to keep them true and faithful. It was a battle royal. We used to have almost stand-up fights. It was a draining experience, but it was exhilarating, too. It was very productive.

I wasn't coming to this fresh when I took on The Street [as Producer] – I'd had years of experience of producing sitcoms, I had all the previous experience I'd gained as a storyliner, sitting in on those meetings in my humble role, then, listening to it all.

The storyliners sit and take notes and they have to go away at the end of the day and make something out of all these ideas, many of them conflicting. The whole thing's a rag-bag of ideas and, often, you've got to throw half of it, but the wonderful thing was, it was extremely stimulating and it would give ideas that even if they hadn't been fully thought out or discussed at the conference, you could pick up in the quiet of your own office later on and make work.

The storyliners were putting down the grass roots of the Street in a scene-by-scene, blow-by-blow account. It was a detailed scene-by-scene breakdown – which actors were in the scene, where it takes place and, basically, the story points. The writer has got no freedom to bugger about with that, not with the story points. He can mess about with the shape of it, but they've got to stick to the story as agreed, otherwise the whole thing falls about like a deck of cards. We were able to commission individuals to write episodes. You have six episodes and you could get six different people to write an episode each and it would all work. In the normal course of events, that would cause untold continuity problems and so on, if you were giving them *carte blanche* to do what they liked within the episode. There are some who would argue it's too constricting and yet it works. It's because of all that and because of the thinking that goes into it, the plotting and the planning, that, for me, it's sustained over 40 years.

Storylining is an artform all of its own. It's about twisting and turning the story so that you're always keeping the audience interested, wanting them to find out what happens next, and it's all very cleverly built around ad breaks and tags of episodes if you do your job well. You've got to leave the audience at the end of the episode wondering where the hell this is going next. The trick, again, for the good storyliners is to create a jigsaw that works. You'd have maybe one main theme running through, with two subsidiary strands. As a main theme would come to an end, one of the secondary stories would be taking over, as a biggie, perhaps, and something else would be coming in in a minor way. There were always one-episode or two-episode stories that were going on just as colour and to fill things in.

There was room for a great deal of invention on the storyliner's part or the individual writer's part. If they felt, when they got their breakdown to write up in dialogue fashion, it was a bit light here and there, they could embellish it or do scenes in the Snug with Ena, Martha and Minnie and let them talk about the price of bread. There was room for all of that and it was good, strong character stuff and good colour for The Street. I'm afraid there's not a lot of room left for that any more because it's so plot-driven and so anxious to get on and tell a story without time to take stock and think seriously about where people are going in their lives and are they behaving rationally? Everybody can behave irrationally and do stupid things as long as they are properly motivated. If you've got the right motivation built into what you're doing or it comes out of the history of the characters, you can do almost anything with anybody, but it all starts to lose credibility when, suddenly, for short term gain, characters undergo complete changes. I don't recognize Rita now. Rita has become a different person altogether, she's changed so often in recent times. The storyliners' job was to go away from these conferences with this welter of ideas, having been guided, to some degree, by the producer at the time.

## Ric Mellis
*Assistant Stage Manager, Floor Manager and Director*

**AM I DOING ALL RIGHT?**

Nobody in telly ever tells you when you're doing all right, nobody says anything to you, you get no feedback at all. They only tell you when you're f***ing up.

After I'd done about three lots of episodes, I went to see Bill [Podmore, Producer] and said, 'I just wanted to know if it's going all right? Is there anything you think I should be doing differently? I want to do The Street the way you want it', and he said, 'I never watch the programme, but everybody tells me you're doing fine.' I just thought that was brilliant! I wandered off in a confused daze, but thought, 'I'm probably doing all right.' I don't know whether it was true.

What was so good about Bill was that he *was Coronation Street*. It was such a great programme and it was because of all its history, but he was part of that history. He was just so immersed in it and he ran it brilliantly. I can't remember any of those daft conversations that you have about soaps, and I've worked on a lot of soaps – 'My character wouldn't do this.

This doesn't feel right. This is a cock-up. What's happened to that story?', that kind of conversation with actors, or reading scripts and you go, 'Wait a minute, this doesn't make any sense at all.' It just worked and, as far as I was ever aware, it just sort of ambled along in its own sort of way, but completely in control. There were never stupid rows and panics about 'We've got too many scenes', not that I was aware of. It was just very neat and tidy and brilliantly run.

The stories were fantastic. You used to come in on a Wednesday afternoon for the tech run – we ran it like a play without the exterior stuff and all the technicians stood round and watched it in the rehearsal room. It took an hour to do, if that, and Bill used to come every Wednesday afternoon with a big smile on his face, watching what was going on. Afterwards, we'd sit down and he'd give his notes. More often than not, his notes were, 'Great, very good' and other times he'd say, 'That's not working and that's not working and a bit more of that' – it was just terribly controlled, in a way that I've never seen from anybody, ever.

## Tom Elliott
*Script Editor and Scriptwriter*

**THE NUGGETS THAT CAME OUT OF THE FURNACE**

When I began working for *Coronation Street* in 1983 as a storyliner, I was working with Esther Rose and it went out Monday and Wednesday – just two a week. They worked on a three-weekly turnaround and we had conferences in Room 600 with the scriptwriters. We'd sit there and the meetings would go on – we were only going for six episodes, but the meetings would go on until half-past six, seven o'clock at night because it was contentious, it really was tough. If you weren't thick-skinned to start with, you soon grew this thick skin. That was Monday.

The producers in those days – the producers I worked for, there were seven – every producer up to Brian Park allowed the programme to be writer-driven. In other words, as Bill Podmore put in his autobiography, he likened those conferences to a furnace where he allowed the heat to grow and where these nuggets came out of this furnace. We went in also with an agenda, which we prepared in the Story Office, because you knew what stories hadn't been completed and also who hadn't played for a week or two and so you prepared this agenda and took it to the Producer. That was sent out to the scriptwriters, so that everybody arrived with an agenda.

There was a point in the afternoons, usually, where someone would say, 'I've got a story for Emily.' Someone might have written it down. I used to write them out, John Stevenson never did and still doesn't. John remembers them off the top of his head and Julian Roach didn't, Adele Rose did and a few people wrote them out. You'd be given the opportunity of finishing what you'd said and then the insults would come and 'You got that wrong, you got that right.' What you'd actually done was stimulate other people into improving what you'd got. There were moments, particularly when I was Story Editor, when I felt the meeting was flagging a bit or we were going off in the wrong direction, so you'd say the first thing that came into your head. Julian, in particular, would leap up. In 13, 14 years of working with him, I never had a wrong word with the man, but, in conferences, I'd be accused of having no sense of the dramatic and no sense of story structure and all this, but what you'd done, again, was spark somebody else. The idea was to come out with as much material as you could – 'Here's a story about suchabody, who can this story influence?' I likened it to firing a pinball off. Now, your ball can either go up and come back or it can light up other areas and your score increases and that's how storyline construction should be put together.

When you wrote a storyline, when I first started, you used to go for 13 scenes. That was an arbitrary figure – six in the first half, seven in the second. One of the other impositions in the early days was that you could only have two pieces of [exterior] film, so everything else had to be interior. We were also in Studio 6, which only fitted five sets. It's the storyliners who have to choose the sets – the 'Where are you going to play this and that?' discipline was tremendous. If you had Brian Tilsley's garage, that meant you could only have four sets because that was a big set. Then came in PSC – the portable single camera. I think it was union agreements that had prevented it being used before that. When I first started, you'd have two bits of film and then you'd be on videotape and there'd be a terrible difference in grain with 16mm, which was awful. When the PSC came in, that gave us more flexibility. You could have some more exteriors, and Paul Abbott and I, with Mervyn Watson's guidance, we had 18 scenes. I think there's a tendency now – and it's throughout television – where they go for even more scenes, and if you cut quick enough, if you edit quick enough, they don't give the viewer credit for absorbing. If you have a good story and a good scene and it's well done, even children will sit like anybody else and watch. Mervyn wanted more than 18 scenes sometimes, but it means a quick edit and no scene is more than 30 seconds long.

When you came out of that story conference your first job was to choose the cast and the sets for that week. With the cast, it was, 'Who do you want to play in this?' and you were governed by, 'He's not played for a while, so we'll put him in the Rovers to order a pint – at least he'll get an episode fee' and then the sets, 'Where is it best to play these stories?'

Exit stories were, 'Give them as good an exit as you can.' I think there was a mood at that time that was wrong. If an actor volunteered to leave, then they wouldn't have them back. If a contracted character left at that time, they wanted him or her dead. Their exit story was final and that was wrong, it was unenlightened. After that came the 'The door's open' and that's how it is now, which is better.

At that time, only the Producer had editorial authority and you made notes to check the continuity and sometimes character consistency. That didn't happen a lot because the writers had been writing it so long and the characters were so well established. You didn't need a lot of stage direction in a Street script for people like Pat Phoenix and Barbara Knox because they knew their characters better than you did.

There was very little difficulty with differences in style between writers. Obviously, with style, occasionally you knew who had written it because they had certain idiosyncrasies, but the viewers wouldn't know. You knew a Julian Roach script, for instance, because of the stage direction. I remember once reading a stage direction in the Barlows' and it said, 'Nicky thrust on by an unseen hand'.

## Ken Farrington
*Actor, played Billy Walker*                          **LEAVING THE STREET**

When I last left, there was a bit of a cloud about it because, when I was in it originally, I played a Jack-the-lad sort of character, a bit like the Johnny Briggs character is now. Then, when I didn't go back, the Briggs character came in and filled that space. Then I think there was a time when I did go back and they phoned me up very late because Fred Feast had been ill and had to leave and I went back for about a year, but, in going back, they'd written the scripts for Fred and had adapted them for me, but there was quite a character change and I felt a bit upset about it. You begin to forget where reality is and where the play-acting is and I got a bit protective about the character and got very upset at some of the things that they were making the character do. I voiced that upset and there were one or two who didn't feel I should have voiced it and, perhaps, I voiced it too strongly. I don't know why they didn't kill me off.

I wouldn't mind going back – I used to love going back. I would like to feel that they would phone me up and call me back in, but they haven't and I would presume it was because the people who are running it now don't even remember who I was.

## Geoff Lancashire
*Scriptwriter*                                                 **NO SWEARING**

One of Harry Kershaw's foibles was that there was no swearing in The Street. Anne Reid, who played Valerie Barlow, wanted to be written out. She had just got married and she was planning a new career. It was never explained to me at the time. In one episode, when she died, she was ironing and something went wrong with the plug. She bent down to pull it out and touched the terminals and died. I wanted to write Ken Barlow at the end saying, 'Oh God, Val, oh God.' I wanted to use the word 'God'.

Harry Kershaw said, 'Are you sure, Geoff?' I said, 'I think so, Harry. You say, "Oh God" when somebody's died.' 'Yeah, OK then,' he said. So, it went through. I think it must have been the first time a swear word of any kind had been used in The Street.

It was a difficult scene. I was quite sad. I didn't want Valerie or Ken to break up, but the storyline had been written and it was up to me to provide the dialogue.

## Dionne Spence
*Fan*                                         **THREE ROLLERS AND A HEADSCARF**

My parents watched *Coronation Street* before I started watching it and so I grew up with it. I was brought up in a working-class area in Manchester, so the characters were realistic to me, but I don't think the storylines were ever quite realistic. When I first started watching it, The Street was black and white and Annie Walker and Ena Sharples and her friend used to be in the pub all the time gossiping about everybody. I remember Alf Roberts used to have the shop on the corner and Rita when she was married to Len

Fairclough. I remember when they first fostered Sharon and she nearly had an affair with Chris Quinten.

I used to watch it with my mum and dad all the time. Depending on what happened, we'd talk about it at school the next day. I remember when the pub blew up, there was a gas explosion and Tracy was outside in her pram. In those days, I think it was on on a Monday and Wednesday. We had to wait then from Wednesday all the way round till Monday to find out if Tracy had been killed or not. I remember talking about that. Then there was Len Fairclough having an accident in his workshop and we all thought maybe he could have been dead and I remember discussing that.

I used to love Stan and Hilda – I loved the way Hilda wore lipstick on the centre of her mouth and those three rollers and the headscarf and she always wore that pinny, fag in the mouth and always singing in that high-pitched voice. Stan always used to wear his window-cleaning jacket with his rags hanging out and that checked shirt. I used to adore Eddie Yeats – he used to make me laugh so much.

The funniest episode I have ever seen on *Coronation Street* was when Stan and Hilda had their second honeymoon and they went to a hotel and she was putting on her negligée and putting on her lipstick and doing her hair, and she came out and Stan was fast asleep. I think he'd actually done his back in as well – that was the funniest.

The saddest was when Stan died and when Hilda left The Street – that was really upsetting. Kevin became Hilda's lodger after Stan had died and then he met Sally. Sally at first wasn't going to be a permanent character in The Street because she came in as a bolshie teenager. She was very aggressive, quite like a Punk the way she dressed. Hilda disapproved – she didn't like Sally at all because she was very rude to her – but they must have then realized that they could do something with Sally and Kevin. Hilda cleaned the Rovers and a doctor's house and then the doctor died and left Hilda money and Kevin and Sally bought Hilda's house.

I loved Bet Lynch. I used to think she was a bit of a tart when I was a kid, but as she matured, she became a nicer character. I loved Elsie Tanner because she was a very strong character – she used to stand up to Annie Walker and the gossipers in the pub. She had a bit of a tarty character, but she was very strong and overcame that all the time. Whatever obstacles got in the way, she always got past them.

# Phil Redmond
Brookside *creator*                                    **SHANKLY'S PASSION**

I didn't want *Brookside* to be like The Street – I didn't want it to be ideal, I didn't want it to be *Coronation Street*, I didn't want it to be a factory, I didn't want it to be that stepping stone for people. In many ways, I shared this with Bill Podmore, because Bill Podmore had this passion for The Street. He even tried to get me on it. I went to three storyline conferences and I said to him, 'It's not for me, Bill' because, actually, I wanted the young people in. This was in the Seventies and they weren't interested in that, but Bill was the same as me in the sense that he would sack people if he heard them talking disparagingly about the show because, basically, he said, 'You're either here because you believe in it or you don't. We're not a meal ticket.'

I took that philosophy with me, and the Bill Shankly thing about the passion and the strength and depth. I wanted this to be somewhere where people would be proud of what they'd done and they would be proud of the product and I wanted it to be somewhere where they'd learn their skills and have the toys and play with them. If they wanted to stay, they could stay. If they wanted to go, then go, that was fine.

# Bob Greaves
*Television Presenter*                              **PODMORE THE PRODUCER**

Jean Alexander – who played Hilda for all those years – could turn her hand to anyone from Hilda to playing any Shakespearian role of her choice. Real actors, nice people. Going back to those who fell by the wayside there was Jennifer Moss, who played Lucille Hewitt. It's not surprising, given the number of people who have been through the sausage machine – runs into the thousands – so I'm not surprised that some proved to be vulnerable.

Bill Podmore – the other long-time producer who sadly died a few years ago – I first knew him when he was a senior cameraman, then he became a producer. I'd known him a long time and I was delighted when he became Producer of The Street – a job he did with a great deal of mental agility, charm, as well as a tinge of having to be a hard man because dealing with contracts and hirings and firings can't have been easy. He was an able soul and liked to stand at the bar and indulge our other passion of pissing ourselves with laughter. His death was another sad, sad loss.

# Brian Spencer
*Film Camerman*                                   **FILMING ON LOCATION**

It was normally just one day a week when the programme needed to go outside of the lot, although even exteriors on the lot were shot on the film. Essentially it was exteriors from the studio sets that were shot on film. So, there was a certain amount on the exterior lot. When I was there, Brian Tilsley was working in the garage under the railway arches, so that story ran for a few weeks.

Gareth Morgan was directing and he persuaded Bill Podmore, the Producer, to shoot in Stockport market. Gareth took it to a new level of realization with dollies and tracks. It was terribly ambitious. We had 23 pages one day and 19 pages the next. I enjoyed it because cameramen like to have these kinds of challenges, but I spoke to Bill Podmore afterwards in the bar and I said to him that trying to do 23 pages of script in a day with a coachload of extras in a high wind on Stockport market was just too much. Bill's reply was *Coronation Street* was not about high tracking shots and cranes and so on. *Coronation Street* didn't need all that, nor want all that; it was bringing to it a level of drama production that was, in his view, unsuited to the format, the story, the people, the feel of *Coronation Street*. As a young cameraman trying to do big dramas, I found that very frustrating, but I recognized, too, that he was right.

# Ric Mellis
*Assistant Stage Manager, Floor Manager and Director*        **FITTING IN THE SHOTS**

The sets were much smaller then – they were tiny. I remember one of the things we did was to rebuild all the sets bigger. They remained apparently the same, but they were enlarged some time in the mid Eighties.

Albert Tatlock's set is the one which always sticks in my head because there was so much going on in there. There was so much furniture in it there was no floor space at all. There were about three places that the actors could stand, but they couldn't move and there were only about two shots you could do. You could set them across a table or you could stand them up on either side of the table, but that was pretty much it.

The Rovers was much more restricted. At the end of the bar, when you come in the door, the bar's facing you. On the U of the bar, on the camera side, there were actually two stools and then a door into the Snug. We used to have to shoot it then as though the door was really there and it was a bugger because, again, that was tiny. Over the years the Rovers has grown and that door has gone and the bar now extends into what used to be the Snug. If you look at the old pictures, it was a proper little Manchester bar. Now it's a big Manchester bar. It was as ambitious visually, but it wasn't about tracking shots – it was about the intimacy.

Having the sets enlarged makes it easier for the technicians to get at it and for the directors to be more imaginative. Years ago, with the kit that you had, Brian Mills couldn't do some of the things that he has done brilliantly over the years – like the famous shot through the fireplace. Sometimes it's been made possible for us to do a bit more and be a bit more adventurous and creative, although sometimes the creativity works against the intimacy of the programme. Over the years, we've been given more and more space and more licence to do things, but it doesn't stop the programme actually being what it is – this very intimate experience.

## Chris Atkinson
*Sound Recordist*                      **RECORDING FOR SOUND**

I started working on The Street about 1978, 1979. I was a boom operator – that's a sound recordist's assistant. I would hold the mike in the air on a long pole, occasionally dropping it into shot! Exteriors were shot on film in those days. Most of it was done on the exterior of the set, in The Street itself. Location work was always around Manchester – you could usually spit on Granada from where the location was. We never went far away and they were mostly streets that were in character with *Coronation Street*. The set in those days used to be down by the Bonded Warehouse, where Tours is now. When we had cars on the set, they always had a problem because The Street was virtually a dead end and, if a car was driving down The Street, they had to slam their brakes on.

Of course, when you opened the front doors of houses on the set, it was just scaffolding. All The Street was was a front, there was nothing behind the front, no rooms or anything like that. You might see a little bit of a wall if a door was open, but not much. There's a lot more now, the houses are more substantial, although they are still not full size. The cameraman always shot slightly sideways to the door so that you could not see far inside.

Sometimes we might use a radio mike if we were doing a long shot down The Street, but, most of the time, we had a boom mike on the end of a long pole. We tended not to use radio mikes because they were so unreliable. They're a lot more reliable nowadays, but, in those days, you'd get three feet away and the quality of sound would go. Sometimes we'd use a gun mike, a rifle mike – it's a directional mike, it gets rid of traffic noise. We'd start at 8.30am in the morning, which was smack on rush hour, so the traffic around was quite heavy, so we used this directional mike that would cut out the surrounding sound. The boom mike used to pick up all that traffic sound. The sound of traffic would bounce off walls everywhere. Traffic noise is always a problem, still is.

We would track down The Street with the actors and the mike as they walked down The Street, being aware of reflections, which you do see now and again. Because of the way The Street is built, it has picture windows, which were always a problem with reflections with the boom. We also used to have to be careful doing scenes over shiny cars, cos, again, you get a reflection and the boom can be spotted.

Our job is to get the dialogue as clean as we can without too much exterior noise. Then they will put sound effects on afterwards. Basically, I sit with a recorder – it was a Nargra in those days, but now it's digital, then it was quarter-inch tapes. I sat with the Nargra and a little mixing desk and, by then, I had a boom operator – somebody who would hold the mike for me. I would have earphones on and had to listen to get the cleanest sound I could. If I could hear traffic, police sirens, planes or anything like that, you would have to stop. Imagine if you're cutting a sequence between two people, you can't have different sounds in the background. Of course, it's very annoying having to stop if the sound is bad, but it has to be done – you can always hear the changes in background sound – but what we then do is to take a wild track, that's an atmos. track – general background sound – and we then lay this over everything, smooth out the edits and then you can't hear the changes. It's just hiding the rough edges. We do the wild track by just telling everyone to be quiet and then putting the boom mike into the air and recording for a minute. That gives us the atmos. track. The secret is to get the background as quiet as possible.

# Ric Mellis
*Assistant Stage Manager, Floor Manager and Director*

**TRANSLATING ABUSE**

The next step was Floor Manager and I did that, on and off, for two or three years, although not constantly on The Street.

In the studio, the Director always worked in the Box [the control room], so your most important job was to keep everybody going and make sure everybody was doing the right thing. You made your notes in rehearsals as to where everybody was supposed to be, the same kinds of notes you made as an Assistant Stage Manager, but not as detailed. Where everybody's to be, where they are coming from, so you check everybody's in the right place, they know what they're doing, check that the props are there for them. But the most important job for the Floor Manager was relaying notes from the Director, who was up in the gallery, to the actor. So, they would rehearse the scene and the Director would want them to be sadder or happier, so you relay that note.

Sometimes someone would say to you, 'Will you tell that stupid cow that if she doesn't stand in the right place the next time, I'm going to come down and kill her' and what floor managers are good at doing is translating that into, 'It would be really helpful to us if, perhaps, you could stand a little bit closer to the table next time you do it.' Floor managers translate abuse into something actors won't be offended by. That happens all the time.

You didn't speak to Pat Phoenix as you would speak to Kevin Kennedy on his first day. You speak to different people in different ways because they respond to different things and there is a hierarchy. There was very much a hierarchy on The Street. You don't give instructions to certain people, but others – especially the younger ones – want instructions and some of them need no instructions at all. Some of them know instinctively what to do or they've been doing it for so long they know what's happening. It just varies from person to person and day to day.

# John Temple
*Storyline Editor and Producer*

**THE BATTLE FOR RATINGS**

When I was producing, we had the fire at the Rovers, we had the good story of the breakdown in the Tilsley marriage, where she had a fling with Brian's cousin from Australia. Then Brian abducted the boy.

Julie Goodyear needed compassionate leave to look after her mother –

she was out for weeks. We had Alec Gilroy go and discover her in Torremolinos, running a bar, and we went to Spain then. We had five days in Torremolinos, filming the 'bring Bet back to Manchester' thing. This all led to her coming back and the ultimate marriage, which I set up, but I left just prior to the wedding episode of Bet and Alec.

I also married Kevin and Sally Webster – they were a young couple. She was a sparky girl, but they lost their way with her, I thought, for some period of time.

I was there the day when Julie was installed in the Rovers. My first story conference, we were discussing the going of Billy Walker and bringing Julie in as queen bee. She came back as landlady.

I was also responsible for bringing Jack Duckworth off that daft window round he had at the time and putting him in the Rovers, and he became a much better character when he started working alongside Julie Goodyear and people like that. We turned the corner shop into Alf's mini-market – that happened in my time.

The burning down of the Rovers was a marker of a new look and new designers. It began with feeling that we needed to revamp this pub and it became a big story. In those days, to get extra filming was unknown. They only worked a five-day week in my time and they used to film on the lot on a Monday morning before the blocking of the thing in the afternoon. So you only had Monday morning and, if you were lucky, you had Thursday morning because the studio didn't start until the afternoon.

So, we had a big thing, like burning down the Rovers. I had to move heaven and earth to get everybody's permission and agreement. The cast used to moan and groan about working at weekends – they all did PAs [personal appearances]. So, it was all set up for a Saturday, a full day Saturday, and we used an old pub down by the river. We actually had a fire, a proper thing for the interiors. It was a big and complicated shoot for that time and Gareth Morgan directed it. We didn't get it finished on the Saturday, so, the following Saturday, we had to come back. This was almost unheard of in those days. The end result was that it was going out in June and there was a World Cup on that year, 1986. By sheer bad luck, this episode found itself up against a World Cup tie. Again, heaven and earth were moved to get the network to repeat an episode of The Street. It got on the network the following night. It ended up with a combined audience of nearly 23 million – a record summertime audience, which, for June, was incredible.

I used to be disappointed when we fell below 18 million. One has to face the fact that there are many more channels now and opposition is wider and greater, but the fact is that we used to enjoy a regular wintertime audience of 17/18 million – 20 million wasn't unknown. We lose sight of that today. I think today they are ratings-obsessed.

After *EastEnders* began – somewhere around autumn 1985 – Michael Grade moved it to give it the same time slot as The Street, but not on the same nights, and started the omnibus on the Sunday. They were allowed by BARB, who measure audiences, to aggregate the figures and, suddenly, for the first time ever, The Street found itself not at number one and trailing for a bit. There was never a lot in it, but they were adding the audience for two shows together and comparing it with our one showing. I kept saying, 'It's not like for like' and great rows brewed. Of course, Fleet Street had been kept at bay from *Coronation Street* for so long by the Granada press people that, suddenly, they had their own soap to blow about. There was never a week when I was Producer when I didn't get a phone call: 'What have you got to say to the latest ratings figure?' It didn't happen until that autumn, but it was an irritating period. Then Plowright [David, Chairman of Granada] said to me a very wise thing: 'We've been going for 25 years, they've just started. Let's see how *they're* doing in 25 years. What do these ratings mean after all? You're quite right, they're not a like-for-like comparison. We don't have to worry about trying to compete, there is no battle here.' The whole ITV schedules were built around Monday and Wednesday nights, so they didn't want to give people a second chance to see it.

## Julian Farino
*Director*                                              **THREE DAYS A WEEK!**

I joined Granada around 1986/87. I started off as a researcher in documentaries, which is what I thought I wanted to do – they were all shot on film. I never did anything in studio or multicamera. I had been on the Granada training scheme for directors. I never thought about anything other than documentaries, but, at the end of the training, the person who had been in charge of my training, Gareth Morgan, said that I should do drama. So, within a few months, I did some studio, such as *What the Papers Say*, and then I was thrown in the deep end with *Coronation Street* in 1991.

It was quite scary because I had never worked with actors before and I didn't really know much about *Coronation Street*, apart from the mythology of it. I knew that there was a celebrity factor, but I didn't know what it would mean working on it and I was quite young. I think what served me best was my naivety, to be honest. I went into it as I did everything – 'How's the story being told, what can you do to affect the storyline?' I went in a little bit blind, so I was not overawed – I didn't quite know the stature of some of the people.

The Street was doing three episodes a week then – we had just changed over from two a week. There were a few ripples, stress on writers and the workload, etcetera. People had got fearful and made a bit of a noise, but I think fairly soon people got into the routine and accepted that it could work and that the actors were not overstretched and the system could cope with it. I never felt too daunted by it all. Sue Pritchard was producing, who was also relatively new to it. Producing is one of the worst jobs on The Street – you're handling the publicity, the scripts, the day-to-day problems, you've any number of people of different temperaments knocking on your door. A job from hell, I would have thought.

Because I was very green when I started, I just got on with it. The quantity of material you got through was enormous – a lot of preparation. On average, we were doing 25 scenes an episode. Some writers liked short scenes, others longer. Of all the stuff I've done subsequently, people are far more impressed and interested in my having worked on *Coronation Street* than anything else. That's what they want to know about. It was real pressure working on it – working out the scenes, how you were going to shoot them and so on. I remember some guy asking me at a dinner party one evening what I did. I told him I worked on *Coronation Street* and he said, 'Oh that must be nice, only working three days a week!' The naivety of what he said was great!

There were different kinds of actors – young novices, the old timers who had been doing it for years, old theatrical hands with great tradition. There is a myth that the characters know The Street better than you and won't like being told what to do, but every story is written for a reason and, with the majority – some were lazy, no doubt, and some were young and were on a rollercoaster – but a lot of the cast there appreciated dialogue. Otherwise it's boring to come in and trot out lines off pat. It's about finding the mood, and attitude of the scenes. That's what good actors like.

# Jim Quick
*Graphic Artist* **PING PONG ON THE STREET**

The Graphics Department developed a very close relationship with the cast during the Eighties. In the studios in Quay Street, the Graphics Department was based on the second floor and the rehearsal rooms, the green rooms, were based in the extension of the building where the library used to be. That was where *Coronation Street* rehearsed.

The people in Graphics were great sportsmen and women – we played a lot of sport together and against other departments. We quite liked a game of table tennis and we bought a table tennis table. We asked *Coronation Street* if we could we put it in their rehearsal room so that we could play at lunchtime, assuming that they weren't rehearsing, and they agreed. Anyway, we ended up having a regular group of people from The Street who used to play. Eddie Yeats ... Geoff Hughes, was one of them. All of the main characters, male and female, used to come and play table tennis with us at lunchtime, which formed a kind of a bond between us. They became great friends with the Photographic Department, because we all lived in the same 'midden', and we developed a social relationship with the show.

# Joan Le Mesurier
*Former wife of Mark Eden, who played Alan Bradley* **FROM ELSIE TO AUDREY**

My mother always missed the North. Then, when Mark Eden, her son-in-law, went into it, she was thrilled. He was, in fact, her ex-son-in-law by then, but he was *actually* in it. He was in twice, in fact, as two different characters. He was a boyfriend of Elsie Tanner's and he dumped her. Then, years later, he turned up as Alan Bradley – quite a different character. I remember being in Ramsgate with him and people were asking, 'What did you do to poor Elsie?' People take things so seriously! He's now married to Sue Nicholls, who plays Audrey.

Mum was very impressed. I might have been married to John Le Mesurier, but it was the name Mark Eden which she dropped most to strangers. Somebody in *Coronation Street* was much important than John you know! Mark used to come over to Sitges in Spain where I had a house after John had died. One day, when we were walking through the town, a crowd of holidaymakers spotted him and Susie and we were mobbed. Some friends who were with us and who knew nothing about *Coronation Street* were astonished. John was never invited to be in The Street. It would never have suited him, although Arthur Lowe had been in it.

# Judith Jones
*Production Assistant*                                        **A PA'S LOT**

As the Production Assistant on *Coronation Street*, I was responsible for all the administration and organization of the programme. In other words, if anything went wrong, I usually got the blame! At the time that I worked on the programme – the mid Eighties – we were only two episodes a week and there were three directors assigned to the programme. Each director had their own PA and we worked to a three-week turnaround. That sounds quite complicated, but, to be honest, *Coronation Street* was such a well-oiled machine in terms of organization that everybody generally knew what should be happening at what stage in the production process.

In the first week, the Director would get his scripts from the office and study them. I would also get a copy and send them out to the actors involved. At that stage, the Director would also decide how many extras he wanted in each scene. For example, in the Rovers Return, whether they would speak (they would then have to be paid more), whether they should be male or female, etcetera, and I would liaise with Casting to book them for the recording dates. It might be that there were exterior filming locations that were not on the *Coronation Street* lot, so the Director would have to go out on a recce to check that a suggested location was suitable.

My main area of responsibility in the first week was to organize the order we would film in. We had to decide in which order scenes would be filmed, what would make the most sense in terms of demands on actors, uses of resources, etcetera. For example, if we were filming exteriors, I would have to estimate how long each scene would take and then work backwards to decide when a particular actor would have to go to make-up and wardrobe in order to be ready. It is particularly difficult when children are involved in filming as there are very strict rules as to how long they can work for in any particular day, so that is an important consideration when preparing a schedule.

On the Monday of the second week, we filmed the exterior scenes. These were shot on one camera, which meant that, in order to get a variety of angles and perspectives, each scene was filmed several times from a different position. That could be quite demanding on the cast and on me as well, as I had to make sure that the continuity would match on all the different takes. For example, if someone knocked on the door with their right hand in one take, they had to do it the same in *all* the takes, otherwise they would never edit together. I found this aspect quite demanding, as you had to concentrate really hard, as well as timing the scene and checking the script. From my notes, I would then prepare an edit script, which would indicate the most suitable takes.

On the Tuesday and Wednesday morning, the Director would rehearse each studio scene and then on the Wednesday afternoon we would have a technical run in the rehearsal room where different members of the studio crew would attend a complete rehearsal of the scenes so that they could anticipate any problems. This gave me a chance to time the programme, as we were given a specific running time, which we had to adhere to. As a result of my calculations, sometimes scenes were cut or the script adapted.

The following two days were spent in the studio recording the interior scenes. I had to call the shots – so that the vision mixer, camera crew and sound crews, etcetera knew which camera was being used next – make a note of the good takes, time each scene, etcetera, so that, when we got into editing the following week, it was as painless an operation as possible. I also had to keep a note of the exact hours each actor worked and how much time was spent in rehearsal and how much in performance, so that they got paid the right amount – a very important consideration!

The third week was devoted to post-production, when we – the Director and I along with the VT Editor – would edit the programmes into the correct sequence and, hopefully, the right running time. I would then have to do what is known as the clearing for the programme, which meant prepare an accurate script, pass all the details of the programme through to the Transmission Department, make sure that the actors were paid, clear copyright on any music we had used ... the list seemed never-ending.

# Graham Seed

*Actor, played prosecuting counsel*
*during Brian Tilsley's court case.*　　　　**A BIT OF A CHARLES ATLAS**

I first became involved with The Street before I joined *The Archers* and certainly before I joined *Crossroads*. I reckon I was in about my late twenties or early thirties. I was employed by the Director Michael David Carson, who must have directed a lot of episodes of The Street in the late Seventies and who had directed me at RADA. I played the prosecuting counsel who prosecuted Brian Tilsley for beating someone up in a garage and was taken to court.

It was shot in studio on a set. This would be about 1980. I had to be quite Southern and snooty. It stretched over two episodes. I remember I had the immortal line, 'You think you're a bit of a Charles Atlas, don't you? Well, a mini-Charles Atlas.' It was quite a good line, I thought. The guy who played Brian was Chris Quinten, who was flavour of the month then, and I had to interrogate him and be nasty to him in court. Indeed, I won the case and he went down for it, but Chris didn't like that line. He was a very fit young actor and I suspect he did bodybuilding, I'm sure he worked out at the gym. No, he didn't like that line, but it made all of us laugh. He was a delight to work with, as was everyone in the cast and crew.

I was only doing The Street for a week, but I'll never forget it. All these programmes are the modern version of repertory theatre. They're a great learning field for those who stay in the programme for only a few months. I think the standard of acting gets better and better in them. Everyone was very supportive and friendly.

From my experience in soaps, when you are a regular, it's very nice having a guest come in, it keeps you on your toes and you are meeting actors from the outside world, so, although you might think it would be a tight-knit community, in many ways it's not.

A couple of years ago, there was a quiz in one of the tabloids that asked, 'Which actor has been in four soaps?' and it was me. I think it was unlikely that I would have ever been offered a longer part because I'm a bit Southern and a bit posh, to be honest, for The Street. I've had enough of TV soaps, I think – I'm quite happy with the radio and I suspect that if I walk under a bus tomorrow, I'll be remembered for Nigel Pargetter and not the prosecuting counsel in *Coronation Street*, which hardly anybody knows I've done. It was just one of those quirky jobs that came up because the Director had also directed me at RADA. It was my first introduction to television soaps. It was a very enjoyable week.

# Peter Baldwin
*Actor, played Derek Wilton*                      **MAVIS AND DEREK**

Initially, in 1976, I was in *Coronation Street* for two weeks because the actor Graham Haberfield had died not long before. He was playing Jerry Booth and I think they were setting up a relationship between him and Mavis, then the actor died, which clearly put paid to that. I think, after a decent interval, they thought they would try to introduce somebody else into her life.

Initially, they asked for someone else and they had somebody in mind who happened to be with my agent and he wasn't available – it's funny how things happen, it's pure luck – and she said, 'Why don't you see Peter Baldwin, he's similar.' So, I went to see Doreen Jones, who was casting, and the director for that week. She wasn't somebody I knew at that time, but we had a lot of friends in common, so we talked about that. Then she discovered that I'd worked with Thelma [who played Mavis] long before that. She thought that it was a good idea and it was literally for two weeks. I was brought in as a rep. – I think I was selling sweets in those days. I went in and we did two weeks of it and, at the end, Bill Podmore said, 'That seemed to work, do you want to do some more?' and I said, 'Yes please.' So that was established. There must have been a few months' gap before I went back, but that was how it began, pure chance in a way.

I thought it was a bit bizarre really because I'm very much a Southern person. I was born and brought up in Sussex and I'd done all my work in the South and in London. I always knew *Coronation Street* was a Northern soap. I knew somebody who'd been in it, but she'd come from the North anyway – she was from Blackpool. To me it was a soap of the North, it was nothing to do with actors like me, so it was amazing that they took me on. They didn't even ask me to read or anything. They didn't ask me if I could drive, and I had to drive, a lot of things like that. It was all a matter of chance, but it obviously worked. Thelma and I, from the start, worked well together.

Acting in a soap was something to get used to at first because the turnover is very fast. Through the years, a number of quite well-known actors, certainly in the profession, have gone into it to play parts and found it impossible and haven't enjoyed it at all. They brought in an actress to play the girl I married before Mavis – Angela, the boss' daughter. Now that was played by a brilliant actress, Diane Fletcher, who's done wonderful things on television and on stage. I thought she was very good in it, but she didn't enjoy it and she found it difficult. It's just this quick turnover. When you're used to – even in television drama and certainly in the theatre – three to four weeks' rehearsal, you've got time to think about it, but [in *Coronation Street*] you've got no time to think – you've got to get down to it and do it. In a way, it's like filming, but you don't have the luxury of time to spend on a single scene. You've really got to get on with it and then get on to the next.

I think characters – and I think it probably applied to pretty well all of them – they just developed almost on their own and gradually over a period of time. I think nowadays – and I think it happens in all the soaps – they cast type more and appearance, certainly with the younger ones. It's a sort of two-way thing between the actor and the writer.

I liked all the storylines involving my character because they were all a bit eccentric. I think this was the joy of the two characters, that they were a couple of eccentrics really and slightly out of it, so they came in for a lot of ribbing and a lot of jibes from other people in The Street, within the story. All the scenes before the final wedding were all fairly extraordinary. Why Mavis ever accepted I don't know because he was pretty awful to her. Every time I went in through the later Seventies and the early Eighties every time we had a story, it always ended with Mavis in tears – that was standard. Derek disappeared and then reappeared and she took him back. It's a terrible thing to say, but I think it was partly because there was nobody else. No, that's not true, there were other people, but they were all a bit strange as well and, I suppose, she had a soft spot for him that eventually ended in marriage. I think they had quite a good marriage. They were both oddballs in a way, but they supported each other. I think eccentricity was the essence of it and slight caricature and I'm not sure that characters have that any more.

## Anne Reid
*Actress, played Valerie Barlow*                    **DYING TO LEAVE**

After about four years, I was having doubts about staying, but it was a good job. I didn't know whether they would write Bill out and he had a wife and family and I was footloose and fancy-free. We used to sign three-year contracts and the next one I signed after that, the minute I'd signed it, I knew it was mistake and I thought 'I'm not doing this any more', but it's a big decision because, as a young actress, it's a very good job.

June Howson was producing it and she said, 'Are you absolutely certain that you won't want to come back, because we want to decide how you're going to go?' and I said, 'Absolutely' and she said, 'You really don't mind being killed off?' and I said, 'No, I'd rather you did that because there's no way I'd want to come back.' June said, 'Would you mind being murdered?' and I said, 'No, not at all' and I think they had some plan that one of the American airforcemen was going to bump me off. Anyway, that was very quickly dropped, I never heard any more about that, but then I heard that I was going to run into the flames. I wasn't officially told, but I heard. They said, 'Have you any strong views about it?' and I said, 'No, I haven't.' In a way, now I wish I'd taken a little more notice, but I really just wanted to go and I didn't care. I think it would have been much nicer if I'd run in to rescue my children, I would rather have done something heroic.

I still get people recognizing me from The Street, even after all these years. When I was killed off, the newspapers were full of it. It was a job. I was in the studio and we had to get it done quickly because we were running into overtime. I wanted to go so badly and I had a party planned for that night. I'd thought about it for a very, very, very long time. I'm not a person who rushes into things and I said to Peter, 'What do you think I should do?' and he said, 'I want no part of it, you must make the decision yourself.' I went and gave my notice in and we had a bottle of champagne because he thought it was the right thing to do, but you don't know what's going to happen. I wish I'd had the courage to leave earlier, but I learnt a tremendous amount.

## Ken Farrington
*Actor, played Billy Walker*     **LEAVING DEIRDRE IN THE LURCH**

There was one particular point when I was getting married – I was supposed to be marrying Deirdre and they'd asked me if I would mind getting married. I didn't mind and then they said, 'We need you to commit yourself for longer than you normally would commit', because I only signed six-month contracts, and I said, 'I'll sign for a year, but you've got to give me something.' My agent went and had dinner with the then producer and agreed that they couldn't up the money, but they'd give me an extra couple of weeks' paid holiday a year. So, I agreed and we got near to the end of that storyline and were coming up to the marriage and the Producer said to me, 'It's all set for April the whatever' and I said, 'That's unfortunate because I leave' and she said, 'I thought you'd said you'd commit yourself to stay', and I said, 'I did, but you'd said I could have this extra paid holiday' and when my agent had discussed it with the contracts people they'd said, 'No, the Producer has not got the right to OK that' and they wouldn't OK it. I said that I was going to leave and they said, 'Oh crikey, you've dropped us right in it because it's too late' and I agreed to stay on for a couple of weeks while they rewrote the scripts and reorganized it so that Deirdre married Ray Langton.

## Geoff Hinsliff
*Actor, played Don Brennan*  **A STREET WELCOME**

In 1977, I came back to play Eric Bailey, who robbed the corner shop.

Julie Goodyear, although she was one of the starry-type people who dressed up, was extremely kind and helpful. In a way, that made things more normal because that's what you expect if you're going into a series, you expect them to be as helpful as possible because you are new and they know the score, and she was and that was a change. I don't remember anybody in particular being helpful in the first one I did. Actually, over the years, it has been learned that people in *Coronation Street* should make a point of being welcoming because we all know now how difficult it can be to come into The Street. You're surrounded by these legends, these household names, and it's very difficult to cope sometimes when you first come in. Everybody makes a point, now, of really welcoming people into The Street.

## Gordon Burns
*Television Presenter*  **BILL AND THE BOMB SCARE**

I got to know some of the characters very well, including Bill Roache. I used to go back to Northern Ireland to host a chat show for the new University of Ulster in their new super-modern theatre up in Coleraine. It wasn't for television, but for a theatre audience. It was a Parkinson-style chat show. My first main guest was Bill Roache. I asked him to come over and he said yes. He didn't ask for money or anything.

I remember we were sitting in the dressing room as the audience was coming into the theatre. It was packed – everyone wanted to see a *Coronation Street* star. I was about to go out on stage to introduce it, Bill was in his dressing room reading a book and there was a bomb scare. The bells rang and, of course, you took bomb scares very seriously in Northern Ireland – this was right in the middle of the Troubles. So, we had to evacuate the theatre. We were all making our way out, but nobody could see Bill – he was still in his dressing room reading his book.

'Do we have to leave?' he asked. 'Yes,' we said.

So, we went out and went into a nearby hall in the university and waited while the police checked the building. Then they came back and said, 'We think it's safe', and I said, 'I'll ask the audience, do they want to do the chat show in this hall that we are in as best we can in the circumstances or see if they want to go back into the theatre, but first,' I said, 'I'll ask my guests.' And every one of them said, 'If you're happy, we're happy,' said Bill.

So, I went back into the theatre with the police and did a tour around it. I then went back to the audience and asked them where they wanted to do the show. Without saying anything, they all got up and walked back into the theatre. It was one of those emotional moments – the bomb will not beat us! It was a very emotional night after that. Bill was the calmest man on earth. From that day, I've always had great affection for Bill.

## Lynn de Santis
*Fan*                      **NOT A DRY EYE IN THE HOUSE**

The whole Deirdre Barlow and Mike Baldwin storyline – that episode where she tells Ken, it was just high drama at its absolute best. I don't think there was a dry eye in Manchester on that night when he's throwing her out and she says, 'I don't want to go' and Uncle Albert's there as well and he's crying. That was fantastic, that was really good stuff. I think the tragedies have always been handled really well. Other memorable episodes? Some of the funny ones, like Bet's car when they take it out for the day and there was that awful barman and they borrow Bet's car for a day and it ends up going into a pond.

# Gary Parkinson
*Fan*                                                             **'COCK OF THE WALK'**

I don't think I've missed an episode of The Street in about 15 years. My memories of it from the Seventies are that it was like a sitcom – it seemed a lot funnier. The abiding memory of the Seventies is that triumvirate of Bet Lynch, Fred Gee and Betty Turpin – and the image that just came into my mind is that one of them sat in Fred Gee's car in the middle of the lake. That kind of thing seemed to happen a lot in the Seventies – there was a lot more slapstick and real larger-than-life characters. Although, in the Eighties and Nineties you get people like Reg Holdsworth and Raquel, the Seventies seemed a lot lighter.

The Eighties is probably my favourite period of it because Bet Lynch is my favourite character and the Eighties were Bet Lynch's decade, when she ruled the roost at the Rovers. I think it was about 1985 when she took over the Rovers and she became this fantastic galleon. She got a new wig and she got all those posh new suits. She was like 'cock of the walk' – I always remember her using that phrase, 'In my pub, Vera, I'm cock of the walk.' She was like this frightening, terrifying but really likeable character. I loved Bet because she looked so outrageous. I'm sure if you were to go to Salford pubs in the Eighties, you would have seen countless landladies like that, but she was like nothing you'd ever seen really and, although she had this reputation for being 'all woman', I was always amazed that no one ever mistook her for a man in drag. That's what she was, she was a drag act – especially in that abysmal *Coronation Street* special that was on just before Christmas where they brought Bet back and she was *so* much like a drag act, it was outrageous. They actually had a real man in drag. Steve McDonald and Vikram stayed in a bed and breakfast that was run by a transvestite and then Vikram encounters Bet and it's his first encounter with Bet Lynch and he doesn't assume that she's a man in drag – it was quite outrageous.

I live on my own, so I watch it on my own, but it's still a talking point with my friends. I think most people I know watch it – not quite as obsessively, but some do. So it's still, 'Did you see *Coronation Street* last night?' – it's still that line, like it was when we were kids. My friend Julie, it's quite a defining thing for us and we have this vision that we will both be working on *Coronation Street* at some point in the future. I don't know whether it's our sense of humour which fits with *Coronation Street* or whether it's that

*Coronation Street* is informing our sense of humour. It does strike a chord with us, slightly over the top sense of humour.

# Barrie Holmes
*Fan*                                        **COMEDY CHARACTERS**

My favourite character was Ged Stone – Sunny Jim, as Minnie called him. He was the first one I remember who injected humour into The Street – I can't remember any before that. There may have been bits of humour, but he was the first out and out comedy character. Since then, we have had much more and I think that is what sets *Coronation Street* apart from the other soaps. Firstly, there is excellent acting and good scripts, but they have this weave of comedy in the scripts and the characters. In the Seventies, that was particularly strong. They did it in a very clever way. They would have a character who had the main comedy role. Geoff Hughes as Eddie Yeats was particularly good at that. He took over from Ken Cope, who had played Sunny Jim.

Since then, we've had people like Reg and Alec Gilroy. There's also been an underlying trend of humour in other areas, such as the Duckworths, who are sometimes very funny, sometimes very serious, but there is a general layer of humour. And, of course, you had that with Stan and Hilda, where there was a great interplay between them. Again, I think that took them into a different sphere with their popularity. They're doing that again now with the Battersbys. They are trying to be the family that have that element of humour. I like that because you can sit there and have a good laugh.

I think that sanitized world almost became a parody. The characters became larger than life. You almost felt, 'Yes, it couldn't happen', but it was good entertainment. It moved from the realistic world to something that was almost like *The Royle Family*. They didn't do a lot, but it was funny to watch. I think *Coronation Street* got a bit like that. There was a stage when it was almost competing to be a comedy show and you would have actors trying to outdo each other with their lines and their comedy roles. That was an enjoyable time if you didn't take it seriously, but then that didn't matter. People did take it seriously, though, as you saw with Deirdre being jailed – the country was in uproar.

# Wally Butler

*Director*        **CORRIE NIGHT AT THE LONDON PALLADIUM**

When I left *Coronation Street*, Julian Amyes was Director of Programmes and he called me up to his office and said, 'We're going to London, we're on the Royal Command Performance. The people I've got on The Street now are television directors, this is a variety show.' He said, 'Your father played the Palladium?' I said, 'Yes.' He said, 'I want to take The Street down to the Palladium. Would you prepare a variety performance, running nine minutes, for The Street?' So I was allocated rehearsal time and we did a stage version of The Street. I took it and all the different people from various companies were there. It was a time when it was variety acts plus the cast of *Coronation Street*, *Crossroads* or whatever. It was meeting the people again and preparing this theatre piece, which everyone was excited about. Then a train was booked and we took over the whole train and went into the best hotel, then into rehearsal, where there was a buffet and bar on all day, then the show at night, the party afterwards and back to Manchester. That was the highlight, being asked to go back.

# Steve Embleton

*Fan*        **KEEPING MUM COMPANY**

I was about 10 when I started watching it – that's about 25 years ago now. I'm not from the North, I was born in Ramsgate, so I suppose *Coronation Street* seemed a strange world, although my dad did come from Newcastle and we had regular trips up to Newcastle, so I did find it true to life, but very different from down here in the South. We're a bit more reserved down here; up there they really did leave all their doors unlocked, whereas down here they never did. The houses down here were not like *Coronation Street*. We lived in a road with about 12 houses and a church and it was quite nice, but it was not a terraced street. Where my dad comes from in Newcastle was very much like that and I can remember the terraced houses as a child.

My brother and I would stay up and watch it with my mum. My dad was a miner and he worked nights a lot, so Mum would have us up watching it with her. We had a bath at seven o'clock and, as long as we were out by then, we could watch it.

I remember that *Coronation Street* seemed a very long street and trying to remember who lived where and who lived with who at the age of ten was

very difficult, but Mum used to fill us in. It was, and still is, great entertainment. It was my mum more than my dad who watched – she's an addict
and has watched it since the very start. You can never phone her between
half seven and eight on a Monday, Wednesday, Friday and Sunday, she
won't pick up the phone.

My favourites were Annie Walker, Ena Sharples, Elsie Tanner, Albert
Tatlock, but Ena was my favourite. She was really bolshie and reminded me
of my dad's mum, she was a bit like that.

## Phil Redmond
Brookside *creator*                    ***BROOKSIDE*, NOT *CORONATION STREET***

I think the thing I have to say, *Coronation Street*'s influence on the early
thinking on *Brookside* was a negative influence, which is just as legitimate
and just as viable as a positive influence. I did not want it to be what
*Coronation Street* was in the Eighties. I didn't want it to be almost a kind
of caricature of Northern life, the fact that dealing with an issue in
*Coronation Street* was somebody walking into the Rovers and saying, 'All
right Bet, how are you doing? Terrible about that bomb in Northern Ireland.
I'll have a half. Where's Ena?' and that was it. I wanted to do a soap which
would have a relationship with its audience, which would actually make
them think about that issue rather than just use it as a touchstone.

So, it was a negative way of interpreting it, but I've always been at pains
to point out that I don't see that as a criticism of *Coronation Street* because,
behind the art, is the practicalities of producing a soap and the reasons why
the soap is there. *Coronation Street* was doing for ITV through the
Seventies, Eighties and Nineties the job that it was asked and that was to
give a very high audience, very high penetration, around which to sell the
rest of the schedule. It had a relationship with its audience in 1980 that was
unbreakable. I've used the analogy of a marriage, like people when they
meet, fall in love, they get married and they age together and you don't
notice the wrinkles and the grey hairs because you've still got the relationship, and I think Corrie has always performed very, very well in that sense;
it's done what ITV has requested of it.

So, I'd never be negative about it or criticize it, it's just I knew what
*Coronation Street* was when it started and I'd seen the way it developed and
I wanted *Brookside* to be something different. I didn't want it to be that.

# CHAPTER FIVE

# The 1990s

## *The years of social realism*

In November 1982, the launch of Channel 4 gave viewers the first glimpse of a new twice-weekly soap opera called *Brookside*. It was different and somehow fitted the mood of the times. It was focused on Liverpool, where the worsening economic crisis had plunged the city into a nightmare of despair. Rising unemployment, a declining population, the demise of traditional industries and all their accompanying social problems, were dramatically portrayed on screen. It was no coincidence that Alan Bleasdale's *Boys from the Black Stuff* was being shown on BBC Television at the same time. Liverpool, more than anywhere, encapsulated the political and economic problems of the time. *Brookside* was about real life. You might not have liked it, but there was no doubting that this was powerful drama.

Ironically, Granada had been offered the idea of *Brookside* back in 1973, but, as *Brookside*'s creator Phil Redmond confesses, the idea may have been right, but the timing was wrong. *Brookside* was far more appropriate to the political dilemmas of the 1980s than ever it would have been to the 1970s. *Brookside* was a *tour de force*, starkly relating the drama of unemployment and a multitude of other social problems twice a week. To the working classes, particularly those in the North, it was grim reality, something they could all identify with. It had all the grittiness, and more, of the early episodes of The Street. Tony Warren himself was impressed by the writing and characterization. However, in terms of ratings, *Brookside* never posed any problem for Granada or ITV. After all, it was on Channel 4, a minority viewing channel, and ratings were never going to be that high.

Viewing figures for The Street were a touch lower than they had been, but the programme still dominated the ratings. *Brookside*, meanwhile, attracted little more than a few million viewers each episode.

What *Brookside* did do was provide food for thought. It was to cause a rethink and set a trend in new soaps. Alongside *Brookside*, *Coronation Street* looked whimsical, out of place in the modern world. Life in any city was now about unemployment, break-ins, car thefts, violence and drugs. Yet these issues never seemed to touch those who live in The Street. At times, the differences were stunningly marked.

The BBC had been short of a soap opera for years. Earlier attempts with *Compact*, which ran from 1962 until 1965, and *The Newcomers* had all come to a sticky end, leaving the way unchallenged for ITV and Channel 4. The Beeb needed a soap of its own, something different, and it took its lead from *Brookside*. Three years after *Brookside* began transmitting, the BBC eventually came up with a new soap opera of its own – *EastEnders*.

Set in inner-city London, in the borough of Walford, E20, *EastEnders* was decidedly not folksy or funny. It was about social realism, working-class families confronting the problems of the day – marriage, violence, money, depression and so on. It may not have been as political as *Brookside*, which at times suggested political solutions, but, without offering the solutions, it certainly portrayed them. However, whereas *Brookside* had been something different and shown on a minority channel, *EastEnders*, screening in an early evening slot on BBC 1, was a distinct rival to *Coronation Street*. It marked the beginnings of a soap war. As far as the press was concerned, it was head-to-head war. It certainly worried Street Producer John Temple, although Granada Chairman David Plowright dismissed any notion of a rivalry, telling Temple and everyone on The Street not to worry about any competition. The Street would always be The Street. It was still one of the most successful shows on British television with ratings as high as ever, he claimed. However, the writing was clearly on the wall.

The Street survived the 1980s intact, much the same as ever, but with the 1990s came spiralling challenges. *EastEnders* had by then firmly established itself and, at times, was winning more viewers. On top of that, the exploits of some of its stars were also scooping tabloid headlines – not necessarily a bad thing when you want to promote a programme.

British television was also changing. For a start, it was fracturing into many more directions. The four traditional terrestrial channels had been joined by new satellite and cable channels, as well as a fifth terrestrial channel. There may have been only a few extra channels in the early 1990s, but, by the end of the millennium, there would be 200 or more channels on offer. The competition for audiences had intensified significantly. Advertisers had become acutely aware of ratings and were not going to pay sky-high fees for any programme that did not deliver its promised audience. Everyone was under pressure to hit targets and maximize their audiences. *Coronation Street* would not be the only long-serving Granada programme to come under pressure.

There were also changes afoot at Granada. A new regime had been installed and David Plowright – for so long one of The Street's strongest champions – had gone. In his place, new decision makers appeared with a more ruthless and challenging agenda. On The Street, the retirement of Bill Podmore in 1988 led to the appointment of David Liddiment as Executive Producer.

David Liddiment, now Director of Programmes for the ITV network, had worked at Granada as a researcher and a producer. Most of his work as a producer had been in light entertainment with little or no drama experience, but he did have an eye for ratings. Given his background, his appointment came as a surprise. It also resulted in changes, with new producers brought in. *Coronation Street* was gearing itself up for the new world of television.

It wasn't only the content that was different, the style was different, too. Above all, *Brookside* and *EastEnders* demonstrated the new world of television. *The Bill* even more so. Both programmes were more high-tech, with hand-held cameras, location shooting, and a repertoire of adventurous camera angles. The Street stuck to its old formula, mainly shot in studio with a few exteriors. One director admits that filming The Street was nowhere near as challenging a job as for other soaps. As a director, he had to film within the established constraints, with much of it still shot in studio, usually with three cameras through a mixing desk. If it works, don't meddle with it was the attitude. However, as the 1990s wore on, The Street was forced to change and take on board at least one or two examples of the new technology and new techniques.

It was also time to ring in the changes among the cast. Old characters disappeared, new ones emerged, old writers went and new ones came. More young characters were introduced to try and win over a younger audience. The profile of The Street seemed middle-aged and Northern; it needed to be more attuned to the changing nature of society. The Street still felt trapped in a class divide that belonged to the early 1960s. The 1990s were about New Labour, not Old Labour.

New Producer Brian Park, who was appointed in 1997, told *Broadcast* magazine that he 'had inherited an established pattern of characters and an ageing, Northern-based audience. It had moved from a show you didn't watch, but your mother did, to a show you didn't watch, but your grand-mother did.' Park went about toning down the comedy and injecting some real life. Sharper storylines – including the Deirdre prison saga – added three million, and more, to the ratings.

There would be other changes as well, some with far-reaching conse-quences. At the end of 1989, The Street had gone from two to three episodes and, then, in 1996, came a fourth episode. The increase in the number of episodes caused a major logistical headache for the programme planners. Actors had always been on a rota system and not used every week, but now the rota became even more important as the demands on actors' time became heavier. The same was also true for programme makers.

Robert Khodadad, who was directing The Street when it moved from three to four episodes a week, remembers the headaches it threw up: 'If you were working flat out before, where did that extra time come from? The answer to that came from being even more efficient than we previously were.' That, as everyone acknowledged, wasn't easy.

In terms of ratings, the new storylines were a phenomenal success. The Street ended the millennium as the most watched programme of 1999, with an audience high of 19.82 million viewing the dramatic Sunday 7 March episode of Sharon's bust up at the altar. Throughout the year, for 4 episodes a week, 52 weeks of the year, it averaged 14.91 million viewers, a 62 per cent audience share.

Not everybody liked the changes, though. One of the biggest critics was former Labour MP Roy Hattersley. A long-time devotee of the programme, who had enjoyed many a wander down The Street on visits to the studios, he launched a stinging attack on the programme in the pages of the *Daily Mail*: 'For more than 30 years, I thought of myself as an honorary resident of *Coronation Street* ... but not any more. ... What was once the home of friendly families has become the squalid refuge of pathetic misfits whose sordid lives can neither inspire nor entertain.' He continued, describing it as 'moral dumbing-down', adding that the programme's producers 'work on a simple formula. The greater the squalour, the better the ratings.'

For Roy Hattersley, the problem had begun with *EastEnders* – a programme he refers to as 'a perverted picture of London life which portrays all of its inhabitants as emotional inadequates'. Even though The Street always had its more roguish characters, there was always a sense of morality, unlike today's characters, some of whom, he claimed, have become anti-heroes.

Fan Gary Parkinson also picks up on this point: 'I do think it's going to be quite dark and there's going to be lots more underworld characters, which we're getting now.'

Roy Hattersley's savage attack might have been a little extreme, but there is no doubting that his views are felt by many, though perhaps with a little less venom. Indeed, in this chapter, more than a few fans have voiced their criticisms of some of the new storylines. Former Granada presenter Gordon Burns is one: 'Abortions, teenage pregnancies, gay problems ... I don't really want that in my soap. It has all changed, and not for the better. I know it still keeps its audience and you can't knock it because of that, but, for me, it is not the *Coronation Street* I enjoyed watching. Yes, I still watch it, though, whereas before I would never miss it, it doesn't bother me now if I miss it.'

'It didn't reflect society to that extent, it was in a time warp and it was its own world,' points out former scriptwriter Tom Elliott, talking about the pre-1990s days. 'There were programmes galore that covered drugs, rape and all the rest of the terrible things that go on in the world in documentary and drama, far better than The Street could. The Street had cornered the market in comedy drama.'

For Merseyside fan Barrie Holmes, the problem is very definitely this absence of humour: 'What is lacking now is the humour. My wife and I have both said that if it's on and we're in, we'll watch it, but, if not, so be it.' The loss of humour has been noted by many. Whereas The Street was famed for its humour in the Seventies and Eighties, it seemed to discard much of it in the Nineties.

If the problem has been in trying to ape *EastEnders*, many insiders feel that it was the decision to go from two to three, and then to four, episodes a week, a decision which has put undue strains on actors, writers and logistics. 'It's inevitable that the quality will go down with more episodes,' says scriptwriter Tom Elliott, pointing out that, in his day, The Street did not try to replicate society and its issues.

John Temple, who produced hundreds of episodes during the 1970s and 1980s, agrees: 'Any criticisms I might make, and anyone might make, result from the day they went from two to three a week, and now four a week. In the old days of two a week, it was a special event watching The Street. It was a big event in people's lives. They've dissipated that to the point that it became three, it became four, with added strains on the whole production team, on the cast. More people are brought in. It's lost its shape because sometimes characters vanish from the screen for weeks or months on end. You can't quite keep the picture in view in the way that one used to – too many characters.'

It's also true that writers, rightly or wrongly, suddenly felt themselves constrained. They were now being told what to write, and being encouraged that they had to introduce more sensationalist storylines. One scriptwriter from the 1960s, Geoff Lancashire, talks of how they were allowed to create scenes that did not take the plot forward, but were about character development. In the 1990s, there was a feeling that this was no longer the case. There were more scenes and most of them plot-driven.

A final criticism has been that The Street is deliberately pandering to a young audience, eager to attract younger viewers. The success of the Australian soap *Neighbours* in doing this has been unprecedented. Prior to *Neighbours*, nobody believed that there was a teenage audience out there interested in soaps. However, as we have seen, most people were attracted to The Street when they were teenagers and watched the programme with their parents, usually their mother. This aside, younger characters have been introduced and younger storylines, many concerning the kinds of social problems that affect youngsters. The Street will continue to reflect modern teenage life, promises the show's current Producer.

In attracting a younger audience, The Street has probably jettisoned some of its older fans. They tend not to want storylines about teenage pregnancies, drugs and so on. The grey audience feels much more comfortable clinging to the humour, nostalgia and the safe, comfortable world of Weatherfield of old.

Therein lies the rub. Although many dislike the current crop of sensationalist storylines, the emphasis on youth and the lack of comedy, they still watch the programme. They may not be quite so enthusiastic, perhaps not quite so committed, but few have actually switched off. Interestingly, Phil Redmond, creator of *Brookside* and *Hollyoaks*, doesn't hold with the notion that more episodes means a lowering of the standards of quality. The Street is still like a drug and the ratings are there to prove it – 18 million are watching the programme today, considerably more than in the 1980s.

Former Granada Producer Jim Walker, in a charming tale, suggests that the programme's durability lies in the simple fact that, as a community itself, The Street has survived the tortuous changes of the last 40 years when most similar communities have been destroyed or disappeared. Certainly, for the older generation, the fact that The Street is still there after 40 years gives us something to cling on to, a sense of hope and optimism in an otherwise dangerous and pessimistic age.

## Ian White
*Director*                    **THE CAT ON A HOT CORRIE ROOF**

The current opening titles are mine – I shot them ten years ago. In the black-and-white era, there were a lot of generic titles, so mine are the second of the colour era. Mervyn Watson [Producer] sent me out round about the thirtieth anniversary. They tried to do some the year before and they hadn't been thought right and Plowright [David, Chairman of Granada] was very keen to do some brand new ones for the thirtieth anniversary year. All that I could think of is, 'What can I do that is better than there is there?' because the pictures were, by then, an institution. They were about 15 years old, so, all I thought was to do something with movement in it, to use the same ideas of life in the backstreets, but to move the camera. They wouldn't give me a crane that was big enough, but we used a Simon tower – they're the things they use to cover the horse racing. You can get them to move by just releasing the hydraulics and, when you switch it off, they'll gradually settle down. At the top, they shake violently and it is only when it settle downs that you get the smooth bit.

The first and second shot are Salford and then we went to Bolton for that shot of ivy in the backstreet. Just as we were shooting, a window cleaner went in the back and left his bucket and ladder there.

In the shot of the cat, it moves from the pigeon loft and stops as if it was going after the pigeons. The reality was that it was take 20 or 30 after a very difficult morning with this cat. The reason the cat moves is that, behind the pigeon loft, is one stage hand and, in front, is another stage hand and the handler and, on 'Action', the stage hand put the cat down. Because it was mid summer and so hot, the cat didn't want to stay, so the reason it moves is that it's burning its feet. Then it sees the stage hand and goes back into the shade, which is the only cool bit which is left. Mervyn and David had run a national competition to find the cat.

## Wally Butler
*Director*                                    **THE DAILY GRIND**

The way that all the soaps are run now, they're going for jaded appetites and they want to hit high spots, with suicides and plane crashes. In those days, there was an evenness about The Street. It reflected the grind. Occasionally we had the high spot and they were only memorable, from my point of view, in as much as we got the opportunity to do something technically and directorially that was different. There was the collapse of the viaduct, for instance. That was marvellous because it was all special effects and we had a great time with that. The actors took second place. For the rest, the characters were almost living life in parallel with the viewers. It was that slow. The viewer would live his life until the Wednesday and then see it repeated with little bits of humour and reciprocal depressions and hardships that they could relate to. This was the substance of The Street – the reflection.

What I think is, nowadays, unfortunately, the characters are reflecting not individuals, but a group. Battersby, for instance, who I dislike intensely as a character. He irritates, he gets me going, which is perhaps what is intended, not because he's Les Battersby, but because he represents a type of person that I know proliferates in society, and this is what they're going for. They're going for key types rather than individuals. Somehow or other, Violet Carson or Pat Phoenix, people could associate with them either personally or with someone they knew in their street, but now what we're talking about with Les Battersby is that we're identifying with a person that we probably know proliferates throughout the country, not the fellow up the street. This is the fellow who is making inroads into our taxes by the money he makes, the black market working and the drinking and the whole thing that we get irritated about nowadays, which is nationwide.

I don't think that old style of *Coronation Street* would have worked today, in as much as people don't live that way any more. You couldn't have held it in aspic, you would have to have moved on, you would have to have introduced television, football, the Internet and all the things that are going on now.

They've gone younger now, because that's where the money is. That's what people are buying, the younger people, they want to be represented. What we represented in the old days was 'Children should be seen and not heard.' There were a few children, but not as characters. It was mainly the older people who were running the show – the mothers and fathers, grandmothers and grandfathers, who ran The Street, ran the shops, whatever. Children were growing up, they were looked after and that was as much as they got. We had a few children in The Street, but the family situation was more how the family, the elders, coped. The children were looked after, that was taken for granted. What was important was how the elders were, in work, not in work, relationships and so on. Now we've gone down further and further to where we're taking notice of the youngsters and the teenagers, which is perhaps a high percentage of the audience.

## Tom Elliott
*Script Editor and Scriptwriter*     **WHY COMPETE WITH THE WORST?**

In my day, we didn't have the introduction of specific issues because, although drugs is an issue and there is now a need for these programmes to reflect society, The Street never did that. It didn't reflect society to that extent, it was in a time warp and it was its own world. There were programmes galore that covered drugs, rape and all the rest of the terrible things that go on in the world, in documentary and drama, far better than The Street could. The Street had cornered the market in comedy drama. It was Julian Roach's quote, and I still remember it, he said, 'Why compete with the worst?' You can take characters out of The Street and put them in any other programme. It's only by recognizing the set that I know which programme I'm watching. It's easy to say it was always better yesterday. It's one of those things and everything changes, but I believe that the evolution of The Street, with a few hiccups prior to 1996–67, was for the good –

it changed imperceptibly almost and you could sit down with your children and be quite safe watching it.

Then people came who said, 'Why should it be cosy? Why should it be like that? Let's change it.' I didn't want any part of it. I talked to a Street writer, who shall remain nameless, this morning on the phone and he was saying that they've just had a long-term conference and they're going for big stories, headlines, tabloid.

It's inevitable that the quality will go down with more episodes. I remember a Granada executive coming in at that time and saying, 'We're going four a week' and Julian said, 'When are you going to go five?' and they said, 'When they impose that, I will write my letter of resignation.' I remember Julian saying, 'Do you want me to help you draft it now?' They've not gone five a week, but they're doing specials, hour-long ones and things like that. Three was absolutely maximum to retain any kind of quality in the writing, in the acting. It's unfair to actors – there's no rehearsal time, there's no tech run at it any more, which was invaluable because, after a tech run, you used to sit down with the director and the producer and everybody had things to say, so, again, it was getting it as right as you could. That's gone now. As I said to this scriptwriter who rang me today, I said, 'Does it matter when you're getting 16 and 18 million viewers?' So, all the things that we did and all the trouble that we took to make it as good as you could in case you lost viewers, I don't think it mattered now, because it's such an institution, they still watch it.

## Jim Quick
*Graphic Artist*                                    **MARKET-DRIVEN**
.......................................................................................................

You don't really see any of the *Coronation Street* characters – very good-looking people in young people's terms – that you could use to sell youth-oriented products. I still don't understand why on earth SAGA haven't got hold of Ken Barlow yet as a character. I still don't understand the mechanics of that – that might be contractual. *Coronation Street* as a piece of television, intellectual property, is owned, I think, by the people of this country.

I don't watch *Coronation Street* any more because it's become something I'm not. I've changed or it's changed or we've both gone in different directions, but I remember with great affection my golden era – the ducks on the wall, Hilda Ogden – that was when I found it was at its funniest. I never watch *Brookside*, *EastEnders*, *Emmerdale*, but you can turn *Coronation Street* on and it's like meeting an old friend or going back to your family. They might look a bit older or you don't like the way they dress any more or what they say, but you can still recall the affection that you had for it when it was, what you thought, a proper show. Now I think it's market-driven. I'm criticizing them for not developing the brand, but you could say that these so-called spin-offs, I don't know what they've got to offer.

## Christabelle Embleton
*Fan*                                                      **IN IT FOR THE MONEY**

I think what's happened is that they are all in it for money nowadays. They went into The Street years ago and they stopped in The Street. It was a living and they enjoyed it, but now there's too much money involved. They go into The Street, make a name for themselves and then leave. Now, Ena and Elsie were in it for years, Ken and even his first wife, Valerie, before she was killed – electrocuted with the iron – she was in it a lot of years. Now, they seem to be in it for six months and then they leave, make a record or whatever, and go off to make more money. There also seem to be a lot of single people in it nowadays.

I've never been up to see The Street. I think it would spoil it. I imagine The Street as it is [on TV], I don't want to see behind the scenes, I want it to be as I see it, not as it might be with cameras stuck behind doors and so on.

We've always had a dominant woman in The Street – Ena, Elsie Tanner, Mrs Walker in the pub, even Bet Lynch – but we don't have a dominant woman now, and I think we're missing that. We need a woman who puts the men in their place. I think Natalie is a bit wishy-washy. I like her, but she doesn't put the men in their place, she's not tough enough to be in charge of the bar. They also need to marry some of them off, they've either got no husbands or no wives.

## Bob Greaves
*Television Presenter*              **THE WOMEN OF *CORONATION STREET***

What developed, certainly in my mind, was that the women characters were the strongest characters in the series and I think that's probably still true today. The women shine in *Coronation Street*. Now whether that's deliberate or an accident, I don't know. My guess is that it evolved.

The men, I always thought, were – not second-rate – but very much second to the women. I'm trying to remember if any of the men had that swagger. No, they didn't. One or two were arrogant, but they were probably the younger ones. There was no genuine air of authority. They probably thought they were something special, but they didn't exude that 'I'm me, behave yourself' attitude. I've always loved the female characters. Julie Goodyear also had that 'Don't you realize who I am?' approach. I don't mean she'd go in a shop and *say* 'Don't you know who I am?', but there was that aura about the big female characters.

In this day and age, although I don't know many of them as I used to know the older ones, there is Liz Dawn, who plays Vera and is a personal friend. She plays that simple woman brilliantly, but is one of the most warm-hearted and generous people in the acting profession I have ever known. My wife Sonia works as a fundraiser for a charity called Disabled Living and I know that you only have to pick up a phone and ask Liz Dawn, who has a busy schedule, talk to her and, in between filming, she'll nip out and show herself at a fundraising do, at balls, dinners, gala events, anything to do with helping a charity. She also runs her own charity in Leeds. She is one of those quietly generous women who never looks for thanks. She's lovely.

## Joan Le Mesurier
*Former wife of Mark Eden, who played Alan Bradley*  **LOVES AND HATES**

I hardly ever miss The Street. I have little discussions with people about what was going on. In fact, I've just been on the phone to someone chatting about it.

I still have my pet hates. I can't stand Deirdre, never could. She has an over-frantic expression – the veins in the neck and that mouth always make me feel exhausted. Although I hear she's an absolute sweetie in real life, I'm not crazy about her. I love Jack Duckworth. Sometimes he's quite sensible and he's getting much more like that nowadays. He's becoming fatherly and kindly. I like him. I'm not mad about his wife. She's a soppy cow, that one. Rita I like, although that hairdo ought to be modified a bit you know, and that make-up – it's still a bit too garish, she still looks too over made up – and those awful jumpers. I used to love Mavis and Derek – I liked their relationship because it was soppy. There was some comedy there because they were such prudes and that's gone now so there's no one to send up. Of course, I love Audrey and I hope she'll get into a romantic situation before she gets much older.

## Ian White
*Director*                                              **BRADLEY THE VILLAIN**

I remember Bill [Podmore, Producer] saying that he wanted to do something with the Alan Bradley character and he went, in a matter of months, from being someone who just came in and had a pint in the bar to being the most riveting of characters.

Mark Eden is a fantastic actor and had not been challenged very much before. He became the most chilling villain and the most inventive actor. I'll never forget when he got released from prison after the court case and he came back. Rita was in the house and someone went out the front door and he came in the back and she was on her own with him for the first time. He was back on the streets.

We did the rehearsal – where would he stand, what would she do, why wouldn't she run out – to make it work and make it real, but it wasn't right. Mark said, 'What about if she had been making some sandwiches for herself and had left them on the table – this was going to be her supper – and he'd come in.' He then sits down at the table, puts his feet up and starts munching away at these sandwiches, talking through the munching, him deconstructing her ability with men and how it had all gone wrong. He had this wonderful air of threat and she was streaming with tears at the end and he wandered off. It was the making of him. It was a great time to be doing it because everybody wanted to know what the story was. They were two great actors – him and Barbara, slugging it out together.

## Geoff Hinsliff
*Actor, played Don Brennan*                    **IT CAN'T HAVE BEEN THAT BAD**

The third time I was asked to go in was in 1987. I did a thing called *Brass* with Bill Podmore, who was producing it and also produced The Street, so I was asked if I'd like to come in and I said, 'I don't think I could be part of all that' and he said, 'It's changed vastly', so I said I'd go in for a few, three or four, weeks and see. So I did that and I found it very different. I found it much much better, much more civilized, much more calm on the money front and really quite enjoyable, so I said, 'Yes, I'll give it a go and see what happens.' I was in for ten years – you never expect that. You think, 'I'll do a year, maybe two years wouldn't hurt me' and time goes by so quickly. As a jobbing actor, a job here for three weeks, a job there for six weeks, a job there for two days, suddenly you have a year's contract, you think, 'This is forever, no problems', but that year goes by so quickly.

You had to learn how to use The Street well. What they would use was what they saw on the screen. There wasn't a great deal of, 'Look, I think my character should this, that and the other.' What they did, invariably, was take up and write what you were doing on the screen, which was difficult. I've seen, in other cases, very good actors come in and they don't know what to do because it isn't in the script. That's what they're used to – you look at the script and that's who you are. In *Coronation Street*, you look at the script and you can play who you like and, really, The Street was set up originally with people playing who they were. They sort of did themselves or did a character that they'd always done and then the writers picked up on that and wrote what they liked about it. You have such a phase of development. Normally, in television, you did one, and your character was set there. Over a period of five years, your character can change completely and radically – mine did. People used to say that, 'When you came in, you were so nice and quiet – now look at you!'

Don Brennan had gone downhill so far – he'd done the lot. Originally, he'd tried to commit suicide in the car and lost his leg. He'd then had another bout of committing suicide in the garage when it went to pot and, then, of course, finally he was quite beyond the pale and blown up in a car. I didn't get many nasty letters. I did get letters saying, 'It must be difficult living with Ivy', which it was for the character.

There are an awful lot of people in the series who are brilliant and I underestimated that before going in. Being a soap actor is not a pushover by any means and they do a terrific job, some of them, and I have great admiration and couldn't do it nearly as well as a lot of them, even though I was supposed to be classically trained. Furthermore, there are some very good friends in it. People were different and friendly and outgoing – there was a lot on the plus side. I stayed for ten years, so it can't have been that bad.

When I went in the first time, it was two a week. There was a lot of fun then, but, honestly, four a week is very tiring. When I started in television, which was 1962 or 1963, what you would do then, for a half-hour play, you would rehearse for two weeks. Then you'd do it from top to bottom, like you would a stage play. And when I did that, you had a fortnight. Now you do four half-hours in one week and, the thing is, technology has only changed so far as it makes better pictures, it hasn't changed in that it has circumnavigated the working requirement – you've still got to learn the lines, find out where you are and what you're doing and you get so little time to do it in. You don't rehearse, you go in and the Director says 'Right' and you say, 'Can we just run it through, just for us?' and the Director says, 'OK, five minutes' and then you're on.

## Ric Mellis
*Assistant Stage Manager, Floor Manager and Director*

**THE UPS AND DOWNS**

I remember directing an episode with Julie Goodyear – a whole long story-line with Bet when she was married to Alec and she lost a baby. There were just fantastic little scenes in the back room of the Rovers and round that table. Right from the very start, there were lovely scenes with Annie Walker and Betty Turpin round that little table – 'What's the problem?' and one woman crying and the other one making a cup of tea. That's what's happening again now with Leanne, who's got this drugs problem and this new girl who's very good sat at that table, sharing their troubles and helping each other and saying, 'It will be all right.' That goes right back to the start of *Coronation Street* – it is absolutely pure Corrie.

The humour's still there. Some of it I don't find very funny, but there's always been awful forced bits. I remember Stan and Eddie Yeats and there were fabulous bits, but there were just as many or more that didn't come off. The same with the Duckworths. Humour is the most difficult thing to do and when it works it's just fantastic. The characters they've had have been fab to do it with, but you remember the good ones and you obliterate the bad ones.

Mavis and Derek were like a little sitcom when they were married and had the budgie. I suppose The Street more than any soap has had these kinds of ups and downs, people trying to take the social realism too far and then somebody going, 'This isn't working' and then it becomes a comedy programme for a bit. I don't think it was ever too much in the extremes for too long.

## Tom Elliott
*Script Editor and Scriptwriter*        **NORRIS AND THE GNOME**

I brought in a story told to me by a friend of ours and I adapted it – it was the gnome's story with the Wiltons. I didn't envisage that everybody would love this so much – the scriptwriters – this was a danger, that everybody wanted to write for it, and so the gnome went on for ages and ages. I actually got a letter from New Zealand with a picture of a gnome on a lawn with a knife in its back. For all the criticism I got – particularly from Carolyn Reynolds who used to pull my leg – for all that, it captured the imagination of the world. It sometimes got a bit out of hand and, at the end of it, we had no idea who had kidnapped the gnome. I had got an end to it, but then it gathered its own momentum, this story.

It was Norris, but it all came to light when Norris was marrying Angela, who was Derek's ex-wife – this was vintage Street in those days. Derek was best man and they went on a stag night together and Norris, having no friends and being unpopular, it was just Derek and Norris. I wrote the episode. They eventually get back to Norris' flat. I'd worked in the theatre with Malcolm Hebden, who I greatly admire as an actor, and eventually he said, 'I've got something for you Derek' – he was stoned out of his head. He opened the wardrobe – and we had a lovely scene were Norris fell into the wardrobe and Derek's going 'Tut', because Derek, of course, had remained sober throughout as, being the best man, he was doing his job properly – and out he came with one of these bags and in it was the gnome with its ear missing. It was kidnapped and the ear was sent in a matchbox, and he'd done it. Derek was livid and was going to kill Norris, but Derek – in the next episode, written by John Stevenson, the wedding – took Norris to the wrong church as part of his revenge and so on, but that's how it was wrapped up.

## Peter Baldwin
*Actor, played Derek Wilton*        **THE AXE FALLS ON DEREK**

At the time, I was sorry to leave – I would have liked to have stayed there for ever. Brian Park dropped the guillotine on me, but I don't think the decision had been his originally. I never discovered whose it was. I think I know because one person must have put the idea into their heads. I was sorry to be killed off because, apart from anything, there have been various spin-offs – that short series at the end of last year, which wasn't as successful, I think.

I'm not sorry now because I don't particularly like the way it's gone and it's changed the focus entirely. I don't watch it now.

Before I left, there was a noticeable difference then and there was this emphasis on the young, which is what all the other soaps do. I thought it was daft that The Street should give way to the pressures and just line up alongside the others. It was always its own show, it was off the ground, it was always a bit different, and the fact that they had stories not only involving the young, but involving older people like us, Jack and Vera, and Rita very often has a good story going, and the much older people, Percy and Phyllis. That's all gone and what was a show about a community of people and their day-to-day lives has just become a series of shock events, mostly. It's silly, I think, in a way.

Last year, I went to a soap awards do in London. Casts from all the soaps were there and we were all sat in blocks. It was in a big studio and the *Coronation Street* lot was all together. If you look along, the people – and mostly the younger members of the cast – they were all interchangeable. You thought any one of them could belong to any one of the other programmes and I think that's what's happened – they've all lined up and they're too much the same.

It was a good time, and at its best, during the Seventies and Eighties. I remember John Stevenson, who's still there – he was a good solid writer. Several of them were axed in that same year, and some were very upset about it. The other writer who was very good was Julian Roach, he wrote well for us. There again, the writers were getting younger and preferred to write for the younger people in it. But it was a good thing to be in and I don't regret it at all.

## Linda McAleny
*Fan*
**DEREK'S DEPARTURE**

I remember the episode where Derek died. I liked Derek and Mavis and I think Derek didn't particularly want to leave. I think it was a mistake because he was a very good character and Derek and Mavis were a good team. It was a shame that he went out, particularly like that because he can't come back again. It's always nice when a character goes out and, perhaps, has a break and then can have the opportunity to come back. But I thought that was rather sad because they were a favourite, I always liked them.

# Ian White
*Director*                                               **CASTING REG**

When we cast Reg, the initial remit was for a tall, dried-up man who had been blocked in advancement and was dour. This list was basically like a dried stick. Then Ken came into this casting session. He was very wary, sat down and did a reading and he was a bit avuncular, but still wary. It was not the best reading in the world, as I'm sure he'd say to this day. He went out and we talked about it for a while and thought about it and what he could do. Because of what we were trying to do, we thought, 'Why not?' You wanted to take a risk every so often, to take a chance to do something slightly different.

I will never forget when he turned up on the first Sunday, five days later, in Bettabuys. He came straight out with a little chat. He was much more relaxed, then, and he launched into this first scene, pulling his watch from the length of his arm into his face and the sudden laughing that stopped, two or three of these 'off the wall' things. We looked at each other and he said, 'Think we'll get away with it?' and I said, 'I don't know.'

It's not very easy to create a comic *Coronation Street* character, because you've got to be realistic, but you've got to be funny and have pathos as well and it's a very difficult thing to do, but, within weeks, he was a favourite character and all the time that he spent on The Street, people loved him. That double act with Curly was one of the best double acts we had. That was another era of successful *Coronation Street* double acts. You had the Duckworths established by then and just going from strength to strength. Mavis and Derek, I think, achieved their best stuff in that era. In the Rovers, Alec and Julie were wonderful because they struck sparks off each other on screen. There was an air of danger, but humour, too.

# Tom Elliott
*Script Editor and Writer*                          **FILLING THE GAPS**

Another story that I was proud of, this was the straw that broke the camel's back. I plotted it very carefully and it was a holiday that Alec Gilroy – in his heyday, when he was behind the bar at the Rovers – he was raffling a Florida holiday. It was a holiday that he'd had given to him, he was losing nothing, and he told Jack that he was going to win and Jack couldn't believe this. I plotted this so carefully, and it was a story that demanded very careful plotting. An old gentleman comes in who can hardly stand up and buys a ticket and Alec was saying, 'If you don't buy, you don't fly.' Of course, when the night of the draw came, this old gentleman had won and he lifted his ticket and promptly collapsed and died. There was no pulse and, of course, Martin in there, as a nurse, he checked the pulse and the man had gone, but Jack gave him the kiss of life and brought the man round. The man was so grateful, he gave Jack and Vera the holiday. What Alec had done, he'd worked with this man years ago on the Golden Mile and he was known as 'Lazarus, the Living Corpse' – in other words, he was able to lower his metabolic rate to such an extent that he hardly had any pulse. So, this was plotted very carefully and it was the last script I wrote for The Street.

Then I got phone calls from various people, 'Can't we put this scene here, can't we put that scene there, wouldn't it be nice if ...' and this is now an epidemic where other people decide how well it should go. It was not arrogance on my part, but I just knew it was wrong and I remember saying to Brian Park, who'd just come out of a tunnel, he was on a train, 'That's it, I don't want to do it any more.' When they played the story, it worked, but there were parts of it that weren't right for me, but I was proud of that story.

That story came out of my head. First of all you think, 'Alec Gilroy, he's not pulled a stunt for ages' and this was vintage Alec and it bounced off another story where he sold a holiday to Derek and he paid for it on his credit card and Julian Roach said, 'If you pay for a holiday like that you can get your money back' and Alec had this holiday then and so he decided to raffle it. So he starts off by saying, 'OK Jack, you're going to win' and he had some reason for wanting Jack to win. Jack was an integral part of the mechanics of it. This is how you put stories together. I've written so many short stories for magazines and this is the way you make it work. I remember reading that story to them and it went through pretty much as read. With it being my story they allowed me to do the denouement.

We could afford in those days – and I think The Street was much appreciated for it and people laughed – to be daft occasionally. We had a gap once – somebody fell ill or something like that. There would be three threads running through a tale, at least – you've got a main theme and two subordinate themes, secondary themes. It was in a secondary theme that we had a gap. It was two episodes. John Stevenson was doing the first one and I was doing the second one, so we talked on the phone and we said, 'What can we do? Jack, he's always good for a laugh.'

Curly has a dormer window in his roof, through which he looks at the stars, and we'd not used that very much, so John and I came up with the idea that one of Jack's pigeons had got in there. At that time, Jack and Curly were at odds and Curly wouldn't give it back. He said he was going to kill it rather than give it him back, and it's whitewashing all over his telescope and he's going to sue him. Jack had had a few drinks and, by the time I got the story in the second episode, Jack was on the roof and he was actually on the dormer trying to get his pigeon. They built a roof and, eventually, when Jack sobered up, he was clinging to the thing and we had the fire brigade get him down. Now, if that happened here, the newspapers would be here, it would be on the television, it would be a *cause célèbre*, a man stuck on a roof and he wouldn't come down, he couldn't, he was scared, he was terrified. Now, in those days, we could write that on The Street and there were even people passing saying, 'Morning, Jack.' This was *Coronation Street* – self-contained, little stories.

John and I, again with another gap, got talking about Maud. She reads teacups, so Phyllis goes to see her, and Sally worked for Maud then in the shop and brought two cups of tea in. Maud starts, 'He's there for the taking, the man of your dreams.' Phyllis gets excited, 'You don't mean it?' 'I mean it,' she says. 'It's never been so clear.' Phyllis can't wait, she's going to buy a new pair of corsets and she's going to see Percy. Sally comes in, 'I don't know how you do it.' 'I'll show you,' she says, 'come and look at Phyllis' cup.' She says, 'But that's not Phyllis', that's yours. *This* is Phyllis' with the bit of sugar in', and Maud had read her own teacup. Percy gets two proposals within ten minutes, and that's the story. Percy was very annoyed by this, outraged! But what happened to comedy? Has television depressed us to the point that we can't laugh any more? Is nobody writing it?

# Robert Khodadad
*Director*                                    **BATTLE OF THE BOYFRIENDS**

There was one scene in particular, it was actually a fight scene and it was between Des Barnes and Alex, Tanya's boyfriend. He found out that she'd been having an affair with Des and you knew, over a number of episodes, that this was going to build up, but what we had to do was the fight scene where the two of them came tumbling down the stairs from the flat above the café and the fight broke into the café itself. We talked about how we were going to do this and, often, with soaps and other drama, one of the key ways of making something like that more dramatic and more realistic is to shoot it a number of times, to put a couple of cameras on it and try to give the thing the pace and energy in the edit and give it a realism through the speed of the cutting, the tightness of the shots. What I decided to do was to try to give it a realism in itself and do it all on one shot, which is almost going back a stage, but I thought, if these two characters can pull it off, it will seem very real. This is going to be one long shot and there will be no edits in it. I think that if the audience has a scene that's got lots of cuts in it, you accept that as being drama, but I think even your colleagues and those who are watching it think, 'You've done a pick-up shot there, you've set up each part of the scene, shot it separately and put it together in the edit.' What I wanted to do was to shoot the whole thing as one continuous scene.

So, we brought in a stuntman to stage this and we basically blocked the scene very slowly and set very specific angles where they would throw punches at each other. Obviously they don't throw *real* punches, but, if you put your camera in a certain position, it will appear that one actor has punched another, particularly if you add sound on to it later. What we had to do was make sure every time a punch was thrown, it was thrown at the right angle for the camera. This was quite a long fight scene, this was going to run for maybe a minute, which, in screen time, and in terms of punching each other, was quite a long time, and the spoons and the forks were all going to be knocked off the top and they were going to tussle and fall on the table and fall on the floor.

So, we brought in a stuntman and we rehearsed it and we blocked it very slowly, imagined walking through the whole thing slow motion. We'd run it for about four seconds and then say, 'Right, at this point, Phil (who plays Des), your hand has got to come off the countertop and knock the spoons off.' The whole thing was also shot in subdued light because it was night-time. We'd do it in slow motion and then we'd rehearse it and block it one stage faster.

One of the big problems was that they really were physically falling on tables and on the floor and, normally, you would use a stuntman to stand in for the actors. Both actors were very keen to do it for themselves and I was very keen to show that we weren't using stand-ins or stuntmen, which would have made it more difficult to film, except that is one of the advantages of being able to put it together in the edit, if Des Barnes falls back, then you cut to a close-up of a body landing on a table, you assume it's his. By doing the whole thing in one shot, it definitely *was* his.

When we came to do the scene, we gave both actors quite a bit of padding underneath their clothes and the first time we were going to go for it for real was the first time we were going to shoot it. We knew that, potentially, they could only do this about twice because, after that, they would be battered and bruised. While they weren't really thumping each other, they were falling on tables and everything was for real.

We came to do the scene, set up for it and we went for it and they went for it in a big way and it looked absolutely superb and we got the whole thing in one take. It looked very effective on the screen. The next day, the pair of them limped in because, even though they were acting, just from that one scene, they felt a bit battered and bruised.

## Bob Greaves
*Television Presenter*                                                   **PLAYING THEMSELVES?**

Somebody like Sarah Lancashire, who played Raquel, is, I think, a superb actress and, once she had left The Street, it was obvious she hadn't been playing herself. Her off screen voice and demeanour is totally different to the character, whereas there have been lots down the years who played themselves and are probably not very capable of playing anyone other than themselves.

## Julian Farino
*Director*                                                               **COMIC CHARACTERS**

I did The Street for a year and a half, doing 39 episodes. Having Jack stranded on the roof was another big storyline I had. I remember Raquel very fondly. I love the character Raquel, and Sarah Lancashire was one of the great treats for me because she was really nice as well. I didn't introduce any major new characters to the show, though.

The Street had a strong element of comedy then. It did more than play just a dramatic storyline. I remember Raquel learning French – that was a great storyline; it didn't have to go anywhere, it was just enjoyable. Curly and Reg at the supermarket was pure comic counterpoint to any of the other drama that was going on. Jack and Vera, Phyllis and Percy – The Street then, as opposed to now, was still populated with far more older characters.

Jill Summers was another diamond for me and Percy was still there. It had that flavour of older, wiser and, often, funnier.

It seems to me, The Street has gone for a more youthful thread, it's more dramatic with more headline stories. What set it apart for me from the other soaps was that we could do nothing and be successful because the others needed a momentum. All good drama is peppered with comedy in my opinion. Great drama can come out of comedy. Look at *The Likely Lads*. Nothing happened, but the amount of character revealed through doing nothing was fantastic. Everybody loves comedy – the most serious of stories should have lines like that.

I do think it has lost that comedy element a bit. Perhaps the writers might have found someone like Reg too comic a character, but it was a shame when he left. I think the balance of drama and comedy has tipped much more towards drama and that's a shame. I do find it relatively thin on humour compared to how it was.

The Street also has always had great losers. Jack Duckworth – he was a great creation, he's such a basic coward. When I first saw the Battersbys, I thought 'alarm bells', but they have bedded them in really well. I think Les Battersby's one of the great comedy characters because the comedy comes from who he is rather than from gags.

## Gillian Jones
*Fan*                                          **RELEVANCE AND REALISM**

I don't enjoy it as much now because the characters are more two-dimensional. It seems as though they change to fit the storyline. It's as though they look round and think, 'What catastrophe can we have in the show this week?' and then people change to fit that situation, rather than the other way round. It's humorous in a different way – most of the time it's not subtle.

The funniest thing ever was Raquel when she was learning French with Ken Barlow and she said, 'Voulez-vous coucher avec moi?' and it was supposed to mean, 'My name is Raquel.' The way they did that was so funny, and Ken Barlow's face!

Now, I think they're trying to have some shocking things in. It seems to be set to a formula, like the other soaps. It was a leader before, but now it seems to be following them. The characters are just not as deep.

I never liked the Battersbys. When they first came, they weren't like real people, they were like caricatures, and, although they've developed a bit, especially the two girls, the mum and dad haven't really got any relevance to me and the people I know. When I used to work for a housing association, I still never met anyone like that and the Battersbys are supposed to have come from that background. I never knew anyone who behaved in that way.

I remember in the olden days my dad used to say, 'It's not realistic because they all go to the pub and that's not what happens in real life', but it still didn't seem false because they had their lives outside. They've spread that out now into the factory and more into the houses, but it still hasn't tackled that problem of being relevant and realistic.

Although I don't tape it if I go away, I do ask people what's happened when I come back. I chat about it to my sister, Barb, and some of the people at work – mainly the kids at school, actually – but I'm not really addicted. You can pick it up easily when you come back.

I didn't like the Curly and Raquel episode because it seemed contrived and Raquel didn't seem very realistic. She kept slipping in and out of an accent. I just thought it was unbelievable, what had happened to her. It was like they just needed something to fill in an episode. I know lots of people thought it was very moving, but that wasn't how I saw it.

I loved Reg – he was so daft. When he did the karaoke, he was pretending it was awful, but he was dying to have a go. I thought that was really good.

## Tom Elliott
*Script Editor and Writer*                    **CREATING A CHARACTER**

All I've heard since is, 'We need another Elsie Tanner.' That's impossible, that's never been achieved. You can never replicate. The nearest one, I think, was Jack Howarth, Uncle Albert, Ken Barlow's Uncle, and then Percy Sugden, but they were different in the way they did it. Percy was a bit livelier, but the community centre was there at that time, so you needed a caretaker. He slotted into that sort of mould, but that never works and, usually, when you introduced a new character, what you couldn't do and what was a mistake was to straightjacket that character – 'We need a character like this, tall, dark, handsome, dashing, debonair, articulate and so on' – because it doesn't work in serial drama. What you get is an actor. He might be able to sustain that for a while, but then he falls back on his own personality, so it was a loose kind of structure, skeleton if you like, that you based his character on and then the character came and you'd look at that character for a while and the strengths were what that character brought with them rather than what we gave them.

We weren't involved in the casting to any great extent. Sarah Lancashire came as Raquel. 'We'll call her Raquel,' Les Duxbury said, but nobody said how she spoke. The most interesting thing about Sarah's performance was her rather vacant and naive attitude and speech pattern, so, when you saw that, then you could write for that, but we didn't plan that at all. You have to say, 'Let's see what the actor brings' and then write for that.

# Gary Parkinson
*Fan*                                              **DOUBLE ACTS**

I thought Reg Holdsworth was great. He used to do a little double act, him and Curly – which is another thing *Coronation Street*'s great at, is double acts, like Rita and Mavis, and Raquel and Curly, Bet and Alec, Mavis and Derek, they were all great double acts. Now they've got Roy and Hayley, who are really sweet and really loveable characters. I'd say Roy and Hayley are going down as a couple of classic characters at the moment.

I like the great tragic moments that are also so ridiculous, like the time when the lorry went through the Rovers' front and everyone thought that Tracy had been crushed, but, actually, she'd been kidnapped. That was great. The excellent Deirdre–Ken–Mike triangle where it all comes out and Ken throws Deirdre against the door and he's got his hand round her throat – that was brilliant.

The other classic triangle of recent times was of Raquel, Des and Tanya – that was brilliant. When she follows him down the street to the flat and it all comes out – that was great because everybody loved Raquel, you couldn't help but love Raquel. I did love the New Year's Eve episode with Raquel and Curly. Over Christmas and the New Year showed the two sides of *Coronation Street* because you had the New Year's Day episode with The Street's celebrations, the street party, which was abysmal and showed the very worst of *Coronation Street*, just so cheesy, so sweet and sentimental, you had Rita up on stage singing 'On the Street Where You live', and then they followed it up with that wonderful Raquel and Curly episode, which was just heartbreaking, so it showed that they can still do it.

As for The Street as a whole, I think quite soon it's going to go quite dark. I don't know whether it's an issue-led thing, like it's starting to be with drugs issues and things like that, but I think it's going to have to move away from the lightness and be a bit darker. I think they are realizing that at the moment because the new Producer seems very keen on making it like *EastEnders*. The Raquel and Curly episode is a good example. They've never done that in *Coronation Street* and it's what *EastEnders* is famous for – two-header episodes. So, that seemed like a very deliberate and quite cynical move towards that, so, maybe that's the way it's going, and *EastEnders* is quite good at that – dark, heavy drama. It's less good at comedy, so maybe that's the way it's going. I do think it's going to be quite dark and there's going to be lots more underworld characters, which we're getting now. It does have a kind of history of that – there have been gangsters at regular intervals throughout it, although I remember, a few years ago, there was outrage with Liz McDonald and her gangster boyfriend: 'Oh, there's never been a shooting in *Coronation Street*', which is a lie because Ernest Bishop was shot. Wasn't Minnie Caldwell held up in her house by a man with a gun? Betty Turpin got mugged. So, there is a tradition and I think it's going to start to move to that.

## Su Garner
*Fan*                                                   **THE WRONG SORTS OF MESSAGES**

I don't like the way it's gone now. It's supposed to reflect society, but there was a bit where Toyah Battersby started a relationship and her auntie was very happy about it. I thought it was wrong, the attitude they were showing of this child. She's only 16 and she was really offensive. I thought, 'What's that telling young kids?' I think they're influenced by it. It's quite worrying because Chloë, one of my daughters, who's ten, is addicted to *Coronation Street* and she'll say things like, 'She's going to bed with him' and I think, as a family soap, should she be watching things like that? I think it's changed just over the last few years – unless it's me because I'm more concerned regarding the children. Looking back, there never used to be anything that was offensive in it, but nowadays I think there is.

I quite like Spider and Toyah now, though. When they came in, I didn't like the Battersbys, and I still don't – especially all the things with drugs and when she was married to Nick, the way she used to behave. I thought that gave the wrong sort of messages out. I don't find them funny. The only funny bits you get now are with Vera and Jack. I used to like Raquel, but I didn't like the episode when she came back because she'd changed. She used to be a wacky person who wanted to be somebody else. You could relate to that, but I didn't like what she'd become. I don't think she'd go down too well in The Street now.

## Dionne Spence
*Fan*                                   **CHANGING CHARACTERS**

When Denise first came into The Street, I hated her, but now I really like her. Vera and Jack are my favourites and they remind me of Stan and Hilda. I remember when the Irish family moved in – I didn't really want them in The Street. It was sad when Des Barnes left and when Chris Quinten left, because he was like the sex symbol of the show in those days, and Jude, that was really sad. I miss Alf Roberts because he was in it for years.

It's quite a diverse show – nothing negative's going on all the time. One family might be having problems, but there's a lot of others that aren't. It's the humour in the show – Jack and his pigeons, the little piece of plaster on his glasses, just things like that make you laugh because it does look funny and you do see people like that.

I don't like the Battersbys. He's a horrible dad – who'd want him as a father? Now they're starting to mellow out, they're not as nasty as they used to be. Maybe that's because I've changed and am more open-minded now.

## Julie Jones
*Fan*                                     **A GROWN-UP PANTO**

I thought the episode with Raquel and Curly was a far-fetched story – French château and all of that. It was a bit too much, but we probably wanted to believe it because she was such a lovely character and so well loved. I thought there was quite a bit of cruelty in it, for her to come back and dangle that horrendous carrot in front of him – 'Oh, you've got a daughter' – and I thought that wasn't picked up well enough because she said 'You've got a daughter' and then she told him about her life and he wasn't saying, 'When can I see her?' So there wasn't that truth about it, to be offered that and then have it taken away so instantly when it made such an impact on him, I didn't think was true and it's not been picked up either. So I'm sure that was just a ratings thing.

I think some of the characters, although real, are larger than life and sometimes it can verge on panto for me, grown-up panto. It's quite sophisticated, but it's that kind of humour. So, to then put real heavy storylines on that jars, but I think they'll be able to do it because we believe and trust the characters. The only thing I've noticed is that they're doing it very, very quickly. I think if they allowed more of a slow build, which has always been their thing – they've done stories over months, even years – and I think that slow burn really takes you with it, but I think now they're looking for instant gratification, like Leanne. She took coke twice, then, by the end of the week, she's having mood swings because she needs her coke. Well, that is laughable, to me that trashes the whole thing. I would have believed that character doing coke and I would have believed her getting into serious trouble, but not in a week. They've wasted a storyline there. I would have built that over four or five months, just a slow burn going on in the background, then I would have believed it and I'd have been with it. I think it was all over in a month. From nothing to a problem within a week, letting people break into the pub and the whole thing going horribly wrong, just too fast.

I don't mind the Battersbys now. They came in and it was too much, too soon. But I think it's a very odd show to have to try and fit into, because some people, there's no reason really, but you just look at them and it's 'No, they're not going to work.' Like Margi Clarke – she was playing it big, she was playing it panto and that was just painful to watch – but you could see that she was playing to what she thought was the style, larger than life.

I think they've given them [the Battersbys] a bit of depth, but, again, it's been all too soon. Like their reaction to Leanne's drug problem. Les totally flipped into this other character and I thought that would have been lovely if it had been a slow burner. I think the sorts of things he was emoting, you would have had to have dragged out of him, yet he was spouting all this stuff, so it's probably just too much too quickly with them.

# Nance Green
*Fan*                                                    **OVER THE TOP**

I do think the more gritty storylines work, though, which is odd because you have these two different strands going on simultaneously – where it's not taking itself seriously at all and there's insignificant stuff going on, and then there's the Leanne business. I'm really pleased that it's in there, that they're covering that particular issue. I rarely feel chilled by something that's happening on *Coronation Street*, but that character Jez is horrible – he chills me, very compelling and very scary. I like him in that sense, he's a good actor. Unfortunately, there are a hell of a lot of people like him around.

I love Roy and Hayley, I could watch them for ever. That was an interesting development, bringing in somebody who'd had a sex change – I think they did it really well. It was very brave and attached to humour. It wasn't totally serious. It was funny, but the reactions of the other people in The Street were all over the top. Everything's over the top, everything's melodramatic in *Coronation Street* and therefore totally unrealistic.

I loved Raquel, I thought she was wonderful. She was definitely a favourite because she was on the funny, taking the piss, side. Maybe the Curly and Raquel episode was just laborious because, actually, there wasn't enough of interest in there. I don't think any of the characters in *Coronation Street* stand up to a special like that – the short snippets are just enough.

The Battersbys took a lot of getting used to, but, looking back, I just wasn't sure whether they were going to be in forever or this was going to be a short storyline. Day one, right from their arrival and over the months, the audience has probably had the same feeling as I would imagine the people on The Street have about the Battersbys – 'Do we have to put up with this lot?' – and gradually I've got used to them. They are a pain, but they're around, they're part of the community now.

The more boring characters where not very much happens are probably the more realistic. Like Bill and Sally, they're quite real people, whereas Jack and Vera are much more entertaining, but they're not real. When they brought in that black boy who immediately started burgling houses, I thought that was absolutely awful and they just don't resolve that particular issue at all. The Asian family I like and I don't necessarily think of them as being the Asian family. I think they are trying their hardest and not necessarily succeeding. They've got a nice, clever woman, but even she can be taken in by some devious man. The lad is verging on the criminal, but he's a good actor, he's very realistic.

This wife-battering issue that's very current with Jim and the new woman, I think that's very interesting, the way they're resolving it – that feels a bit unusual in *Coronation Street*. The undercurrent is people can change, let's give people a second chance. I'm just tingling thinking about that – I obviously feel comfortable with things working out, I've never liked the idea that people can't change. Like in the episode with Les Battersby weeping at his wayward daughter, maybe he will turn out to be something more than he is. I can cope with overnight changes in character quite easily, because it's a soap. I know it would take years in real life. There's nothing subtle about *Coronation Street* anyway, ever, but I love that.

# Gordon Burns
*Television Presenter*            **HILDA AND HUMOUR**

I was never into *EastEnders*. I always thought it was dark and heavy. I didn't want that; it reflected everyday life a bit *too* much. I didn't really want everyday life when I got home from work. *Coronation Street* gave me something different. There's a lot of humour in *Coronation Street*, especially in the Seventies and Eighties. Hilda Ogden, who is my favourite character of all time – Hilda, Stan and Eddie were just a terrific comedy trio and yet there were times when they could move you with a storyline. The character of Hilda was so special, particularly the voice. Yet if you spoke to Jean Alexander in real life, as I have done many times, you'll hear that she has quite a posh voice. She did something so different with her voice. I can still hear that voice ringing in my ears.

It wasn't *quite* everyday life. People say it was nothing like life in Manchester, but it was. You can go down streets in Manchester and in pubs and there are similar characters and similar things happening. But you don't have to be dragged through abortions, teenage pregnancies, gay problems and so on. I don't really want that in my soap. Alas, it has all changed, and not for the better.

I know it still keeps its audience and you can't knock it because of that, but, for me, it is not the *Coronation Street* I enjoyed watching. Yes, I still watch it, though, whereas before I would never miss it – and if I was not there, I would get my wife record it and we'd watch it together later in the evening – it doesn't bother me now if I miss it. I'm not into having situations were the 12-year-old daughter of Gail is getting pregnant. I'm not for that sort of storyline particularly. I know you can say, on the one hand, that it is good and that these things happen and it helps show people the problems and how you deal with them. I'm sure you can put a good argument as to why it should be there and why it is helpful, but I'm an old cynic at heart and I think that these things are put in to get audiences. *EastEnders* went down that road and got bigger and bigger audiences and then *Coronation Street* had to hit back and give bigger stories and get bigger audiences, but I don't like it. I want to be entertained by my soap. I don't want to sit there and be depressed. I want to have a laugh and a giggle, which Hilda gave me or Reg or the butcher who's in it now. I want to come home from work, put my feet up and be entertained.

## Barrie Holmes
*Fan*                                                                     **ISSUES**

There has been an attempt to broaden the attraction of the programme, but the thing that strikes me about the current programme is that it is broadly based on Salford and yet you never see any scallies hanging around. It is a safe environment. You get individual acts of violence, such as Emily's husband being shot, but, generally, it is a fairly safe environment to live and walk in. Nobody's house gets burgled or nobody's car gets vandalized. In *EastEnders*, every time someone turns a corner there's a gang of lads up to no good. So, although they deal with current issues, it's almost sanitized.

I don't think they have gone down the road of reality. They've never had a gay character, they've never had a major black character. They recently had an Indian family, but they're being written out. Over the years, they've dealt with some issues, but they are the softer issues – like the Benefit fraud – whereas the really sensitive issues – such as racism or homosexuality – have not been picked up as they would be in *Brookside* or *EastEnders*. Even drugs tend to be on the peripheral. None of the main characters has been into drugs.

## Robert Khodadad
*Director*                                          **CHANGING CHARACTERS**

I think during my time, what I have seen is the storylines get a bit more *risqué*. If you take the story of Hayley and Roy, the concept of having a transsexual on *Coronation Street* maybe as early as ten years ago would have been horrific to most of our viewers. I think it was Brian Park's idea to introduce this, but he took a risk on it – it was a calculated risk, but it worked very well.

I think the other changes have been the acknowledgement that it needs to appeal to a wider, and potentially younger, audience. I think, as you will see now, a lot of the younger members of the cast are very much in the public eye and they have an association with The Street, but they have almost a separate career outside The Street – whether it's a pop record or a modelling career or some such occupation – which throws them into the public eye a little bit more. I think that has been a big change, the awareness of the appetite for the younger audience, which, if we go back 15 years ago, it wasn't so much the younger members of the cast that were the prominent ones, the ones in the public eye, whereas now you see them on the front covers of many magazines. If you look in the bookshelves and the magazine racks of any shop now, you may see four or five of the young *Coronation Street* cast on the front covers of magazines in any one week.

I think The Street has lost quite a few of what were the fabulous characters. I think some of the key characters who were there, and had been there for many years, were a sad loss to The Street – people like Bet, Hilda Ogden, Alec Gilroy, even the characters like Reg Holdsworth, who now I see is returning, but these were great characters. Like them or loathe them, they were great characters and, to be a successful soap, there have to be those characters you loathe as well as love. That's important and, whilst a lot of people say, 'I don't like that character', they still watch the programme. They do need to not like a character. I don't know that a lot of the younger characters coming in are as strong as some of the older ones.

The changes have been good and bad. What they've done is that, by introducing a lot of younger people, they've opened up the potential audience base and opened it up to younger people. Younger people can identify that little bit more with the programme. I think that, in terms of soap and pure characterization and pure humour, they are a loss.

One thing I think The Street has lost. When I used to talk to a lot of people about The Street, they used to say the one thing about the Street is its humour, its comedy. It's very subtly done, but it's comedy and I think it has lost a big element of that. Inevitably, when you knew a scene was coming up with Reg and Curly, you knew it was going to be funny. You looked forward to it because you knew it was going to be a humorous scene because the characters worked so well against each other. Or, again, with Bet and Alec, there was a certain chemistry there, a certain on-screen chemistry, that you can never design. You can only hope for it and, when it works, it works superbly and whether Alec and Bet were being serious with each other or comical with each other, their scenes would always work. I don't know that you get that kind of chemistry from a lot of the younger, newer characters. That's not to put them down and you could argue that it takes many years to build up that on-screen chemistry, which is fine, but I think you have to be careful not to dilute some of the very good characters too much or too soon.

## Gary Parkinson
*Fan*                                            **DRAMA AND TRAGEDY**

In the Nineties, you had fantastic creations, like Reg Holdsworth and Raquel Wolstenhulme, who just took it to new heights in the early Nineties. Raquel was a fantastic character. I didn't mind the Brian Park year or two years that he was Producer, when he got rid of all the characters. I had always liked Maureen Holdsworth, I thought she was a great character, but most of the characters they got rid of I wasn't bothered about particularly. I do think he gave a bit of life to it. Raquel and Reg seemed to come in at the same time and leave at the same time and, when they left, it did go a bit flat. And Bet left soon after that. So, there was a bit of a nothing period when the main characters were the McDonalds. They were just flat and never really worked for me.

The thing about introducing all the young characters is that you get the feeling that none of them is going to last, except perhaps Toyah Battersby. I think she's excellent. It was a deliberate ploy to win over a young audience, but I can't see that it has been successful. I can't imagine that young kids and teenagers watch *Coronation Street* in the same way that they might watch *EastEnders*. I don't know why that is. *Coronation Street* has got a kind of nice cardigan feel about it. There's nothing smart, nothing clever about it. Even the introduction of Adam Rickett as Nicky Tilsley was just a bit sad, really. It's always been the old characters and the middle-aged characters who have been the real winners with *Coronation Street*, whereas something like *EastEnders* had been run by the young characters, like Bianca and Tiffany. *Coronation Street*, as far as I can think, has never had major storylines involving the young characters.

It's only through that drama and tragedy that you get the tremendous comedy and I think that's always been its strength. It plays the comedy and the drama off each other. But, yes, there was a period in the Nineties when it was cosy and safe and now they're deliberately trying to tack on issues, such as illiteracy and drugs, but The Street has never been issue-led. That was always their credo, that it was character-led rather than issue-led, so I think this adding on of issues seems a bit forced and it does not work for me.

# Lynn de Santis
*Fan*  **FAVOURITE CHARACTERS**

I think it has kept pace with what life is all about. When it first started, it was gritty reality – the cobbled streets. There was far more definition between working class and middle class, hence the conflict in the Barlows' household, whereas now that is much more nebulous. What they have done now is bring in characters like the Battersbys, who are like the scummy side of society. They're not really poorer than anybody – it's not to do with money, it's to do with attitude and that's the differentiation between the different strata on The Street now.

I think they lost a lot with Annie Walker because I think that sort of 'I'm superior', I think it's a shame they haven't got that any more because everybody's a bit the same really. Obviously, you've got the Duckworths – the victims and failures, everything always happens to the Duckworths – who took over from the Ogdens quite nicely. They were always my favourite people.

I think it's got a lot sexier than it used to be. In the early days, it was very innocent – there was none of that sort of stuff.

I loved the Ogdens. They weren't in right at the start. I think probably Ena from the early days – in fact, the coven of the three witches: there was Martha Longhurst, Ena Sharples and Minnie Caldwell. I used to love them sitting in the Snug with their stouts and passing judgement on everything with Ena Sharples leading the fray. I never really liked Elsie Tanner; I thought she was a trollop. I remember thinking, 'I wouldn't want her as my mother.' I quite liked Dennis Tanner, I suppose. There used to be a guy in it called Jerry Booth, who was Len Fairclough's sidekick. He was a bit soft in the head, but a really nice chap and I always liked him. Then, as soon as the Ogdens arrived, I loved Hilda Ogden – she was just wonderful – and Hilda Ogden and Annie Walker in scenes, it was so delightful.

As it went on, then the Duckworths came in and then we had Bet. I quite liked Bet in her heyday when she used to come out with the one-liners.

I always liked the funny characters and I think that's the other reason why it's the superior soap, because there are always things to laugh at, which is what real life is – people do laugh a lot. It isn't like *Brookside* and *EastEnders*, where everybody is permanently depressed and horrible things happen. The Street has that reality where at least there is humour – there are nasty things that happen but there is always another side to it.

The whole thing just recently, with Jude's death, the wedding's going on and you've always got this juxtaposition. He's making a really nice speech at the point where she's gasping her last breath. It's so well done, it's just so well written, because that's what life's about. In *EastEnders*, someone would be murdering somebody else round the corner while this one's dying while someone else is having a car crash and somebody else has just been diagnosed with a brain tumour. *Coronation Street*'s got that lightheartedness, which balances out. It's real life.

## Robert Khodadad
*Director*                                    **FOUR EPISODES**

During my period on The Street, one of the main changes was going to four episodes per week, which, effectively, if you said it took six working days to make three episodes and you worked flat out, it was now going to take six working days and you had to make four episodes. So, if you were working flat out before, where did that extra time come from? The answer to that came from being even more efficient than we previously were. What went was the tech run that we ran for the Producer, which could take half a day. The tech run was quite an important thing because, at the end of it, when we ran all the three episodes, the writers would attend and we would make any adjustments or any changes to parts that weren't quite working and any episode that was running over we would make the cuts then – we lost that.

Really, what happened was that the scripts had to be slightly tighter. You had to know that they were going to run pretty much to time. If you over-record by three scenes, you've used up a lot of studio time that might not end up in any episode, which was a waste of resources and time when you're already short of time. When we used to do three episodes a week, we would have episodes that were two and three minutes over, which would require firm editing. As you're recording, the PA is not only telling you whether you're on schedule or not, they're also telling you how the episode is running in terms of time.

Every scene goes through several stages of timing – when it's written, when it's blocked in the studio, when it's rehearsed, at the tech run and when you actually record it. That's five stages of timings. A scene that may be a couple of minutes long can spread by 50 per cent between reading the script off the page and actually recording it. Now, if any scene ran over by 50 per cent, then you would end up with an episode that was three-quarters of an hour long. You can't just chop stuff out willy-nilly because, hopefully, every scene that's written is important, there's a reason for it being there. You also have the added problem that if you drop a scene, have you dropped a character from the episode? There are certain contractual reasons that actors and actresses are in a certain number of episodes. If you drop that scene and drop them from the episode, it gives the Producer a potential problem administratively. It's extremely difficult.

The whole machine is so complex and the whole machine of characters – are characters available, who's in which episode – even the order the scenes are recorded in. We don't record the scenes in programme order. What we do is take a block of scenes. For example, if we try to do the scenes in the Rovers in blocks, we'll do eight Rovers scenes and then we'll move to another location and do maybe three Kabin scenes. The actual scheduling of the order in which we do the scenes is highly complex and involved and it has to take into account make-up changes, because you could record a scene for Monday's episode and then the next scene you're planning on recording is for Wednesday's episode, so you've got costume changes, make-up changes, character changes, lighting changes, a huge number of changes.

It's also a little bit unfair if you call an actor in at eight o'clock in the morning to do one scene and their next scene and last scene of the day is at seven o'clock in the evening. A lot of the actors live in London, so if they've come up just to do that scene then what do they do all day? They have to hang around. Similarly, if you give them the first scene on a Thursday and the first scene on a Friday then they're not going to be very happy. All of that has to be taken into account as well. Once the PA has set the schedule, you will always get actors calling up saying, 'Look, I've got a real problem with this. I want to get back to London for Friday night and you've put me in last scene on a Friday, it's going to be impossible.' That has a knock-on effect – if you pull that scene up, it then affects another actor.

The timing of the programme is very strict – about 24 minutes 30 seconds for 30 minutes, because you've got to account for commercial breaks and the titles and credits at the end and the break bumpers. There is a little bit of latitude – maybe literally about eight or nine seconds, but that's about it, unless you get special permission for an over-run, but then an over-run is a matter of seconds. So, the programme has to come out pretty much on time, give or take a couple of seconds. With drama, that's not so easy. With The Street, or with any drama, every shot or every line of dialogue has a value and a meaning.

There are certain scenes often identified by the writers as cuttable. A writer would send in the script and, once it was timed, as the Director you would go back to the writer and say, 'Look, this is running over a minute or two' and give the writer the chance to cut some scenes. It might mean rewriting some of the others to accommodate them. It's very embarrassing, though, when you go to the writer and you say, 'This is running a minute or two over' and they cut some scenes and you record the whole programme and you find you're 30 seconds under. That is difficult. Somehow you always do it. Don't ask me how, but sometimes you are in the edit, you cut the episode, it's two-and-a-half minutes over. I've had an episode that was four minutes over and you think, 'Where the hell are we going to pull this time out of?', but you always manage it somehow.

## John Temple
*Storyline Editor and Producer*  **CREDIBLE CHARACTERS**

The fact is, I don't honestly think that the viewers today believe in the characters as such in the way that they used to believe. They totally believed in these characters as real people. They didn't know their actors' names. It was such a protected little world of its own and the stories were more credible. They were told with a credibility that, somehow or other, doesn't exist any more. The sheer demand of churning them out now, at a far greater speed than ever they used to, means, I think, there's less belief in it all. The days when people would send presents because they believed these two people were getting married, those days have gone. They did exist at one time, but I think it's reached a point where that has gone. You've got to watch it on the credibility front.

We used to be very much more careful about details. I notice nowadays that it's all about churning out four a week and, let's face it, any criticisms I might make and anyone might make result from the day they went from two to three a week and, now, four a week. In the old days of two a week, it was a special event, watching The Street. It was a big event in people's lives. They've dissipated that to the point that it became three, it became four – the added strains on the whole production team, on the cast. More people are brought in. It's lost its shape because, sometimes, characters vanish from the screen for weeks or months on end. You can't quite keep the picture in view in the way that one used to – too many characters. The whole thing has become diffused and weakened. Again, you lose sight of people, where they're at in their lives. You find yourself saying, 'Wait a minute, where does he live now, what does she do for a living and why is so and so in this café when she should be at work? What's Curly doing in this café in the middle of the day when he runs a supermarket? Would any supermarket manager come back to have his lunch in a café on The Street?' There's a whole load of unrealities that creep into it now, which they seem to think don't matter any more because they can take artistic licence. They have to do it to tell the story. We wouldn't have done it; I wouldn't have allowed it. In the end, you would do it in a way that would make it far better. You found that, when you had a problem like that that came up and you insisted on the reality of the situation being adhered to and you worked that through, you would find it was a better story in the end because another twist would come in.

## Phil Redmond
Brookside *creator*                                  **MAINTAINING QUALITY**

I think, again, that's another one of those bogus arguments that are put out by vested interests – that the more episodes you have a week, at some stage, inevitably the quality is going to go down. It's usually because they don't want to put the money up for it. It's all to do with gearing up the production. So long as the production is geared up properly and provided you build in the thinking time, which broadcasters are not very good at so you have to educate them, but it's the canal boat principle. It doesn't really matter how long the canal is providing that the canal boats are all coming at the same speed. So, what you have to do, is build in the time into the storyline and scripting process and build in the people to read that. The production end is not a problem.

There's two ways of doing it. One is that you can either expand the cast – but, again, you've got to remember, critically, that the audience only look at one in three episodes anyway, so that's what I mean about you have to have the model in your head about how you're going to deal with the story-telling, so some stories might only go every other episode instead of being every episode and then you'll rotate your cast, mix your cast, the combinations and permutations of your cast will change slightly. You can expand the cast in that way or you can do it in the storylining, so that it's more focused in fewer locations, which means that the time that you then lose jumping around from set to set is actually spent just driving through a simpler, but perhaps intellectually more complex, storyline. The reality is that it's a combination of both. It's not that end of the process that's the worry – that end of the process can be dealt with and handled – it's the front end of the process, it's the storylining and scripting that is the important thing.

I think the interesting thing about *Coronation Street* is that they're fantastic at rewriting history. One of their big puffs is that it's never been out of the Top Ten, which is nonsense because, in the Seventies, it dropped completely out, it dropped completely off the scale. That was when they had a producer in there who had a very strong social conscience and actually wanted to drive it with social issues. Of course, Bill Podmore was brought out of retirement again.

Bill Podmore's career in Granada linked to *Coronation Street*, which underlines the cyclical thing, because Bill would come in, get it all up again, get the plates spinning, go away again and then they'd go, 'Bill' and he'd come back again. There's like a mini-cycle every year. Every year, coming up to Christmas, it's, 'Oh', because we're going into the dark, the winter, and you come through Christmas and, as soon as the clocks go forward, it lifts up again. You go through summer, everyone's knackered again, so there's a mini-cycle that we have to plan for and, then, I think, there's somewhere between a three- and five-year one, where stories and characters go through a natural cycle of familiarity. So, you'll get really excited about it, like a Jimmy drugs storyline and it will drive everybody on for two years and, in the third year, it's, 'What do we do with Jimmy now?', so either you have Jimmy abducted by aliens to keep the storyline going up and up or you think, 'He's got to go back to just being in the back of the bar or the chip shop' and, to judge those things – nobody's ever got it right.'

It doesn't matter who you talk to, whether you talk to producers in the UK or in France or Italy or America or Australia, it's the same thing, because intellectual enthusiasm and energy drives things on for so long and then it moves on. So, you have to go in every now and then, 'Where are we, what are we up to, what are we doing?' As an executive producer you're probably on to that 12 months before everybody else is because you chair the long-term meetings, you see the stuff coming through six months before it's coming into production, six months before it's on screen, so, by the time the tabloids have picked it up, we're already moving to go in one direction.

# Linda McAleny
*Fan*                                                            **KNOWING THE CHARACTERS**

I would think it would go on for *another* 40 years if they can keep the same quality and not go down the road of other soaps that have to have mega-dramas. It has changed in that they have different locations and that adds interest, that you're going into different places. Every soap seems to have to have a meeting place, which was the Rovers, but now that they've got the hairdresser's and café and different places, that all adds a bit of interest. They've got a good variety of characters in it now. It's changed, though, perhaps being on at half past seven, some of the things these days are not as suitable for young children as perhaps they were years ago. For family entertainment, you never get many bed scenes, but they're going into rela-tionships – I think that's probably true to life. You want to be able to watch it with children of all ages because it does appeal to the young ones as well.

I think they've got plenty of variety of characters. I like Hayley and Roy – they're perhaps the Derek and Mavis that used to be. You always need somebody like that in and other soaps don't seem to have such good char-acters. They have characters that flit in and disappear and move house and go, but *Coronation Street* seems to have more continuity. You feel you get to know the characters and, if something happens in a script that you don't like, you always feel 'Sally wouldn't have done that' and you feel you get to know that particular character.

# Phil Redmond
Brookside *creator*

Soaps in the future will roll on for as long as television as we know it rolls on. They always make this comparison between soaps and Dickens, don't they? Well, Dickens put out his penny pamphlets on a monthly basis because that was the only way to do it, but then that form passed into history. I think, sooner or later, television as we know it will change. Whether or not soaps will survive the way they are, I don't know. They might survive in shorter bursts. There might be a weekly or a monthly episode or show or continuation. I'm thinking more about the on-line world now. As long as terrestrial channels are running and they'll need to pull in audiences, soaps will survive, but, once people are starting to buy the programmes, not the channel, that's the only time that people start to question their future.

Soaps are great drivers for terrestrial television in a structured broadcasting universe. When that changes, it will change. They might want an hour-long episode per week. Then you could just say, 'I've got an hour, I'll have that' and then watch it, but I think this thing of every night at 8.30, although I think that's the way for the next five years. I think it will have another five years after that, really, because it's the one in three dipping in. I've been saying this for five years, we should be on five nights because, if they're only watching one in three, the more opportunities you give them to watch, the more you'll retain. The broadcasters have got to write the cheque. Any commercial organization, like ITV or Channel 4, to me it's a no-lose situation, but they've got to have the nerve to do it.

# CHAPTER SIX

# The Queen Bees

'She was a star, she should have been in Hollywood, she was Joan Crawford.' Who else but Pat Phoenix? Pat was, without question, supreme – the finest of all Street stars. She had everything – glamour, sex, style, flashing eyes, clicking heels, even outrageous red hair. What's more, she wasn't afraid to flaunt any of it. She even had a temper to match.

Everyone talked about her – from Ena Sharples to Keith Waterhouse in the *Daily Mirror*. Wherever she went, headlines followed. People loved to gossip about her and there was plenty to gossip about. There was usually a man somewhere in her life – a husband, an ex-husband, a lover, an ex-lover, a fancy. Young men dreamt of her, older men fantasized. 'The tart with the heart,' says a former *Brookside* scriptwriter. 'Who couldn't love her?'

In real life, she was Pat Phoenix, but there was little to distinguish her from her screen personality – they were one and the same. In its obituary to her, *The Times* called her the 'brash and blowzy heroine of *Coronation Street*'. After meeting her at No. 10, Prime Minister Jim Callaghan called her 'the sexiest thing on television' and when she swept into Granada dressed in all her furs, Tony Warren christened her, 'Catherine of all the bleedin' Russias'.

Street Director Les Chatfield remembers going to a party at Pat's house: 'Suddenly the lights were dimmed, music started and these curtains parted electrically and the whole of that wall was glass and the glass parted and she'd made all of the garden into an indoor swimming pool.' They all changed and went for a swim, but, 'at one point, we all had to clear out because Pat was going to swim in the pool on her own. She was the star, she was very much the queen.' It was typical of Pat, swimming unimpeded, glamorous and the centre of attention.

There was no doubt that she could also sting – what more could you expect from a queen bee? There are countless stories of Pat's temper, some best left in the past, but one or two have been included here – not out of malice, but to remember Pat as she really was, a highly charged, larger-than-life star, an icon.

She could be the most difficult person from a production point of view, as Producer Wally Butler remembers: 'Pat threw a few wobblers in my day – not serious things, but serious in those days, when you didn't expect them. Apart from that, you just negotiated it and got on with it.' She was also The Street's unofficial shop steward, always ready to march upstairs and complain if something was not right.

If the Sixth Floor found her difficult, then the juniors found her impossible. Clarissa Hyman, now a well-known food writer, briefly worked on the show as a 'call girl' and remembers being humiliated after Pat had arrived late on set. She insisted that Clarissa had failed to call her. In fact, Clarissa had been repeatedly knocking on her door, only to be told to go away by Pat. 'I felt terrible and humiliated and angry,' she remembers. 'If she behaved like that with me, she must have behaved like that with others.'

She could infuriate. On a personal appearance, she once told 700 soldiers that the 'drinks are on Granada'. Little wonder there was a stampede for the bar and, of course, Granada eventually had to foot the bill. Pat Phoenix unquestionably had a reputation for awkwardness and even admits in her autobiography that, 'I had some notoriety as a firebrand at Granada … some might say I was just a damned nuisance.' Pat, though, was Pat, and she was a star. To be fair, as Leita Donn, the programme's Press Officer recounts, there were times when she did apologize.

When The Street started, in December 1960, it kicked off with three queens – not only Elsie Tanner, but Ena Sharples and Annie Walker, as well. Ena ruled The Street with her sharp, sometimes wicked, tongue, her high morals, her fearlessness, her godliness. She was a proper Edwardian lady. José Scott, who cast her, remembers Violet Carson as 'a kind of Queen Mother, a tough old biddy', adding that 'we were all terrified of Ena, really, or terrified of Vi. When I say "terrified", I mean they all paid her a tremendous amount of respect.'

Granada presenter Bob Greaves remembers almost bowing to her and holding a door open as she gracefully swished down the corridor: 'She would give you an imperious wave or a shimmy of those Ena Sharples hips and sashay through with hardly a word. You didn't get thanked for opening the doors. It was expected because she was the queen.'

On screen and from the word go, her slanging matches with that lady of dubious morals, Elsie, were high drama – the kind of thing that had you perched on the edge of your seat with glee. They both gave as good as they got and there was never a winner. Alongside her drinking pals, Martha and Minnie, she would castigate, lecture and infuriate. Nobody was more opinionated than Ena and she was always right.

If Ena occupied the moral high ground, Annie Walker occupied the valleys. She could look down her nose in that true blue Tory way of hers and dismiss you. There would never be any nonsense in her pub, though, at times, you did wonder how an earth a woman of her standing finished up managing a pub. Yet Annie, in real life, was quite the opposite. For true blue Tory on screen, read red hot socialist off screen. Doris Speed was, all her life, a member of the Labour Party – Old Labour at that – and as committed to the working class as anyone. After Ena and Elsie had departed from the series, Doris assumed the role as queen of The Street for a short time. She had no competition.

That Tony Warren could have conjured up three such fearsome characters is, in itself, testament to his creative abilities. Julie Jones provides an interesting insight, recalling hearing Tony Warren talking about *Coronation Street*: 'His viewpoint was that he was brought up in a very female-oriented home and it was all women talking about women's stuff and him, being a child, could soak it all up and they wouldn't think he was listening. He's done it with an affectionate eye and not cynically and I think that really showed in the early days.' There are few male writers who can write with such affection and sensitive understanding of women as Tony Warren.

After Doris came Bet Lynch, another archetypal queen bee. She had all the looks of an Elsie and all the vulnerability as well – a chequered love life, a brashness – but not quite all the glamour of an Elsie, and you always felt that she erred, ever so slightly, on the side of respectability. She was never as passionate about life as Elsie, never as tempestuous, but she certainly had her moments.

In recent years, no female characters have matched those created by Tony Warren. Sarah Lancashire as Raquel was as near as any, but her disappearance from The Street in 1999 has left a hole that is waiting desperately to be filled. Somehow Rita is not quite a queen – a princess, maybe, but not regal enough to take the throne itself.

It's undoubtedly true that the women characters have traditionally been the stronger characters in the series and is probably still true today. As Bob Greaves says, 'the women shine in *Coronation Street*'. He also wonders if that is deliberate or accidental. It probably all stems back to Tony Warren and his ability to conjure up such wonderful female characters. Once Elsie, Ena and Annie Walker had been established, it just continued. Of course, you could devise an argument that strong women characters will attract a female audience and, ultimately, most soap operas are aimed at women rather than men. However, the fact is that the strong women were there long before *Coronation Street* became an integral part of the ITV schedule.

Think of *Coronation Street* and you think of Ena and Elsie. Ask any fan over the age of 40 and they automatically think of the two. They are, and always will be, *Coronation Street*. It will be another 40 years and another generation before we fail to associate the Street with Ena and Elsie. They were the queen bees – two of the finest female characters ever created for British television.

## José Scott
*Casting Director*                          **CASTING THREE QUEENS**

There was the big stumbling block with Ena. I was always travelling somewhere or other to try and find an Ena. Every actress that was on earth, from God knows where. If we could have dug them up, we would have done. Then, one day, Tony had a brainwave. He said, 'I remember when I was at the BBC,' because he'd been a child actor, 'Vi Carson. Phew, my word, she was a tough lady.'

So, she eventually came and, of course, when the thing went on the air … she didn't exactly stick to the script either, but that is what made it. She was such a strong character. I can't remember now what the original lines were, but she was a very good-looking woman. She had this lovely iron grey, naturally wavy hair, very smart, lovely complexion. It was very difficult to make somebody look like an old bat, so, I don't know whose brainwave it was to get the hairnet, but, I can remember, we were all sitting in the viewing room and she'd gone into Florrie Lindley's shop and, whatever the dialogue was before, and she said, 'Are those fancies fresh?' and she said, 'Yes.' 'Well, I'll have half a dozen and no ee-clairs.' The way she timed it, the way she did it. It wasn't in the script either, but that was it. We all roared with laughter. It was just the pitch of what she said, 'I'm not having that' and 'Put that away for start', so that's how her character came to life. Tony had written it, but that came to life through her own inventiveness.

Annie Walker was easy to cast because Doris – who became a very, very close friend – she was such a funny, lovely woman. There was always something rather grand about Doris and the idea of putting Annie Walker, who was always a bit above herself – you know, 'I'm one of the Beaumonts from Clitheroe' – it seemed just perfect. In the early days, Doris did put on this slightly sort of posh accent, but eventually that went. So, really, there was no problem with her. I don't think there was with Jack either – Arthur Leslie, he seemed to fit in just like an old glove.

Violet Carson was a kind of Queen Mother – a tough old biddy. We were all terrified of Ena, really, or terrified of Vi. When I say 'terrified', I mean, they all paid a tremendous amount of respect, as they did with all the older members, and that was quite different from probably how it is now.

Pat *was* Elsie Tanner, in a way. I'd been in rep with Pat, so I knew her very well. It's strange because, of all the people, Margaret was absolutely adamant that she didn't want Pat in the thing. She said, 'Oh, she'll go miles too far, she'll go right over the top.' Margaret was always the one who kept the finger on that – 'We don't want anyone going too far.' Tony and I fought like mad – I had been in rep with her and I said, 'I'm sure she won't', because Pat had got a tremendous sense of the theatre. She really was a kind of Joan Crawford – she should have been in Hollywood. You would see her coming into the canteen with the white mac and the collar, all this sort of thing, but, nevertheless, nobody could have been better than her in The Street.

I remember going to one of her houses and she opened the door and there were about five million pairs of shoes – talk about Imelda, shoes, shoes, shoes, jewellery and God knows what. She was tremendous – everything had to be so opulent. She bought Wilfred Pickles' house. Then, of course, her marriages, they were sensational.

The Street visited Australia and Pat came back with a kangaroo coat. They had a wonderful time in Australia. They were fêted wherever they went.

# Norman Frisby
*Granada Press Officer* **MINNIE AND MORALS**

*Coronation Street* was an extremely moral show in the early days and Harry Kershaw would never allow anybody to swear. I'm not sure there's a great deal of swearing now. Certainly adultery was hinted at, but it was never openly there. Elsie Tanner always married her lovers – she didn't just live with somebody, she actually married them.

Margot Bryant was a mistress of the four-letter word. Little Minnie Caldwell! Butter wouldn't melt in her mouth in the show, but she'd been a chorus girl in her day and she certainly knew how to toss around the four-letter words.

# Leita Donn
*Press Officer* **DORIS AT DOWNING STREET**

Doris Speed played Rovers Return landlady Annie Walker from episode one to the day she retired, both on and off the screen, and everyone thought that Annie and Doris were identical, but they weren't. For a start, although Annie Walker stood as independent councillor in Weatherfield's elections, her own attitude marked her down as a 'dyed in the wool' Tory, while Doris was a life-long, very committed socialist, who was welcomed to Number Ten Downing Street by her great admirer, former Prime Minister Harold Wilson. Annie gave out the distinct impression that her natural habitat would have been an up-market Cheshire hostelry rather than a little back-street Lancashire pub, but Doris lived all her life in unfashionable Chorlton-cum-Hardy and, until Granada put a stop to it, she came to work every day on the bus. Annie was an out and out snob, while Doris had a wicked sense of humour and would quite happily tell a naughty joke. She would, with great glee, regale everyone with hilarious stories and she didn't mind a bit if, in so doing, she sent herself up.

# Ken Farrington
*Actor, played Billy Walker* **DORIS AND THE TABLOIDS**

It's like a family, especially when Doris was around. She really did look upon me as her son. She had no family herself. She used to phone up and chat and, when she went into a home, I used to go and see her once a month. She said she was going to put me in her will, but she forgot to do it.

One of the tabloids did a nasty trick on her [about her birth certificate]. I really went anti-newspapers at that point because they got somebody to move into the rooms opposite and take a picture of her when the postman knocked on the door. She was lovely, she was adorable and I was very, very fond of her.

## Norman Frisby
*Granada Press Officer*                                    **FANS AND FUNERALS**

Harry Kershaw was dead against anybody wanting to push any kind of message. There's rarely any mention of politics. Interestingly, Doris Speed was a shining light in the Labour Party, whereas Annie Walker could not have been any more of a true blue Conservative.

One of my personal highlights with *Coronation Street* was when Number Ten rang up and said that the Prime Minister, Harold Wilson, was having one of his soirées and wondered if Doris Speed would like to come. I said, 'She's in the studio, but I'll pop down and ring you back.' I went down and knocked on the dressing room. I said, 'Doris, this is absolutely wonderful, Harold Wilson would like you to go to Ten Downing Street, they're having a reception for Pierre Trudeau, the Prime Minister of Canada. It's in a fortnight's time. I've checked upstairs, you're not actually working that week, would you like to go?' 'Ooh, I'd love to, darling, oh yes.' I said, 'You can actually take a guest.' She said, 'Oh well, I'll take you, as you've brought me the good news.' So, I had a good night at Ten Downing Street with Doris – one of the great occasions. Doris and Harold had met before. When we went to Australia, one cringe-making stunt had been to take them to Downing Street before we went to the airport and we met Jim Callaghan, who was then Chancellor, and Harold, who was PM, so he did know her. I think it was really Lady Wilson who was more taken by her – she was a huge fan.

I got on very well with Violet Carson. She was not the most popular person in the Press Office because she didn't have much time for the newspapers. She didn't want to do interviews, but we became quite pally. It was rather sad – when Vi died, I went over to the funeral. She had no family, except her sister Nell, and, in fact, myself and a friend of ours were almost the only family mourners. There were others there, but no actual family. I don't think any of the cast were there, but there must have been some reason for that. She had been left quite a while by then. She also didn't get on very well with Pat Phoenix – they suffered each other, but they were a bit rude about each other.

Pat's funeral was the other end of the scale. Tony Booth rang me and said that Pat wanted this, this and this for her funeral. So I said, 'Sure, if you want a jazz band in the church and so on.' It was a huge production at a church in Oxford Road. We stopped the traffic – thousands and thousands turned out – huge.

## Leita Donn
*Press Officer*                    **THE MAGIC OF THE HAIRNET**

Like her screen self, Violet Carson never suffered fools gladly. She had a great respect for her God and her religion and she valued the important things in life, like morality, punctuality and good manners. She didn't like nosy parkers, which was unfortunate because bus drivers taking tourists around the Blackpool area would tell their passengers, 'And this is the bungalow where Violet Carson – Ena Sharples, you know – lives with her sister Nelly Kelly' and the whole busload would descend and curious noses would be pressed against the windows of Vi's front room. Vi solved that one by switching her living arrangements around and transferring her front room to the back.

As I said, she was a stickler for punctuality and she hated it when the Blackpool to Manchester train arrived late and made her late for rehearsals. Now, Vi was a perfect lady and perfect ladies don't kick up a fuss, but Vi knew she would have to do something about British Rail. As she explained to me at the time, 'As my courage failed me, I just imagined myself into Ena Sharples' hairnet and into her persona and then I was able to write and tell them a few home truths.' The result was a grovelling apology from British Rail and a promise that they would do all in their power to ensure that the trains, and Vi, arrived on time.

## Christabelle Embleton
*Fan*                              **ENA'S 'EE-CLAIRS'!**

I can remember Ena going on about her 'ee-clairs'. She'd go into the shop wanting some cakes, but add that she didn't want 'no ee-clairs'! It sounded so funny to us. I can remember Florrie in the shop – she'd moved in and that's how it started. That first scene was in the shop and she was being shown it. Then Ena came to welcome her and told her not to give certain people tick.

For me, Elsie Tanner was the great character of The Street, without a doubt. She had spirit, she had something different. I think Ena was good, too, because she ruled the roost, she *was* The Street. They had lovely fights, her and Elsie Tanner, literally fighting in the street. That also was something we didn't do down here [in the South]!

## Bob Greaves
*Television Presenter*                              **MAKING WAY FOR THE QUEEN**

What developed, certainly in my mind, was that the women characters were the strongest characters in the series and I think that's probably still true today. The women shine in *Coronation Street*. Now, whether that's deliberate or accidental, I don't know. My guess is that it evolved.

Violet Carson was a bit of a Tartar – a friendly enough woman, but not the sort of woman you could, or I could, get close to. I remember vividly one day walking down the corridor that led to the Wardrobe and Make-up Departments where a lot of the dressing rooms were. I was walking along and there were two sets of double glass doors. She had entered the corridor and was walking towards a set of doors and she was probably 10 or 12 feet from the doors. I was coming in the opposite direction, 50, 60, 70 feet away. There was no way she was going to open those doors before the man – i.e., me – scurried to open the doors for her. She was a queen and you do not expect real queens to have to open doors. She would stand there until you scurried along and opened the doors. Then she would give you an imperious wave or a shimmy of those Ena Sharples hips and sashay through with hardly a word. You didn't get thanked for opening the doors, it was expected because she was a queen.

## José Scott
*Casting Director*                                          **STARTING OUT**

Tony wrote superbly for women. He based all his women characters on his relations, aunts and grandmas. I never really had any tremendous like or dislike for any of the characters because, in relation to each other, that's what made them good – one was no good without the other.

Barbara Knox was a wonderful character, terribly funny, and, as an actress, too, she was terribly clever and very, very funny. You'd see that part of her in The Street. They'd go on barmy holidays. I think she and Julie went to Benidorm or Majorca. In relation to each other, you couldn't say, 'I particularly like that character' until you saw them with one or two of the others.

Joanna Lumley [Elaine Perkins, Ken Barlow's girlfriend] was more or less a star when she came. I never thought she'd do it, actually, but, when they wanted this posh girl, I said, 'Wouldn't it be lovely to have Joanna Lumley?' but they said, 'She'll never do it', but, to my absolute astonishment, she did and never looked back really because that put her on the way.

There were one or two people who you kind of knew. A lot of them started with terribly small little bits. Eileen Derbyshire [Emily Bishop] started with a tiny little part and I remember saying to her at the time, 'Look, there's a part that's in two or three episodes, but, later on, there's a part coming and it's only tiny, but it could very well go on, so you can choose which you want to do.' She chose the small part, which went on and it paid off.

# Wally Butler
*Director*                                        **CLICKING HER HEELS**

When I was working on it, the actors were an ensemble. Eventually, as it grew more popular, you had favourites, from the point of view of the audience, and they tended to get more press. Pat Phoenix was *the* character. Vi Carson, although she was an elderly character, she got a lot of press because of her presence and the type of character she was playing. I would say that Vi Carson and Annie Walker and Len Fairclough and Pat Phoenix, Hilda and Stan Ogden, seemed to reflect the Street, from the viewers' point of view. The others – Ken Barlow – mosied along – as he still mosies along.

I suppose, like a repertory company, there were one or two ... this was reflected in the writing – the more popular they became, the more lines they got. The stronger the character was, the more press they got and, therefore, the writers elevated them. So there was a hierarchy, but they didn't use the star syndrome – they didn't demand a bigger dressing room – they played as an ensemble company, but, obviously, some were greater than the whole. The lesser artistes were older, wiser and they were glad to be working and they were quite happy to take second place. The younger ones who came in were happy to be among this clan and they kept their place, so it was very pleasant.

Pat used to play it up – she used to come late for rehearsals and change her clothes about twice, three times a day. After lunch, she'd come in in a different outfit than she'd had in the morning and she had these high heels and she'd come in a few minutes late for afternoon rehearsal, after lunch, and she would click her way up the stairs to the Green Room and you knew Pat was back. She'd go in and do herself up and have a coffee and come out. She wasn't needed right at the beginning, but she made her presence felt.

Pat threw a few wobblers in my day – not serious things, but serious in those days, when you didn't expect them. Apart from that, you just negotiated it and got on with it. I was brought up with actors who respected you because you respected them and that was the end of it. You never talked money. If you got your photo in the papers, everyone would huddle round in the Green Room to have a look. They were all paid pretty much the same in those days – latterly, I think one or two, like Pat Phoenix, got a bit extra because their parts were heavier and they were getting more attention, there were more demands made of them. The rest of cast realized this and knew, quite intelligently, the better they did, the longer they would stay.

## Clarissa Hyman
*Researcher and Producer*                    **WHERE THE HELL'S ELSIE?!**

It was my first job. It must have been the early Seventies, I was about 21 or 22. I got this job attached to Granada as a POA [production office assistant]. It was seen as an entrée into television. It was a gopher's job, nearest equivalent would be an assistant stage manager. I was a runner, fetcher/carrier, but it was a good way of learning about television production. It was accepted that one would proceed upwards from that job. It was a good scheme in its time, but it was a very junior position. There were about three or four of us at any one time. You got shunted around and put on different productions, mostly drama productions because you could help out with the cast. Everybody had to do a stint on *Coronation Street*. All you had to do was be on hand in case anyone wanted messages running.

Your biggest area of responsibility was to make sure that the right people were in the right place at the right time. So, you got a script, a breakdown of who was appearing in what scene, and you had to keep tabs on everybody and make sure nobody went AWOL, and they were in the studio at the right time. You didn't want them in studio too early as they only got in the way, so you got a call sheet and you worked from that. Mostly on Corrie, it just ran itself – most people were true professionals, theatricals who had come up the old-fashioned way and you didn't have to worry about them at all. People like Albert Tatlock and Annie Walker, you knew that they would be there. You might have a little flutter wondering, 'Where's Annie?' but ten out of ten times she would be there and so would Albert – they were solid, true professionals.

As a POA, I didn't have much to do. I had to keep the extras in check a bit, make sure they didn't run riot, mithering everybody. There was a great pecking order among the extras; if someone had a speaking part – maybe just one word – then they were up the pecking order.

It was taped when I was there, not live, but they would tape each half of the show for live and only go and do it again if there had been a major mistake. They tried not to stop because it was costly, but sometimes they had to. I remember the corner shop falling to pieces once and they had to stop. It was very carefully plotted.

Anyhow, my worst experience was with Elsie Tanner, who was always a bit of a diva. I found her rather scary. I was young, raw and nervous and not sure what I was doing there. I found her absolutely terrifying. I tried not to get in her way, but there was this one occasion I knew she was wanted on set. I had to knock on her door and say, 'Ten minutes, please.' They were still very much rooted in the old theatrical traditions. Then I went back and said, 'Five minutes.' I kept knocking on her door and she kept saying, 'OK, OK', but she never appeared. Time was ticking away and she was not in the studio, so they started taping. She wasn't in the first scene, she was in the second scene. I kept racing between studio and her dressing room and she kept saying she was coming. Finally, it got to her point in the script and she wasn't there, so there was a great business – 'Where the hell's Elsie?!'

All eyes are on me. I said I had been knocking and knocking and she kept saying she was coming. Then, suddenly, she swans into the studio, as cool as a cucumber. God knows what she had been doing in her dressing room, but she obviously thought the world stopped for her. She turns around and says out loud, so that the whole studio can hear, 'Well, I've been waiting for my call! I've been waiting for the POA to come and tell me when I was wanted on set.'

I thought I was going to die – the end of my glorious career in one stroke. Anyhow, they had to get on with it – there was no time for an inquest at that point. By the end of studio day, of course, it was forgotten, as so many other things had happened. I was absolutely upset, I felt terrible and humiliated and angry. If she behaved like that with me, she must have behaved like that with others. I had a word with the Floor Manager, who was my immediate boss, and he said, 'Don't worry.' But it was good experience working on The Street. Just the thrill of leaning on the real Rovers Return bar was unforgettable.

## Les Chatfield
*Cameraman and Director*                    **QUEEN OF THE NORTH**

I had a very close working relationship with the cast. Everyone used to socialize together as well, especially in Pat Phoenix's heyday – she was forever giving parties and everyone used to go. She was with the taxi-driver, Bill, then. She was queen of the North. She used to have this enormous house in Disley and used to give these extravagant parties there. Violet Carson was still in The Street then, but she never came to the parties, nor did Minnie Caldwell or Martha Longhurst.

I remember going to a party that Pat Phoenix gave. We were all invited to this semi-detached house in Macclesfield. We didn't know it was semi-detached. We had to meet at a pub and then go on in convoy – a pub just outside Macclesfield, between Poynton and Macclesfield. We arrived at this house, thought, 'What are we doing here?', went into this semi-detached house, which was very ordinary, and went into the living room, which was just about big enough to hold us all, clutching the bottles that we'd brought.

One wall of this semi-detached living room was all curtains and, suddenly, the lights were dimmed, music started and these curtains parted electrically and the whole of that wall was glass and the glass parted and she'd made all of the garden into an indoor swimming pool. It was quite a big swimming pool and it had its own changing rooms and a bar. There was a swimming costume laid out for everybody and it turned out to be a very good party. At one point we all had to clear out because Pat was going to swim in the pool on her own. She was the star, she was very much the queen.

I worked with Jean Alexander and she was dramatically different to her character. She didn't naturally socialize a lot with the others. She got on her train to Southport and, by that time, Ena was getting on the train to Blackpool, so it was the younger ones and Pat and whoever was in tow at the time.

## Denis Parkin
*Set Designer*                                    **A COACH AND FOUR**

We used to go to Pat Phoenix's house in Sale at Christmas. She used to hire a stagecoach and four horses and go round Sale. She was a lovely, flamboyant lady. We used to go there quite often at the weekends. My daughter was about three or four then – she was dangled on Pat Phoenix's knee. When she grew up, she was make-up artist at Granada and Pat Phoenix always pretended that she didn't remember her because she didn't want to say it was 17 years earlier!

## Leita Donn
*Press Officer*     **FLAMING RED HAIR AND A TEMPER TO MATCH**

Pat Phoenix had flaming red hair and a temper to match, but she was warmhearted – too generous for her own good, a marvellous character and a great friend. We hit it off from the start.

It took me all of two minutes to suss out that Pat was one of the few people who could genuinely be described as a star. There are actresses and there are stars. Actresses I was used to – I'd worked with quite a few of them before I became involved with the cast of *Coronation Street* – but I hadn't met anyone who had the same kind of star quality that Pat exuded. You could never mistake her for the girl next door – she wasn't into that kind of image. When she went out to make a personal appearance, she put on the glamour because that was what she believed the public wanted to see. Why should they turn out to look at someone in jeans and a T-shirt? Pat never wore that kind of casual gear, even for rehearsals, but when she went out to meet the public, she made sure that she looked every inch the star she was. I still have this vision of her standing in Reception at Granada, waiting for the car to take her off to her evening's engagement. She wore a long, sequinned evening dress, which glittered from *décolleté* cleavage to hem. Around her shoulders was a white fox-fur stole, which looked marvellous, it glittered and flashed under the lights. Girl next door? Never in a million years. Not surprisingly, many people were in awe of Pat and, because of that legendary, fiery temper of hers, they tended to walk on eggshells so far as she was concerned. It was safer not to cross her.

The reason that she and I got along so well was that I wasn't a bit afraid of her and if I didn't like something she had said or done, I would tell her to her face, instead of whispering about it behind her back, and for that she respected me. An example of this occurred when I needed a new photograph of her for publicity purposes and I arranged with our photographer to take it on the set in the studio when she had a break between two scenes, but I warned him not to photograph her smoking – something she was apt to do between scenes or whenever she could. The photo was going to be reproduced postcard-size to send out to fans and I didn't want any young, impressionable girls to see her with a cigarette. I decided to go down to the studio myself, just to see that there were no problems. Unfortunately there were. Pat was puffing away on this cigarette and the photographer tactfully took it off her saying, 'Let's have this out of the way for the moment – I'll put it over there until we're finished.' Green eyes flashed a warning and Pat's temper erupted like a volcano: 'Don't you *ever* take a cigarette off me when I'm smoking,' she stormed. A shocked silence descended on the studio and the poor photographer turned bright red. I stepped forward and said, 'Pat, I asked him to take a photo of you not smoking, so don't blame him, please.' She posed for the picture and then stormed off the set into her dressing room. I followed. The door wasn't locked, so I went in, sat down and said quietly, 'I think you owe that young man an apology. He was only doing his job and you bawled him out in front of everyone on the set. We were all embarrassed. I think you should go and say you are sorry, don't you?' For a moment, I thought the volcano was going to erupt again and, then, suddenly, the warning light went out and she grinned. 'You're right,' she said, 'I shouldn't have lost my temper, I'll go back and apologize to him', and she did.

## Norman Frisby
*Granada Press Officer*                    **THE DRINKS ARE ON ME!**

Pat Phoenix was a kind of Hollywood-style actress. She was wonderful, but she got into some terrible, terrible scrapes. One of my favourite funny stories is when the King's Own Yorkshire Light Infantry had chosen her as their pin-up girl. They were going to Borneo and they asked us if Pat

Phoenix would go and say 'goodbye' to the boys in the NAAFI the night before they set off on the troop ship. I said, 'Do you want to do it?' and she said, 'It will be fun, will you take me?' so off we went to Pontefract.

There was a complete battalion – about seven to eight hundred men – in the NAAFI, having a big booze-up on their last night in the UK. Pat Phoenix gave them a wonderful show, dressed to the nines. She leapt up on to a table and she shouted, 'Boys, the drinks are on me!' I said to the Adjutant, 'She can't afford it and I certainly can't, so you'd better send the bill to Granada.' So the bill came through and it wasn't an astronomical sum and I thought, 'There's only one person who can OK this and that's going to be Cecil Bernstein.' So, I assembled all the splendid cuttings that we'd got and these wonderful photographs of this glamorous person with her arms outstretched on the table in the barracks and I took this sheaf of cuttings, saying what a wonderful show this was. Then I said, 'By the way, it's cost us eighty pounds (or whatever it was) to buy drinks all round for seven hundred soldiers.'

I suppose Pat caused me the most problems in a way. She was a superb publicist herself. If she went to open a bingo hall in Wigan she would get an outfit from that place near Kendals and she would dress up to the nines. She'd have a limousine laid on and she would be a star! She would give her money's worth, she was absolutely superb.

## Alistair Houston
*Sound Engineer*                                              **BEHIND THE BAR**

The year after it started, they decided to have a party. There used to be a pub behind Granada called the Pineapple, which was little used, so, for this Christmas party, they took over the pub and the cast served the drinks. There were three old locals in there when we went in, having their pint in the corner, and they stayed there and all the drink was free. They were going to the bar and getting whatever they wanted from Pat Phoenix. They were absolutely rolling by the end of the night and you could imagine them saying, 'Elsie Tanner's been serving me drinks.' We had some good times in those days. Granada was more family-oriented than it is now. It's just a business now. The last time, I worked on *Coronation Street* about three years and Bill Roache and I were the only two people there who had been in the very first episode.

# Mike Newell
*Director*                         **HANDLING WOMEN**

I would have been the baby among the directors. Some of the actors were sweet. Some of them were formidable – you know, Vi Carson didn't suffer fools gladly, Pat Phoenix was a big drinker and if she had a hangover, then you knew about it – but they were pretty kind. I don't think dealing with them as actors was particularly useful because there was very little creativity left to put into it, you could only do grace notes, but handling Pat Phoenix – she was an adorable woman, but also she was tricky. Vi Carson was tricky – they all could be.

# Julie Jones
*Fan*                                       **STRONG WOMEN**

I've always watched *Coronation Street*. It was just totally part of my life. My mum reckons that the pilot episode was on while she was in labour with me. She remembers watching it and thinking it was great but being distracted by these labour pains!

It seemed to reflect the life that I lived – people like Ena Sharples, there *was* an Ena Sharples. Different accent, because it was Liverpool, but the same thing. I always found it very matriarchal, especially in its early days – strong, memorable women characters. That's, I suppose, how our family was – it was led by the women, the men were just something that tagged along and showed up, a necessary evil almost – so I always related to it.

I watched it with my mum and my nan. Of course, when you grow up, you start getting snotty about it because if your parents like it and your nan likes it, it's obviously crap, so why would I want to watch it? So, I went away from it for quite a few years in my teenage years. I suppose I came back to it in my mid twenties and then I got caught up in the stories, because it is always character-led. I find a lot of their characters really credible – they give them lots of layers. It's not just a two-dimensional soap character – I think a lot of the other soaps do that. I always find they're much warmer, they're icons aren't they? People like Elsie Tanner – the tart with the heart, brilliant. Who couldn't love her?

I think sometimes they've taken quite an old-fashioned male view in recent years in the storylines. Like when they had Sally have to go away to look after her mum and she was gone a couple of weeks and Kevin was having a fling with Natalie. All through that, it was almost like there was an undercurrent of, 'Well, what did you expect? You weren't servicing your husband and that's your job.' Now that made me really mad and I know that the rest of the women on the team really argued madly against that because it's such an old-fashioned view – 'If you're not attending in that department then obviously he's going to go off, what else can he do?' So I find it quite annoying when they do things like that.

I don't think there are any strong women now. I know that's what they're trying with Natalie. They've put her in the pub, behind the bar – they've always liked that strong woman in the focal point behind the bar – but she's not done it for me because, again, I've not believed what they've made her do. I just haven't believed it. I think she had the makings of it, but, in a way, I think they've sold her out, they've diluted her. There's Vera, but she's too much of a comedy character to carry any weight. Maybe they were trying it with Linda – that very manipulative, 'in control' woman, but the *way* she controlled is a very typically old-fashioned male view of women controlling.

Raquel was a lovely character because she came in as the traditional airhead – 'We're not going to expect much of her except stupid remarks that we can all laugh at' – but they gave her an emotional depth and a self-awareness. She knew that she could be stupid and that men in particular could take advantage of her and that made her all the more likeable and believable. She wasn't some hapless, witless woman. I thought they had some lovely scenes between her and Bet, because they're two of a kind, with Raquel being much softer.

If I did write for it, I'd want to see some more of these brilliant strong female characters, not just for their sake, but, for me, that's the truth and for a lot of people it's the truth – females getting on with it day to day. I think if you go too much for the big storyline, you can miss out on the day-to-day business of people getting on with their lives. That isn't boring to anyone. It's interesting to see other people making a cock-up of being a mum or make the wrong decision and have to pay for it – how are they going to get themselves out of it? To me, drama is going back towards that. I think we've done all the big, shouty storylines – murder and everything you can think of. I think it's more interesting to actually relate to somebody and watch them live their lives.

We went to see Tony Warren talking about *Coronation Street,* which was fab because his viewpoint was that he was brought up in a very female-oriented home and it was all that, women talking about women's stuff and him, being a child, could soak it all up and they wouldn't think he was listening. He's done it with an affectionate eye, not cynically, and I think that really showed in the early days.

## Gary Parkinson
*Fan*                                               **'WOMAN, STANLEY, WOMAN!'**

It's hard to say if the characters today are as memorable as the old ones. You mention *Coronation Street* and you immediately think of Ena Sharples, Elsie Tanner, Hilda Ogden. Some of them were caricatures and some of the best episodes came from Hilda, but it's not that long ago that we had Raquel, who was wonderful, and is one of those larger-than-life caricatures, and Bet. At the moment, there is perhaps Spider, who is a bit larger than life. They've tried it with the Battersbys, but that didn't work.

It's always been the women in *Coronation Street* that you remember – you never remember the men, they are always shifty and weak – but I can't think of any particularly strong characters at the moment. There's Natalie, but she's not got the gusto of a Bet Lynch. I suppose Rita is the queen of The Street at the moment, but, for me, she isn't – she's just someone in a terrible jumper with big hair. Rita symbolizes that sweet chocolate box image for me – she's got no bite, like the classic *Coronation Street* women. You notice all the classic *Coronation Street* women have red hair, except the women who run the pub – they have to be blonde.

Bet is my all-time favourite, but I also like Hilda. I was never keen on Ena or Elsie Tanner, but Stan and Hilda – that was classic comedy. I remember their second honeymoon and that line. Hilda is stood there in all her finery and putting her lipstick on. She's sipping a cocktail and she gets Stan to give her a kiss and he says, 'What does that taste of?' meaning the lipstick and she says, 'Woman, Stanley, woman!' The best line ever!

## Robert Khodadad
*Director*                                               **CROCODILE TEARS**

One thing as a director that's always amazed me – and I think I probably saw it on The Street more than anywhere else – is the ability of actresses, when the script calls for it, to cry and shed real tears. There were one or two actresses who were absolutely superb at it and one in particular was Julie Goodyear, who, if the script called for tears, she was able to produce these tears. I don't know how they do it, because I think crying is a natural reaction to a certain set of personal circumstances. It probably comes from the fact that, when some of the more professional actors or actresses are playing the parts, then they are actually living the part of that character. It did make me wary of trusting a woman's tears ever again! It was the ability to do it that was quite astonishing.

They couldn't do it take after take – generally you had to do it in the first take. As you got to know them, you got an idea that they were probably going to be able to do it and that the first take was probably going to be the one. Maybe you gave it a little bit more rehearsal, so that when you came to record it in the studio, it was spot on the first time. After a fairly emotional scene, you would shout 'Cut' and the place would just be completely silent and nobody would say anything. That's when you knew that a scene had worked very well.

## Geoff Lancashire
*Scriptwriter*                                    **RAQUEL AND IRMA**

She [Geoff's daughter, Sarah Lancashire] had been in The Street before Raquel – she played a girl called Wendy Farmer, a district nurse. It was only three episodes. Then Mervyn Watson said, 'If anything comes up, I'll get in touch.' Then the part of Raquel came up and he got in touch.

She did the little thing with the voice and I thought it sounded all right. So she went in. The Raquel character never came straight away, but, after a few weeks, it began to develop. I think the writers began to cotton on and picked up on it and what they could do with her. I think she was one of the few genuine characters in the show.

I loved Sandra Gough – she was a good character. She had a quick mind. She played Irma Ogden and married David Barlow, Ken's brother. I always liked her. I think some of the best stories I did were with her. She hadn't done much acting, but we took her on. I remember the way she used to say 'mortgage', smashing. She had a wicked sense of humour. I used to play her off against Kenneth.

# CHAPTER SEVEN

# A Street Far Away

In April 1966, Australia was honoured with a royal visit. Her Majesty the Queen Mother had arrived to tour the country. There was much pomp and circumstance, overly rich dinners, school visits and plaques unveiled. Yet it was a tour that was to pass almost without mention. That's because, at precisely the same time, another visit was taking place and this one was far more important to the people of Australia. Pat Phoenix, Doris Speed and her screen husband Arthur Leslie were also visiting Australia to meet their southern fans. In contrast to the Queen Mum's low-key trip, the *Coronation Street* stars were to be mobbed wherever they went. The press went wild, too.

'By now the word will have reached Buckingham Palace,' warned the *Melbourne Truth*, 'never send the Queen Mother to tour a country at the same time as stars from *Coronation Street*.' It also caused another newspaper to reflect that the older, more supposedly level-headed fans of *Coronation Street* would, in future, have no cause to criticize the antics of teenagers in welcoming their idols. For Beatle mania, read Street mania.

The *Coronation Street* tour was simply extraordinary. Norman Frisby – then Press Officer for Granada – made the trip with the three stars and watched, astonished, as they were mobbed and fêted wherever they went:

'If anybody had told me about this, I wouldn't have believed it, but, because I was there and saw it, I had to believe it. We did a visit to the Town Hall in Adelaide to meet the State Governor and they actually closed down the centre of Adelaide because people were ten deep on the pavement either side of the road. There were motor cycle outriders and police to keep people back and, when they actually got into the Town Hall, the massive gates had to be shut to stop people storming in.'

The *Adelaide News* reckoned that a crowd of more than 50,000 had lined the streets of their city as the party made the six-mile journey from the hotel back to the airport for the next leg of their trip. They also visited Sydney and Melbourne and, everywhere they went, the crowds flocked in their thousands to greet this other family.

Since the 1960s, the popularity of the show and the enthusiasm for its stars may have waned a little. Australia has, after all, matured in the past 30 years, with its population not quite as enthusiastic for all things British as it once was. Anyhow, Australia has its own soaps with its own glamorous stars these days. Yet the programme still goes on – no longer shown on any of the main channels, but still transmitting every week on one of the cable channels.

*Coronation Street* makes headlines wherever newspapers are printed. When Pat Phoenix announced that she was leaving the programme, the news was carried in papers from Rochdale to Miami and, today, hardly a day passes when the tabloids do not have something to say about the programme or its stars. *Coronation Street* is news. In New Zealand there is even a *Coronation Street* web page. Nor was it unusual for press enquiries to come from all four corners of the world, especially from the Commonwealth countries and, in particular, from Australia, New Zealand and Canada. Press clippings that Granada received from an international agency clearly showed that the programme was watched everywhere and made headlines, even in Japan. Such was the influence, and worldwide appeal, of the show. Could Tony Warren ever have dared to imagine that his six-part series about a street somewhere in Salford would find its way into homes across the world?

When the idea of *Coronation Street* was first mooted, Granada's Programme Committee had wondered if people in Norwich and London would be interested. Would they understand the Lancashire idioms, the strong accents, would they, in fact, be in the least bit interested in an alien landscape of back-to-back Victorian terraced houses, as far removed from their semi-detached houses with their cultivated lawns as Timbuktu? The answer turned out to be a surprising 'Yes', for the same reason that we would later be just as interested in *Peyton Place*, *Dallas* and *Neighbours*. It's not the landscape that is important, but the characters who inhabit that environment and we can – most of us, anyhow – find some affinity with the characters who make up *Coronation Street*.

The same question must have been asked a hundred times when it comes to wondering why anyone living thousands of miles away – often in a totally different climate, sometimes with a totally different language, let alone different idioms – should find anything remotely compelling about *Coronation Street*. Why should people on the other side of the world find it so compulsive? That's not an easy question to answer.

Over the years, *Coronation Street* has been sold to, and shown in, Australia, Belgium, Denmark, Eire, Finland, Gibraltar, Greece, Holland, New Zealand, Nigeria, Singapore, Sierra Leone, Sri Lanka, Sweden and Thailand, and no doubt a few other places never recorded in Granada's annals. Today, the programme sells best in New Zealand and Canada.

In the burning heat of Phoenix, Arizona, Jenny Lingo, once of Swindon, adjusts her satellite dish, pointing it towards Canada, then settles down, four days a week, to watch another episode in The Street. 'I still get homesick,' she admits, as she indulges in the realism of a street far away. 'The thing about *Coronation Street* is that it is not like the soaps over here, where all the women are dressed in their furs and don't seem to ever do any work.' Jenny is a podiatrist who takes care of the feet of Arizona's sports stars. The Phoenix Suns basketball team and the Rattlers football team are subjected to regular updates on the Battersbys or Mike Baldwin's love life as their feet come into Jenny's hands for careful inspection.

'The most important thing about the show is that it keeps home close and that is important when you are so far away,' argues Sandy Charbonneau, once of Fareham, but now living in the wilds of Nova Scotia. Nostalgia is a forceful and dynamic intuition. For half an hour a day, those exiled abroad can jet back over the airwaves to England and Manchester. They can remember what it used to be like, what their relations and friends back home are thinking and experiencing and, when they call them on the phone – or even contact them by e-mail these days – there is something to chat about.

'I have other friends who were born in England, who I have met over the years and this is a common bond with us,' claims Janet Smith, once of Davyhulme in Manchester, but now living in Kingston, Ontario. 'We love talking about the show and guessing what will happen next.' It's a bond, not just with the UK but also among those ex-pats living in a community thousands of miles away. It's a means of forging friendships, having something to talk about, something to share.

You can understand former UK residents in New Zealand, Australia and Canada still retaining an affection for a programme they began watching when they lived in Britain, but why should people native to Singapore, Sierra Leone or Phoenix, Arizona, bother with a programme that is as parochial and Mancunian as *Coronation Street*? There are plenty of people in these pages, though, without any British connection, who love The Street as much as the ex-pats. As New Zealander Diane Walker points out, there are few similarities: 'All our houses are completely detached and surrounded by a yard, which makes it more difficult to get to know our neighbours. Neither do we have a pub culture.'

However, the strength of The Street is not in its environment – important though that may be – but in its characters. Icons such as Ena, Elsie, Bet or even the Battersbys, are archetypal in many ways. They all produce strong responses of love or hate. Every community has an Ena or an Elsie. The comedy is crucial, too, even for those of a different culture where many of the idiosyncrasies of English humour are probably lost.

'I think the most important thing about a show like *Coronation Street* is the language – sayings, slang, local expressions and the like, familiar sayings, like "collywobbles" and "clever clogs". All those Lancashire sayings you don't hear in Canada, but which, nevertheless, you need to hear sometimes. It's these little things that keep home close and, of course, The Street itself; no matter where you are from in England, streets are all the same, so it's familiarity that you are looking for,' claims Sandy Charbonneau.

In Canada, there are what are colloquially known as 'pingfests'. 'A pingfest, or a ping, is a friendly get together for *Coronation Street* fans,' explains Ken Wong in Vancouver, 'usually at a restaurant, pub, boat or train for drinks, food, trivia quiz, photos, to show off of memorabilia, raffle, scavenger hunt, games, etcetera.' A pingfest is essentially an Internet invention, an actual gathering of fans that has resulted from people communicating on the Internet. Apparently, on one of the first Corrie Internet relay chat channels, users were buying cyber-pints to drink, but someone made a typing error. On the keyboard, the letter 't' is just above the 'g', turning 'pint' into 'ping'. The word stuck. A group decided to get together in August 1995, at the Duke of York in Toronto, to meet face to face and it was dubbed a 'pingfest'. Since then, there have been dozens of pingfests and the phrase has now spread from Canada across to New Zealand.

So, not only has the name *Coronation Street* been donated to the English language, but also the word 'pingfest'. If you have difficulty in understanding all that, don't worry – the chances are that Ena wouldn't understand either!

In 1980, there was a second trip made by the cast to the other side of the world – this time to Singapore. Pat Phoenix, Anne Kirkbride and Johnny Briggs, as well as Street Producer Bill Podmore, went this time. It was organized by the *TV Times* to celebrate the 2,000th episode of *Coronation Street*, providing a photo opportunity among the palm-fringed beaches of sunny Singapore. Would you believe, even in Singapore, The Street stars were mobbed. Ironically, The Street was transmitted in the wrong language, with Mandarin subtitles rather than the island's most common language, Tamil. Half the city couldn't understand, but, after huge protests, a solution was found. A kindly local radio station agreed to provide a simultaneous radio translation. It meant that viewers could turn down the sound on their television sets and switch up the sound on their radios.

A couple of years later, the cast was off again – guests of a Canadian company that wanted some of The Street's stars to open a new chain of English-style pubs in Toronto. This time it was the turn of Julie Goodyear, Chris Quinten and Johnny Briggs. The programme, by then, was screening on CBC and, in order to catch up, they were transmitting five episodes a week. 'By the time we arrived, the cast were almost national heroes,' claimed Bill Podmore in his autobiography. 'The welcome was unbelievable.'

Street Director Robert Khodadad remembers going on a shoot with the cast to Holland. When they were in Amsterdam, they needed a few extras to play bit parts, such as a taxi driver and a boat owner. They decided to audition and were astonished to discover that they had attracted a number of leading Dutch actors to the audition. They weren't interested in the money or the fact that the parts were minor – they simply wanted to be in *Coronation Street*. The Casting Director told Khodadad that, even though the programme had not been shown in Holland for ten years, it was still one of the most famous programmes to have ever been transmitted on Dutch television. 'I was gobsmacked, it was absolutely bizarre,' remembers Khodadad. 'Such is the power of *Coronation Street*.'

Fanaticism for The Street, particularly in New Zealand, continues to this day. Cast members still visit. Helen Worth, who plays Gail, was in New

Zealand only recently and New Zealand fan Cheryl Drinkwater also reports on the outrage among Street fans when Television New Zealand recently announced that it was going to cut The Street: 'This would have put us even further behind Britain – we are six months behind at the moment. There was a national roar of disapproval that was heard from one end of the country to the other. Someone soon started up a petition that grew to enormous lengths and the powers that be very quickly reconsidered.'

She also says that, last year, one episode was replaced by a party political broadcast just prior to the general election, which caused a national outcry: 'We were all sitting in our armchairs ready to watch Roy and Haley's wedding and they didn't play it! Imagine! Some folks just have no sense.' Quite so.

Back to that famous Australian tour party of 1966. As they arrived in Adelaide, Norman Frisby remembers looking out of the window as the aircraft taxied towards the terminal. There were huge crowds gathered on the balconies. He nudged Doris Speed, who was sitting next to him, and nodded towards the window. She stared out: 'Who are they waiting for, darling?' she asked naively. 'Doris,' replied Norman, 'they're waiting for *you*.'

# Leita Donn
*Press Officer*                              **FANS AROUND THE WORLD**

There was a couple who lived way out in New Zealand – they'd emigrated from England – and they discovered, to their great delight, that they could plug their portable television into the car and, while they were out, they could watch it on picnics.

There was a wonderful man and, every year, he used to lead a round-the-world tour of New Zealanders and it was called the *Coronation Street* tour and it was a busload of fans, some of them elderly. He wore khaki shorts and jacket and he just looked as though he was going to meet Livingstone at Victoria Falls. They went to Thailand, Tahiti, the most exotic places, but it was called the *Coronation Street* tour and this was the highlight of their visit. Every year I used to go and hostess them and take them down The Street and explain who lived here and so on and take photos of them outside the Rovers and they were a lovely group. There was one lady who'd taken ill, somewhere in France, and they wanted to rush to her to hospital, but there was no way she was going into hospital until she'd seen Violet Carson,

Ena Sharples, and she made it. He wrote to me a few weeks later that an elderly couple who'd met on the tour were getting married, so we sent a telegram from the cast to the wedding.

We got attention from all over the world – Canada, Australia, New Zealand. In fact, we had Granada International and all the features I wrote would be mailed out to them all over the world. When we wrote press releases, which went out to all the papers – all the nationals and the evenings and the Sundays – copies would go to Granada International and they would send them out all over the world. We had a foreign cuttings service and, one day, I got a lovely piece, all done in chrysanthemums, from a Japanese newspaper.

## Norman Frisby
*Granada Press Officer*　　　　**VISITORS FROM NEW ZEALAND**

We once had a letter from one of the New Zealand television stations saying that they had a tie-up with a travel agency and they were trying to put together something that they were calling the *Coronation Street* tour and it would be led by a television personality from New Zealand called Selwyn Toogood, who was a comedian-type person. He would bring these 30, 40, 50 people, whatever they were, and it would be a world tour and they would stop off in Hawaii, San Francisco and New York, then fly across to London, but the highlight of the thing would be their day at *Coronation Street* – they would come up and spend a day at Granada and have tea with the cast. They used to do it on a Thursday, which was convenient with the cast – they could break a bit early. The first time they came up, we decided we would push the boat out and we decorated the Grape Street set, as it was then, down at the bottom end. We did all kinds of back-breaking things. We had special picture postcards printed and rubber stamped 'Posted in Coronation Street', we had the letterbox put up in The Street so that they could write their postcards and post them. At three o'clock, a little mail van came down from Newton Street and collected the post and the postman was applauded as he emptied the box and took the postcards away and we photographed them. Then we took them across into Committee Room A and they had tea with the cast of *Coronation Street*. Then they used to have a dinner in the evening and I asked a few of them to go along to that at the Piccadilly Hotel. It was quite touching really. They were going on, then, to Rome and Athens and these people would write back to us afterwards and say, 'We had a wonderful time – the highlight was the afternoon we spent at *Coronation Street*.' They were mainly retired, elderly people, the backbone of your *Coronation Street* audience as it was then.

## Angela Larson
*Fan, Canada*                                                    **THE STREET AS THERAPY**

I was widowed at a very young age and had to return to the workforce to support my children after my husband became mentally ill and subsequently drowned. Without trying to make light of it or expand on the horrendous circumstances associated with his death, it was only through the repetition of ordinary daily activities that I was able to function at all in those dark days. *Coronation Street* was a lifeline for me then. I knew there would be at least 30 minutes when I could suspend the pain that was my life and focus, instead, on the activity on the street.

I cry with the anguish of the characters on screen and I laugh when they laugh and I applaud when they deserve recognition.

## Lin Cripps
*Fan, Canada*                                                    **IN TOUCH WITH MY ROOTS**

I moved to Canada in 1969. I don't really remember when Corrie came to Canada, but I have been watching it since about 1987/1988. I used to watch it when I was a young girl living in England.

I remember being very sad when Martha Longhurst died. I think a big part of the attraction of watching it was being able to see the inside of a pub! It was the first one I ever saw, it made me feel so grown up! Ironic really, because that's what I do for a living now, run a small pub in a hotel. Maybe that's why I liked Bet so much, maybe that's why I am so sarcastic sometimes at work – I had a good role model.

I really liked Elsie Tanner, too. She always looked so sophisticated, with her hair all done up, her plunging necklines and always a fag in her hand. She never took any guff from anybody either – a woman of the Nineties way back then. I wasn't so fond of her daughter Linda and her husband Ivan, though.

My daughter, Stacy, who is 27, and I tape an earlier version of Corrie (currently March, 1992) Monday through Friday. We also tape the current episodes, Monday through Thursday. When we get home from work, the first thing we do is rewind and watch and enjoy. Some of our associates think we're nuts! I feel closer to home through Corrie – it keeps me in touch with my roots. We both love it and hate to miss an episode. When we were visiting England last year, we had a friend come over and tape all the shows for us and we had a marathon when we came back from holidays.

Several of my customers at work who have to travel with their jobs ask me for updates because they'll miss the show when on the road. I am happy to oblige!

## Sandy Charbonneau
*Fan, Canada*                           **TRIGGERING MEMORIES**

I was born in Portsmouth in 1947 and lived in Fareham until I was 15. My family then moved to Australia and we stayed there until 1965. On my return to England, at the tender age of 18, I went to Europe and it was there that I met my future husband. He was in the Canadian Air Force.

There was no *Coronation Street* in my life until we were posted to Canada. I am now retired and live in Nova Scotia with my husband of 32 years and have 3 children, all married, and 4 wonderful grandchildren.

*Coronation Street* does not seem a million miles away. In fact, it's been on TV so long here that it is a natural part of life. The most important thing about the show is that it keeps home close and that is important when you are so far away. I have finally got my youngest daughter, Natalie, 25, to watch it on a regular basis and she really enjoys the show, especially now that she has been to England and experienced life over the pond. I don't have many British friends and only a few of my Canadian friends watch the show. I think it is very different for them as they don't have the roots to fall back on.

I will often see some little thing on the show that will trigger a memory, such as the corner store. I grew up with a corner store much like Rita's Kabin. Also, it is amazing how a character on the show will always remind you of someone you knew as a child. Another thing, my best friend lived across the road in the Chequers Inn and I have memories of the Snug in her dad's pub and peeping round the corner and watching the little old ladies drinking, just like Minnie, Ena, Martha, Albert Tatlock and the like.

I stay with this friend when I visit England – she still lives in Fareham. She doesn't have time to watch *Coronation Street*, which is a crying shame.

I also have another friend in Fareham who never misses the show and her and I have a good laugh at what's going on. Also, if I want to cheat, I can call her and find out what's going on three months ahead, but, most times, I don't want to spoil things, so I am patient and wait.

I think the most important thing about a show like *Coronation Street* is the language – sayings, slang, local expressions and the like, familiar sayings like 'collywobbles' and 'clever clogs'. All those Lancashire sayings you don't hear in Canada, but which, nevertheless, you need to hear sometimes. It's these little things that keep home close and, of course, The Street itself. No matter where you are from in England, streets are all the same, so it's familiarity that you are looking for. Fred Elliot is just like the butcher in Fareham. His name was Frank Buzzy – so loud!

Also, with modern life, we have lost the closeness that a small community brings – there are no more little butchers and grocers. I also remember my mother buying one – yes, one – egg for supper. Try getting a big grocery store to do that for you today. Knowing individuals by name – that's unheard of today; at least it is like that here. So, all the more reason to watch the show and hang on to every word.

I came to Canada as a new bride in 1967. I had left England in 1962. It was 1994 that I went home for the first time and a lot of people had said I would be very disappointed. Well, the little town of Fareham had changed some, but all the things of any importance to me were as if time had stood still – my old home, school, park, street, some stores and old school chums were all there.

The same goes for *Coronation Street*. On *Coronation Street*, things don't change as far as how they are living, it's just a new generation with more modern problems, things that would appeal to a younger audience. I suppose that the writers need to catch the interest of the next generation before us oldies die off! I think the show keeps up to date on most things, but I suppose that, if I had my choice, the good old days were a little funnier. You feel safe with familiar things, especially old familiar things.

I was 19 years old when I came to Canada and, although I was ready to embrace all that Canada had to offer, you still need a little connection to home. That's where *Coronation Street* came in. I still see Ken Barlow in my mind with his first wife, still remember the twins, and what about Florrie in the corner shop and Ena Sharples? All those laughs and tears. Then there was Annie Walker, with her touch of class, and Hilda Ogden, with her not-so touch of class, but, nevertheless, a jewel of a character. I think that, to some of us, when we suddenly get homesick, that maybe these people become real and, for a few minutes a week, you can be transported back home. It's great to get a little shot of the living room in the Rovers and see Jack and Annie's picture on the mantle, still there after all these years. And Elsie Tanner – don't we all know an Elsie Tanner, tough as nails, but, under-neath it all, as soft as butter. And Mavis – dear, aggravating Mavis. Well, just how often was she flummoxed? And Bet Lynch, all dolled up to the nines – what a tart?!

I watch it with my Canadian husband and he gets a laugh, although I do have to explain the sayings. The brick walls – I still miss the brick walls, strange isn't it? The show has changed a lot. I recognize that they have to keep up with the times, but I still think it has kept its charm and still brings home back to a lot of people abroad.

## Norman Frisby
*Granada Press Officer*                    **LANCASHIRE SAYINGS**

There were a lot of Canadian and Australian production people in those days and they were completely baffled by all these Lancashire expressions. That caught up with me later because, in 1971, we had somebody over from WNET in New York, the Channel 13 public broadcast station, to look at some of the things we were making. We tried to interest them in *Coronation Street* and Denis Forman [Granada executive] actually gave them the first 50 episodes. I think he gave them to them in the hope that they might be intrigued enough to actually buy and I was dispatched to the States to sell this programme to Manhattan.

One of the first things I had to do was to get out the first 50 scripts and quickly go through them and lift out all the Lancashire expressions, like 'By heck', and I remember there was a reference to 'panda cars' in one of them. I compiled a glossary of Lancashire expressions, a kind of dictionary of Lancashire phrases, which could be printed in their programme magazine called *13*. You had to watch *Coronation Street* with this little dictionary at your elbow so that you could understand when Len Fairclough said that he was 'going out for a fag', it didn't mean what the Americans thought it meant. It was not a huge success. I had a fortnight there and I stayed for its early transmission and the American press were very intrigued by it all. We got a few fan letters from the States, but they all had a common denominator: the father of the family had served in the US Air Force at Burtonwood, so he knew Manchester and he would watch it and say to the family, 'That's what I remember it was like'.

## Cheryl Drinkwater
*Fan, New Zealand*                     **ADDICTED TO THE STREET**

I'll admit it, I am addicted to *Coronation Street*. The Street has been part of my life for over 20 years now and the residents feel like an extended part of my family. Although two of my grandparents came from Britain, that doesn't have anything to do with my love of the show.

No, my addiction started because of a very fondly remembered acting teacher. Part of the assignments she set involved watching and observing the characterizations of the cast of *Coronation Street*. They were then, as they are now, superb. Of course, very soon, I felt as if I was getting to know the characters and wanting to see what happened to them. I was definitely hooked.

I have a real soft spot for my favourite, Ena Sharples. She was in full flight, along with Elsie Tanner, Annie Walker and Uncle Albert when I first started watching. Ena was lovely. A battle-axe with a big heart who had had a tough life. Not at all backward in saying her piece, but always ready to help – she really was a joy. It was because of characters like Ena and Elsie that I got hooked. I must say, I miss them. I know that the producers need to bring in new blood to keep The Street alive, and new storylines, but we seem to be losing so many of the old characters – the ones who've seen it all before and are not afraid to tell you so, characters with years of life's experiences behind the wrinkles and a twinkle in the eye that tells you that they are not washed up yet.

I remember when Elsie Tanner [Pat Phoenix] came to visit New Plymouth when I was living there. My, it was exciting. It was a lovely sunny day. The square in the middle of town was closed off and a stage put up in the centre. I, along with so many others, waited so eagerly to see her. It was like a royal visit and I remember thinking how glamorous and how much larger than life she was. I don't remember why she was there, but do I remember the thrill from seeing her.

More recently, Television New Zealand proposed to cut the amount of time we spent viewing *Coronation Street*. This would have put us even further behind Britain – we are six months behind at the moment. There was a national roar of disapproval that was heard from one end of the country to the other. Someone soon started up a petition that grew to enormous lengths and the powers that be very quickly reconsidered. Just last year, one episode was replaced by a party political broadcast just prior to the elections and that caused a rumpus. We were all sitting in our armchairs, ready to watch Roy and Haley's wedding and they didn't play it! Imagine! Some folks just have no sense.

It's played here on Monday and Thursday nights. Morning tea and often lunch conversations at work on Tuesday and Friday are all about last night's events – 'What did you think of Kevin talking to Alison like that?' and 'Oh, that Sharon annoys me' and so on. Great bonding stuff. When I phone my parents, who live four hours' drive away, I know they have been watching and the same conversations take place. The man in my life maintains it's just another TV programme, but if he happens to miss it, he insists on a rundown of what happened.

I wouldn't say I am obsessed, even though I have watched this programme faithfully for the last 20 years. I wouldn't put other parts of my life on hold for The Street. Thank God for video recorders or I might.

About a year ago, I discovered an on-line Internet community who have a love for *Coronation Street* as their bond. I joined up and have had some wonderful moments – happy and sad – with great people who I probably will never meet in person, but whom I feel I know in some way. We meet through e-mail every day and share our lives as well as the lives of the folks on The Street. If it wasn't for *Coronation Street*, I would be missing out on all this good company and witty repartee.

The Street is real. The uniqueness of The Street is that it deals with the little everyday incidents in life – the funny times and the sad ones. It doesn't have to go for the big, gritty storylines, some of which I believe detract from the appeal of 'Our Coro'. Who can forget scenes like the look on Jack's face when Tyrone presents him with one of his favourite pigeons, stuffed, Fred and Audrey running round the countryside with Sid peacefully dead in the back of the car, the waiting to see if Danny and Sally are going to get together?

It's the people in the show we love. The characters are real. There have been one or two who didn't quite make it over the years, but they are quickly forgotten or sent to Canada. When I start to think about the characters I loved, the list can just keep growing: Elsie, Ena, Annie, Hilda and Stan were special, as was Eddie Yeats, Charlie Whelan – mmm … always remembered. Bet was, well, just Bet – unforgettable. So many gone, but not forgotten – Raquel, Des, Percy Sugden and his memories.

I cried when Des died and I cried at Roy and Haley's wedding. I would really miss them all if The Street disappeared tomorrow. I hope it goes on forever or at least as long as I do. I want to be able to sit in my rocking chair when I'm 80 and watch my Corrie.

# Jan Bowditch
*Fan, Australia*                                    **WATCHING IN WOLLONGONG**

I started watching *Coronation Street* when I was at home with a young baby, so it must have been in 1963/64, as she is now 36. From memory, it was broadcast daily in the late morning or afternoon and, as I like all things British – I had grandparents from Lancashire and Yorkshire – I was immediately hooked and involved with the Barlows (David included), Hewitts, Tanners, Walkers, plus Ena and Minnie and the third one, Martha, not to mention Florrie Lindley in the shop. It had started in the UK some three years prior to Australia.

After some time, it was discontinued on Sydney television, but resurfaced on a different commercial channel some years later, and in both Newcastle and Wollongong, the state of New South Wales' second- and third-biggest cities. It died in Sydney again, but continued in the country areas. In 1980, we went to live in an area served by Wollongong television and, as I was not working at that time, I was able to watch daily at 11am and catch up with all the people I remembered and acquaint myself with new characters. Even if we were out in the car, as WIN 4 Television Station shared an FM frequency with the radio, we could pull off the road and listen to the programme, even if we couldn't see it, and I remember doing this often between 1980 and 1983.

In 1983, we moved to the Blue Mountains, west of Sydney, and, due to good reception and a tall antenna, we were still able to receive television from Wollongong, so continued to watch until they unceremoniously stopped broadcasting the programme. Despite phone calls and letters, it seems to have permanently disappeared from the free-to-air television screens of Australia, although early episodes are appearing on Pay TV, which we don't have.

I have been able to see it a few times on trips to New Zealand in the late Eighties and Nineties, and have also been to England in 1990, 1992, 1995, 1996, 1997 and 1999, so have been able to catch up a little, although, with such radical changes to the character list, this becomes harder and harder. I must say, it has become more difficult to follow recently with all the new characters they have introduced. I am very pleased to get the weekly updates from Sunderland because the Granada official web site has changed and I find it very difficult to access, whereas you could click on recent goings on before and print out the previous week's show synopses. I just can't get into it at all now.

It has always seemed odd to me that British serials do not succeed here, although they do well in Canada and New Zealand. *Eastenders* lasted here about a year on the ABC and *Brookside* suffered a similar fate on SBS (Special Broadcasting Service), which shows ethnic programmes, slightly offbeat things, Channel 4 sort of thing. *The Bill* continues to be one of the top-rating programmes here and British drama and comedy are well received, particularly on the ABC – *Cold Feet* and *Playing the Field* are on at the moment on commercial channels and people are watching, despite the fact that they are made in the North.

## Sandra Gough
*Actress, played Irma Barlow* **DOUBLE GOUGH**

I went to Australia by myself and Gough Whitlam was Prime Minister at the time and, in the papers, they said, 'We've got one Gough in the country and now we've got another one and she's great, she's a breath of fresh air.'

## Jennifer Lingo
*Fan, Arizona* **THE HIGHLIGHT OF MY LIFE**

I come originally from Swindon in Wiltshire, but have lived in Phoenix, Arizona, for years. I have been working as a podiatrist for 20 years, taking care of the sports stars' feet. I look after the Phoenix Suns basketball team, the Rattlers football team and the Coyotes ice hockey side.

I started watching Corrie back in the Eighties. I get it on a satellite station, which brings it here from Canada. I only get it four days a week, but I wish it was on every single day, as it is the highlight of my life. That doesn't say much for my exciting life, does it?! Sometimes, the electricity goes off or the satellite moves a little and I go 'nuts' until I have it back on the television.

I really love the series and hope it will go on forever. I tape it every day and then pass it on to my sister and her husband, who is a minister, and he loves it almost as much as I do. I also pass it on to some of my co-workers, who really get a kick out of it as it is so realistic, not like the soaps over here where all the women are dressed in their furs and don't seem to ever do any work. My grandson, who is in his twenties, tries to watch it whenever possible and you should hear him mimic the accent – he's quite good. He mimics me as well. I even call my cousins every weekend to get an update – I know that's cheating, but then I know what I have to look forward to! It really is the highlight of my every day.

As for memorable stories, well, there are so many, I wouldn't know where to start. However, I do recall Rita and that rotter, Len Fairclough, and then there was Deirdre in jail. I wore my T-shirt to work when Deirdre was in jail, but, of course, I had to explain to all my co-workers and patients what it was all about.

I cried for 30 minutes when Judy Mallett died. I loved so many of the characters, especially Vera and Jack, Curly, Mavis, Alma and a host of others. I did not care too much for Fiona – I like Maxine a lot better – but wish that wimp of a husband would get some 'get up and go'.

I have always thought Mike Baldwin was a rotter. Sharon was an airhead, Gail needs a little romance in her life and they need to get Fred another woman. I also liked Percy, the nosy neighbour – I have one just like him, but he's a dear! I did like Mavis and Derek so much – she was like my Auntie Evelyn, so I could relate to her quite easily.

Yes, Corrie seems just like I am at home. Even though I get home quite often, I do still get homesick. The Rovers Return could be in my home town – it is the centre of attraction – although I never could go into a pub, as I left England before I became of drinking age, but my dad was a member of a working men's club and I did go with him sometimes for a packet of crisps – my big night out on a Saturday!

# Andrea Morgan
*Fan, New Zealand*                                    **LIKING AND LOATHING**

I was born in Otorohanga, New Zealand, in 1963. I live on my parents' dairy farm. My sister and brother-in-law do too. We've all come back to the family. It's a bit like *The Waltons*. My 82-year-old great aunt is here, too, and we all watch *Coronation Street* together. My parents bought their first TV when I was born. It was a major decision as they had to put it on hire purchase. I started watching *Coronation Street* when I was about 11.

The men say they are not interested, but always know what's going on! The consensus here is that Ena Sharples made *Coronation Street* in the early days.

Characters that gave me the heebeejeebees were Alan Bradley and Don Brennan. Don especially – he was really quite freaky and showed pretty good acting as it seemed quite real his madness. I loathed Reg – quite revolting little man, I could never see why people liked him.

When Bet Lynch left the show, I did not watch for quite some time. I really did think that Granada made a stupid mistake letting her go and still do. Also, I do think that they made a mistake putting Jack and Vera in the Rovers and the Alec Gilroy story of takeover was pathetic – a stupid storyline.

I am amazed at all the marriage break-ups and affairs that have happened recently – totally unnecessary. Even though it has not screened here yet, I already know that, for the umpteenth time, Martin and Gail will go through another affair. We've been down this road before with Martin – it's old hat and boring.

I loved the Natalie–Kevin–Sally saga. Probably because it was quite well acted and some of the things Sally got up to, like turning the bath water on, etcetera, is quite real. I do, however, still have a concern over Natalie's cat – was it ever found? That reminds me, where are all the pets in *Coronation Street*. Surely you Brits have pets.

Hilda Ogden, Stan and Eddie Yates were a favourite bunch. Her singing was classic. Eddie was a great loss as well. In those days, the storylines were good. Great wit. Just a look said many a word. They don't do that any more.

One area that The Street could do with is a nice young couple starting out in life with a couple of kids and, for the next 20 years of the show, have them living happily ever after. Their storylines won't be boring if they just have them going through a normal life. Not everyone has affairs and break-ups by running off with their best mates, or whatever!

I loved Elsie Tanner and Ena Sharples having a go at one another. My mother used to tell me that Elsie was a 'loose woman'.

Other episodes I remember vividly are when Ken's first wife got killed. My favourite characters are Bet Lynch, Rita, Elsie and Hilda. I also loved Eddie Yates. I loathe Ken Barlow, Sally Webster, Reg Holdsworth, Fred Elliot, and despise Audrey. I can't stand her, in fact, but that's the character so she must be doing her bit well.

At the moment, I loathe the storylines – everyone has to have a gory past and that's just not right. Also, just about everyone's marriage has split up except Jack and Vera, or had an affair, which brasses me off.

## Patricia Parsons
*Fan, Canada*                                    **A GREAT PICK-ME-UP!**

There are many *Coronation Street* fans here in Gander in Newfoundland. It was the single reason why many of us working mums were motivated to learn how to programme our VCRs – we couldn't even wait for the repeat on Sunday mornings, we have to see it every day! We discuss it at length on coffee break – going over every funny line, speculating on how the storyline will evolve.

The show is a great pick-me-up – no matter how serious any subject matter is in an episode, you're guaranteed a laugh somewhere in the 25 minutes! We love to follow up reading stories of the actors and actresses, which one often sees in *Hello* magazine.

My very first memories of *Coronation Street* go back to my childhood. My dad, who was from Londonderry, in Northern Ireland, always watched it on CBC. There had to be complete silence when he was viewing it, and Mum would gather us all up, out in our small kitchen, saying, 'Sshh! Not a peep, your father's watching his story.' Meanwhile, the rich assortments of accents pouring into our living room were as foreign to us as Chinese or Japanese. I couldn't figure out for the life of me why he would want to watch something I thought he couldn't understand! Little did I know, 30 years later, I'd be in a similar trance in front of the TV, demanding the same silence from my family, not wanting to miss one single syllable.

The characters in the show are very much like Newfoundlanders – great sense of humour, taking each day as it comes and enjoying a beer while dealing with any joy or tragedy. I feel like I know these people so well that, if I bumped into any of them on the street, I could chat with them like they were my next door neighbour. Congratulations on 40 years of a great series! I look forward to a few more years of watching the show myself!

## Jill Kennedy
*Fan, New Zealand*                                    **A WORLDWIDE FAMILY**

We had one of the first televisions in Dunedin because my father loved anything new. I vividly remember watching *Coronation Street* in my early twenties. I'm now 57 years old, so that's a good portion of my life. TV was such a novelty then that we didn't watch it casually like we do now. Instead, visitors used to come and watch it with you. We would sit glued to it for hours, having tea and coffee and snacks. *Coro Street* soon became a big draw card, even though we found it very foreign and strange at first – the grimness and blackness of the North of England, the terrace-joined houses and the accents almost making it like another language to us Kiwis. Being a teetotal family, it was amazing how quickly we adapted to visiting a local pub so often.

I don't think I really liked Ena Sharples that much, but Minnie Caldwell looked a lot like one of my favourite aunties. Doris Speed as Annie Walker was a great favourite and, strangely enough, was very similar in appearance to my mother, who watches it still at 90 years. We used to be kind of shocked by Elsie Tanner [Pat Phoenix], we thought of her as a kind of Jezebel. To this very day I'm always staggered by the attractive women I've seen coming out of such old, rather humble houses in UK. I've noticed how *Coro Street* women to this day still copy Elsie – the way they do their make-up at the kitchen table and carry on conversation. Quite different to the USA, Aussie or New Zealand.

I've always liked Ken Barlow [Bill Roache] and it's been great to see his son acting so well, too. William Roache still looks handsome and wonderful for his age, and it used to puzzle me how he would be so more upper-class and educated than the rest of them, yet they all come from the same roots.

Gradually we came to know the language of The Street, though, and love the grimness and I can remember resisting very strongly when the others were thrilled about colour TV coming in. Now, of course, I wonder how I could have been so slow to change.

For some years – with marrying in my early twenties and moving to the UK with a new husband and then back again – my viewing became interrupted, and then a young family to take all the attention, but I never really lost touch with *Coro Street* and could always link up again if I missed a few episodes.

We recall the death of Jack Walker, Martha Longhurst passing away in the Snug, the horrible death of Valerie Barlow – now amusing us in *Dinnerladies* – and a lot of laughs with Rita and Mavis. We all miss Mavis and Derek – we didn't want them to go – and good to see her in comedy as well. The acting of Rita was wonderful when Alan Bradley was after her in Blackpool and also when she became poisoned by fumes. We miss Alec, too – a funny man and you could always see his mind working and scheming.

I'm jolly glad they've got Natalie in the pub now – she is very sexy, great arms – and they needed a successor to the powerful, sexy Bet Lynch. How many times did I think of her when I saw outrageous earrings on travel to the Far East on the ship? I wanted to send her some, but felt shy – perhaps I should send some to dear Vera, who needs cheering up at the moment with despicable Terry on the run. My husband loves Jack and Vera, some of the terms Jack calls her will never be forgotten – I think Jack and Vera are a bit like us two really.

It is great we don't miss our fixes of The Street away on our ship. My husband is a UK-born Captain from the North and always has some British pals there as well. A pal in Auckland keeps us going with Kiwi episodes. We call it the *Coro Street* Club.

We never thought we would want the old characters to leave, but we have made new friends with the later ones. Brilliant acting from Sally, Kevin, Deirdre and her dreadful lover John. Manchester Airport Tie Shop will never be quite the same now. We all think Fred and Ashley marvellous characters. In fact, our Auckland pal sends us messages calling himself Fred, to me, Mavis, and my husband, Mike – a bit of a mix-up there, but my husband likes the keen mind of Mike's persona while Mavis and I have similiar features, I believe.

None of us wanted Des, the bookie, to die and we still miss him. It was the same when Raquel left Curly. We are looking forward to when she returns with a Curly offspring, soon, to our screens. We loved the wicked ways of Greg, if you can love badness, and his father Les will always be a favourite, a loveable rascal. Just recently, we suffered all through Gary's grief when Judy died and will never forget those poignant words of his echoing out, about always cherishing the one you love, with the still portrait of Ashley's and Maxine's wedding group.

In New Zealand, *Coro Street* is on, at present, twice a week on TV 1 for one hour at 7.30 on Mondays and Thursdays and sometimes on Fridays for half an hour catch-up. There was a dreadful fuss some years ago when an Aussie management figure tried to cut our episodes down – in Aussie, it is only seen on one kind of special channel, I think. A man who got up a petition here, with great support, eventually took it to the UK and met the stars at The Street.

It is amazing how many young members of families watch it now and love it, too. When our youngest girl arrived after a long and exhausting journey from New Zealand to Manchester, a few years ago, she had to fill in time before her hotel room was ready. Into a nearby mall she went and came upon Helen Worth [Gail], who was at a display. Feeling quite unreal, she conquered her shyness for Mum and Dad's sake and went to speak to her. A delightful meeting it was – she was made to feel so at ease and a lovely photo resulted.

That is the power of *Coro Street* realism and, though such streets may not exist now, it makes us into a worldwide family – all with the same interests at heart.

## Greg Wadden
*Fan, Canada*                                          **ON THE INTERNET**

I was born in Canada and almost started watching by accident. When I was a kid at our cottage up north, I remember seeing *Coronation Street* listed in the TV guide every Sunday morning on the CBC and, since we only got one channel up there, it was a choice of either watching it or playing outside. For some reason, I had it in my head that it was a religious show, so I always went out to play.

When I was about 17 – this would have been about 1979 – I happened to be home sick from school and there it was on TV one afternoon. I watched one episode and I thought it was wonderful, funny, dramatic and down to earth and I've watched it ever since. It's very hard for me to believe that I've been watching The Street for over half of its run on TV, but I guess I have.

I think it was about 1985 that I got connected to the Internet. I had no idea what to look for. The first thing I did was to search for *Coronation*

*Street* things. I figured, well, at least I know about that! I've been a part of the on-line *Coronation Street* community ever since. In 1996, I started a Corrie chat room that's been a wonderful part of my life. In the beginning, I would have to park myself there in hope that someone would happen upon it. Gradually, people started to find it and it became busier and busier. Now it's filled with people almost 24 hours a day and you'd be surprised at how friendly and warm a place it is. It turns out that *Coronation Street* fans are the best.

*Coronation Street* is broadcast here on the government-owned Canadian Broadcasting Corporation and has a very loyal following. I wouldn't say it's part of the average Canadian's life by any means – in fact, most people around here wouldn't know much about it, but you'd be surprised. I worked in an office about 10 years ago with a group of about 30 men, mostly in their thirties, none of them from Britain. About five years after I left there, I recognized two of them at a *Coronation Street* Internet fan gathering (pingfest) and we got to talking. It turns out that a dozen of them were Corrie addicts and spent a good part of the day talking over what had happened in the show the day before and I had known nothing about it!

Just last year, in another office, a woman working near me happened to say, 'I have to hurry home today, I can't miss *Coronation Street*.' The guy beside me asked her excitedly, 'Do you watch that? Did you see yester-day's?' She said, 'No, why, what happened?' He told her, 'Judy collapsed, I think she's going to die.' She let out a loud gasp from deep within her and clutched her heart. I thought she was going to collapse.

Again, another four or five people joined in the conversation, people I hadn't known to be fans, people who hadn't known each other to be fans.

So, although it is popular, it tends to be a solitary pleasure, which is why Canadians are so much a part of the *Coronation Street* Internet audience. If you live in Britain, you can talk about it with almost anyone. Here, it's a rare thing to find a fellow fan.

I just love *Coronation Street*. My all-time favourite characters are Hilda and Eddie, Jack, Raquel, Tyrone, and a few obscure ones – Debbie Webster, Billy Williams, and probably my all-time favourite, Becky Palmer.

I really don't remember Debbie that well, but I do remember that I had a huge crush on her. I couldn't believe it when she left with Bill and Kevin stayed. I still think it would be a brilliant idea to bring her back one day.

I know a lot of people were put off by Becky at first, but I found her hilarious right from the first episode she appeared in. 'I don't mind' – she must have said that 30 times before she ended up telling her mother that Des was a plonker.

One of my favourite scenes was Billy Williams tending the bar in the Rovers. Every time someone told him, 'Have one for yourself', he would reply, 'I'll just have the 'alf', and then actually have it. He ended up drunk, and happy, and singing at the piano. I'm not sure, is it a coincidence or not, that the Mallet children are called Becky and Billy?

Of course, Hilda was a classic – I absolutely loved her. Jack is just lovely, and Tyrone is perfect as his protégé, and I find myself admiring Betty's work more and more. To me, she keeps everyone in their place and gives the show a link to the past.

*Coronation Street* is the only show I watch every week, and I can't wait to see how it goes on in the next 40 years.

# Diane Walker
*Fan, New Zealand*                    **PART OF THE STREET FAMILY**

I first started watching *Coronation Street* in the Sixties in the days of Ena Sharples, Annie Walker and all the old actors. I was a child then and New Zealand only had one channel, so the whole family used to watch it. I caught on almost by default and also enjoyed it, although, at that time, I didn't always understand all the storylines. We all used to gather around the black-and-white set and I remember, when colour television came in, in 1973, and we were all excited about seeing what colour Hilda Ogden's pinnie was!

My favourite scene was when Hilda Ogden left and she sang a song in the Rovers. She always did have a dreadful singing voice, but this scene was quite touching. Hilda, however, was not my most favourite character. Like so many others, initially, it was Ena Sharples and now it has to be Natalie Barnes, as she's such a strong character who also has a sensible streak, but still makes mistakes. She seems to have brought a lot of colour and life to The Street and I was delighted when she ended up with the Rovers Return as she is tailor-made for this role. Natalie is a likeable character and I can't understand why so many people tend to dislike her.

My least favourite character is absolutely Sally Webster! Her double standards and manipulation really grate on me and I find her extremely irritating. Most people seem to think of her as sweet, but I see her as a spoiled brat who always demands her own way and her treatment of Kevin when she was doing exactly the same thing as him, with a lot more people, turned me right off her. I'd like to see the girls go to Kevin, as he is by far the more stable parent.

In New Zealand, The Street is on Channel 1 for an hour and, at the moment, it's shown on our screens twice a week, although, from time to time, we have what is known as '*Coronation Street* Catch-ups', where it will screen for a half hour for an extra night, just so we don't lapse too far behind Britain. I watch it on my own and try very hard not to miss an episode and, although my husband says he is not a follower of it, I find it interesting that he always seems to know exactly what is happening and who every character is – I'm sure he's a closet Street fan! I also follow it on the Internet as I like to know what's happening in the future.

For an extremely long time, I was of the impression that *Coronation Street* was a very typical portrayal of British life and that this was how all the English people lived and was quite surprised to find that this was not so when I travelled to Britain for a year. It didn't stop my enjoyment of it at all, but perhaps my next visit should be to Manchester, so I can see how true to life the show actually is. It is certainly different to New Zealand life, where nearly all our houses are completely detached and surrounded by a yard, which makes it more difficult to get to know our neighbours. Neither do we have a 'pub culture', such as the Rovers Return Inn, which is a pity.

The storylines have changed a great deal over the years and are now more realistic. Certainly, many controversial issues are now addressed and, in this day and age, this is a good thing. I don't like it, though, when the writers go through a 'killing off' stage and I get annoyed when the characters are killed off instead of just having them leave The Street – particularly when three or four of them are killed off in succession. This is a bit too over the top in my opinion! It would be nice if some of the characters from the past could revisit The Street from time to time, because this does happen in real life and would give it an added dimension.

Having grown up with *Coronation Street*, I almost feel part of the 'Street family' and I do hope that it will continue to screen for many more years to come. It's nice to see that the New Zealand following has not been ignored and, of late, we have had quite a few of The Street actors visit New Zealand.

We have quite a cult following down here and the actors have almost been treated like royalty!

## Norman Frisby
*Granada Press Officer*                    **THE 1966 TRIP TO AUSTRALIA**

On the trip to Australia, I went out a week before to get things sorted out, like where the toilets were when they went on PAs [personal appearances], all those essential things that you had to do, and check the timetable and the rest of the arrangements. We started in Sydney. I learnt a lot on that.

I remember I had to meet Doris Speed and Arthur Leslie when they flew from Sydney to Melbourne – I'd gone a couple of days before. I had to go out to the airport and meet them and explain to them in the car, between the airport and the television station, how they had to play this game that they were going to be in. It was quite a complicated contestant game and they were the star performers. I was rehearsing them in the car all the way down to the station. Harry Kershaw had done a little sketch for them to do on these occasions. They did a lot of PAs – opening shops, motor showrooms. They got a huge reception – quite frightening on some occasions – I couldn't believe it.

We were quite used to crowds turning out at bingo halls in Salford and so on when Elsie Tanner [Pat Phoenix] went to a personal appearance, but, to go to Australia … I used to say afterwards, 'If anybody had told me about this, I wouldn't have believed it, but, because I was there and saw it, I had to believe it.' We did a visit to the Town Hall in Adelaide to meet the State Governor and they actually closed down the centre of Adelaide because people were ten-deep on the pavement either side of the road. There were motor cycle outriders and police to keep people back and, when they actually got into the Town Hall, the massive gates had to be shut to stop people virtually storming in. I had had to go and get some more film for my camera and, when I got back, I couldn't get in because the gates were closed. I missed the reception by the State Governor of South Australia. Wherever we went, there were hundreds and hundreds of people.

We went to a place called Elizabeth, which is a suburb of Adelaide, which is mainly English immigrants, and it was to do a PA at a supermarket. We went up on the roof because there were so many people. People couldn't get into the shop, they were just on the lawns outside, thousands and thousands of them.

When we left on the Sunday night from Adelaide at about six in the evening to drive to the airport, the entire route was lined by people, five or six miles, kids in pyjamas. People had driven hundreds of miles to bring their kids to watch this procession, this open car with Elsie Tanner and Jack Walker and Annie Walker making its way to the airport. I, personally, was so concerned – I thought we were going to miss the plane because we had to drive so slowly because of the people. It was really totally extraordinary. They actually held the plane up and let us drive on to the tarmac and we got straight out of the cars and on to the plane.

I remember landing at Adelaide and, as we taxied along in front of the airport building, it was absolutely covered with people who were standing on balconies and on the canopy over the doors and on the roof and so on and Doris Speed looked out of the window and said, 'Who are they waiting for, darling?' I said, 'Doris, they're waiting for *you*.' The cast couldn't believe it either.

## Robert Khodadad
*Director*                                        **GOING DUTCH**

Another memorable time on The Street was when I went to Amsterdam with Hayley and Roy – 1997 or 1998. It was a storyline that required Roy to go and search out Hayley because Hayley had gone to Amsterdam for her operation as a transsexual. I went out there beforehand, because we were going to use one or two Dutch actors and actresses and we ran some auditions in Holland. We got some of the best actors and actresses from Holland. We were offering them very small parts – the part of a taxi driver and a boat owner. The Casting Director, who was from Holland, said, '*Coronation Street* has not been shown in Amsterdam for over ten years. It used to be shown there in black and white, but, even to this day, ten years on, it is still one of the most famous shows in Holland and that's why these actors are happy to come and audition. Even though it's a small part, they'd like to be associated with it.'

When the actors came in, one of them said, 'Yes, I used to watch *Coronation Street* in black and white. Is it still in black and white?'

As each actor or actress came in to audition, we videoed them. This one girl was 22 years old, she was Dutch and she was operating the videocamera for us. I asked her if she'd ever heard of *Coronation Street*: 'Have I ever heard of *Coronation Street*?' she said. 'I've never seen it, but I know it. My mother used to call me Ena Sharples because, as a little kid, I used to run round with curlers in my hair, and that is what my mother still calls me today.' I was gobsmacked; it was absolutely bizarre. Such is the power of *Coronation Street*.

When we came to film the scenes in Amsterdam – we're used to it in the UK, when people come up – even in Amsterdam, the Dutch people, when they heard it was *Coronation Street*, they were quite enthralled and they would stand and watch and try to get autographs.

## Angela Larson
*Fan, Canada*                                        **A GENERATION OF FANS**

I've been watching *Coronation Street* for a very long time. I remember watching the first ever episode in my grandmother's kitchen/front room in Glasgow on ITV.

From the start, I was interested. At that time, I was a teenager and totally into the world of mods and rockers and the great groups that were around at that time. Despite my preoccupation with boys and music and all the trappings of youth, I still watched *Coronation Street*. After that first exposure, I became a loyal viewer – as were a lot of my friends. We didn't talk much about our delight in the programme because we had other lofty matters to discuss. However, whenever there was a big fight or a sad or extremely humorous event, then you can bet that we talked about it. Somehow, it was OK to talk about the notable events on The Street, while we never exchanged views about the day-to-day ones.

I emigrated to Canada with my family when I was 18 years old and started a new life here. I was thrilled when the CBC here in Victoria began to air *Coronation Street*. It aired in the afternoon at three o'clock two days a week and I watched faithfully when I was at home raising my children. It connected me with my past and, I had left so many of my extended family members behind, I felt an affinity with my far-off loved ones when I could watch The Street and know that we could still share in the lives of the people of Weatherfield.

My children grew up knowing who the characters were on The Street and, at any opportunity after I returned to the workforce, I would try to catch episodes of my favourite programme if I was at home sick or on holidays.

Then the VCR was invented and I was in hog heaven. I set my timer to tape the show every day and eagerly came home from work on the days that *Coronation Street* was on. My children knew that if anything was going to ruin my day, it would be if the VCR didn't operate properly and I would miss an episode. I wasn't actually missing the episode as it aired in an omnibus fashion on Sunday mornings, but I never wanted to wait until Sunday to see my show. I know that, over the years, there were countless tears and mindless rants when I came home from work to find that 'somebody' had messed with the TV set and I didn't have my *Coronation Street* to watch.

Now I am a grandmother and my grandchildren are as familiar with the characters as my children were. Everywhere I go, I can find *Coronation Street* fans. I belong to a *Coronation Street* mailing list, where we discuss episodes, storylines, character development, etcetera, etcetera. Sometimes we get together in person to talk about the show and meet one another for the first time – we come from all across North America, as well as other countries and the UK. Invariably, somebody who's in the pub or restaurant will hear us talking and come over to share their own favourite *Coronation Street* memory.

I hope *Coronation Street* continues for another 40 years and, I can honestly say, that it gives me great pleasure to be a loyal watcher and I find it to be different from any of the other soap operas that abound.

## Anne Flack
*Fan, Turkey*                    **TURKISH DELIGHT**

I'm a 39-year-old British woman who has been living on the south coast of Turkey for the past six years. I've been a fan of the programme since about 1981. I've never really been a TV fan at all, but *Coronation Street* was the one programme I used to watch in the UK. I loved the mixture of drama and humour.

My favourite episode from the Eighties was in May 1983, when Fred Gee was chasing after Bet Lynch and persuaded her to go for a drive with him in, I think, Mrs Walker's Rover. Bet, of course, knew that he had in mind more than just a drive in the car, so she took Betty along as a chaperone.

Fred parked the car by the riverbank and got out, but hadn't put the handbrake on properly and the car – plus occupants – rolled into the river.

Fred waded in to rescue Bet, then put her down on the riverbank and went back for Betty. There was a priceless bit at the end where Bet berated him for his stupidity and, best of all, for putting her down 'right in the middle of a great big cow plop'!

The first two years I was here, I was working in a hotel frequented by British guests, so my first question to new arrivals was, 'What's been happening in Coro?' and, thus, I managed to keep up to date. In 1997, I worked for a British tour operator, so, again, was able to grill the guests to find out the current storylines.

In February 1998, my daughter was born, in the UK, and I was able to actually watch *Coronation Street* myself for a few weeks. I decided to invest in a video recorder, which some friends brought out to me in May that year – they're really expensive here in Turkey – together with ... roll on the drums here ... videos of all the programmes from the time I returned to Turkey in mid March. These friends continue to record and send out to me every episode of Coro, plus any extras like 'Our Vera' and 'After Hours'. They've even started sending some chocolates out with the videos as the adverts at the beginning of each episode get my mouth watering.

My Turkish neighbours find it amusing when these packages arrive every six weeks or so. I've tried to interest some of them in the programme, but none of them speak much English and those who do are baffled by the accent! Madeleine, my daughter, having grown up with the regular videos, does a wonderful rendition of the theme tune, which is reminiscent of Hilda's singing in the Eighties as she cleaned the bar at the Rovers.

It's amazing to think that The Street is almost 40 years old – in fact, it's seven weeks younger than me – and that Ken was a student in the first episode and is now receiving his pension. I wonder if we'll see Toyah receive hers in or around the year 2040?

## Sue Siddeley
*Fan, Chile*                                              **A CHANGE OF SCENE**

I think I qualify as a far-off link, since, for the last 20 years, I have woken up to a view of the Andes Mountains from the west side of Santiago, Chile – as opposed to the first 20, when it was of the Pennine Hills from the north side of Huddersfield.

At the moment here, we are harvesting grapes for Concha y Toro wines

– an exhausting task, which is lightened every evening by watching an hour of *Coronation Street* videos sent by obliging offspring. This has been going on since 1984!

It is hard to conceive of life without The Street – it has been an integral part of mine since the first episode in December 1960. At that time, I was studying for A levels at Greenhead High School for Girls, Huddersfield, where watching TV, especially ITV, was frowned on. It was, however, one of the few things that I could agree about with my father – i.e., that the programme was well acted, realistic, funny and satisfying. He normally favoured cowboy serials and, since he had first call over family viewing ...

After I left home – first to go to University and then to Canada with a geologist from Lancashire – the latest happenings on The Street were as eagerly discussed as family news whenever we returned to the North of England to visit. Catching the latest episodes was one of the first things we did, along with eating fish and chips and eagerly reading the Sunday newspapers.

Besides Canada, we've lived in Jamaica, Bolivia, Uruguay and, for the last 20 years, mostly in Chile. We've never lost our Northern roots and, passing on the essence of these to our four children – now grown up and living in Toronto – has been made much easier with this continuous, brilliant audio-visual back-up. They and their partners are all avid fans and are now responsible for taping and forwarding every episode.

The Street and the people in it are so real, that, on retiring from our farm, with its acres of vines, fields, woods and beautiful garden, I, at least, still want to live in No. 1, so I can nip into the Rovers of an evening and finally be home with Ken, Rita and Alma – free to commiserate, advise and moan. The Street and its characters have been a reference and focal point – a constant thread linking my diverse and dispersed family for most of my life.

My favourite moments have included Len telling Elsie she could have had him anytime, Ken telling Deirdre she is beautiful, Jack dealing with Jamie, Alec and Charlie showing Raquel the Flea Circus, all the street outings, the production of the *Importance of Being Earnest*, the trip to Majorca, Ivy and Vera as 'Maidens of Plenty' on a float, Derek's funeral, the sausage incident in France (Fred and Alf), Audrey practising hairdressing in the front room, the 'Miss Better Buys' competition, Victor, Mavis and the foot massage, Percy's ironing, Emily's nighties, the birth dramas and the nice handling of Hayley's situation.

I now have to go check with grapepickers, count the day's cut, watch the sunset over the Andes and then pour a Pisco Sour [delicious cocktail of grape liquor and lemon juice] ready for tonight's treat – a *Coronation Street* tape ... Linda and Mike? Sally and the disappearing Danny, Deirdre coping with her mum – maybe a few pointers there – Jack's heart bypass ... are we behind?

# CHAPTER EIGHT

# The Price of Fame

When *Coronation Street* began, the press were barely interested. The *Daily Mirror* even slated the programme. Ken Irwin's review of the first programme predicted that 'the programme is doomed from the outset – with its gloomy tune and grim scene of a row of terraced houses and smoking chimneys'. Others didn't show much enthusiasm either. Most of them didn't even bother to review it. Indeed, it was to be some years before the press really latched on to the show.

Granada's then Press Officer Norman Frisby remembers trying in 1966 to persuade some of the tabloids to accompany them on their trip down under. Pat Phoenix, Doris Speed and Arthur Leslie were to tour Australia where the show was big news, but the British press were simply not interested. The tour, of course, turned out to be a huge hit, attracting headlines in the Australian press wherever they went. All that the British papers could do was to pick up on stories from the Australian papers.

Even back home, it wasn't that often that *Coronation Street* made it into the papers. A death, wedding bells, maybe the occasional sneaky preview of what was about to happen – and that was rare in those days, as the press were considerably more obliging when it came to keeping storylines secret. That, however, was about it. It was Granada who had to do the work, pouring out the press releases in the hope that someone, somewhere, might write a few paragraphs and create a little publicity for the show.

If the tabloids were not interested in *Coronation Street* in that 'golden era of newspapers', it was certainly changing by the late 1970s. The success of the *Sun* brought untold pressures to Fleet Street as a tabloid war flared up. In the 1980s and 1990s, the *Sun* and the *Daily Mirror* battled it out in a fearsome circulation war. Fleet Street suddenly became about the four S's – sensationalism, sport, sex and soaps, with *Coronation Street* at the centre of this vicious war to attract as many readers as possible. Both papers realized that millions watched the soaps and, consequently, there were readers to be gained by running *Coronation Street* stories or any soap stories for that matter. To satisfy circulation managers, editors demanded a soap story a day; it didn't matter if they were true or not.

'The newspapers in Manchester assigned one particular reporter to handle *Coronation Street*,' remembers Norman Frisby, 'and he had to get a story a day, which was the beginning of the made-up stories, because there *wasn't* a story a day out of *Coronation Street*.' The material for a story each day just wasn't there, so they simply made it up.

There were tales of affairs, booze, drugs and so on. Much of it was tittle-tattle, but some was genuine. What it did was to put untold pressures on those involved in The Street. Photographers snapped at them here, there and everywhere. They couldn't turn without a flash bulb blinding them or go anywhere without being recognized.

'Laurence Olivier could walk down the street and seven out of ten people wouldn't know who he was immediately, but, with Elsie Tanner, ten out of ten people knew … It was fame in the sense of notoriety,' remembers actor Geoff Hinsliff, who, until recently, played Don Brennan, husband of Ivy Tilsley.

Jennifer Moss, who played Lucille Hewitt, recalled how she had been treated: 'I was opening a garden fête and this large lady came up to me and whacked me straight across the face, knocked me to the ground and said, "That's for being cheeky to your dad!" ' Phillip Lowrie, who played Dennis Tanner, got similar treatment from a so-called fan who found it difficult to distinguish between fact and fiction.

'I used to go up and down the streets in Manchester, shopping, to see if anybody recognized me. They recognized me now and again, then it got that they recognized you all the time – it would drive you mad. They won't let you go, feel they own you and then they get rude,' says Sandra Gough, who played chirpy little Irma Ogden, who married David Barlow, Ken's younger football player brother. That was more than 30 years ago – what must it be like today?

It got to Ken Farrington as well, who played handsome young Billy Walker, Annie and Jack's son: 'You weren't left alone. You couldn't go to a supermarket, you couldn't go and have a drink in a pub without somebody pulling you over – there was an invasion of privacy.'

Bill Roache, who has played Ken Barlow since the opening episode, reckons fame comes in three phases. In the first phase, you're delighted – doors are opened and so on. Then, in the second phase, the awful truth hits you: you can't escape. If you're lucky, you come through that phase and come to terms with fame. 'I remember going to the Orkneys,' he wrote in his own autobiography, 'which is about as remote a part of the British Isles as you can find ... within a few minutes of arriving, the whole village knew I was there.'

Some, of course, never managed to reach that third phase.

Not everyone could take the pressure. As ever, it was the young who were the most vulnerable. Like footballers with a recognizable face and a pocketful of money, they can so easily be tempted. Drugs, drink, sex were, and still are, all readily available. Some fell from grace. Jennifer Moss, who played Lucille Hewitt, had her problems, as Bill Podmore recounted in his book: 'Jenny simply couldn't handle the life of a celebrity and her world took a fast downhill spiral through heavy drinking and five marriages.' Thankfully, Jenny Moss is now fully recovered. Peter Adamson, who played Len Fairclough, had his problems as well, with a well publicized court case and, finally, broke his contract by selling behind-the-scenes stories to the papers leading, in part, to his dismissal. A face that was once the most recognizable in the land has, for years, been hidden away, nobody's quite sure where.

More recently, Sarah Lancashire, who played Raquel, admitted that she was heading for a nervous breakdown towards the end of her days in The Street. It may not have necessarily had anything to do with The Street, but it's hard to believe that the pressures of working on The Street did not in some way contribute.

As The Street has introduced more young characters and carefully developed a younger image, the youngsters in the cast have found themselves splashed on the front covers of a variety of 'young' magazines. They have become superstars and role models. Personal appearances, modelling, records – the rewards, and pressures, are enormous.

The tabloids could also be unnecessarily cruel. It was the press who destroyed Doris Speed. Although old, ill and clearly defenceless, they ran a story revealing her true age as 84 when she claimed to be only 69. She no doubt had her reasons for not admitting her age, but, there it was, one Sunday morning, in large print, showing that she was well into her eighties. Doris was on sick leave at the time; she never returned to the show, upset that the press could be so cruel.

The *Sun* headline of 2 March 2000 'Corrie Les In Booze Clinic' was typical, as the paper revealed that *Coronation Street* star Bruce Jones, who plays Les Battersby, had booked into a clinic with severe stress and drink problems.

Strangely, some of the worst excesses of the press came at funerals. When Graham Haberfield, who played Jerry Booth, died very suddenly, scores of photographers besieged the picturesque church near Knutsford where the funeral was taking place. 'There were scores of photographers there,' remembers Norman Frisby. 'Graham had two little boys and I thought it was absolutely nasty because the photographers were fighting among themselves to get near the gravestones to photograph these two little boys at their father's funeral.' It was pretty much the same at Bernard Youens' funeral. It was all very unsavoury.

Norman Frisby also recalls one extra who was elevated by the papers, becoming '*Coronation Street* Star' after he died, even though he had made only a couple of appearances in the background of the Rovers. The regular cast never even knew his name, but, when he died, 'some lively young reporter decided to do some checking – and, sure enough, nobody from the cast had gone to the funeral'. The next day, he was dubbed 'TVs forgotten star', with Pat Phoenix being accused of having snubbed him.

There wasn't much you could do about it. Occasionally, Granada complained to the Press Complaints Commission, but it brought little satisfaction. If anything, it only served to make matters worse.

The papers also had another ruse. Journalists would frequently ring up, looking for a quote to attach to some made-up story. Frisby, or whoever, would deny the story, but it made no difference. 'I'd come into the Press Office, the next morning,' says Leita Donn, former Press Officer, 'pick up a paper and it would start, "A Granada spokesman denied that ..." and then they'd print the whole story and, by the time you got to the end of it, you'd forget that it had ever been denied.'

Storylines were regularly divulged, so that the element of surprise for the viewer was destroyed. It might have made a good headline, but it undoubtedly spoiled the effect for millions. It was simply unnecessary and the only gainers were the tabloids, which would put a few thousand more on their circulation totals. No doubt they would argue that it was good for The Street's viewing figures, guaranteeing a huge audience, but Granada never wanted that. Producer Harry Kershaw would go apoplectic when he picked up a paper to see their painfully worked out, carefully kept secret plot revealed. As often as not, the papers would get it wrong.

There were pressures on the staff as well, and not just because of the lengthy hours. The shift to four programmes a week had put new pressures on the actors and staff. Working six days a week is not unusual for many of them. Young, often inexperienced, directors found themselves having to direct The Street's superstars – actors who had been doing the show for years. It could be daunting. They had to prove themselves. It was not always the technical side that was demanding, but, rather, directing stars who could be tetchy and were often ready to test the youngsters. They had to show that, even though they were young, it was the director who was in charge and had the final say.

The Street was always regarded as a useful training ground. It was generally a smooth operation, staffed by personnel who had been doing the job for years. It was a well-oiled machine and, for that reason, the company liked to try out talented and ambitious young directors. For many, it was a first opportunity to direct drama. Michael Apted, who became a major Hollywood director, and Mike Newell, who later directed the Oscar-nominated *Four Weddings and a Funeral*, cut their drama teeth on *Coronation Street*. Julian Farino, another director who was to go on to greater things, began on The Street and recalls in these pages how he was tested by Barbara Knox. Fortunately, he passed his test. Of course, it wasn't always the case that young directors, or whoever, would be probed; mostly the cast were as professional and helpful as possible, as many testify.

Of course, publicity can work the other way as well. Programme executives need headlines for their show and regularly feed the tabloids and other papers with a steady stream of press releases and stories. There are plenty of soap stars lining up to sell their tittle-tattle to the tabloids as well, though rarely with the programme's approval. It's a difficult line to tread – the need for both publicity and control of that publicity. There are stories that Granada would prefer not to see in the papers and, inevitably, on a programme employing a cast of stars, including many youngsters, problems will arise. It's back to the football analogy that one producer has suggested. Star names, money, young people and outside interests only add up to problems. As in any football club, not everybody likes each other and there will inevitably be internal tensions.

As long as there are soaps and as long as they are successful, they will continue to attract the attention of the tabloids and down-market, star-struck magazines. Television has also mushroomed, with a hundred and one different channels, all on the look out for stories, guests to appear and so on. The pressures are phenomenal. Whereas 20 years ago, Granada employed one press officer to deal with The Street, today there are half a dozen. As more episodes are introduced, so those pressures will continue. It can, as one cast member has said, be something of a merry-go-round where jumping off is impossible.

## John Finch
*Scriptwriter, Script Editor and Producer*    **WRITING THE STREET**

Tony Warren worked through Harry Kershaw and Harry Elton. He wrote the first 13 scripts himself. I think he and Harry worked on them towards the end, shaping and doing stories. I've always thought Tony was a very innovative writer.

Granada needed *Coronation Street* to continue once it got this momentum. They wanted more from you than you wanted to give and I think Tony was overwhelmed by the sheer progression of The Street and Granada's need and he just couldn't cope with it single-handed. I did 39 hours of a series called *Sam* and I wrote them all myself, but it nearly killed me. The pressures are enormous and Tony was a young lad then. I think that must have been very tough for him. I've always felt for him in that respect.

I moved from being a writer to a story editor, because the pressures were so much on Harry that somebody had to do it. I was the only one who'd been with it from the beginning, apart from Tony, and he obviously didn't want to do it. Tony was thinking about other things then. I remember Jack Rosenthal talking to him and Tony said, 'I want to cut my links with The Street finally so I that I can go on to other things.' Jack said, 'Go and get John to fire you', as I was Producer at the time. Tony came in and explained, so I said, 'OK, Tony, you're fired' and we both burst into tears. I was terribly emotional about it. I said to him, 'You've changed so many people's lives. As far as I'm concerned, this is a joke, but, if you're taking it seriously, don't ever think that people don't appreciate the difference.' As Jack says, too, he changed so many people's lives by creating these marvellous characters. He did a great job for the working class because they had been very badly represented on television.

## Ken Farrington
*Actor, played Billy Walker*     **SORTING OUT THE MEN FROM THE BOYS**

With The Street, the first episode was live and the second episode of the week was recorded. I loved it – I wish they'd bring it back. It sorts the men out from the boys because, when the pressures are on, that's when you get the adrenaline going and the performance goes up a notch. I'd like to see it come back because, by bringing editing in, it's opened the door to a lot of second-rate actors who can't actually do it. If you do three or four takes and go back and redo it and do it in bits, they can fill in the inadequacies, which, to me, is a sadness for our trade.

## Les Chatfield
*Cameraman and Director*     **A DEATH THREAT**

I remember the time when Elsie married Steve Tanner and I actually got a death threat for marrying the flower of British womanhood to an American, to a Yank. It was written to me as the Director. I thought it was a joke and I showed it to Harry Kershaw and he called the police in. He took it seriously. I think it came from Nottingham and when the Manchester police got on to the Nottingham police, they knew who it was, so they went round and read the riot act to him.

We used to get letters. If a family was moving out of The Street people would write in and ask if they could have their house, rent their house – most peculiar.

## John Finch
*Scriptwriter, Script Editor and Producer*     **TROUBLE-SHOOTING**

I had no intention of staying with The Street for ever. I was Story Editor for about a year and then I became the Producer 1968/69. Harry then went back to writing scripts. At the time I became Producer, he became Executive Producer, so he was always there – thank God, because I hated producing. Really, it was only the fact that I'd got some marvellous directors and Harry there that kept me going. As a producer there was so little that you could do.

They used to say to a producer when they were talking to him about the possibilities, 'What would you like to do?' and, when they asked me, I said, 'Well, I'd like to run it for a bit and then take it off' and they took a very dim view of this. I said, 'I'm only joking.' Really, I thought it had had its time then. It went through a dip, mostly when I was producing. Soaps do have to go through dips. It's a natural cycle because the actors get tired. I went through a period when the actors were tired and we had a couple of alcoholics on the show, which was very, very difficult. Pat used to complain to management about me because she said I was too hard on her, though we were the best of friends really. I think it's a natural process. Harry knew I didn't want to go on for ever and I came up with an idea for a series – *A Family at War*.

When I left *Coronation Street*, I did have some regrets and, in fact, I kept going back. I became a sort of trouble-sorter in that, if they got problems on a script, they called me in. I seemed to develop a facility for sorting out problems. For example, one actress absolutely refused to get out of bed to come and do this script and you couldn't do it without her because there were two episodes that were entirely her story. I think she knew this. So, Harry called me in and said, 'What the heck are we going to do about this?' and I had a brainstorming session and came up with the idea that we rewrote the scenes in her bedroom, so that sorted her out. She came in in a wheelchair, face-saving. She was in the Green Room for about ten minutes and then she was hopping about!

## Ken Farrington
*Actor, played Billy Walker*                                    **A STREET SUPERSTAR**

I thought I was doing what I wanted to do, but there was a price to pay and that was that I didn't get the financial rewards of being recognized as a soap character. I would go in and earn good money for about six months and come out and there were certain things that I would get, like touring or jobs that I might not have been offered if I'd not been in *Coronation Street*. You also have to put up with the loss of privacy and I wasn't getting the money for it.

I think the loss of privacy is not so bad now. In the early days of soaps that loss of privacy, especially up in Manchester, it was very much, but, now, you have so many soaps that there is a glut of soap stars. In the past, you weren't left alone. You couldn't go to a supermarket, you couldn't go and have a drink in a pub without somebody pulling you over – there was an invasion of privacy.

## Sandra Gough
*Actress, played Irma Barlow*  **LEAVING THE STREET**

I kept on saying, 'I want to leave. Write me out.' I gave them three months to write me out and they didn't, so, on the Friday, when we were packing up, I said, 'I'm not coming in on Monday' and they all laughed. I said, 'I'm not, I've given you the chance to write me out. I'm going, I've had enough' and I went to Spain. I don't know what they did with the programme, but I know it was in all the papers that I was missing, nobody knew where I was, which was not true because I'd told them.

When I came back, my solicitor said you must offer to go back and I said, 'No, I don't want to.' He said, 'You've got 18 months left on your contract, they could sue you for it.' I thought, 'I've worked hard for that, but I've never had the sack from anywhere, I'd be so ashamed.' He said, 'Would you rather have the sack or be sued?' So, I had to offer to go back and they said 'No'.

## Geoff Hinsliff
*Actor, played Don Brennan*  **THE NATURE OF FAME**

I was not too long out of RADA – I left in 1960 and went into *Coronation Street* in 1963. At that time, actors were terrified of soaps, in that they killed you off. You feared that you'd never work again because of being in a soap. It was a steady job, but, after it, you were virtually finished. That was the difficulty.

In the theatre, knighted actors would turn up in jeans to rehearse; people in The Street would turn up in fur coats. I recall seeing Minnie Caldwell in the canteen in a fur coat and rings – she couldn't get any more on her fingers – and eating fish and chips. It was a very homely, friendly place, though – that was the kind of aura that there was around it. People would come in in the kinds of clothes that you'd wear for a cocktail party. They did that especially on Wednesday, which was the Producer's run through. Even when I joined, people used to dress up for it. All those things were utterly surprising to the rest of the profession. It all spoke of the difference and the basis was money and fame.

Laurence Olivier could walk down the street and seven out of ten people wouldn't know who he was immediately, but with Elsie Tanner, ten out of ten people knew – that was it. It was fame in the sense of notoriety. I never went along with this. I thought fame was about doing something extraordinary, like climbing Everest – that's fame, you did something that no one else could do that was a tremendous feat and you were famous, whereas soap stars, especially, were … It was just that, twice a week, their face was on the box and people loved it and lived by it and practically treated it as reality. There are notorious stories about people ringing in to do with something that's happening in The Street and treating the whole thing as real. One story that Bet Lynch – Julie Goodyear – used to refer to was that, when she was turned out of her flat in The Street, the telephone exchange was jammed with calls saying, 'Come to my place, she'll be all right. We've got a nice room there, it won't cost you a fortune.'

## Leita Donn
*Press Officer*                                        **DORIS' RETIREMENT**

Doris Speed had done a lot of acting before she got her part in *Coronation Street*. For years, she was just another unknown radio and rep actress and then she was a star with fans around the world, but there was a downside to this instant recognition. Like most women, she had always enjoyed going to the sales and hunting for a bargain. 'I can't do that any more,' she told me mournfully. 'If people saw me rummaging through the clothes they'd say, "Look at her, with her money. Fancy her being so mean." '

In all the years I had known her and in all the interviews and features I'd done with her, I had never asked her her age. I don't think it had occurred to me to wonder about it. If I had thought about it at all, I suppose I would have put her somewhere in her late sixties, so I was astonished when one very ungallant tabloid newspaper journalist took it upon himself to root out the records and published her birth certificate, which, unbelievably, showed her to be in her eighties.

She was actually on sick leave when this happened and she was so devastated by this very public invasion of her privacy that she never came back. A storyline was hastily concocted, with Annie, on holiday, deciding to leave the running of the Rovers Return to her son, Billy Walker, and, without any announcement or fuss, Doris slid quietly out of the programme and into retirement.

## Bob Greaves
*Television Presenter*                    **FALLING BY THE WAYSIDE**

Like any big team of people, with the throughput of different faces over many years, a fair number, sadly, fell by the wayside – Peter Adamson, who played Len Fairclough and was famous throughout the nation, fell from grace and disappeared. The last I heard was in a Sunday tabloid and he was living somewhere down South in a one-roomed place. Chris Quinten, who always had a touch of arrogance about him – if he didn't fall by the wayside, he drifted out of sight. He went to Hollywood and always thought he was a finer actor than he was, like some others in The Street over the years. A lot of them are inclined to play themselves and then get carried away with the idea that they are rounded actors and the proof is in the pudding.

## Norman Frisby
*Granada Press Officer*                    **THE EXCESSES OF THE PRESS**

I think the worst excesses of the press came when Graham Haberfield, who played Gerry Booth, died very suddenly. He lived near Knutsford and the funeral was going to be in Knutsford Parish Church and one or two of the cast went. When we arrived – I'd always go early to events like this, just to get the lie of the land – the press were beginning to assemble. There were scores of photographers there. Graham had two little boys and I thought it was absolutely nasty because the photographers were fighting among themselves to get near the gravestones to photograph these two little boys at their father's funeral, but there's not much you can about it. That kind of thing tended to happen. I remember Bernard Youens' funeral was pretty much the same, except even Granada reporters turned up for that one.

My most difficult decision ever that I had to make on *Coronation Street* was when Pat Phoenix married Alan Browning, who played opposite her for a time, then they parted. Anyhow, Browning died and Pat was on holiday in Cornwall. I had to ring her to tell her and she said, 'Norman, do you think

I should go?' Well, I knew he had been married before and had a family. Anyhow, I established that that wife was going to be responsible for the funeral arrangements and, obviously, she and her family would be there. So, I said to Pat Phoenix, 'No I don't think you should go, because Alan's first wife and family are definitely going to be there and the press will just turn it into a circus and it will be very unpleasant.' So, she didn't go. I did spend a lot of time afterwards wondering if I had made the right decision, but I think I did because it would have been beastly.

## Sandra Gough
*Actress, played Irma Barlow*　　　　　　　　　　**THE STAR SYSTEM**

I used to go up and down the streets in Manchester, shopping, to see if anybody recognized me. They recognized me now and again, then it got that they recognized you all the time – it would drive you mad. They won't let you go, feel they own you and then they get rude – 'How much money do you get for that job and what do you do really during the day? You don't work' and silly things like that. You might only have your lunchtime to do some shopping and if you say, 'I'm sorry, love, I'm in a hurry. I'll sign something', it's, 'Oh, you're a snob.'

There was a kind of star system and, of course, we got letters every week from different people saying, 'You're the best, we love you. You should have a show of your own. You're better than any of the others.' Well, you have to stop and think that all the others are getting these letters, too, from a different type of person who prefers them, but some believed that only *they* were getting letters and started getting bigheaded.

I find a very big problem for actors in soaps is that they join acting to play different parts, to travel, to have a challenge, but, then, there's not much money coming, not many jobs. Then they get into a soap and love it, which I did, and get money and stability and you get recognized. Doors open that wouldn't before and, really, they want to leave, they're fed up. Can you imagine even *two* years playing the same part, three, four, five, eight, nine, ten, twenty? A lot of them went into it not having a lot of other experience. If you went into it famous, there's a better chance of you getting other jobs afterwards. And the work now, you've no idea – 14, 16 hours a day, 6 days a week and then you've to come home and learn your lines for the next day.

These are people's lives and they don't ever give young people a talk-to when they go into it – 'You do realize, save your money and there could be an end to it.' Some people think that it will never end and I've tried to tell younger people, 'Please, save your money.' They get big cars, big houses, get into debt, then they daren't leave. They did look after us better in *Coronation Street* in those days. It was quieter, slower then, now there's no time.

## Ian White
*Director*  **PROVING YOURSELF**

It was daunting for me as a young director who hadn't really done drama before to go into *Coronation Street*. You walk in there and everybody else in the room knows what they're doing and you don't. Some of these people had done this job for 20 years. They had got used to it over the years, but, undoubtedly, they wanted to know if you could do your job. You had to win them over – that was the challenge – and you had to prove yourself. Sometimes artistes would say, 'I don't think he or she would do that' and you'd have this very complicated camera plot all worked out and then it would all change. It was a frightening thing to join because it was so big, but I can never remember when any of the actors would have really jeopardized the programme.

## Julian Farino
*Director*  **A TESTING TIME**

The very first episode I had to direct had a big storyline in it where Rita Fairclough hears that her husband has a brain tumour. I remember you used to rehearse all the studio scenes with an average of about five minutes each, so that you could block the actors, get as much dialogue in as you could, before coming back two days later to shoot the scene.

The first scene I had in that storyline was with Barbara Knox and William Russell, who played Ted Sullivan, her [Rita's] husband. Barbara Knox hears the news and starts crying in the scene. I looked at her and thought, 'That wasn't quite what I had in mind.' I said I wanted her to play it dead straight, I didn't want her to cry in this scene. She looked at me like, 'Who do you think you are, boyo?' – it was a look to kill. Then she said, 'Why?' and I said, 'Well, there are five scenes in this episode and maybe the first reaction should be shock and the tears are what we should see in the final scene.'

After that, I was on trial with her. It was like, 'I'm going to test you' at every stage of the week's work. When I walked away from that scene, after maybe 20 minutes, instead of 5 minutes, the Assistant Floor Manager, walked away with me to the next scene in the Kabin and said, 'That's the bravest thing I've seen' and I said, 'What do you mean?' He said, 'If Barbara Knox cries for you, you're supposed to go down on a bended knee.' To be quite honest, it was my naivety that saw me through – I was just trying to find my way through the enormous amount of things I had to cope with. If I had been in awe of it, I could have been eaten for supper.

On arrival, there was a degree of testing and why not? They wanted to know how you would cope. Julie Goodyear definitely put you through your paces when you were a newcomer, but not in an unreasonable way – not tantrums, but questions, do you know your onions. There were certain tensions between members of the cast, which were unspoken but open secrets. I never thought Julie Goodyear and Barbara Knox liked each other, but, on screen, they acted as friends and confidantes. They both had that queen bee status.

## Norman Frisby
*Granada Press Officer*         **THE STREET AND THE PAPERS**

Another very good example led to me taking a newspaper to the Press Council, which was an interesting exercise. I only did it really to see what would happen.

Liz Dawn used to do some fundraising work for a school for the deaf in Moss Side and they were having some event. She said to some of the cast, 'Will you come with me and help entertain these children? It's good PR.' The two who went were Sally Whittaker, who plays Sally Webster, and Kevin Kennedy – Curly Watts. Of course, there were some photographers there. Sally and Kevin were sitting pretty close together, but newspapers don't like white space in pictures, so the photographers said, 'Would you mind getting a bit closer', so he put his arm round her shoulder and said, 'Come on, Sally, let's get together', so they were actually closer together. Flash, that was the end of it, nothing appeared in the paper. It was not the kind of story that was going to make the paper – nothing went wrong, they *did* turn up, they didn't get drunk, they didn't fight with anybody, so there wasn't a story in it.

About a month went by and, suddenly, I picked up the paper one morning and there is this picture with a totally fabricated story, that these two were having an affair, that their behaviour was such that the Producer had had them in and warned them they were not to behave like this in the rehearsal room, their colleagues were complaining about the way they were canoodling when they should be rehearsing and learning their lines, they were out nightclubbing all over Manchester together night after night, they were an item. I thought, 'There's not a word of truth in that.' In fact, the embarrassing thing was that she had got a regular boyfriend who didn't much approve of her mixing with other actors, so that was very difficult for her. He was very upset about it and they came to me in floods of tears and said, 'This is terrible. What are you going to do? Let's sue them.' I said, 'Let's sit down and think it through first of all.'

In the end, to pacify them really, I thought there was no point in suing over a thing like that because the damages would be negligible. It would cost you a fortune, so it wouldn't be worth it really. Plus, all the excitement of discovering all the other things that would come out. I said, I'll take it up with the Press Council, so I wrote to the paper's Legal Department and told them, 'We're going to take you to the Press Council over this totally inaccurate and damaging story.'

We did get an apology in the end, but it took months to extract from them. There was a great exchange of letters, including letters from their Legal Department, saying, 'We are absolutely certain that this story is true. Our source is absolutely watertight.'

## Leita Donn
*Press Officer*                                    **A STORY A DAY**

Do you remember the Ken–Mike–Deirdre triangle? Well, as you know, Australia and New Zealand work while we're asleep, so, at twenty past eight in the morning, I used to start getting calls from places like the *Liverpool Echo*, the *Manchester Evening News*, so that had to be done before I went to Granada. I'd get into Granada at half-past nine, the phone would be ringing on the desk. Standing there in my coat, I'd pick it up and it would be calls from everywhere in the western hemisphere and, as I put it down, it would ring again. One morning, when we were coming up to the final days of this 'would Deirdre choose one or the other?' I stood there and, after half an hour, a secretary came up and, as I had the phone in one hand, she took my coat off and said, 'Would you like a cup of tea?' and it would go on all day, through lunchtime.

All the British papers would phone every day to see what they could get out of me. It would go on all night at home. I know that the Press Officer now doesn't, but I used to take calls all round the clock and even one in the morning because, when the early editions of what was Fleet Street came out, every paper would get every rival's first edition. They would scan it. If a rival had a story they hadn't got, they would ring me up, so, at one o'clock in the morning, one tabloid would come on, 'There's a story in such and such a paper' and they'd read it to me. What they didn't know was that there was a journalist who told me frankly that his boss had put him on to soaps and he had to produce a soap story a day and if there wasn't anything going, he had to make one up. So, he would do a soap story and, of course, the rivals would ring me up to find out, even if I said, 'There isn't a word of truth in it.'

I'd come into the Press Office the next morning, pick up a paper and it would start, 'A Granada spokesman denied that ...' and then they'd print the whole story and, by the time you got to the end of it, you'd forget that it had ever been denied.

## Norman Frisby
*Granada Press Officer*                        **FACT AND FICTION**

I used to find difficulty in selling *Coronation Street* stories. The newspapers didn't seem to want to know, and there is a very good example of that. When I took three of the cast to Australia in 1966 for a personal appearance tour of those stations in Australia that showed the programme, I had great difficulty in interesting Fleet Street in it. I virtually had to bully the representatives of the Fleet Street papers in Australia to do something about it. It was very hard to persuade Fleet Street that this was interesting. If 16 million people watched the programme, they might buy their newspaper. We didn't get a lot of publicity. I can just imagine what would happen if they were to go to Australia now – it would be a front-page splash on these tabloids.

I think it was really in the early Eighties that it suddenly dawned on them – the point that I'd been trying to make for all those years – that if millions and millions of people watch the programme and you write about it, millions and millions might buy your newspapers and so it became a kind of circulation war-led thing.

The newspapers in Manchester assigned one particular reporter to handle *Coronation Street* and he had to get a story a day, which was the beginning of the made-up stories, because there *wasn't* a story a day out of *Coronation Street* – I wish that there had been – but that would mean that they would come on in desperation, saying, 'Norman, have you got anything for tomorrow? I've got the News Editor breathing down my neck. Is somebody leaving or somebody new coming?' It became an absolute obsession and the material wasn't there.

There were classic made-up stories. They used to hang around in the pubs and there were plenty of people behind the scenes at Granada who were happy to flog them a tip-off on what was going on. Harry Kershaw used to be apoplectic about them blowing the storyline – the number of times I've had to mop the tears of Harry Kershaw because his story's been blown in some newspaper.

What used to intrigue me was that you'd tell them that the tip-off that they'd got from behind the scenes was accurate, but it was the way it was dressed up in the newspaper office, it got garbled. It became laughable really. I would say to Harry, 'Look, it isn't true' and he'd say, 'There's a bit of truth in it.' I'd say, 'Yes, there's a bit of truth in it, but the reader of the newspaper doesn't know that until they've watched the programme to see *how* true it is.' In many cases, they were *so* wildly inaccurate that I thought it did the programme a service rather than a disservice.

I remember a guy ringing up one day from a Sunday tabloid, saying, 'Norman, I've had a tip-off about *Coronation Street*.' Our attitude was that we would always say we would neither confirm nor deny any rumour about *Coronation Street* because, to tell you the truth, it would, in effect, spoil the enjoyment of the programme for millions of viewers. That was the stuff we churned out every time. This chap rang and said, 'We've had this tip-off. I know it's true, our source is impeccable. Gail Tilsley [who was pregnant at the time] is going to fall downstairs, she's going to be carted off to hospital and she is going to lose the baby, but she is going to be reunited with her wandering husband.' I said to the fellow, 'Well, it doesn't sound quite right to me.' 'Oh, I'm absolutely sure, the source is faultless.' I said, 'I would be a bit careful if I were you. I don't think it's quite as right as it should be.' Anyway, I couldn't stop them from doing it.

The paper came out on the Sunday with a story saying Gail's going to fall downstairs, have a miscarriage, lose the baby, etcetera, and, of course, it was not at all true. They didn't care about that, and that was curious, because it meant, did they really stop and think what their readers would make of it? If you read the paper and told your family and your friends and it didn't actually happen in the programme, you'd feel a bit miffed. I suppose you could say, 'Oh well, they changed it after it had been in the paper', but there were no end of these sorts of stories that just had no basis in truth at all.

## Norman Frisby
*Granada Press Officer*                           **CREATING STORIES**

They were always wanting to sue the newspapers in those days and I was always a bit opposed to it. On the *Express*, it was part of the style book that, if anybody threatened to sue, you were never to actually argue with them.

I remember Peter Adamson wrote a series for the *News of the World* before he was sacked – it was why he was scalded in the end – and he described a scene in the rehearsal room where there had been some horseplay between one of the actors and actresses. It was one sequence where they were supposed to be sleeping in a tent and there was some fooling about in the rehearsal room. Peter Adamson wrote about this, but he got the wrong actors. His memory failed him or he wasn't there and somebody had told him about it. Peter Baldwin was named and, of course, he was a very serious actor and didn't like any suggestion that he fooled about in the rehearsal room.

He came to me and said he would like to sue the *News of the World* for this because he thought it was damaging. I said, 'I don't think it's the kind of thing that Granada would actually encourage you to do, but, if you want to go and see a lawyer yourself, we would support you.' I think he went to see his solicitor, who said, 'If you put £1,000 down on the table we could talk about this' and he decided not to bother. That was such a glaring libel that they did, in fact, correct it the next week, so we were happy about that.

It was this obsession with finding a *Coronation Street* story that was rather pathetic, I used to think. I used to consider myself something of a professional and I didn't like to see newspaper men reduced to such a level.

Newspapers have changed so dramatically over the years. In my day, if you got a tip-off for a story and you made a few enquiries and it was clear that there was absolutely no truth in this story, you would spike it. They don't now, they run the story and make it into a row and then the next day they do a follow-up saying, 'It's died, this story.' It's just creating stories when they're actually not there.

## Geoff Hinsliff
*Actor, played Don Brennan*  **COPING WITH FAME**

In my final stint, there were obviously people who had a great following in The Street and were an institution as characters in the piece, but it wasn't the same. It hadn't gone to people's heads. In a sense, people matured over the years and behaved in a different way.

It was very difficult, being that much of a celebrity – it's very difficult to cope with your life. It is something you have to cope with and some people don't cope with it very well. There's nothing like previous experience. You see it most in the young kids who come in. A young boy comes into the series, an 18-year-old who has done very little, if anything. Within three months, all his mates are saying 'Wow' and girls are making offers and, suddenly, you can easily think, 'I really *am* terrific.' I think it's practically impossible for a young actor *not* to go through that phase – either off at the deep end or be a pain in the arse. At some point, you'll go through that and, hopefully, you'll come out the other side. It really is a lot to cope with. Suddenly, you are notorious and it's very difficult. I think the cure, like for myself, is to have been around for 20 years and know who you are and *then* go in. Then, I think, it won't go to your head.

## Robert Khodadad
*Director*  **WORKING AGAINST THE CLOCK**

The biggest pressure then, and even now, in directing – particularly programmes like The Street – the biggest pressure and your biggest enemy is time. The biggest pressures aren't 'Are the actors behaving themselves? Is the scene working? Is the episode working? Are the performances right? Is the camera shot working? Is the crew working well together? Am I going to work up with some decent television?' – all those factors come into it – but your biggest pressure, that's working against you, is time.

When you go into that studio, the obvious difference between working on location and working in the studio is that location is shot single camera in the same way a normal film drama is shot, so, if we've got two actors in a scene in a coffee bar, you'll shoot all of actor A's lines and then you turn the camera round and shoot all of actor B's lines and they'll be put together in the edit. The difference with the studio is that it's shot multicamera – i.e., two or three cameras, all recording simultaneously, so you can do the actions and reactions all at the same time. By shooting multicamera, it is very efficient in some ways and it creates a whole host of problems in other ways, but the thing about the time element is that, in the studio, you always knew which actors and which scenes were your bankers, those that you knew you could rely on, and there were those that you were always concerned about, because some actors can walk into the studio and be super-efficient, they will know their lines from day one of rehearsal. Some of the actors will know every line and have it word perfect, some of the other actors, by the time you go into studio to record it, still don't know their lines. So that was one element. The other factor to take into account is which actors are working with which others, because you could have one actor who is absolutely superb with their lines and one actor who isn't so good with their lines and you knew that that scene could potentially take a lot longer. Also, it's the complexity of the scene and how you're going to shoot it. So, you're always thinking in your mind. You have a first assistant and a PA who are constantly telling you. We allot so many minutes of shooting time to each page of script, irrespective of how complex that script is, so, as you're shooting, you have to know in your mind, 'I know they've allotted 15 minutes to shoot this scene, but it's a very, very complicated scene. Therefore, I know it's going to take me a lot longer', so, straight away, you could be 10 minutes over on the schedule, but you have to keep an idea in the back of your mind that you're going to make that 10 minutes up later on. You're always thinking ahead and you're looking towards the end of the day, knowing that, 'OK, I know I've run over on this one, but I know I can make time up on the other because I've got two very good actors or actresses who will come in and they will do it and, within two takes, we'll probably get it.' So time's your biggest enemy, and even more so when we went to four episodes.

Effectively, *Coronation Street* is run over a maximum working week, it works six days a week in production and, if it wasn't for the fact that you use the same actors, it could work seven days a week by changing your crew around, but the actors have to have a day off. For the actors, it's very, very, very tough. They could have a location scene to do at eight o'clock on a Sunday morning, which means they may have been in make-up from seven, which means they may have been called for six-thirty in the morning. They will be expected on the set at eight o'clock on a Sunday morning. They will have to know their lines.

The difference with the location stuff is that there is no rehearsal. We effectively go on the set wherever the location is – it could be in a school hall, it could be in a library, it could be in a church – and we will block it, rehearse it and shoot it almost immediately. So the actors and actresses will have no time to go away and learn their lines. When they go in that Sunday morning, they have to know their lines for all the scenes they're doing that day, and that's true of a Monday as well. So, they're working Sunday, Monday, Tuesday they're blocking. Tuesday afternoon, they've got time to rehearse and learn their lines, as they have on Wednesday, and on Thursday and Friday, it's record, so they have Saturday off. So, they could have had their last scene on a Friday and they could be in their first scene again on the Sunday, but they finish Friday exhausted and they have three more episodes for next week to get their heads round.

I've worked with actors and actresses who've had a very heavy storyline and they are in a huge number of scenes in every episode over a number of weeks. So, Friday night, they are absolutely exhausted and, come Sunday morning, they've got a make-up call at six-thirty and they're on the set at eight o'clock and they could have a whole day's filming and, the difference is, there's no breathing space. They have to know their lines on that Sunday.

## Robert Khodadad
*Director* **LEARNING YOUR LINES**

One or two of the more mature characters of The Street did, on occasion, have problems learning their lines. What would happen – particularly in Rovers scenes where they were always very complicated to shoot because there are a lot of characters and a lot of scenarios going on – this one actor would write his lines on the beer mats in the pub, so that he could tap the beer mat and just remind himself of his lines. I remember one scene in particular where we were doing the whole thing in one shot and a lot of little cameos would happen and, at the end of a two-minute scene, this person would have to come in and say something like, 'A pint of bitter, please, Betty' and he'd blow it. He'd blow it for everybody because, then, we'd have to go back to square one to record. So, what he did was, he'd write his lines on his beer mat to remind him and it all worked very well in rehearsal, but, I remember, on one occasion, Phil Middlemiss, who was always a bit of a prankster and a joker and had a devilment in him, during the actual take, he leant next to this person and put his elbow on the chap's beer mat. I could see out of the corner of my eye, as the scene was progressing and we're closer to this person's line, that he was getting more panicky. When it came to his line, it was, 'Oh, I'm sorry, I've dried, I've forgotten my line', but it was very funny to see it unfold. He couldn't budge Phil because he was on camera and, in theory, he should have known his lines.

# The Interviewees

**Jim Allen** The late Jim Allen was one of Britain's finest screenwriters, who wrote many television and film successes, usually in collaboration with director Ken Loach. They include *Land and Freedom*, *Days of Hope* and *United Kingdom*. Jim Allen was a scriptwriter for *Coronation Street* during the 1960s. He died in 1999.

**Michael Apted** A film director who directed *Coronation Street* in 1966. Later, he became a major Hollywood film director, whose credits include *Agatha*, *The Coal Miner's Daughter*, *Gorky Park*, *Gorillas in the Mist*, *Nell* and the James Bond movie *The World Is Not Enough*.

**Chris Atkinson** A sound recordist who worked on The Street during the late 1970s, doing location and exterior set recording. He fondly remembers doing the sound for Bet Lynch and Alec Gilroy's wedding. He now works as a freelancer.

**Peter Baldwin** An actor who was born in Chichester and trained at the Bristol Old Vic. He appeared in a variety of stage productions before auditioning for the part of Derek Wilton in *Coronation Street* in 1976. Over the next 12 years, he appeared, off and on, in the show, becoming a more regular character. Having jilted each other at the church in 1984, Mavis and Derek finally married in 1988. Peter left The Street in 1997, when Derek died.

**Jan Bowditch** An Australian fan, aged 58, born in Sydney, but now living in Balgownie, a suburb of Wollongong, 50 miles from Sydney. Jan Bowditch worked as a secretary for the British Motor Corporation and then at the University of New South Wales and the University of Western Sydney. She is married to a retired academic and now retired herself. She started watching The Street back in the early 1960s and continues to watch via various satellite stations and on regular trips to New Zealand and the UK.

**Gordon Burns** Born in Northern Ireland, Gordon Burns worked for Granada Television for many years as a producer and presenter. He was formerly the presenter of *The Krypton Factor* and now presents BBC Television's *Look North West*. He is a long-time *Coronation Street* fan.

**Wally Butler** A director, he directed over 1,000 episodes of *Coronation Street* as well as the spin-off programme *Pardon the Expression*. He became Head of the School of Film and Television at the former Manchester Polytechnic, but has now retired.

**Sandy Charbonneau** Born in Fareham in Kent, Sandy Charbonneau emigrated to Australia just as *Coronation Street* began. She married a Canadian Air Force man and now lives in Nova Scotia in Canada, but keeps in touch with home every week through *Coronation Street*.

**Les Chatfield** He joined Granada as a cameraman in 1957 and later became a director. Les Chatfield did both jobs on The Street before going on to direct *A Family at War* and being the producer/director of *The Lovers* and *The Dustbinmen*.

**Lin Cripps** A fan who was born in Exeter in 1950, emigrated to Canada in 1969 and now enjoys life in Sudbury, Ontario where she works in a pub in a large hotel.

**Lynn de Santis** A Salford-born fan, now in her mid forties, whose sister lived in the street where the opening titles were shot. She is a lecturer in Exercise Physiology at Salford University.

**Leita Donn** She was *Coronation Street*'s Press Officer from 1965 until 1987, during which time she was responsible not only for getting *Coronation Street* stories into the press, but also for scotching many of the absurd stories that appeared in the tabloids. A close friend of Violet Carson, Pat Phoenix, Doris Speed and Jack Howarth.

**Cheryl Drinkwater** A New Zealander living in Tauranga, aged 42 and a *Street* addict for more than 20 years. Cheryl Drinkwater grew up in New Guinea where her parents were missionaries. An office clerk by day, she is a student by night, studying for a degree in psychology. She keeps in touch with other *Street* addicts via the Internet.

**Tom Elliott** A script editor and writer who joined *Coronation Street* as a storyliner in 1983 and wrote his first episode in 1991. Tom Elliott left The Street to write for *Emmerdale* and has also written stage and radio plays.

**Christabelle Embleton** A fan who watched the very first episode and has rarely missed one since. She gave birth to her son, Steve, at 3.30pm and was propped up in bed, watching The Street just four hours later. She lives in Ramsgate.

**Steve Embleton** A fan, now aged 35. Born and bred in Ramsgate, he now co- runs a baker's shop. He regularly visited Newcastle where there were houses just like those in *Coronation Street*.

**Julian Farino** He joined Granada as a researcher in 1986 and began directing *Coronation Street* 5 years later, which he did for 18 months. Later, he directed the award-winning drama *Our Mutual Friend* for BBC television and, more recently, the full-length movie *The Last Yellow*.

**Ken Farrington** An actor, he played Billy Walker, son of Jack and Annie Walker. Ken Farrington originally screen-tested for the role of Dennis Tanner, but sufficiently impressed the Producer so that the role of Billy Walker was created for him. He trained at RADA and joined The Street soon afterwards. His *Street* appearances have been punctuated with long spells in the theatre and appearances in numerous television dramas, including *Heartbeat* and *Casualty*.

**John Finch** He wrote roughly 100 scripts in the first 8 years of The Street, becoming Script Editor in 1961 and Producer in 1968. He is probably the only person to have done all three jobs for The Street. He also created and wrote *A Family at War* and *Sam*.

**Anne Flack** She was born seven weeks before Coronation Street began but didn't become a fan unti 1981. She has lived in Turkey for the past six years.

**Norman Frisby** In 1959, Norman Frisby joined Granada as Press Officer.

He was heavily involved with The Street from its inception until he retired in 1987, and probably knows more *Coronation Street* secrets than anyone alive. He toured Australia with three of the cast in 1966, and throughout the 1980s spent much time protecting stars of The Street from the excesses of the tabloids.

**Sandra Gough** An actress, Sandra Gough played Irma Barlow, daughter of Stan and Hilda Ogden, who married Ken Barlow's brother, David. She left the programme in 1968, only to return two years later. Her last appearance as Irma was in 1972. Since then, she has played parts in various television and radio shows, including Nellie Dingle in *Emmerdale*.

**Su Garner** A life-long fan living in Childwall in Liverpool.

**Bob Greaves** For many years, Bob Greaves was regarded as the public face of Granada Television. He joined the company as News Editor in 1963 after working for the *Daily Mail*. Soon he became a presenter and presented *Granada Reports* and *Granada Tonight* for years, as well as a host of other local and national programmes. He retired from Granada in 1999.

**Nance Green** A Manchester-based fan and homoeopath who started watching *Coronation Street* while at University. She lives with her partner, the playwright James Stock, and their two children, in Chorlton.

**Lord Denis Healey** Former Chancellor of the Exchequer, Defence Secretary and Labour Member of Parliament for Leeds East, now he is Lord Healey of Riddlesden. He is a life-long fan, who was captivated by the programme during its early years.

**Geoff Hinsliff** After training at RADA, Geoff Hinsliff appeared in many West End plays. He played characters in *Coronation Street* over three different periods from 1963 to 1997, but is best known for his role as cab driver Don Brennan, who married Ivy Tilsley in 1988.

**Barrie Holmes** A life-long fan living on Merseyside, Barrie Holmes has a *Mastermind*-level knowledge of *Coronation Street* trivia and has been watching the programme since it began. His other passion – Liverpool Football Club.

**Alistair Houston** He worked as Sound Engineer on the first episode of *Coronation Street* and many subsequent episodes. Alistair Houston also worked on a wide variety of other programmes in over 40 years at Granada, later in his capacity as Senior Sound Supervisor. He has now retired.

**Lord Doug Hoyle** Former Labour MP for Warrington and President of the Manufacturing Science and Finance trade union, Lord Doug Hoyle is another and a life-long fan of The Street. He has watched the programme since the early 1960s, but thinks that today's *Street* is a far more accurate reflection of life in the North than was the case 20 years ago.

**Clarissa Hyman** A well-known food writer, Clarissa Hyman worked for Granada for many years as a researcher and producer. She still vividly recalls a tense encounter with Pat Phoenix when she briefly worked as a 'call boy' on The Street.

**Gillian Jones** A teacher living in Chepstow, but originally from Liverpool, Gillian Jones has been a fan since the early days.

**Judith Jones** A former production assistant at Granada who worked on *Coronation Street* during the early 1980s, Judith Jones is now a lecturer in media at John Moores University, Liverpool, and an author.

**Julie Jones** A freelance writer and life-long fan of *Coronation Street*, Julie Jones' writing credits include *Brookside*. She lives in Manchester.

**Jill Kennedy** Living in Dunedin in New Zealand, Jill Kennedy is a 57-year-old fan. Her family had one of the first television sets in Dunedin and friends would come around and watch The Street in their house with cups of tea and sandwiches. She is now married to a ship's captain.

**Robert Khodadad** A director, Robert Khodadad started working on The Street in 1994, and was heavily involved in the switch from three episodes a week to four. He was born in Manchester.

**Geoff Lancashire** One of The Street's finest ever writers, Geoff Lancashire worked alongside Tony Warren and Jack Rosenthal in promotions at Granada, but told Warren the programme would never last. He later went on to write many hundreds of scripts for it himself between 1964 and 1981. He also wrote *The Cuckoo Waltz* and *Birds of a Feather* for Granada. He is the father of Sarah Lancashire, who played Raquel.

**Angela Larson** A Canadian fan, who emigrated to Canada from Glasgow in 1967 when she was 18, but clearly remembers seeing the first programme. Angela Larson is now a grandmother living in Victoria in Canada and Administrative Assistant to the Speaker of the British Columbia Legislative Assembly. Widowed at an early age, she found her half-hourly escapes down The Street of great solace and comfort.

**Joan Le Mesurier** Formerly married to Mark Eden who played Alan Bradley in The Street, Joan Le Mesurier vividly remembers living in a street exactly the same in Chadderton in Manchester. Later she married the actor John Le Mesurier.

**Jennifer Lingo** A *Coronation Street* fan, Jennifer Lingo is originally from Swindon, but has been living in Phoenix, Arizona, for more than 20 years, where she is a podiatrist to the city's football, basketball and ice hockey teams. She picks up The Street on satellite via Canada.

**Linda McAleny** A fan of The Street for over 30 years, Linda McAleny lives at Moreton on the Wirral.

**Ric Mellis** Assistant Stage Manager, Floor Manager and later Director of The Street, Ric Mellis directed the programme for many years. He is now a freelance director and has also directed and produced *Brookside*.

**Andrea Morgan** A New Zealander, born in Otorohanga in 1963, Andrea Morgan is now living back on her parents' dairy farm in Whakatane in the Bay of Plenty. She works as a gardener and watches The Street with her mother, great aunt and sister.

**Mike Newell** A major film director, whose credits include *Four Weddings and a Funeral, Donnie Brasco* and, most recently, *Pushing Tin*, Mike Newell cut his teeth directing *Coronation Street* in the mid 1960s.

**Denis Parkin** A set designer, Dennis Parkin designed the original *Coronation Street* set – houses, interiors and all. He spent weeks wandering the streets of Salford with Tony Warren in search of ideas.

**Gary Parkinson** A fan, 34-year-old Gary Parkinson is a copywriter, designer and astrologer, living in Manchester. He has done astrological charts for many of The Street's characters.

**Patricia Parsons** A fan living in Gander in Newfoundland, Canada, Patricia Parsons is a librarian at the Central Regional Library at Gander.

**Jim Quick** A graphic artist, Jim Quick worked on The Street during the 1970s and 1980s. He oversaw technological changes that changed the nature of his job.

**Phil Redmond** One of the foremost scriptwriters in British television, Liverpool-born Phil Redmond is creator of *Grange Hill, Brookside* and *Hollyoaks*. He admits that watching The Street in the 1960s helped shape his view of television and writing. He now runs Mersey TV.

**Anne Reid** An actor who played Valerie Barlow, first wife of Ken Barlow, from 1961 to 1971. She asked to leave the programme and her character was killed off. Since leaving The Street she has appeared in a wide variety of programmes, including *The Upper Hand, Heartbeat* and *Playing the Field*, as well as providing the voice of Wendolene in Wallace and Gromit's *A Close Shave*. Most recently, she has appeared in Victoria Wood's *Dinnerladies*.

**Prunella Scales** She briefly starred in The Street in 1961 as Harry Hewitt's bus conductor girlfriend, Eileen Hughes. Now a well-known television and film actor, Prunella Scales is perhaps best known for her role as Sybil in *Fawlty Towers*.

**José Scott** Casting Director José Scott cast the very first *Street*. She is the person most responsible for discovering and casting a host of memorable characters, such as Ena Sharples, Elsie Tanner, Albert Tatlock and Annie Walker.

**Graham Seed** An actor who appeared in The Street as prosecuting counsel when Brian Tilsely appeared in court. He is possibly the only actor to have appeared in *Coronation Street*, *Brookside* and *EastEnders*, but is perhaps better known as Nigel Pargetter in *The Archers*.

**Sue Siddeley** Born in Huddersfield, Sue Siddeley became a *Coronation Street* addict from the first episode. She emigrated to Canada, but has since lived in Jamaica, Bolivia and Uruguay. Now she lives in the foothills of the Andes mountains, where she and her husband grow grapes, in between watching videos of The Street.

**Janet Smith** She emigrated to Canada from Davyhulme in Manchester in 1967 with her mother, father, brother and sister. She keeps in touch with life in Manchester through her weekly trips down The Street and recently returned to Manchester for a memorable tour of the set.

**Dionne Spence** Manchester-born and a life-long fan, Dionne Spence works at Burnage High School in Manchester as a Learning Mentor.

**Brian Spencer** A director, Brian Spencer joined Granada as a freelance director, having worked at the BBC. He directed film inserts for The Street in the early 1980s. Now he teaches film and television at Manchester Metropolitan University.

**John Temple** Storyline Editor and later the Producer between 1985 and 1987, John Temple is one of the most influential figures in The Street's history. Later, he produced *Take the High Road* for Scottish Television, as well as many comedy shows for Granada.

**Graham Twyman** A 47-year-old funeral director living in Ramsgate, Graham Twyman is a self-confessed *Street* addict. He still remembers being traumatized by Martha Longhurst's death – the first death he had ever encountered.

**Greg Wadden** A 38-year-old Canadian living in Cobourg, Ontario, Greg Wadden is married to Gill, formerly of Wythenshawe in Manchester. He now runs a highly popular Corrie web page in Canada.

**Diane Walker** A New Zealand fan, born and bred in New Zealand, and living in Auckland. Diane Walker spent a year in England as a nanny and five and a half years in Singapore. She is now a personal assistant for a sporting company, is 40 and married to a teacher.

**Jim Walker** He was a producer at Granada Television for more than 20 years. Although he never worked on The Street, he retains fond memories of the many actors and technicians who worked on the show.

**Harry Whewell** Former Northern Editor of the *Guardian*, Harry Whewell was born and bred in Manchester. He joined the *Guardian* in 1950 as a journalist, finally became News Editor and then Northern Editor, which he was until his retirement in 1985. His late wife was, for some years, a scriptwriter on *Coronation Street*.

**Ian White** A director who joined Granada Television in 1978 as a researcher, Ian White went on to direct *Coronation Street*, which he did from 1989 until the end of 1992. Now a freelance director, more recent credits include *Lovejoy, Casualty* and *The Bill*.

# Bibliography

Betjeman, John, Lycett Green, Candida (Ed.), *Letters*, Volume II,
  Minerva, 1996

Forman, Denis, *Persona Granada*, André Deutsch, 1997

Kay, Graeme, *Life in The Street*, Boxtree/Granada, 1991

Kershaw, H. V., *The Street Where I Live*, Granada Publishing, 1981

Kilborn, Richard, *Television Soaps*, Batsford, 1992

Little, Daran, *The Coronation Street Story*, Boxtree/Granada, 1995

Little, Daran, *Around the Coronation Street Houses*,
  Boxtree/Granada, 1997

Little, Daran, *The Women of Coronation Street*, Boxtree/Granada, 1998

Phoenix, Pat, *All My Burning Bridges*, Arlington Books, 1974

Podmore, Bill, *Coronation Street: The Inside Story*, Macdonald, 1990

Roache, William, *Ken and Me*, Simon & Schuster, 1993

Winter, Gordon, *Here We Were*, Granada, 1984